AT THE
ELEVENTH HOUR
AND OTHER TALES

AT THE ELEVENTH HOUR AND OTHER TALES

KEITH FLEMING

Edited and with an introduction by
Gina R. Collia

Published by Nezu Press
Queensgate House,
48 Queen Street,
Exeter, Devon,
EX4 3SR,
United Kingdom.

This edition published 2024

At the Eleventh Hour first published by George Routledge and Sons Ltd., 1891. *The Sins of the Fathers* first published in instalments by the Forfar Herald, etc., 1893.
Short stories: The Courage of Kathie', *The Sunday Sun* (Australia), 28 April 1907; 'An Audacious Wager', *Irish Weekly Independent,* 3 February 1912; 'Garth Austin's Strategy', *Weekly Freeman* (Ireland), 14 June 1913.

ISBN-13: 978-1-917113-04-5

In the interest of preservation, the punctuation and spelling of the individual first edition texts have been maintained, and the original formatting has been used wherever possible. Only minor publisher errors and spelling inconsistencies have been silently corrected.

CONTENTS

'Most Unassuming in Demeanour' The Life of K. E. Fitz-Patrick

by Gina R. Collia

When I began looking for information about the author Keith Fleming, I had very little to go on. The only thing I knew with any certainty, based on the contents of the publishing contracts she signed with George Routledge, was that her real name was K. E. Fitz-Patrick.[1] It was thought that her first name was Kathleen and that she had been born in Ireland in 1858 or 1859, so I began by searching for a record of Kathleen's birth in Ireland.[2] But I found nothing. This wasn't surprising, as it turned out, as her name wasn't Kathleen, and she wasn't born in Ireland.

Next, I turned to the census books, where I found that Miss Fitz-Patrick had been recorded under four different names. Though it's not unusual to come across errors in census books—generally speaking, the ages given have a tendency to be a bit off—in Miss Fitz-Patrick's case the information is particularly unreliable. Within the 1851 Scotland census, both her name and age are recorded incorrectly. The same is true for the 1891 Wales census, in which her birthplace is also incorrect. The 1901 Wales census has her name down correctly, but it knocks nine years off her age. When presented with so much contradictory information, it can be difficult, without access to the original census forms, to know which is correct.

The main reason for errors being present in Victorian census information is that the records were produced by a third party, based on householder forms that could contain incorrect or illegible information. The average Victorian did not attach quite so much importance to providing accurate details about their own birth as we do nowadays, and it would have been no great surprise to find both men and women knocking several years off their age at census time to recapture their lost youth. In addition to the human tendency towards vanity, a person's exact date of birth was sometimes forgotten by their parents unless recorded somewhere early on (for example, in a family Bible), so guesswork played a much greater role in filling out forms than it does now.

The first national census for England, Scotland and Wales took place in 1801, but the information gathered before 1841 was statistical; for the most part, very few personal details were taken. This changed in 1841, when the first truly modern census was taken. From that point forward a census form was delivered to every property in the land, and the head of each household was responsible for recording the personal details of all individuals residing under his or her roof on a given date. The forms were then collected, and the enumerators transferred the information contained in them to census books. Unfortunately, the original forms were usually destroyed; this changed in 1911, from which time they were retained.

In Ireland, the first national census was taken in 1821. Few early Irish census records still exist—many having been lost when the Public Records Office in Dublin was destroyed in 1922—but those for 1901 and 1911 have survived. And when I looked at the individual householder returns for 1911, I found that 'Kate Elizabeth Fitz-Patrick' filled in and signed 'Form A' as the head of her particular household; she was living at 20 Richmond Hill, Dublin, at the time and recorded the country of her birth as Scotland.[3] Interestingly—and as if to prove beyond doubt how unreliable information recorded by the census enumerators can be—when I turned to the sections of the 1911 form that were filled in by the official enumerator, I found that Kate's name was recorded by him as both 'Kate E. Fitzpatrick' and 'Catherine Fitzpatrick'.

Over the years, various enumerators renamed her Catherine, Katherine, and Kathleen, but she signed herself as Kate. In addition to this, as I later discovered, her name was recorded as Kate in her mother's will, in her own will, and in the records of the cemetery where she was buried.[4] So, based on this small amount of census information—the name and birthplace provided by Kate herself—my search began in earnest, and what follows is the result.

Kate Elizabeth Fitz-Patrick was born in Edinburgh on 12 November 1849.[5] Her father, Peter Fitzpatrick, was born in Dublin in 1813, the third son of Peter Fitzpatrick (c.1768-1819) and his wife, Margaret (née Meighan, 1781-1842).[6] Peter Fitzpatrick Snr was a solicitor, and his son followed in his footsteps, being sworn in as an attorney of the court on 23 June 1838.[7] Peter Jnr's two older brothers, James and O'Keefe, were also solicitors, and the family business was run from 64 Capel Street, Dublin.[8]

On 21 November 1843, Peter Fitzpatrick Jnr married Georgina Elizabeth Queely at St Thomas's Church, Dublin.[9] Georgina was born in Dublin in January 1818, the only daughter of John Queely (c.1790/1–1869) and his wife, Catherine (c.1789/90-1840).[10] Georgina had only one sibling; her brother, Edward, 'a most lovely and interesting boy', died in 1828 at the young age of five, having suffered from hydrocephalus.[11] John Queely operated a 'general agency and discount office', supplying cash to 'persons requiring discounts, or wishing to raise Money on Mortgage, or other securities'; he was a money broker.[12] His premises at the time of his daughter's marriage were at 29 Lower Abbey Street, just half a mile from the Fitzpatricks' office on Capel Street.

Georgina, her brother and mother were involved in a serious

Carlisle Bridge, Dublin, c. 1840.

accident when she was just a child. In December 1825, while crossing Carlisle Bridge in the centre of Dublin—about half a mile from Moore Street, where they lived at the time—Catherine and her children were 'most violently thrown down' by a horse which, ridden by a boy who could not control it, had galloped furiously onto the bridge.[13] Catherine was carried 'in a state of insensibility' to Doctor Butler's Medical Hall—located about four hundred yards away at 54 Lower Sackville Street—along with Georgina, 'a fine and interesting little girl' of seven, and Edward, who was two.[14] Edward escaped 'without receiving the least hurt', but his sister and mother 'received very serious injuries, particularly about their heads'.[15] 'Everything their deplorable condition required' was done for them, and a week later they were pronounced 'out of danger'.[16]

Just one month later, Catherine opened a boarding and day school, 'for the Instruction of Young Ladies in every branch of Polite Literature, &c.', at her home at 22 Moore Street.[17] In 1829, she and her family moved to 15 Hardwick Place, where she re-opened her school and placed advertisements in local newspapers, promising to pay 'unremitting attention to the religious principles and general deportment of her pupils' and offering instruction in French, English, history, geography, 'the Use of Globes', writing, arithmetic, music, dancing, drawing and needlework.[18] 'Mrs. Q.' wished to 'impress on the Public, the peculiar advantages of her School in the Writing and Arithmetic department', as 'Mr. Q.' devoted his entire time to those subjects.[19]

In May 1839, the Queelys moved to 18 Lower Abbey Street, which later became no. 29.[20] When Georgina Queely married Peter Fitzpatrick at the end of 1843, he moved into her family home, and he took an office a short distance away at 53 Middle Abbey Street.[21] But this is the point at which things began to go wrong. By the end of 1846 he was in financial trouble, and six months later insolvency proceedings were initiated against him.[22] His case was set to be heard on 23 June 1847,[23] but he appears to have managed to pay his creditors before the matter got to court, thereby avoiding imprisonment. His father-in-law was not so fortunate.

Catherine Queely died on 5 April 1846,[24] and her husband remarried the following year. In his mid fifties, John Queely married twenty-two-year-old Emily Jessie Dunne on 25 September 1847.[25] Just three months later, in January 1848, notices of his insolvency began to appear in the local newspapers.[26] He was arrested and imprisoned for non-payment of debts, and his case was heard on 17 February; he was in bad health and was allowed out on bail for the sum of £200.[27] More notices followed, warning 'all persons indebted to the insolvent' not to pay him; they were to pay no one but the assignee responsible for the distribution of his assets.[28] He managed to repay his debts and remained in business, and in 1851 he moved his office to 85 Marlborough Street, 'opposite the

Education Board'.[29] But he was insolvent again in May 1860, and again in July 1864.[30] He died on 25 May 1869.[31]

Some time between the summer of 1847 and that of 1849, possibly as a result of financial difficulties, Peter and Georgina left Ireland and moved to Edinburgh, where their only child, Kate, was born at the end of 1849. In 1851, they were living in lodgings at 75 Parkside Street.[32] Around the spring of 1854, Peter started working for the North British Railway Company; he no longer worked as a solicitor and was employed as a clerk in the cashier's office.[33] By the spring of 1855, he and his family had moved to a house belonging to his employer in St Leonard's Hill.[34] Less than two years later he was in prison.

In his capacity as clerk, Peter was responsible for depositing funds into a bank account at the National Banking Company of Scotland on behalf of his employer, but on 5 January 1857 he failed to deposit the amount of £43 16*s* 11*d* into the account, choosing instead to keep the money.[35] He was arrested for theft on 9 January, but he could not be questioned at the time as he was 'labouring under delirium tremens'; he was examined before John Clark, magistrate, a week later and charged with 'wickedly and feloniously, upon the Fifth day of January Eighteen hundred and fifty seven within

St Patrick Square, Edinburgh,
by Alfred Henry Rushbrook, 1929,
National Library of Scotland.

the premises in Canal Street Edinburgh occupied by The North British Railway Company stealing the sum of Forty three pounds Sixteen shillings and Eleven pence Sterling'.[36]

When the crime was first reported to the police on 6 January, 'criminal officer' Michael Reilly went to Peter's home in St Leonard's Hill to look for him.[37] Finding him not at home, he searched various places around Edinburgh but failed to locate him. It turned out that, on the evening of 5 January, Peter had gone to the house of two drinking companions, Elizabeth and James Baillie, where he had spent the night with their lodger, Mary Ann Goldie; he had remained at that address until he was apprehended by the police.[38] Reilly searched the Baillies' home on 9 January and found Peter 'in a bed in a closet'.[39]

In his defence, Peter claimed that he had no memory of receiving or stealing his employer's money on account of being 'much addicted to drinking'.[40] But according to George Henderson, a witness who had spent time with him on the day the crime took place, Peter had been drinking 'but knew quite well what he was about'.[41] A warrant was issued, and he was committed to prison for further examination on 17 January.[42] Then, on 21 January, he was committed to Calton Prison—the largest and most brutal of Scotland's prisons—pending trial.

Peter's trial took place on 2 March 1857, and he pleaded not guilty, maintaining his claim that he was too inebriated to remember what had happened on 5 January.[43] The jury was unanimous in finding him guilty of breach of trust and embezzlement, and he was sentenced to four years' penal servitude.[44] The sentence of penal servitude consisted of three stages: separate confinement, labour in a 'public works' prison, then release on licence. Peter began the second stage of his sentence at Chatham Convict Prison, the largest prison in England, which had opened the previous year to house prisoners who would hitherto have faced transportation.[45] Cells inside Chatham were 'excellently ventilated, and furnished with a hammock, a bench, a tin water jug and basin, and little else'.[46] The prisoners were well fed, 'to enable them to perform the hard labour they have to undergo.'[47] When Peter arrived at Chatham, in the spring of 1858, he was healthy, but by the spring of 1859 he was an invalid.[48] On 8 March 1859, he was transferred to Dartmoor Prison, which was by that time a light labour or invalid prison, though the work performed by inmates was not in any way light or suitable for invalids.[49] His behaviour throughout his time in prison was 'very good', but he was not released on license; he served his full term and was released on 1 March 1861.[50]

Immediately upon his release, Peter returned to Edinburgh. Perhaps he did so to look for his wife and daughter; he took lodgings at 32 St Patrick Square, in St Leonard's Hill, describing himself at the time as a 'landed proprietor'.[51] As an invalid and ex-convict, he most likely needed someone to look after him. It would appear, however, that he did not find Georgina and Kate; he returned to Ireland alone some time between his release and his death on 30 December 1864.[52] He was buried in the churchyard of Drumcondra Church, Dublin, alongside his father.[53]

Kate was seven years old when her father was sent to prison. Whilst there is much we will never know about her life at the time, or that of her mother, we do know that her father was an alcoholic and thief who mixed with bad company and spent several nights with a woman who was not his wife—the type of woman who, six months after Peter was sent to prison, was charged with 'causing a disturbance, swearing and rioting and fighting' and was sentenced to thirty days imprisonment.[54] We also know that, as a result of

Peter's criminal behaviour, his wife and young daughter were left to fend for themselves and to find new accommodation; they could hardly remain in the house in St Leonard's Hill, the landlord of which was the very company that Peter had stolen from.[55]

According to the various census returns, Georgina and Kate lived on their 'own means' on 'income from land'.[56] Their income must have belonged solely to mother and daughter; otherwise, given the fact that his need for money drove him to crime, it would most certainly have been appropriated by Peter Fitzpatrick. Perhaps, like Mabel and Katharine Arden in *The Sins of the Fathers*, after Peter 'had done his best to shame and beggar both wife and child', Kate and her mother lived on 'the only source of income which her father had been unable to alienate from them'.[57] And perhaps, being to some extent financially independent, Georgina saw Peter's imprisonment as an opportunity to cut ties permanently with a husband who had brought her nothing but shame and pain.

As a result of John Queely's remarriage, Georgina had two half-brothers and a half-sister, and Kate had several half-cousins—one of whom was L. G. Wyndham Shire, chief engineer for the famous Midland Red bus company—but I have found no evidence to suggest that Kate or Georgina resided at any point, for any period of time, with any relative following Peter's imprisonment.[58] Kate and her mother appear to have been entirely self-sufficient and to have gone their own way.

For the years between 1857 and 1887, I have found no record of Georgina and Kate Fitz-Patrick—they always preferred to use this spelling of their name rather than Fitzpatrick. So, we don't know where Kate received her education. That said, given the fact that Catherine Queely ran a school for a number of years, Georgina was most likely educated by her mother, and she most likely passed on what she had learned to Kate who, as is evident from her writing, was well-read. But we know nothing of Kate as a child, adolescent or young woman.

Whilst we don't know when Kate and her mother left Scotland, or where they lived following their departure, we do know that in October 1887, by which time Kate was thirty-seven years old, they were living in Mid Wales. Both the *Aberystwyth Observer* and *Cambrian News and Merionethshire Standard* named them as two of the people involved in elaborately decorating Trinity Church in Aberystwyth for the harvest festival thanksgiving services that year, and the latter gives Georgina's address as Trinity Place.[59] Apparently, the services were so well attended that many parishioners could not find space within the church and had to leave.

By the time Kate's name appeared again, in an announcement in the *Carmarthen Journal and South Wales Weekly Advertiser* on 10 May 1889, it was common knowledge in Aberystwyth that she was the author 'Keith Fleming'.[60] The following day, a review in the *Aberystwyth Observer*, revealed that she had 'been for some time a resident of Aberystwyth.'[61] Kate, described as 'most unassuming in demeanour', was 'well known to the Holy Trinity congregation, which Church has the honour of numbering her amongst her members.'[62] She was a friend of Rev. D. W. Jenkins, the curate of Holy Trinity, and it was he who acted as witness to her signature when she signed a publishing contract with Routledge for "*Can Such Things Be?*" in December 1889. By that time the reverend had taken the living of St Mary's in Pembroke, but, despite his new parish being about seventy miles away from his old church in Aberystwyth, he and Kate had remained friends.[63]

Kate's first volume of fiction, *By the Night Express: A Psychological Romance*, was published by George Routledge and Sons in May 1889.

It contains three novellas—'By the Night Express', 'Dolores', and 'Love Stronger than Death'—in each of which it is 'not easy to mark the line between the real and the supernatural'.[64] Each tale contains 'enough of the horrible to satisfy the reader of morbid tendencies', and there are no happy endings for these characters.[65] In 'By the Night Express', the best of the three stories, Maurice Donovan is travelling to Ireland by train when, having become involved with an attractive fellow traveller, he finds himself mixed up in a gruesome murder mystery and unable to tell the difference between dream and reality. In 'Dolores', when Colonel Frank Oswald is found dead, presumed by most to have committed suicide, Arthur Wilmore receives the solution to the mystery of his death by means of a supernatural vision: 'it was not drowsiness or sleep. I swear it was not sleep'. And in 'Love Stronger than Death', Norah Desmond 'sees' an end to all her hopes and dreams when she suffers a 'terrible mystic revelation'. The book was well received; the *Bookseller* wrote:

> 'The wonderful dreams, which are the groundwork of the plot, might, if they were true, form useful matter for the investigations of the Society for Psychical Research. They will, however, at any rate keep the most sleepy traveller awake for the two or three hours' railway journey he may spend in reading them.'[66]

Announcements for Kate's next book, *"Can Such Things Be?" or, The Weird of the Beresfords: A Study in Occult Will-Power* began appearing just seven months later, in December 1889, and it was issued at the beginning of 1890, in both cloth and 'fancy boards', as part of Routledge's Railway Library series.[67] The decidedly atmospheric tale is that of the fulfilment of the Beresford family curse, in part narrated by Arnold Dysart of Trinity College, Cambridge, based on his father's account of Maxwell and Eunice Beresford and the events surrounding the latter's supernatural experiences and death. As with Kate's first book, *"Can Such things Be?"* received positive reviews for the most part. *Punch*'s 'Baron de Book-Worms' objected to the number of 'twaddling interruptions about "spookikal" research and metaphysical problems', but he seems to have missed the point served by the interjections:[68] to reinforce the idea that the story is based on real events, presented by a man of learning, a Professor of Modern Philosophy, a 'poet and philosopher, dreamer and thinker, imaginist and scientist'.[69] The *Bookseller* wrote:

> 'An old haunted manor-house, a lady who leaves her coffin and re-appears in society, and a violin of "astral" properties, are the main elements of the "Weird of the Beresfords." No one can say that the ingredients of the story are wanting in psychological spiciness. An air of realism is thrown over the tale by the introduction into it of a Cambridge professor, who patiently investigates the mystery and is persuaded of the veraciousness of these occult phenomena. Take it all round, Mr. Fleming's book, for its kind, is distinctly to be recommended.'[70]

Kate's third book, the sensation novel *At the Eleventh Hour*, was published by Routledge a year and a half later, in the summer of 1891. Lionel Hartley Dacre, up-and-coming architect, has been engaged by the Marquis de Vallanelle to design a château on the French Riviera and to make improvements to other properties, so he and his wife, Helen, relocate to Paris with their young son. But the French nobleman's designs are not restricted to his various homes; he has a bad reputation where women are concerned and has set his sights on beautiful Helen Dacre. When Lionel discovers that his wife has gone missing without a trace, he fears the worst: that she has abandoned him, and taken her son with her, to run off with the villainous Frenchman. The mystery of her disappearance is later revealed… at the eleventh hour. *The Scotsman* described *The Eleventh Hour* as 'a novel of conspicuous power and deep interest… that may be read with a great deal of pleasure.'[71] The *Carlisle Patriot* wrote:

> 'The author… here achieves a distinct advance in his art. His previous work proved him an expert in plot and incident; and he has developed a charm of manner and breadth of treatment which add grace to a stirring story. The analysis of character and descriptions are all well done; and altogether the novel takes rank among the best that have been produced of recent months.'[72]

Kate and her mother, like many 'unattached' middle-class women at the time, lived in lodgings, moving from one reputable establishment to another when want or need dictated. By the time that *At the Eleventh Hour* was published, they had left Trinity Place and taken lodgings at 7 Sea View Place, situated just a stone's throw

Aberystwyth, c. 1896.

from the beach in one of the town's most desirable locations.[73]

By the time of Kate and Georgina's residency in the town, Aberystwyth had long been one of the favourite watering places in Wales, praised by fashionable physicians for 'the virtues of its health-giving air'.[74] There were lodging houses all around the main streets of the town, no shortage of hotels, and the local authorities 'spent money freely' to increase its attraction to people in search of health.[75] From 1883, Aberystwyth's water supply came from Llyn Llygad Rheidol reservoir, at base of Pumlumon Fawr, and residents and visitors alike were assured that what they drank was 'pure and unadulterated'.[76] The beach was known to be a good hunting ground for precious pebbles, and every facility was provided for sea bathing. In short, Aberystwyth was an extremely pleasant and attractive place to live.

Kate's final novel, *The Sins of the Fathers*, was never published in book form; it was issued in instalments in several newspapers between 1893 and 1895; its earliest publication appears to have been in the *Forfar Herald* from July 1893.[77] It tells the story of a mysterious disappearance during a party at great, grey Arden Grange on a wild, stormy All Souls' Night. And aside from being a gripping yarn—involving theft, supernatural visions, revenge, kidnapping, and murder—that was popular enough to be picked up by Australian newspapers, *The Sins of the Fathers* provides us with an insight into Kate's views on capitalism and inequality.[78] It also gives us an idea of her views on the hunting of defenceless animals—the victims of 'cruelty and strength' and 'that insatiate, horrible desire to destroy and ruin so strong and rampant in man's evil breast'—in the name of 'sport', perpetrated by 'them cowardly creatures that call themselves "men".'[79] On the subject of the unfair distribution of 'money and lands and worldly goods' she wrote:

> 'And what are these things? Do they not belong to all alike? Are they not the inheritance of all who know labour? Not the monopoly of a few drones in the world's busy hive. Are they not the natural heritage of civilised, toiling humanity? In the beginning the Great Creator made no distinctions. He gave the earth and the fulness thereof to man, to have dominion over it, and over all things upon it. This was to man in the aggregate—mankind; not to the swollen capitalist—the human sucker of the people's blood.'[80]

Various themes run throughout Kate's work. She seems to have been fascinated by the idea that individuals—people with 'peculiarly organized minds'—who are possessed of 'mesmeric power' could, whether living or dead, influence the thoughts or actions of fellow human beings, even at a great distance.[81] Professor Dysart, in "*Can Such Things Be?*", thinks it possible that the minds of the dead remain active and capable of exerting influence on both people and objects, working as an 'invisible, unimagined force' for good or ill.[82] And Maurice A. Donovan, in 'By the Night Express', suggests that proximity to a severed head, 'that even for one short hour had held the mind… that for all we know, in our dark and groping ignorance, was not then yet dead, though the body was but dust', could account for his uncanny experience.[83]

Kate was a Christian and believed in the survival of the human soul; she also appears to have believed, certainly at the time of writing her supernatural fiction, in the survival of individual human consciousness. As Cyril Raymond explains in "*Can Such Things Be?*", 'We bury the brain', but 'the immaterial, divine spirit of that mind, the condensed, sublimated essence of the man's being, has surely separate existence'; the soul, he suggests, is 'the spirituality of his mind'.[84] Kate's characters exist in a world where the dead are with us always, 'crowding round us… blessing us as we go', separated from us—imperceptible for the most part by our physical senses—by a 'shrouding veil' that, now and then, becomes 'transparently thin', thin enough to permit us to interact with the 'just beyond' and to 'move amidst a mighty host of the dead'.[85]

As I mentioned before, Kate was described as 'most unassuming in demeanour' by a local journalist. And she may well have been quiet and shy, maybe even painfully shy, like several of her female characters—like Lettice Willoughby, Ula Ferguson, Kathie Ormsby, and Helen Templeton who was 'reserved, shy, almost timid, in the presence of strangers'.[86] But she was an intelligent woman with strong opinions, and she injected those opinions into her writing. And no doubt she did so with less fear of reproach under a male pseudonym; though local journalists appear to have known that *Mr* Fleming was in fact a *Miss*, those working for the national papers thought her to be a man.[87]

Kate opposed war, pointing out the hypocrisy of those who, whilst professing to be Christian, spent their 'highest ingenuity' in 'fashioning devilish instruments, or discovering chemical combinations, that would be most deadly in their slaughter of our fellow-men'.[88] She also opposed capital punishment, that so often, based on little evidence, resulted in the innocent man dying, 'calling God and man to witness that he is murdered'.[89]

With regard to Kate's views on members of the opposite sex, the male protagonists in her stories tend to lack the strength, faith, and determination of her female characters. When their trust in a woman close to them is tested, as is the case with Hugh Denver in *The Sins of the Fathers* or Lionel Dacre—and to a certain extent his son too—in *At the Eleventh Hour*, they are weak and relatively quick to think, and accept, the worst; they lack 'a perfect faith'.[90] In contrast, the women in her stories, such as Mabel Arden's mother, Katharine, in *The Sins of the Fathers* or Helen Dacre's aunt, Dorothy Templeton, in *At the Eleventh Hour*—even Helen's landlady, Mrs. Graham, for that matter—never doubt; they keep perfect, unwavering faith. In the words of Aunt Dorothy:

> 'Oh God! they are all alike, these men—weak, selfish, pitiful cravens where women are concerned; they cannot value any of them, a true, loyal, faithful woman; but are ready to condemn her as vilest of the vile, if but a whisper is breathed by some evil, jealous tongue; ready to think her as false as they are ready to be false themselves, to honour and love and truth.'[91]

Selfishness, Kate explains, 'is essentially man's attribute', and he is very good at keeping things all to himself when he wishes to do so; he 'skilfully arranges it' so that when women encroach upon his 'self-established privileges', if they dispute the 'masculine monopoly in certain directions, they find matters made rather rough for them.'[92]

Following the publication of *The Sins of the Fathers*, no new work by Kate appeared for several years. By August 1895, she and her mother had left Sea View Place and were living at Rossnalee, 2 Trinity Road, a boarding house run by one Mrs W. Bubb.[93] And by the spring of 1901, Kate and her mother had moved again, this time to rooms at 21 Lower Portland Street, about a third of a mile from Holy Trinity Church and their old lodgings in Trinity Place.[94]

Georgina Fitz-Patrick died, 'after a lingering and distressing illness', on 31 December 1903,[95] leaving the sum of £361 13*s* 7*d* to Kate.[96] At the time of her death, she and her daughter were living at 'Grogwynion', 1 Penglaise Terrace, a short distance from

Holy Trinity Church, but she was buried in Mount Jerome Cemetery, Dublin, alongside her mother, Catherine, on 8 January 1904.[97] Every year for the ten years following Georgina's death, on the anniversary of that event, Kate placed memorial notices in Welsh newspapers 'in ever-mourning memory' of her 'beloved mother': 'Soul of my soul, we *shall* meet again, And with God be the rest.'[98]

It is likely that Kate resided in Ireland for a short time after travelling there to arrange her mother's funeral at the beginning of 1904; she was resident in Dublin in February 1904 when probate was granted.[99] But by the summer of that year she was back in Wales and living again at 'Grogwynion', where she remained until the end of August.[100]

Routledge republished *"Can Such Things Be?"* as a sixpenny novel, under the title *The Weird of the Beresfords*, in the spring of 1905, and it was still available for sale in 1911.[101] But following the death of her mother, Kate appears to have turned her attention entirely to writing short stories, none of which have a supernatural theme. Possibly, all matters concerning death and the supernatural were then too painful for her; or, in order to please newspaper editors and readers, she was forced to shift the focus of her fiction in order to get it published. Whatever the reason, she appears to have given up on all things supernatural, in her writing at least.

The short story 'So Innocent' was published in *The Idler* in October 1905. In it, Fred Glover of the *Western Light* is covering a political speech at Park Hall in Cardiff when his assumptions about a pretty young, and seemingly helpless, girl get him into trouble.

The spring of the following year, 'The Transfiguration of Lettice Willoughby' was published by *The Novel Magazine*. In it, Greville Newcome, rising young politician and Member of Parliament for Blackmore, is looking to marry well in order to advance his career.

When his mother advocates a match between him and the youngest daughter of the Attorney-General, Sir Francis Willoughby, a man of great influence, Greville pooh-poohs the idea. He doesn't want his wife to be 'a limp creature without any backbone'; he wants a woman with character. And 'poor little Letty', according to Greville, is a 'colourless little creep-mouse that is frightened at its own shadow'. But when he makes a bitterly sarcastic speech in the House of Commons that puts his life in danger, Greville discovers that Lettice Willoughby is a woman with character and courage in abundance.

'The Red Skirt' was published in *The Pall Mall Magazine* in September 1906. May Palliser is in love with the poet Percy Wyndall, a man she believes is capable of doing great deeds and of rousing others to 'great and noble action'. He is a man with 'heroic impulses'. Most of all, he is 'a champion and defender of women and children'. But Percy's deeds are not so great when May finds herself stuck up a tree with an angry bull waiting for her in the field below. And he is no champion of children when a little girl becomes the frustrated beast's next target.

The following spring, 'The Courage of Kathie' appeared in *The Sunday Sun*, an Australian newspaper. Its heroine, painfully shy Kathie Ormsby, is travelling by express train from Cardiff, on her way to Llandrindod Wells, when she uncovers and determines to thwart—in order to save the man she secretly loves—a plot to assassinate a Russian aristocrat.

By July 1908, Kate had returned to the boarding house at 21 Portland Street, which was run by Jane Bateman.[102] But some time between then and 1911, she left Aberystwyth and travelled to Ireland, where she took lodgings at 20 Richmond Hill in the Rathmines district of Dublin; she occupied a single room and was still living on 'income from land'.[103] Her short story 'An Audacious Wager' was published in the *Irish Weekly Independent* in February 1912. It is the story of the downfall of Adolphus Treherne, captain of the Lancers, who makes it a rule 'never to look twice at an ugly woman'. Over confident regarding his own irresistibility to the fairer sex, he bets Major Lawrence O'Reardon 'a pony' that he can win over a young woman he barely knows.

By the summer of the following year, Kate had returned to Aberystwyth. In June 1913, a short story entitled 'Garth Austin's Strategy' appeared in the *Weekly Freeman's Journal.* It was the 'Prize Story of the Week' and was written by Keith Fleming of 'Isfryn', Llanbadarn Road, Aberystwyth'.[104] 'Isfryn', not far from the sea and station, was a 'homely' boarding house run by a lady called Mrs Jenkins, who offered 'healthy rooms' and 'every comfort', and Lanbadarn Road was less than half a mile from Kate's previous home at Trinity Place.[105]

In 'Garth Austin's Strategy', Arabella and Eleanor Freeman, both of whom are journalists, are identical twins who 'get themselves up in duplicate fashion'. While cycling at headlong speed through the little village of Creswell, one of the 'Sisters Freeman' is involved in an accident in which an old woman, Mrs. Musgrave, is knocked down and later dies, but nobody can tell the two sisters apart in order to decide which one was responsible. Dr. Garth Austin, who has a deep interest in physiognomy, has 'made brain-study a speciality', and he devises a plan to discern the difference between Nell and Bell.[106]

Of all Kate's short stories, 'Garth Austin's Strategy' is the most like her earlier work, with its male protagonist, a man of science who has dedicated his time to 'brain-study', hatching a plan to solve a mystery. It also marks a return to a subject that seems to have fascinated her: 'that strange mystic affection said to exist between twins'.[107] In addition to the twin sisters Arabella and Eleanor Freeman, in *The Sins of the Fathers* Agatha Hargrave and Walter Oliphant are twins, and Bernard and Brian St. Lawrence are twin brothers in 'Love Stronger Than Death'.

Unlike her earlier short stories, there was no mention of Kate's previous successes alongside 'Garth Austin's Strategy', just the statement that she was awarded two guineas for it. Kate was sixty-three years old when the story was published in the summer of 1913, and I have found no work by her published after that date.

For the years 1913 to her death, I have found no mention of Kate Fitz-Patrick. At some point, she left Wales for the final time and travelled to Dublin, where she lived at 8 Dunville Avenue, Rathmines. Prior to her death, she was a resident of the Home of Rest for Protestant Dying at 20 Camden Row.[108] Kate died at the age of ninety-five on 19 January 1945; she was buried alongside her mother, Georgina, and grandmother, Catherine, in Mount Jerome Cemetery, Dublin.[109]

Notes

1 James Doig, 'Archives of British Publishers/Keith Fleming', online at *Wormwoodiana*, 26 December 2011.

2 Ibid.

3 *Census of Ireland, 1911*, Dublin, Rathmines and Rathgar East.

4 Georgina's will, see *Calendars of Wills and Administrations 1858-1920*. Kate's will, see *Calendar of Grants of Probate of Wills and Letters of Administration, 1945*. Burial records of Mount Jerome Cemetery and Crematorium, Dublin.

5 *Dublin Weekly Nation*, 24 November 1849, p. 14.

6 Peter Fitzpatrick was baptised on 4 May 1913 (see *Ireland, Catholic Parish Registers, 1655-1915*, Dublin, St Mary's). His father died on 22 Jan 1819 and was in the '52nd year of his age' at death, so, assuming that his age was recorded accurately, he was probably born c. 1767 (see *UK and Ireland, Find a Grave Index, 1300s-Current*). Margaret Meighan was baptised on 1 May 1781, see *Ireland, Catholic Parish Registers, 1655-1915*. She died on 11 April 1842, see *Dublin Evening Post*, 14 April 1842, p. 3.

7 *Dublin Morning Register*, 25 June 1838, p. 4.

8 Edward Keane, P. Beryl Phair and Thomas U. Sadleir, *King's Inns Admission Papers, 1607-1867*. Dublin: Irish Manuscripts Commission, pp. 168-169.

9 *Statesman and Dublin Christian Record*, 24 November 1843, p. 3

10 Georgina was baptised on 11 January 1818 (see *Ireland, Catholic Parish Registers, 1655-1915*, Dublin, St Mary's). John Queely's age at death was recorded as 78 when he died on 25 May 1869, so he was probably born in 1790 or 1791 (see *Calendars of Wills and Administrations 1858-1920* and I*reland, Civil Registration Deaths Index, 1864-1958*). Catherine died on 8 April 1846, and her age at death was recorded as 56, so she was probably born in 1789-1790 (burial record at Mount Jerome Cemetery and Crematorium).

11 Edward was born in May 1823 (see *Ireland, Catholic Parish Registers, 1655-1915*, Dublin, St Andrew's), and died 15 April 1828 (see *Dublin Evening Post*, 19 April 1828, p. 3).
12 *Thom's Almanac and Official Directory*. Dublin: Alexander Thom and Sons, 1859, p. 1112, and Saunders's News-Letter, 14 October 1846, p. 4.
13 The accident, *Dublin Morning Register*, 20 December 1825, p. 2. Following its reconstruction it was renamed O'Connell Bridge in 1882. The Queelys' address, see *Dublin Morning Register*, 23 January 1826, p. 1.
14 The accident, *Dublin Morning Register*, 20 December 1825, p. 2. As an aside, Charles Butler, M.D., 'Apothecary and Chemist to his Majesty and the Lord Lieutenant of Ireland', the proprietor of the Medical Hall, produced *Butler's Medical Hall 'Medicine Chest'*, a guide to drugs and doses.
15 Ibid.
16 Ibid.
17 *Dublin Morning Register*, 23 January 1826, p. 1.
18 *Saunders's News-Letter*, 28 September 1829, p. 4.
19 Ibid.
20 *Saunders's News-Letter*, 13 May 1839, p. 3. The numbering was altered in 1844, see *Saunders's News-Letter*, 29 October 1844, p. 4.
21 *Thom's Almanac and Official Directory*. Dublin: Alexander Thom and Sons, 1847, p. 633.
22 'John Byrne v. Peter Fitzpatrick, Gent. Attorney, bill of exchange' (see *Saunders's News-Letter*, 1 December 1846, p. 2)
23 *Dublin Evening Post*, 10 June 1847, p. 3.
24 *Dublin Evening Packet and Correspondent*, 7 April 1846, p. 3.
25 *Ireland, Select Marriages, 1619-1898*. The marriage took place on 25 September 1847.
26 *Freeman's Journal*, 29 January 1848, p. 1.
27 *Freeman's Journal*, 17 February 1848, 4.
28 *General Advertiser for Dublin, and all Ireland*, 15 April 1848, p. 2.
29 *Freeman's Journal*, 6 August 1851, p. 1.

30 *Bankrupt & Insolvency Calendar*, 28 May 1860, p. 2, and 11 July 1864, p. 3.

31 *Ireland, Calendar of Wills and Administrations, 1858-1920.*

32 *1851 Scotland Census.*

33 Declaration of Peter Fitzpatrick, 17 January 1857, AD14/57/313.

34 Valuation Rolls VR010000004-/15, Edinburgh, 1855, p. 15 (National Records of Scotland). Also, John Queely and Peter Fitzpatrick v. John and Edward Harper, 28 August 1856, NRS ref. SC39/8/33.

35 Indictment Against Peter Fitzpatrick, 'Theft; As also, Breach of Trust and Embezzlement', 2 March 1857, JC26/1857/356.

36 Petition of Robert Lockhart Dymock, Procurator Fiscal, 12 January 1857, NRS ref. AD14/57/313.

37 Criminal officer: detective. Statement of Micheal Reilly, 19 January 1857, NRS ref. AD14/57/313.

38 Statements of Elizabeth Baillie (or Fisher) and Mary Ann Goldie, 19 January 1857, NRS ref. AD14/57/313.

39 Closet: a small room. Statement of Micheal Reilly, 19 January 1857, NRS ref. AD14/57/313.

40 Statement made on 17 January 1857 before John Clark, magistrate, NRS ref. AD14/57/313.

41 Statement of George Henderson, 19 January 1857, NRS ref. AD14/57/313.

42 Schedule in precognition, NRS ref. AD14/57/313.

43 High Court Minute Book, NRS ref. JC26/1857/356.

44 Ibid.

45 W. Bayne Ranken, *Prisons and Prisoners*. London: Longmans, Green and Co., 1874, p. 9.

46 Ibid., p. 10. The author's descriptions of prisons were based on his visits to them in 1857.

47 Ibid., pp. 11-12.

48 *Criminal Lunatic Asylum Registers, 1820-1876, Quarterly Returns of Prisoners in Hulks and Convict Prisons*, March 1859.

49 Ranken, op. cit., pp. 9 and 13.

50 *Criminal Lunatic Asylum Registers, 1820-1876, Quarterly Returns of Prisoners in Hulks and Convict Prisons*, March 1861.

51 *1861 Scotland Census.*

52 *UK and Ireland, Find a Grave Index, 1300s-Current.* He was buried in Drumcondra Churchyard and shares a grave with his father.

53 *UK and Ireland, Find a Grave Index, 1300s-Current.*

54 *North British Daily Mail*, 23 September 1857, p.4.

55 Valuation Rolls VR010000004-/15, Edinburgh, 1855, p. 15 (National Records of Scotland).

56 See the Wales census for 1891 and 1901, 'living on own means'. The Ireland 1911 census has 'income from land'.

57 See pp. 346-347.

58 The Birmingham and Midland Motor Omnibus Company, known colloquially as 'Midland Red'. The company operated in the Midlands from 1905 to 1981, and during L. G. Wyndham Shire's time the vehicles it used were built entirely to his design and specifications.

59 *Aberystwyth Observer*, 22 October 1887, p. 4, and *Cambrian News and Merionethshire Standard*, 28 October 1887, p. 5.

60 *Carmarthen Journal and South Wales Weekly Advertiser*, 10 May 1889, p. 2.

61 *Aberystwyth Observer*, 11 May 1889, p. 4.

62 *Carmarthen Journal and South Wales Weekly Advertiser*, 24 July 1891, p. 3.

63 *Welshman*, 20 September 1889, p. 4.

64 Morning Post, 15 May 1889, p. 2.

65 Ibid.

66 *Bookseller*, 4 May 1889, p. 17.

67 *The Athenaeum*, 21 December 1889, p. 873.

68 *Punch*, 15 February, 1890, p. 75

69 Keith Fleming, *By the Night Express and Other Tales*, Nezu Press, 2024, p. 203.

70 *Bookseller*, 14 December 1889, p. 1365.

71 *The Scotsman*, 22 June 1891, p. 3.

72 *Carlisle Patriot*, 26 June 1891, p. 6.

73 *1891 Wales Census.*

74 Askew Roberts, *Gossiping Guide to Wales.* London: Simpkin, Marshall. Hamilton, Kent & Co., 1894, p. 30.

75 Ibid.

76 Pumlumon Fawr: the highest point of the Cambrian Mountains in Wales. Re the water source: Royal Commission on the Ancient and Historical Monuments of Wales. Quotation: from Roberts, op. cit., p. 30.

77 The first instalment appears in the *Forfar Herald* on 7 July 1893 (p. 2). Its final appearance appears to have been in the *Southern Press*; the final part was published on 25 May 1895, p. 7.

78 *The Sins of the Fathers* was published in Australia in the *Gippsland Times* from the spring of 1894.

79 See p. 349.

80 See p. 387.

81 Fleming, *Night Express* (2024), p. 225. (n 69)

82 Ibid.

83 Ibid., p. 48.

84 Ibid., p. 226.

85 See p. 37.

86 Lettice Willoughby from 'The Transfiguration of Lettice Willoughby', Kathie Ormsby from 'The Courage of Kathie, Ula Ferguson and Helen Templeton from *At the Eleventh Hour.*

87 *Carmarthen Journal and South Wales Weekly Advertiser*, 24 July 1891, p. 3.

88 Fleming, *Night Express* (2024), p. 264. (n 69)

89 Ibid., p. 279.

90 See p. 214.

91 See p. 45.

92 Fleming, *Night Express* (2024), p. 264. (n 69)

93 *Aberystwyth Observer*, 2 August 1895, p. 4.

94 *1901 Wales Census.*

95 *Aberystwyth Observer*, 7 January 1904, p. 2.

96 *Ireland, Calendar of Wills and Administrations, 1888-1920.*

97 Ibid., and burial records of Mount Jerome Cemetery, Dublin.

98 See *Aberystwyth Observer*, 7 January 1904, p. 2 and 3 January 1907, p. 2; *Cambrian News and Merionethshire Standard*, 29 December 1905, p. 8 and 30 December 1910, p. 8, etc.

99 Probate was granted in Dublin on 6 February 1904, *Ireland, Calendar of Wills and Administrations, 1858-1920.*

100 *Cardigan Bay Visitor*, 30 July 1904, p. 6, 6 August 1904, p. 3, and 20 August 1904, p. 6.

101 *Bookseller*, 9 May 1905, p. 36, and *Wells Journal*, 9 March 1911, p. 7.

102 *Aberystwyth Observer*, 23 July 1908, p. 2.

103 *1911 Ireland Census.*

104 The address is printed incorrectly in the newspaper as 'Is. Fryn, Lanbadarn Road'.

105 Mrs Jenkins advertised in several newspapers, for example the *Runcorn Examiner*, 17 June 1911, p. 6.

106 Physiognomy: the deciphering of character from head and facial characteristics.

107 Fleming, *Night Express* (2024), p. 117. (n 69)

108 *Calendar of Grants of Probate of Wills and Letters of Administration, 1945.*

109 Burial records of Mount Jerome Cemetery, Dublin.

AT THE ELEVENTH HOUR

A NOVEL IN THREE PERIODS

"Life is not as idle ore,
But iron dug from central gloom,
And heated hot with burning fears
And dipped in baths of hissing tears
And battered with the strokes of doom."

ALFRED, LORD TENNYSON

FIRST PERIOD
"THE OLD ORDER CHANGETH"

CHAPTER I
TOO LATE

A DREARY, miserable November night, or rather earliest morning, as the first hour after midnight has just rung out from many brazen throats upon the dank, sodden air. It is raining in torrents, and Paris, even Paris, whose very name insensibly conjures up visions of brilliancy and airy lightness is shrouded in a mantle of greyest gloom, heavy, depressing gloom. It seems as if the gay city had taken an enlivening trip across the Channel, and returned in the disguise of a British fog, so thick and murky is the atmosphere. In terse phrase, it is true November weather, that is, according to our insular traditions, though one might hope for other experience in the French capital. And the gloom, and drear, hopeless misery of the night, seem to have entered the heart or at least rested on the face of a man who is splashing heavily along through the soaked streets, in the immediate neighbourhood of the terminus of the South.

When the few passengers, who had rushed through those hours of dripping darkness, alighted at that chill, unwelcoming moment, they found fewer *fiacres* awaiting them:[1] the truth is, the race of French cabbies have not served the apprenticeship to heart-breaking, deplorable weather, which our stolid, seasoned "Jehus" have, and consequently resent its darker moods;[2] and so the drivers and

---

[1] *Fiacre*: horse-drawn four-wheel carriage for hire.

[2] Jehu: coachman, especially a fast or reckless one.

owners of the *voitures* stayed shivering at home, as well as all the rest of the world that could;[3] and the surplus passengers, who were not happy enough to be in time to fling themselves headlong into the two or three carriages that stood in melancholy, drenched wretchedness (generally depositing themselves on the coachman, who was forgetting his sorrows in sleep under cover of his own cab), had to trudge it.

But the particular pedestrian we have elected to follow on this miserable November night, heeds not the rain, or the chill, creeping fog—cares not whether he walks or drives—is scarcely conscious of aught around him, but tramps on drearily, persistently, rather slackening than hastening as he goes, with despair at his heart and on his brooding face.

Some thirty hours before he had started for the Riviera; he reached L—— (where he was to remain for a day or two before continuing south) at four in the morning, wearily found his hotel, and went straight to bed; at eleven o'clock he was roused from placid slumber by the landlord himself, who, with many and profuse apologies, was the bearer of a telegram for Monsieur; it came last night before Monsieur himself arrived; but, alas! through the *bêtise*, the deplorable carelessness of an infamous *garçon*, it had been forgotten, mislaid, and only this moment had been discovered;[4] would Monsieur pardon, excuse, would he have the complaisance to overlook such a misfortune? Monsieur, sleepily and unemotionally, took the ominous, greenish-blue paper from the hands of the verbose landlord, and proceeded slowly and uninterestedly to open it. Something connected with the business that was taking him

---

[3] *Voiture*: carriage, vehicle.

[4] *Bêtise*: stupidity. *Garçon*: waiter.

South, of course. Monsieur le Marquis had changed his somewhat capricious mind about some direction already given with regard to that wonderful Riviera château that was to be, and at the last moment flashed him his new whim, his fresh suggestion, thus—— And then, the paper lay open in his hands, and he sprang from his bed with a curse, as his face grew ashen white with indignant rage, while a cold, horrible fear crept round his heart. Who had sent him that warning? the ostensible name of the sender of the telegram was unknown to him; if it was all a baseless lie, would any one have the fiendish malice to carry it to such a pitch as this? Notes he had had, anonymous, one or two, telling him to beware—to watch—to guard his honour while he could; but a telegram was a different matter. He stormed, he swore in vigorous Saxon (and was consequently utterly unintelligible to his host) at the delay in receiving the direful message; he dressed, and breakfastless tore to the station, to find the fast train to Paris just gone. Was there ever such diabolical fate? He would have to wait hours, many hours for another—wait inactive, with fierce anger, wild grief, and agonised, torturing suspense raging and contending in his breast.

By-and-by he was tearing back over the ground he had travelled so tranquilly the night before, frantically chafing at each moment's delay.

At last he reached that gloomy station which he has just left, and would have been amongst the first to take bodily possession of a *fiacre* by sheer strength of will or body, but a note was thrust into his hand. He tore it open, glanced hastily at it by the dim, flickering light of the platform lamps, and then—staggered back half-fainting against the wall.

He was too late! too late to save his honour; too late to save what was dearer than honour, or life, or name; too late to save that good old name from being smirched, being trailed and dragged in the dust; and—*by her!* the woman he had idolised, the woman he had believed in as he did in his God, and this was the end; his home was deserted, he was dishonoured, and a despairing, broken-hearted man.

Thus he reflected, after reading those cruel lines, that cowardly, anonymous note, which stabbed the man to the soul, and then left him to writhe in bitter, helpless pain. For a few moments he was half stupefied, partly stunned by misery; but then he roused himself. How did he know that the venomous thing was true? He had had a couple of these poisoned barbs within the last month—those nameless notes that are craven's blows that strike you in the dark, and you know not from whom they come—but he had heeded them not. He had looked in his Helen's eyes, fresh from reading those slanderous hints and innuendos, and seen there—love and truth, and faithfulness unto death.

And now—why should he believe? And yet—that telegram that summoned him so urgently!

He stumbled out of the station like a man blindfold, mechanically repeating over and over to himself the brief, terrible sentences of that cruel note, as if the words had lost their meaning for his stricken ears, as if he sought dazedly to unravel some hidden mystery, and repeated a bidden formula automatically:—

"*Too late!* The bird has flown. Your hearth is desolate. Madame Dacre, the adorable, the facile Helen, eloped with the Marquis de Vallanelle while your farewell kisses were still warm upon her lips. You trusted 'all in all,' and thus your trust is rewarded."

On and on he tramps, through the deserted, drowned streets, his pace ever slackening as he nears his home, or rather, the house in which he has lived during the one short month he has been in Paris. It, or no place on this earth, will ever be really "home" to him again, if what he has read under those dim platform lamps to-night be true.

The Marquis! His patron—his employer—his only friend in all that brilliant city. And this, then, was the reason of his condescending friendship, his apparent simple kindness, which had been accepted in perfect good faith, partly as a natural tribute to his wife's rare beauty and charm (a tribute paid, as he supposed, in all honour), partly to that fact of their being aliens, and quite unknown.

The Marquis had brought him—Lionel Hartley Dacre, the clever, skilful architect, whose great talent was just beginning to be acknowledged—to France, to design for him an ideal château on the Riviera; also to devise certain improvements and decorations for his stately old mansion in the Faubourg St. Germain; besides suggestions for alterations he wished effected in his beautiful country-house, a few miles out of Paris.

He (Lionel) had been so fortunate, as he then thought it, to meet the Marquis de Vallanelle at a public *fête* in London, at which he and his wife were present, and where he was something of a personage, having just achieved the success which he hoped was a foretaste of the fame that would be his by-and by. An English patron, who esteemed his talent highly, introduced him to the French nobleman, hoping to obtain for him this very commission. The Marquis was wonderfully affable, he spoke English perfectly, and chatted in pleasantly familiar fashion, with the architect and his wife, and then made an appointment to talk business for the morrow. That interview was eminently satisfactory. Mr. Dacre should make his own terms; the one thing stipulated for by the Marquis was, that he should come to France as soon as possible;

he wished to have the work entered upon at once, and, from what his friend Lord —— had said of Mr. Dacre's talents, he had determined that no one else should design that château of which he had dreamed for the last twelve months, and that was to be a marvel of airy elegance, a home of delight.

Lionel Dacre felt duly impressed and flattered, and said he would make arrangements for leaving England at once. In another week the Marquis was returning, and he would follow in a few days.

Of course Madame Dacre would accompany him; his stay was uncertain, might be indefinitely prolonged; besides, it would be a charming opportunity for her to visit Paris. So spoke the Marquis, with kindly consideration. And so Lionel and his lovely Helen,—lovelier even after her ten years of matronhood, than the girl of twenty who stood with him at the altar in the bloom of her brilliant youth, and had been the sunshine of his life ever since, sunshine unchequered by even a passing shade,—and their little son, found themselves very delightfully settled in a luxurious *appartement* in the "Chaussée d'Antin;" much too ambitious a residence for their still simple ideas; they would have preferred to live in a less pretentious quarter; but the Marquis took the rooms, hired the servants, and insisted on bearing all expense, in short they must consider themselves his guests, though under another roof, as long as they remained in Paris. How wonderfully kind and affable he was, they thought, and how scrupulously courteous and polite, quite as much so as if they were his equals in rank, and these old Faubourg aristocracy were so apt to be haughtily exclusive. With what chivalrous respect and deference he uniformly treated Mrs. Dacre, and how considerately thoughtful and attentive he was; almost daily sending a carriage of his own to take her and her little boy an airing, because they demurred at his supplying them with one for their own especial use; sometimes even himself driving with the architect and his wife in the Bois, where ladies of the highest and most exclusive rank and fashion wondered as they bowed—perhaps a trifle frigidly—who was the lovely woman with the fair English face, who reclined with such easy grace in the Marquis de Vallanelle's carriage. She was a stranger; she was not of their set; and they would have shaken their heads and whispered scandal but for the presence of the stalwart Englishman at her side; even as it was, that protecting presence scarcely quite shielded her: there were some who glanced askance at that sweet face, with suspicious looks and suggestive shrugs.

But Lionel Dacre and Helen his wife, knew nothing, heard nothing, of Paris gossip. They did not know that the Marquis de Vallanelle was notorious as a profligate. They did not guess, when looking at his frank, almost boyish face—he was scarcely thirty, and looked younger than his years—that the fact of a woman being seen much in his society, was sufficient to cast a slur on her reputation; that his dearest delight in life was to damage the fair fame of any pure, trusting creature who was thrown in his way.

Rotten to the heart's core, was Louis, tenth Marquis de Vallanelle; and the beauteous, unsuspicious Helen Dacre, whom he had marked for his latest victim, felt pleased and flattered at his courteous notice; congratulating herself with fluttering pride on the good fortune that had given to her darling Lionel so influential and kindly a patron. How completely at her ease she felt, with this friendly, handsome, young French nobleman; and how distressingly the reverse with the pompous, laconic, elderly Lord —— on the one or two occasions of her meeting the English aristocrat. And to the young man of the gracious, simple, familiar manners—though not intrusively so—the lovely unconscious creature—innocent and confiding in spite of her thirty years,—shewed, unintentionally, the pretty enchanting tricks of face, and voice, and gesture, that always took fright and vanished when in the presence of strangers,—that were only seen to the best advantage by those who had the privilege of watching her in her home, in sweet familiar intercourse with those she loved. For this woman, in her single-hearted simplicity and loyal faithfulness, unlike many of her sisters, appeared at her very winsomest when with the dear ones that formed her world; she wanted no audience to admire, to applaud, when she smiled her sweetest smile and glanced most radiant glances; she was bright and playful and witching when happy in the still seclusion of her home, with her beloved husband and her idolised child, and knew not her own wondrous powers of fascination, powers quite apart from her beauty that was indisputable. All these subtle, indescribable charms, blossomed forth in unrestrained, unconscious perfection, before the eyes of Louis, Marquis de Vallanelle, who exercised an influence not unlike that of the fabled upas-tree, blighting where his shadow fell. He seemed so friendly and natural and unaffected, and so young—much younger than herself, she imagined,—that Helen Dacre lost all sense of strangeness and formality in his presence, and was her own sweet, arch, captivating self, smiling in the young man's face with serene security, little guessing, never dreaming that he would extinguish for ever the light of her happiness, the happiness that had been so true, so perfect.

That her whole life to come would be deformed and hideous, torturingly seared and twisted by those few weeks' acquaintance with this gentle-spoken French nobleman.

And so, during that short month in Paris, Helen has been on the very verge of a precipice, though she saw it not; a precipice, over which she must inevitably go. Though she imagined it not, she was bidding an eternal farewell to the dear old life, the life that seemed a very part of herself, from which she could never be dissevered, save by death, but which was fast slipping from her loving clasp.

Her Lionel, by whose side she looked forward to spend a long, and happy, and honoured life, God in His great mercy, she often thought and prayed, would let them both live to be very *very* old; they loved each other so intensely, He would have pity, and not separate them till the last possible moment.

And she thought not that soon, horribly soon, the time would come, that would see them parted as effectually as if the grave yawned already between them.

Her Lionel.

Her husband; her beloved, from whom she had never been separated but once or twice for a brief period since her marriage, to drift asunder in a fiercely short week or two; never again in all the cruel, distant, despairing years, to meet, to kiss, to speak, to look into each other's eyes—*until*——

CHAPTER II
IN THE SILENCE

ON and on, through the dreary dripping night, splashes the lonely wayfarer. How inexpressibly dismal and depressing are the silent sodden streets, so empty, so deserted, so still; how insidiously creeping and penetrating the thick yellow fog. The man shudders involuntarily, but whether from physical wretchedness or mental misery (the misery of a crushing terrible despair coupled with a sickening agonised suspense, a vague shadowy hope that is more horrible than downright torturing certainty), none can tell.

And now—he turns into the street, grown already familiar in those few weeks. He reaches the house that but a few hours ago he left with joy and pride and calm trustful love reigning in his breast, the house that had held for him all he cared for on earth.

And now!—He glances fearfully at the windows—the windows of his *appartement* that look upon the street—all is darkness, profound, inscrutable.

How will he have courage to enter and know his fate? And the strong man, weak in the moment of his anguish, walks a few yard from the threshold, which he dreads to cross, and there, in the pitiless rain, in the gloomy hushed street, he stands for a minute or two bareheaded in silent prayer for strength to bear as a Christian this awful blow with which it has pleased the Lord to visit him; for now and then a wave of wild demoniacal wrath, which almost staggers him, sweeps over him, making him feel more like devil than man. And then, in a few seconds more, he is in those rooms whose blank rayless windows he had gazed at from the street.

What brooding ominous darkness and boding stillness dwells

around, and yet what else can he expect at this hour? With trembling hand he strikes a light and kindles a small lamp, and to his nervous disordered fancy the weak flickering flame sheds a ghastly weird light through the lofty handsome salon, the room that has become so dear and familiar in those few latter days, though but a short month ago it seemed so strange and unhomelike. Is it not love, the presence of a beloved one, that oils with sweetest unguent the harsh new hinges of life, making all, however dissonant and jarring, soft and smooth and melodious?

How intensely it speaks to him of his Helen; are there not traces of her late presence around him everywhere? If she is gone, surely it must have been suddenly, without premeditation.

But no! How wrong, how wicked it is of him to think so devilish a thought. She is in her chamber but a few yards off quietly sleeping, doubtless dreaming loving dreams of him while he is desecrating her noble purity and faithfulness, by harbouring belief in such hideous slander even for a moment. What did that note, with its fiendish scorpion sting, say? He can't remember; and he again looks round the room slowly, while a strange wild troubled gleam grows in the clear calm steadfast eyes. There is the book she had been reading, thrown face downwards, open where she had flung it when he came in early in the afternoon with the more or less sudden intimation that he must start for the South that night. He remembered she cried a little and clung about him, and he had laughingly told her not to be a little goose, that so antiquated a matron as she was ought to care nothing for her husband's goings or comings, save a general feeling, that his absence was a good riddance, and she had given a little hysterical sobbing laugh and kissed him, and then, after some almost nonsense lover-talk, she had gone off to see after his portmanteau, &c. And there in the far window was her work-table and the pretty artistic cap, she was embroidering for Master Lion, who insisted, young rascal, on calling it his "smoking cap," the needle was still stuck in it where she had laid it down carelessly to come to dinner, which was served a little earlier owing to his departure, and the piano stood open, and his favourite song was on the desk, that she had sung at his request shortly before he left; how well he remembered every trifling incident of that afternoon and evening, and how the sweet voice trembled and broke a little at the words:—

> "O! that 'twere possible,
> After long grief and pain
> To find the arms of my true love
> Around me once again;"

and he had lovingly chided her for a nervous darling; and then, he moved a step or two, and his eye caught something on the carpet. He stooped and picked it up. Ah! the little odorous bunch of violets and heliotrope that she had worn in her bosom through the evening. The morning's post had brought a letter from dear friends in England, enclosing a few Torquay violets and a sprig of sweet-scented heliotrope; violets and heliotrope in November. Well, it sufficiently marked the contrast between the Paris season and that of Devonshire; it seemed like a little bit of their own dear land to the exiles, and after carefully keeping them in water all day Helen Dacre had pinned the tiny nosegay in her breast for dinner, and they had diffused a sweet faint perfume as she moved about. And her husband recollects that as he caught her to his arms for a final embrace almost his last impression was the clinging penetrating odour of her flowers, and now he holds the poor little withered posy in his hand, still it exhales a shadowy sweetness. Why has it been thus tossed aside? and why are the flowers so strangely, utterly dead? They seem as if they had lain there many, many hours, and yet, his train went at eight, and it is now not quite two.

Great God! he is going mad, stark staring mad!

He is losing all count of time. He had grown oblivious of the fact that nearly thirty hours have elapsed since he stood in that room and held his wife to his heart and smelt the rich sweet scent of those little dead blossoms; time for them to die, aye, and for a body and soul to die too. He has been looking round on all these tokens of her late presence, as if he had parted from her but the evening before, whilst a whole horrible day and night stretches between, and yet everything remains as he last saw it as if none had entered the room since. Where is Rosalie? Why does she not come and tell him of her mistress? He had asked no question of the servant who admitted him. His pride had revolted from doing so; but it had struck him that the man looked somewhat pale and troubled. But his wife's maid, where is she? If Helen had gone anywhere, she would have left a note, a message, with her. He will ring and question her. No, he will search the rooms himself first.

It is all some horrible coincidence. Helen perhaps has been poorly, not able to rise and enter the salon since he left, and the servants, taking advantage of her indisposition, have neglected to arrange it; or—and a wild gleam of hope darts across the thick pall of doubt and deadly conviction that has enveloped him the last few moments—possibly she has been summoned to her aunt, an elderly maiden lady, who lives some fifteen miles out of Paris, and whom Helen has driven out to see constantly since they came. Some dozen years before, Miss Templeton, feeling desolate and lonely in her English home, from which the dearly loved members had been carried forth one by one to the not far distant graveyard, had come to France to join a lady who, in their far away youth, had been her and her sister's governess; but as well as teacher and pupil she and Dorothy Templeton had been dear friends also, and this friendship had remained firm and unbroken through the years; and so she left her native land, probably never to return, taking with her one faithful servant who had been with her since they were both girls, who had been with her through the sorrow of her life and had proved herself a true, staunch, steadfast friend. Miss Templeton was much attached to her niece, her only brother's only child, and Helen would have been with her daily since they came to Paris but for the inconvenience of the situation where she lived, a village near which no railway passed, and twice fifteen miles is a long drive in one day.

But she had promised to spend a fortnight, perhaps a whole month, with her aunt when they returned from the Riviera, if not before they went; but as yet their plans had been too uncertain to permit of her staying beyond a day.

Three days ago Helen was with her last, and he remembers now her mentioning that Aunt Dorothy was ailing. Perhaps the lonely old woman had grown worse and sent for her niece, and Helen had gone, leaving Rosalie to look after little Lion, and also doubtless leaving with her a note to forward to him, her husband; for the dear girl could not guess the malign influence that was at work, that had sent that diabolical telegram and written that hellish note.

And so thinking, trying to cheat himself as long as remorseless fate will let him, he takes up the lamp and leaves the salon. He will not summon Rosalie yet awhile; perhaps he will not need to do so; perhaps God in his infinite mercy will grant that he may find his darling resting peacefully in her quiet chamber. How shall he explain his return? How shall he speak in that pure presence of the hideous mystery of devilry that encompasses them, that dares with foul and dastard tongue to assail *her*, his angel, his wife!

From the salon the wretched man passes with hurried uneven step into the small dining-room adjoining, and thence through a small chamber which has served him as a study, or place rather to keep his plans and papers in since they came. A hasty glance scans in an instant the mantel-piece in each room. A note in his wife's handwriting he half dreads, half longs to see. This room opens on to the landing, and facing him is one closed door. What lies beyond that portal? Is all that forms his world hidden but by that plank of wood? or does it mercifully screen for a moment longer the death of his happiness, his honour, the death of the very meaning life had for him hitherto?

What a frenzied look of tension there is in the set white face (the man has aged twenty years in those few hours) as he turns the handle and enters. How silent it is in that large and stately room, the very stillness of death itself. Surely no warm, living, breathing presence is within these cold, responseless walls. He holds the lamp aloft with trembling hand, and its rays fall on buhl and ormolu, and brass and oak, on full length mirrors with burnished candelabra, on soft low chairs, on full shrouding curtains at the windows and at the bed. This last stands in an alcove, at the further side of the room, and the light scarcely reaches it, except faintly to touch those long shielding rose-satin hangings; and with a heart that throbs furiously at this culminating supreme moment, a head that reels and limbs that bend and sway beneath him, Lionel Dacre dashes across the intervening space and tears the curtain aside to see the deadly confirmation of the horror he has been fighting against. The empty, smooth, unruffled bed meets his tortured gaze, and the agony that will be controlled no longer is wrung from his lips in a fierce wild groan.

"Gone! Gone! The cursed leprous thing is true. Helen, wife, mother of my child, fled from her home, and with *him!* She lay on my breast and planned this. She, whom I thought more saint than woman—she, who for ten long years has been a model wife, a devoted mother, a woman in ten hundred thousand, true as steel, pure as snow, and suddenly to sink into such an abyss of depravity and crime. It is monstrous, hideous! I refuse to believe it. It is some frightful demon plot to divide us; but it shan't succeed. My darling, my beloved has been fooled, cheated, duped in some way by some hell-loosed fiend; but she'll come running back with outstretched arms to her husband, from whom I swear one thought of her heart has not wandered, and de Vallanelle, I am convinced, he knows nothing of it. It is some practical joke concocted by some French ruffian, perhaps to see how the Englishman would take the aspersion of his wife's honour. He—whoever he is—had better not cross my path. If it were the Marquis himself I would strangle him where he stood ere he could gasp out a prayer to his Maker. God forgive me! I am mad and wild, and know not what I say."

And the distracted man stopped suddenly short in his fierce rapid walk up and down the long room, and dropped on his knees, burying his face in his hands. He had spoken the foregoing sentences in a frenzy and passion of grief, of horrified despair at the apparent awful confirmation of his anonymous warning; but after a minute or two he rose calmed, strengthened, hopeful.

"She is gone to Aunt Dorothy," he murmurs quietly, decidedly, as if in some strange occult way he had become convinced of the fact. "And she has either written me a note to L—— or left one with Rosalie to send. Fortunately I told the landlord of the hotel to forward any letters that might come. My dear one said she would write every other day, so if I hadn't rushed back like a fool, insulting her by doubting her, I'd have had a second letter to-day written from Miss Templeton's. I'll see Rosalie, and she'll tell me all about it, and as soon as morning breaks I'll drive out and see my dearest, and entreat her forgiveness for my temporary want of perfect faith."

And with another long, slow glance round the room, which took in mantel-piece and dressing-table, on either of which a letter may lurk, he crosses the threshold of the room for the last time; but before he is quite through the door the child occurs to his memory, and he glances back to where the boy's little bed stands. It also is empty! Where is Lion? Where is his son? Surely Helen would not take him with her: yet she might not like to leave the child to servants. Possibly Rosalie had him, the little fellow would doubtless be afraid to sleep all alone; and then returning to the salon he rings the bell, and as he stretches out his hand to do so, he sees that it still unconsciously clasps the tiny faded bouquet; he raises it, and inhales for an instant the clinging sweet odour not yet dead, then touching it reverently with his lips he thrusts it hurriedly into his breast out of sight; and ever after, through all the long and dreary years to come, the combined scent of heliotrope and violets, makes his heart grow sick and faint within him, recalling as it does so vividly, the night when his heart and his honour were so cruelly slain.

Then the door opens and a servant enters.

"Send Rosalie to me at once," speaks the master, and his voice sounds in his own ears harsh, strange, unfamiliar.

The man withdraws silently, but not without casting a mingled look of curiosity and pity on Mr. Dacre's averted face. Up and down the spacious handsome salon he paces as he waits for the slightly delayed coming of his wife's maid: not the simple, honest girl who had been with them since little Lion was a baby. Coming first in the capacity of nurse, she had remained on, though Lion had long repudiated the infantile word; but she looked after his wardrobe, and tended the little fellow with loving interest. She had grown very fond of her charge, and having more or less instituted herself Mrs. Dacre's maid (a luxury which that lady had not previously indulged in), she hoped to remain for many years near the boy she had carried in her arms as an infant—and who had awakened those mysterious maternal instincts in the young girl's heart. But this French visit had divided them, though only for a time, as all supposed. Though her heart was so warm with love and loyalty, yet poor Susan was woefully prejudiced, bigoted, and timid, and with deplorable insular ignorance, and dogged, immovable obstinacy, she hated, despised, and also feared all foreigners—more especially the French. No tongue, however eloquent, could persuade her that they had any virtues, that they had religion or morals, or cleanliness, or that their larder ever held aught but frogs and toads, and still more noisome creatures; as to going amongst them she would rather, she declared with energy, go and "live in a wood with a lot of 'bamboos' and 'orange-o-tanks' (presumably baboons and ourang-outangs) than with them jabbering Mossoos."

Hard to credit such thick darkness of national superstitious ignorance and narrow-mindedness in our boastedly enlightened country; yet isolated cases of equally lamentable prejudice linger even to this present day of light and leading.

So Susan, with much grief at her heart, but sturdy determination in her stupid head, refused point-blank to go abroad. She would seek no other place, but go home to her old mother while they were away, and would fret day and night, she knew, for Master Lion and her dear lady, and think the hour would never come that would bring them back again; but in spite of the dog-like fidelity and faithfulness of the honest, silly creature, go with them she would not.

And I scarcely think there could be a more striking instance of the awful and significant importance which the most trivial accidental circumstances sometimes exercise in a life or lives: a trifling miserable little chance act, word, rencontre, a mistake in a name or a number, an innocent forgetfulness or stupidity, will make or mar a history, will leave an impress that time cannot obliterate, or death destroy. And perchance the wrong or sorrow, and heart-breaking despair and wretchedness, that overtook and crushed these two people, whose life-tragedy is roughly sketched in these few pages would not have been if poor ignorant, mulish, loving Susan Barnes had not unhappily chosen to nourish in her crazy head a wild, outlandish hatred of all things outside of, and beyond, our insular domain.

And Rosalie—her supplanter, her rival? She was another witness of the Marquis de Vallanelle's considerate, kindly attentions to the Dacres. Hearing by chance an allusion to the English girl's obstinate refusal to cross the Channel, he immediately insisted on filling the blank in the Dacre household that Susan's absence caused, and though Helen protested that she did not want a maid, that she would much rather be without one, that never, long ago, had she been accustomed to such a pretentious item in their modest *ménage*, explaining how Susan had come to stay on in their service, but now Lion was getting a great boy, and independent of all the world of women save herself, yet the Marquis had his way, as marquises have a knack of having, and next day there appeared in Helen's dressing-room a bright, pretty, coquettish-looking, French girl, who proved herself, without delay, a perfect treasure; smart, deft, clever, sweet-tempered; she wormed herself without difficulty into the good graces of mother and son, and Helen began to wonder how she could part with her, though her sensitive heart told her that there was disloyalty to poor, faithful Susan, even in the very thought. But the newcomer's apparent devotion and undisguised admiration for little Lion unconsciously won the maternal partisanship, and though Mrs. Dacre knew the stranger could not have the true, deep love for her boy that filled honest Susan's heart, yet the girl showed her regard and fondness for the child in so bright, winning, and spontaneous a manner, as to carry all before it, and the memory of loving, stubborn Susan Barnes, who was guiltless of all winsome little graces, all small airy prettiness, and subtle, insidious, coaxing ways, that win love and liking without desert, was growing a little dim and blurred. Poor Susan, far away in England, is missing, and fretting, and longing for the boy she nursed, the employers whom she loved, and little dreams that never will she lay her earthly eyes on any of the three again.

And in the meantime, she who has temporarily taken her place, softly, hesitatingly opens the door of the salon, and with a pale scared face, and nervous, reluctant demeanour, appears before her suspense-tortured master.

"Where's your mistress?" he asks, sternly, with searching, flaming eyes bent upon the face, that flushes and pales, pales and flushes, in such swift alternation.

"Madame Dacre is—is, *hélas*—gone! *Voilà tout*, Monsieur; *et moi*——"[5]

"Gone!" echoes the despairing listener, interrupting the halting, faltering girl, whose speech generally flows with such pretty,

[5] *Hélas*: alas. *Voilà tout*: that's all, there's nothing more to say.

confident rapidity. "Gone! What do you mean? Gone where?—to Miss Templeton's?"

"Ah, Monsieur, I am desolated, *c'est un malheur terrible, un désastre affreux*. Madame Dacre is no more here: she goes the night of last, and returns never. I tremble *moi*, I wait and watch *toute la nuit*, but she comes not again ever; *et le chéri, le pauvre petit* Monsieur Lion——"[6]

"Woman! Can that cursed French tongue of yours speak to be understood, and speak truth? I ask you where my wife, Madame Dacre is, and you jabber in your villainous way that none can comprehend. When did your mistress leave this? where did she go? and with whom? Answer truly as you hope for salvation; and be quick, or——" and he abruptly ceases. The girl, feverishly lacing and interlacing her trembling hands, gives a swift, panic-stricken, questioning glance at her interlocutor's face at this unfinished, doubtful termination of his sentence; then her eyes quickly seek the floor again, and she involuntarily moves a step or two nearer the door.

"Monsieur, my best I do *vraiment*. Madame has gone *hier au soir*; about eleven hours she departed. *Une lettr*e came for Madame but a little *demi-heure* before——"[7]

"Ah, from Aunt Dorothy as I knew," mutters the man, while a spark of hope illumines the sick despair of his eyes.

"*Le cher pauvre petit* has the sleep upon the sofa, *eh bien!* Monsieur le Marquis arrive in minutes few *après la lettre*; he and Madame talk, *parlent doucement, eh Mon Dieu! si doucement et si vite*—quick *je veux*

---

[6] *C'est un malheur terrible, un désastre affreux*: it's a terrible misfortune, a frightful disaster. *Toute la nuit*: all night. *Et le chéri, le pauvre petit*: and the darling, the poor little.

[7] V*raiment*: truly, really. *Hier au soir*: yesterday evening. *Une lettr*e : a letter. *Demi-heure*: half an hour.

dire; pardon, Monsieur, *mais j'ai peur*, and I forgot the English—if I may say slow, I vill remember," she interpolates in frightened tones, as he to whom she speaks makes a wild gesture of impatience.[8] "*Tout le temps la voiture* of Monsieur le Marquis waits, *et bientôt* Madame and le Marquis leave the salon to depart.[9] Madame *a l'air* pale, *distrait*—what you call—how you say it—flurried, *agité n'est ce pas*?[10] Monsieur le Marquis *chuchote*, persuade; Madame *en hésitant*, lingers *pour un moment; elle a le cher petit fils* still sleeping under below *un manteau noir* which goes to *envelopper* Madame from *cou aux pieds*, not of *chapeau, mais simplement la capote du manteau* folds her head.[11] Monsieur le Marquis is in hurry; Madame *ne parle pas un mot*, but she has *des frémissements un peu; ils vont partir*, and I demande Madame from where she goes at the hour so late.[12] She not responds, *mais les yeux* have *un air effarouché, et Juste Ciel!* in a little moment they are gone!"[13]

"That letter your mistress got was from her aunt, Miss Templeton? Prevaricate not at your peril."

---

[8] *Après la lettre*: after the letter. *Parlent doucement, eh Mon Dieu! si doucement et si vite*: speak softly, oh my God! so softly and so quickly. *Je veux dire*: I mean. *Mais j'ai peur*: but I am afraid.

[9] *Tout le temps la voiture*: all the time the car. *Et bientôt*: and soon.

[10] *A l'air*: looks. *Distrait*: distracted. *Agité n'est ce pas*?: agitated isn't it?

[11] *Chuchote*: whispers. *En hésitant*: hesitatingly. *Pour un moment*: for a moment. *Elle a le cher petit fils*: she has her dear little son. *Un manteau noir*: a black coat. *Envelopper*: wrap. *Cou aux pieds*: head to toe. *Chapeau*: hat. *Mais simplement la capote du manteau*: but just the coat hood.

[12] *Ne parle pas un mot:* doesn't say a word. *Des frémissements un peu:* the quivers a little. *Ils vont partir*: they are going to leave.

[13] *Mais les yeux*: but her eyes. *Un air effarouché*: a frightened look. *Et Juste Ciel!*: and good heavens!

"Monsieur, I not know; but I think, *au moins* imagine, q*ue la lettre* was of the Marquis."[14]

"The Marquis! take care what you say. Will you take your oath of that?"

"*À Dieu ne plaise*, Monsieur, I swear never; I say only as I think."[15]

"And what message did your mistress leave for me?"

"*Message? Je ne vous comprends*, Monsieur," twisting and twining her hands still more nervously.[16]

"Don't lie, woman! Where's the letter she wrote and left with you? have you sent it? or had you the infernal insolence to forget it? Take care of yourself. By Satan, you shall suffer if you deceive me! Where's my letter? Answer me, I say."

Lionel Dacre is half frantic, and feels a wild, senseless rage against the pretty, frightened girl, as she stands there confronting him. How he loathes and detests, with an irrational, fierce hatred, the sound of the French tongue, of the broken English, as it falls from her lips; and never in all the years to come will a foreign tone in a voice, a French phrase, an un-English rendering, fail to thrill and jar his nerves with a throbbing pain, a sick, shrinking, creeping of the flesh, as if some noisome creature had crawled over him.

"Lettare, Monsieur?" and the girl goes from a brighter red to an intenser pallor than any previous fluctuation. "*Je n'ai aucune de lettre moi.*[17] Madame write no lettare *à* Monsieur. *Eh! Mon Dieu!* what for

[14] *Au moins*: at least.

[15] *À Dieu ne plaise*: God forbid.

[16] *Je ne vous comprends*: I don't understand you.

[17] *Je n'ai aucune de lettre moi*: I don't have any letter.

should I have lettare?" She cries, with more vehemence than she has yet evinced. "*Sainte Vierge!*[18] I take no lettare of Madame: she carries she with her; *comme* she carries *le cher petit fils—il est trop*, how you say—beeg? *pauvre chéri*, for the arms of Madame, *il faut qu'elle*——"[19]

"Cease, woman—you'll drive me mad! Have you the heart of a fiend in your bosom that you torture me thus? Leave me to my misery, to my despair, to the horror of thick darkness that your accursed country has brought on me. It is some diabolical plot, some foul conspiracy. But let all who are involved in it—beware! To the death I will punish the traitors—ay, to the death! Do you know what that means? Death—death—you French witch!" shaking his clenched hand in the girl's terrified, pallid face, as he almost shrieks out the last few words, and she gives a faint, gasping scream, and flies from the room.

---

[18] *Sainte Vierge*: blessed virgin.

[19] *il est trop*: he is too. *Il faut qu'elle*: she must.

CHAPTER III
THROUGH THE DARKNESS

POOR Lionel Dacre! He is indeed distraught. His kindly, generous, gentle nature, seared and scorched by the magnitude of his misery, by the intensity of his anguish. An impotent ferocity, horribly foreign to his native calm sweetness, his mild, equable serenity and justness, had taken temporary possession of him. Who is it says—"There is a savage element in most natures, which only requires waking to be dangerous," and Lionel Hartley Dacre feels not unlike some poor desperate frenzied (*mother*) beast, who has been basely, cruelly robbed of her young, has seen them wantonly slain at her side, who howls and roars in her boundless rage and agony; and who, though ordinarily gentle and peaceable, would tear, and rend, and slay any that approach, in her wild, senseless craving for revenge on the cravens who have murdered those, her little ones, her cubs, the delight and desire of her loving, tortured, brute's heart.[20] The *animal* is in us all, and will assert itself at times, in spite of the thick-coated veneering gloss of centuries of civilisation; the savage instinct to hurt, maim, kill, rises up giant-like, in its overmastering power; devil-like, in its insatiatc thirst for evil; brute like, in its ferocious, unreasoning haste; and Christ, and his divine teachings, and the great, glorious, eternal example which He has left for us, of a sublime, supernal submission for all ages, is forgotten—faith, intellect, culture, habits of thought and life, the qualities that make the barrier between barbarism and civilisation, go to the wall.

[20] Taken from *Maxwell Drewitt* by F. G. Trafford (Charlotte Riddell): 'There is a savage in most which only requires waking to be dangerous.'

And for a brief moment (happily 'tis but a moment with the greater number) we are monsters more than men. A hellish wrath, a fierce, terrible hunger for vengeance, swift and deadly, rages in Lionel Dacre's breast, as he strides up and down that lofty salon, alone in his despair. Alone, unfriended, unconsoled, in this, the hour of the most horrible grief, the most awful trial that can come upon a man.

For is not dishonour a thousand times worse than death? The one is dissolution of the soul; the other, but the decay of the physical tenement where that soul has had its habitation; and would not a man who truly loved and trusted a woman, who believed in her purity and her virtue, rather lay, with his own hands, that woman in her coffin, himself closing down the cruel lid, the impenetrable door that for all time would shut away her who lay within from the sights and the sounds, the joys and the sorrows of life; the door that none may open to greet the quiet inmate of that darkened chamber, but which seals the captive fast until the day of resurrection; would not a man, I say, a million times rather bury—aye! even slay—the woman so loved, so trusted, the wife who had lain in his bosom, the mother of his children, than have to assist with wild loathing, with quivering, tortured rage and remembrance, at the obsequies of the soul he thought so white, so spotless?

Helen,—his wife,—his beloved;—the woman who seemed to him a creature apart in her moral loveliness, a loveliness as entire, as perfect, as indisputable, as her physical fairness. A woman, as he had believed, of a noble purity, who held a lofty, high-souled standard of human excellence, of a wife's duties, a mother's responsibilities. A woman who had seemed the very essence of truth and loyalty, and loving devoted faithfulness, to have suddenly fallen so hideously low; to have voluntarily thrown herself from her pedestal of safety and honour, and stainless rectitude, into the deepest depth of the mire, the mire that would engulf her in its foul loathsomeness; mire, that the slightest touch of clings, and obstinately will not be brushed away; and she, in one fell moment, had plunged therein, and—was lost, lost for ever . . . .

And for a man whom, a month ago, she met for the first time. A man, whom she had never appeared to notice, beyond what courtesy compels; whom she had discussed freely, unreservedly, with him, her husband, talking frankly of de Vallanelle as "a pleasant young fellow," "a boy" (as she often styled him) "who was so unlike her preconceived ideas of the French noblesse;" laughing a little with sweet, arch, brightness, that never degenerated into ill-nature, or aught of unkindliness, at the foreign courtesy, the mannerisms that often seem, to unaccustomed English ears, as exaggerated and strained. A woman to whom deceit seemed a horror, who appeared to detest, and had no patience with pretence or false seeming; who seemed to scorn a lie; to have descended to such degradation of hypocrisy——

"It is monstrous, inconceivable," he groans as he throws himself into a chair with his arms out flung on the table before him, and his head bent low upon them in a passion of despair.

An hour and more passes, and still he maintains that attitude of pitiful abandonment, his form from time to time at first shaken by terrible heart-straining sobs that convulse his frame, and are evidence of the fiery anguish within, but sobs that bring no blessed relief of tears; the man's eyes are dry and burning, tears he weeps this night are not outward tears of innocent brine, but tears of blood, that none but God may see.

Nearly two hours have passed away since he entered that room; could agony so great be compressed into so fearfully short a space? He raises his head, and gazes with hollow eyes about him, then the same words fall from his lips, with the same strange accent of mysterious conviction: "She is gone to Aunt Dorothy, and taken the boy with her." He rises slowly to his feet; he feels weak and giddy, as if he had been long ill, and grasps the table for a moment or two to steady himself; then deliberately, without undue haste, he makes his preparations to go out again into that terrible drenching night, or rather morning. The weather has grown much worse, wilder, fiercer, since he has been abroad; the rain now lashes the panes furiously; while the wind, only lately risen, shrieks, and moans like a creature in pain, a creature flying for its life, hunted through the darkness, through the night, that struggles in desperation, and with clamorous, wailing pleadings, to effect an entrance by door or casement, to seek shelter from its pursuers. Calmly, methodically almost, Lionel Dacre puts on coat and hat that had been thrown aside; a great peace seems suddenly to have settled on him, while his haggard eyes have a distant, far-away look, as if he was straining to see something beyond.

"Aunt Dorothy sent for her, and she is gone. De Vallanelle lent his carriage. She will have written to me to-day to L——. I'll have her letter to-morrow, but before I see her letter I'll see her face; my darling, my dearest, my Helen, I am coming to you now; you want me. I hear your voice crying for me through the stillness; my angel, whom I have cowardly wronged by foul suspicion, I am coming, coming," he murmurs in a dreamy way, with the same fixed absent look in his eyes; and then, in another moment, he is again in the desolate, wind-swept street, with the rain dashing in his face, and the creeping, raw, November cold, subtly penetrating his whole being. By great good fortune he meets a *fiacre*, the driver of which is disengaged, and the horse fresh; the driver, in fact, has just come out; he is an energetic man, and shrinks not from the weather like some of his brethren. He was abroad the night before till nearly ten o'clock, went home wet and tired, had a few hours' sleep, and finding the rain not abating, was out again at three, with a fresh horse to meet the early morning trains: he is on his way to the nearest station when met by Mr. Dacre. Here is a fare, ready and willing to pay almost anything that cabby's elastic conscience may demand; and he hugs himself in delighted congratulation, and doubtless neglects not to mentally recite the French rendering of a certain pertly, odiously familiar proverb, anent the aggressively "early bird," and the aggravatingly wakeful "worm." Straight to the Marquis de Vallanelle's residence in the Faubourg St. Germain Lionel Dacre is driven; the wild, mad, improbable story he has heard, wants some confirmatory proof before he can let it enter his mind at all; not that anything he may hear, he solemnly vows, can alter his belief that his wife is with her aunt, safely sheltered under the roof of that dainty cottage *ornée* in that distant sleeping village.[21]

At the de Vallanelle mansion he hears but what appears thoroughly to substantiate Rosalie's narrative. Monsier le Marquis left there the evening but one before, at about ten o'clock, in his small close brougham, that he always uses for night driving;[22] he directed to be driven to Monsieur Dacre's residence in the Chaussée d'Antin, and he has not been seen since by any of his household; neither has the carriage returned, nor his valet who accompanied him, though the coachman somewhat strangely was sent back almost immediately.

They know nothing of their master's whereabouts; he has not gone to "Sans Souci" (a charming château some four or five miles

---

21 *Ornée*: ornate.

22 Brougham: light, four-wheeled carriage that could be drawn by one horse.

out of Paris), because the head gardener was in town yesterday, wanting to see the Marquis with regard to the new range of hot-houses; that was about three o'clock; it would be possible, of course, that the Marquis might have gone to "Sans Souci" since, but it was not probable. The Marquis generally mentioned when he was going out of town—that is, any distance by rail that would detain him a day or two; besides, there remained the peculiarity of the non-appearance of the carriage; such a thing may have happened two or three times before, but it was rare. Mr. Dacre has no reason to doubt the information thus received; the man's manner is perfectly natural, he speaks English fluently, and seems unaffectedly surprised at his master's absence.

But in spite of this singular corroboration of the anonymous letter, and the girl's statements, Lionel Dacre still refuses to believe, still fights desperately against the gradually swelling roll of evidence, evidence that by-and-by will seem to him clear as Holy Writ. The first shock crushed him with its very weight of horror; the first tremendous wave rushed over him, engulfing him in its awful, unexpected suddenness; he was drawn under, and had struggled despairingly for a terrible minute or so, and almost given up; and then he had been buoyed to the surface again, and gaspingly breasted the on-coming giant billows, each colossal wall of water seeming more deadly than the last; and yet still the struggling human waif rides those stormy waves, sinking, perhaps, a little, as each rolls on unsparingly; but still with the pallid white face raised imploringly skywards; but soon, horribly soon, if the strength does not give out before, the creature, to whom no help can come, must inevitably be dashed upon those terrible granite cliffs, rising rugged and pitiless, just in front.

Yes, the granite cliff of "certainty," that is what Lionel Dacre is hastening on to when he bids his coachman drive out to G——, the village where Aunt Dorothy resides; and though it is fifteen miles, in darkness, rain, and wind, the driver of the *voiture* rejoices exceedingly; his horse is young and fresh, he himself is well made up against the weather, and he again reflects with amazement and many inward benisons, on the wonderful luck that has been sent him, on this miserable November morning. Most likely his fare—who seems a queer, excited *pauvre Anglais*[23]—will want to return to Paris, and if he can only get him to wait long enough to rest the horse, what a handful of money he will bring back to *la chère Marie, et les petits Jean et Jacques.*[24]

Fifteen miles—*Peste!* what are fifteen miles when the heart is light and the pocket prospectively heavy?[25] And the man whistles softly from sheer gaiety of spirit as he whips up his horse, and rattles through the dismal, saturated streets, and out on the villa-bedecked roads, and by-and-by, through lonely country lanes where darkness reigns profound, impenetrable, on deserted, dreary highways, where the lamps shine dim and blurred at desolate intervals.

Fifteen miles—and the man on the box almost wishes it were longer if the horse would hold out, for the pay would be higher, and his heart dances in his breast, for he is young, and happy, and life seems sweet, so sweet, though his lot does compel him to drive through rain and darkness.

And the man inside the vehicle groans as he thinks of those out-stretching miles, and his own imprisonment in that small,

---

23 *Pauvre Anglais*: poor Englishman.

24 *La chère Marie, et les petits Jean et Jacques*: Dear Marie, and little Jean and Jacques.

25 *Peste*: an oath, damn, darn.

gloomy cell. Fifteen miles; alone with torturing suspense, and a sick weight as of lead crushing down his heart; not even to have the relief of restless movement to assuage the mental fever. Fifteen miles in darkness, with the grim blackness of the night abiding in his breast; but he shrinks not, and on they go—a fair example of how the light and shade of life are ever just touching, jogging each other in the streets, sitting elbow to elbow in car and train. Here—the darkest, deepest, most desperate care, wretchedness, despair. There—radiant happiness, hope, joy; and yet, the light in one breast never illuminates the gloom, or even detects its presence in another; nor does the shadow—thick and murky though it be in one heart—dim, by the slightest veiling, the faintest penumbra, that clear brightness steadily shining in another at its side. How close we are, how near to each other, and yet—how immeasurably, how mysteriously distant! Slight is the barrier, yet none may penetrate it. Each individual dwells alone with his own soul; and none may enter in but God!

An isolation, a solitariness incomprehensible, is that of each human spirit as it journeys in this dual solitude through the years of its earthly pilgrimage. None may enter and share that long, long loneliness; the nearest, the dearest, must stand without, and in vain seek admittance. Each temple of flesh has its innermost chamber, its "Holy of Holies," where the dweller in the temple talks alone with his soul and with his Maker. This "inner self," how strange, how mysterious is its existence, this quiet, silent inmate, which looks on at life, and says no word to betray its presence to the world; and yet—it (that indefinite "*It*") is much more the real man or woman than that we know or talk to. Each individual walks about with this second self invisible, undiscoverable; they hold converse together, unsuspected of men. It, and "It" only, sees the real heart of the man, bared and free from disguise. Are "It," this secret, inner, wondrous self, and the soul one and indivisible? or have each a separate and distinct existence? But this is no place for such discussions, and we are wandering far afield from Lionel Dacre, driving swiftly through the night's darkness, with a blacker depth of care and woe unutterable in his breast, and yet still clinging desperately, frenziedly, to one faint, shadowy hope, the dim, flickering rush-light, whose feeble, uncertain ray is the only speck that pierces the heavy gloom.

He looks at his watch; it is not far from four o'clock; the horse is young and fresh, the roads are tolerably good; he may expect to reach the village where Dorothy Templeton resides by half-past six, if nothing occurs to delay him, he calculates, as he throws himself back with a groan, and looks out with blank, non-seeing eyes, on the sleep-bound city, on the muddy, wet pavements, and the flaring gas lamps that have the streets all to themselves, save for an old, skulking, hurrying figure here and there. Soon the markets will be open and astir, but not yet. Even already, on the distant country roads, heavily-laden carts and wagons are rumbling slowly towards Paris; but still night and sleep hush and rock the great throbbing heart of the city to rest; and how often those who are by chance awake and abroad at such a time feel somehow either a terrible loneliness, or else a strange sense of guilt and secrecy. They are active, waking, moving, thinking, while all around is sleeping, helpless man; and it seems to them, as they hasten through the night, fearful and abashed, unheard by these dulled ears, that if all those sleeping ones could suddenly awake, and see their hurrying, gliding figure passing alone through the silence and the shadow, they would point with gibing finger of scorn and derision at him who was striving to come abreast with "Time" by rushing him through the night, taking an unfair advantage by going forth to meet the morning and the world ere each had risen. Either that, or they would shrink from him, as a nocturnal, noisome creature sinuously winding his secretive way through the labyrinths of dark and sleep.

What weird, fantastic fancies come to us in the small hours, irrational imaginings for which we cannot account.

A sense of horrible loneliness and desolation oppresses Lionel Dacre as if it were a tangible weight, it presses him down. He feels as if the whole world were dead, and he alone moving ghost-like through its deserted silence. He looks out into the black void surrounding him (they have now left the city, and are in the open country) and shudders; it seems to him as if they were passing over graves, innumerable graves, the graves of that world that is hushed in death. Eerie, superstitious thought shape themselves in his mind as he is borne along through the night's gloom, which serve for a brief space to divert him from the miserable, hideous errand on which he is bound.

He feels as if he were on a sort of dim, mysterious borderland between the known and the unknown, the real and the unreal; as if it suddenly came to him, inspiration-wise, that in these loneliest watches of the night, in the darkness, in the silence, the shrouding veil that hides "the just beyond" from our straining eyes becomes transparently thin; and that we hover unconsciously on the confines of the other world; that if we had but a patient, perfect faith our eyes would see what no eyes have seen, our ears would hear what no ears have heard; that the dark realms of air round and above us are peopled with the unseen; that countless numbers—far exceeding the living on earth—are coming and going swiftly, silently; that our own—

"Those we have loved, long since, and lost awhile,"[26]

come crowding round us, and touch us with their spirit hands, strengthening us by that touch for the fray and battle of life, blessing us as we go with their spirit voices, that reach not our earth-clogged ears; that, in short, in the dark, during those hours of human sleep and silence, we who are awake and astir move amidst a mighty host of the dead. A wild, fantastic idea you will say; and yet, which of us would be rash and confident enough to assert positively that such a thing cannot be? No message reaches us from those who have journeyed to that country, which is perhaps so awfully distant, or so mysteriously, fearfully near. We know not where our dear ones are; and would it not be sweet and consoling to think of them, not as infinitely far off, lost to our mental comprehension in the limitless regions of space, but that nearer, closer, in the air around us at times hover those emancipated spirits, guarding—blessing (though we guess it not), helping (though we see no hand outstretched), holding with us a species of mystic communion, unsuspected by our unspiritualised humanity, yet that insensibly purifies and supports and heals and strengthens when we are bruised and crushed under the relentless cart-wheels of the world?

"Surely a sorry lot for our beloved dead"—you will probably make answer—to be conscious of the misery of those dear to them on earth, and yet powerless to avert it; but, may it not be, that they, with their spirit eyes, see the end! and seeing, all the griefs and sorrows and distresses that tear our hearts and wear our lives are to them but the little accidental roughnesses and unevennesses on the path on which we must walk to gain that end, the path which

---

[26] Based on a line from the hymn 'Lead, Kindly Light' by John Henry Newman: 'Which I have loved long since, and lost awhile.'

leads to that glorious goal that is beyond mortal sight. And Lionel Dacre gazes with rapt eyes out into the (to him) peopled darkness, and fancies he hears the rustle of garments, a faint echo, as of voices, spoken across a gulf of time or distance; surely—he catches a murmur of tones once dear and familiar—the mother he loved so passionately in the bygone years. She is there, somewhere near. He can feel her presence. In that strange, soundless voice she breathes words of encouragement and love.

"Hark!" And he bends still closer to the open window of the carriage. *That* is not her voice; that is one clearer still, one who has not yet entered into "shadow-land;" that is a living voice. For the second time to-night Helen has called him. Erect, expectant, he sits, his eyes no longer gazing into the black void beyond the window, but looking straight before him, with a strange, introspective, intensely listening expression in their mournful depths . . . . And quite clearly through the silence come the words,—"*Lionel, love,—husband, come to me! Life of my life, come quickly!*" And he stands up, as if he would go faster, "*Coming, darling! Coming, coming!*" he cries, and the coachman turns round on his box and asks him did he speak; and seeing, by the faint light of the carriage lamps the man as he is,—standing, looking as if he saw something beyond his surroundings, and muttering to himself,—he promptly concludes that his fare is a lunatic as well as an Englishman, who, it is to be devoutly hoped, does not carry fire-arms; and, with a prayer to the Virgin for protection, he lashes on his horse, and, for the first time, thinks with something like dread of the long miles still stretching between them and their destination. He even, for a moment, entertains a wild idea of, in some way or other, tumbling the occupant of the *fiacre* out on the road, and then leaping on the box and galloping swiftly back to Paris, but this he immediately rejects. The *pauvre Anglais* may be harmless, and will he run the risk of losing those golden louis that he has already handled in imagination? and so, on they rattle through the darkness. But to Lionel Dacre the gloom is no longer peopled; he no longer hears voices, living or dead; the prosaic interruption of the driver's question banished his weird fancies, and he sinks back on the seat, with his eyes closed, in dreary, miserable musing.

But soon these wretchedest, saddest thoughts that can possess the soul of man are soothed in sleep. Nature, who has been so badly used, asserts herself, and the man, worn out with fatigue and want of food, exhausted by mental suffering, slumbers peacefully, profoundly.

How strangely often this is so, that great grief, heavy trouble, acts like a narcotic, and that those who are, in the usual way, light and easily awakened sleepers, will fall into deep and dreamless slumber after hours of mental misery. The sleep may be short and the awakening terrible, but while it lasts oblivion is complete, unbroken.

And now, Lionel Dacre, who would have sworn that he never could sleep in a cab, especially one jolting through uneven country lanes, and above all, that unconsciousness could not weigh down his eyelids while despair and suspense tore at his heart, sleeps sweetly and restfully as a child.

CHAPTER IV
AUNT DOROTHY

AT exactly twenty minutes to seven o'clock, and nearly two hours after Lionel Dacre fell into that heavy sleep, the cab stops at the door of Miss Templeton's residence. The village they have just driven through is waking into sleepy life, though but the very faintest sign of the late and sickly dawn of this gloomiest November morning appears in the east; a slight grey tinge, more depressing than the actual black it dispels.

The rain is over, but there is a raw penetrating cold in the air, an almost imperceptible drizzle that makes one feel more completely wretched than does a fierce honest rain or boisterous winter wind.

Lionel Dacre somewhat roughly wakened from sleep—the sleep that has been so profound—by the stopping of the cab at the gate of Miss Templeton's pretty cottage, opens his dazed, haggard eyes, and looks around in the early, dreary dawn with non-comprehending miserable stare, and shivers with a chill, dull sense of foreboding ere his sleepbound senses realize where he is, and why?

Early as is the hour, Miss Templeton's household is astir; for nine months of the year that lady herself rising at half-past six. During the remaining three, December, January, February, she lies in an hour later, but as November has still a week to run and her habits are methodical in the extreme, she is in the act of dressing when her nephew arrives and is shown into a little breakfast parlour, where a fire has already been kindled. He asks no question of the maid who admits him; if it had been the English servant—the elderly woman, who is Miss Templeton's friend as well as serving woman in her voluntary exile—he would have spoken the words that seem to burn his brain, and yet that his lips feel as if they could not frame; as it is, he possesses his soul in the patience of despair. The foreboding of a moment ago has become a certainty; he feels instinctively that his wife is not beneath that roof, that his journey has been in vain, and so thinking he sits down in brooding silence to wait for Aunt Dorothy, as he has learned to call her.

And she does not keep him long, in little more than five minutes the door opens, and the mistress of the cottage appears. The struggling light of early day has grown stronger in these last few moments, and we see her plainly as she enters—a slight, delicate, fragile woman, not to say old, being but little past fifty, with an intensely interesting face, one of those faces with a pathetic sweetness, a pleading mournfulness in its tender gentle lines that one is apt to see in the faces of the sensitive deformed, for Miss Templeton is misshapen, slightly but decidedly, though one ceases to remember the imperfect figure (the result of an unhappy accident in her bright early womanhood) when looking in the face so full of a sweet holy calm, a loving lovely sympathy, and yet withal that look of rooted, patient sorrow.

Her niece is very dear to her. She had had a sincere love for her as a child, and they had corresponded most affectionately ever since Miss Templeton left England.

When she heard of Helen's engagement and marriage she had felt genuine regret and compassion: the girl was going forth surely to meet sorrow and disappointment of some kind when she placed her happiness in the hands of any man, of this her aunt felt convinced, but she forbore to exhort, to try to influence, the young creature who in the first glamour of her young joy would have laughed at Aunt Dorrie's dismal croakings; the light of *her* life could not be quenched, no matter who else's might be extinguished, so the girl would argue, in confident rash security, Miss Templeton knew instinctively, knowing by the light of her own wretched experience; the radiant brightness of her own youth and hopes she would have once declared to be "undimmable," when the shadow suddenly fell and blotted it out for ever. Besides, Helen had her mother, who had a better right to guide and influence her; and so the loving, lonely soul, far away in a foreign land, contented herself by praying earnestly for the welfare and happiness of her dead brother's only child, and when by-and-by she heard that the woman was even more perfectly happy than the girl, when the years rolled on, and she heard of nought but peace and trust and unity, and ever increasing love in that married home, a strong unconscious affection grew in her breast for her unknown nephew, which had been deepened in the three or four times they had met since he came to Paris. And now, as she looks at him as he sits unconscious of her approach, his head sunk on his breast with haggard gloomy eyes fixed on vacancy, a great fear rises in her heart. What has changed him so fearfully? A week ago, when he was last within those walls with Helen at his side, he looked the impersonation of vigorous manhood, with serene content and quiet happiness written on his brow; now he looks actually an old, broken man, with cruel lines of suffering, grief, horror—which is it?—traced around those dark hollow eyes, about the painfully compressed lips.

She pauses just a moment close beside him before she speaks, before she rouses him from that strange absorption into which he has fallen. A queer little catch in her breath from sheer nervousness at seeing him thus makes speech difficult, and so dumbly she lays a soft, gentle hand on the poor fellow's shoulder, and looks with anxious, eager inquiry into his face. At that light touch he starts horribly, and glares at her for a moment, with a strange wild fierceness in his glance; she shrinks back a little, while a dread springs new-born in her heart, "Can it be that Helen's husband drinks?" Surely such a terrible fate is not to overtake her darling. "A drunkard's wife!" But the next instant this fear is dispelled for ever.

"My wife!" gasps the wretched man. "What have you done with her? Where is she? Speak, Aunt Dorothy! for Christ's sake speak, and tell me where to find her. Where is my Helen, my beloved?" And there is such a depth of agonised despair in his tones, that the woman's soul turns faint and sick within her; what misery is this that is coming—or already come—after all those years of tranquil peace?

"Lionel, my nephew, what is it? What do you mean? . . . What of Helen? don't speak so wildly, you terrify me . . . . What has happened to my dearest girl?" And Miss Templeton sinks down tremblingly into the nearest chair; she has but a frail body, though a brave heart, and her throat feels dry and husky, and her lips so parched that she can scarcely form her words, and yet she strives to speak calmly, soothingly, not to excite unnecessarily the man who gazes at her with a hungry, desperate questioning in his eyes.

Another thought flashes like lightning through her brain as he looks at her thus, "Can he have gone mad, suddenly, hopelessly mad?" but the thought is gone as soon as formed; there is no fire of madness in those terribly sad eyes, so near her own, nothing but the desperation of a mighty sorrow. "She is gone!" he cries hoarsely. "Gone?" echoes Miss Templeton in distracted non-comprehension. "Gone where? For God's sake, Lionel, calm yourself, and don't let excitement carry you away; be rational, and tell me what you mean. Where is Helen? my darling, my dear one; she—she—c-can't be—oh Lionel. Surely she can't be—you're not trying to tell me that—that she—she is dead!" ends the poor affrighted lady in an awed whisper, with her hand pressed to her heart to still its nervous throbbings.

"Would to God she were!" cries the unhappy man vehemently, and Miss Templeton cowers and shrinks at the flame of lightning wrath that for a moment displaces the misery of his eyes. "Death would be blessed, 'tis the hand of God, while this—this—" and his face grows dark with passion, while a note of wildly discordant pain jars his voice, and cuts down into the very heart of his listener. "*This* is of the devil! Helen, my wife whom I worshipped and thought of only as a little lower than the angels, to be——, Great and merciful Father, I cannot say it, it is like blasphemy. Aunt Dorothy, bear with me, I am half mad, I think, with grief and horror. I started, as you know, for L—— two days ago: a diabolical telegram from an unknown sender brought me back instantly. Last night when I reached Paris, having had an accursed delay, *this* was thrust into my hand on the platform, the light was dim, and in the confusion I did not see by whom; read it and tell me it's a lie, a fiendish, cursed, malignant lie." And so saying he draws from his breast pocket that serpent's fang, the anonymous note we have already read; poor Miss Templeton takes it in her trembling hands, but for a few seconds the characters dance up and down before her dazed eyes, and she cannot gather the meaning of those brief, cruel lines. When they do at last reach her brain a great cry of indignation bursts from her pale lips, a cry of burning, righteous indignation, that rises up giant-like in that frail misshapen body to do instant battle with this outrage, this gross vile calumny, on her dead brother's child; a woman—as she conceives—of unblemished, immaculate purity, a cry that does Lionel good to hear, for is not it a proof that she at least does not accept this fearful thing?

"And you believed this lie!" she cries in horrified reproach, rising to her feet, with worn face flushed, and faded eyes alight, with loving partisanship. "This heinous, hideous lie!" dropping the paper from her fingers, as if it were some loathly thing, and spurning it contemptuously with her foot.

"I, who am only her aunt, believe in her implicitly, undoubtingly; and yet you—you, her husband—oh God! they are all alike, these men—weak, selfish, pitiful cravens where women are concerned; they cannot value any of them, a true, loyal, faithful woman; but are ready to condemn her as vilest of the vile, if but a whisper is breathed by some evil, jealous tongue; ready to think her as false as they are ready to be false themselves, to honour and love and truth.

"My Helen, my pure, noble, devoted girl! how can you—how dare you, Lionel Dacre, believe aught of ill of her, for one cruel moment?" and Miss Templeton pauses for breath, and grasps the back of the chair, from which she has risen, panting from the force with which she has spoken. Her words are bitter, bitingly bitter, in the ear of him who listens; but the very magnitude of the shock she has received goads her into stronger speech than she would wilfully indulge in; her own miserable experience stands suddenly out in relief, and for the moment she hates and despises all men, most of all him who can, even for one instant, let doubt of her niece linger in his mind; but the next moment the gentle loving heart softens, as she looks at the changed, haggard, grief-lined face before her.

"You come to me," she continues, before he can collect his distracted senses to answer her, and tell her of the horrible proof he has had that there is truth in that paper; "you come to me to show me this, to ask me where she is, instead of gong to your home, and there, where the truest, purest, sweetest wife sits lonely, asking her pardon on your knees for being led into a momentary suspicion of her faith, her honour, her love."

"But I have been there," he passionately cries. "Do you think I am so accursed a ruffian, such an infernal drivelling idiot, as to come to you with such a story with no better foundation for it than that scrap of paper? Didn't I tell you she is gone! gone! gone!" he almost shrieks in gradual crescendo of despair, and the listening woman grows pale and feeble again, her temporary strength fades out, and she shrinks with frightened eyes from the wild, uncontrolled anguish before her; she begins to comprehend at last the length and breadth and depth of the agony that wrung that cry from the man's very heart.

"Gone?" she repeats, in a dull, mechanical tone.

"Yes, gone, and left no word, no sign."

"And the child?" gasps Aunt Dorothy.

"Ah! the child!" and the man laughs a terrible laugh. "She was determined to rob me of all domestic joys!" (with a savage sneer) "she has taken the child with her, so I am free and unencumbered." Then the mood suddenly changing again: "Aunt Dorothy, as I stand before Heaven, I don't believe she has gone with *him*; yet where—where is my darling, my angel? Where in that wide, strange city am I to look for her? She has been tricked, deluded, deceived, and now she wants her husband. I heard her crying for me through the night, and I came to you; I felt so sure,—oh God! so sure, that she was here." And then, for the first time, hot, scalding tears rain from the man's eyes, and he bows down his head and weeps, while the woman sits speechless, almost appalled by this evidence of violent emotion; for who can see a strong man in the vigour of his days weep and wail, and not be strangely impressed? But those blessed tears will do much to save the tortured brain.

By-and-by he tells her everything; every word of Rosalie's narrative, which is written in letters of fire upon his heart. The confirmatory proof which he had of the truth of her statements, in his inquiries at the Marquis's town mansion—the princely old hotel in the Faubourg St. Germain—and Dorothy Templeton listens in mute amazement, in dumb sympathy, and silent dread. No doubt of her niece enters her mind; her belief in her is unshaken, unassailable; but a great fear is growing in her breast, a fear that she breathes not to the man at her side. A fear that the niece and wife so fondly loved has come to some harm, that some disaster has overtaken her. The dear girl, she reflects wretchedly, is impulsive, warm-hearted, charitable to a fault; how easy for her to be decoyed away from her home on some pretence, and then robbed, and perhaps even murdered. Her fancy at once pictures the most terrible images. Helen, a stranger in a strange land. God alone knows what horrors might befall her, in that unfamiliar, wicked city. As to the story of the Marquis's presence, it was a mere coincidence, she says vehemently; she attaches no meaning whatever to it. The girl Rosalie, like all other Frenchwomen of her class, sees, and imagines, intrigue in everything; to their ill-regulated and ill-balanced minds, fed so frequently on pernicious literature, the idea of a *liaison* is always delightful; it gives tone and colour to the ordinary monotony of their existence; but as for herself and Lionel, it is too vile a thing for either to contemplate for a moment. In spite of her long residence, so comparatively near the French capital, she knows as little of Parisian gossip as these strangers fresh from England's shores. She is entirely ignorant of the character which the Marquis de Vallanelle bears. She met him once in the company of her niece and nephew, and was charmed with him: his courtesy, and frank kindliness to herself, quite won her, little as she is predisposed in favour of the sterner sex. Sweet and sensible as she is, Miss Templeton, like all the rest of the world, has her little weakness, that smallest of small weaknesses, that prevails among so many, an instinctive reverence for a title, and to be treated with deferential respect by a real live Marquis she thought a pleasant sensation, and was duly impressed thereby. She tries to speak cheering words of hope and encouragement to the broken-hearted man, stifling her own new-born terrors; and she feels, and shows, such genuine contempt and unbelief for Rosalie's statement, the telegram, and the anonymous note, that he at last grows to think with her. But then there remains the extraordinary absence of his darling. How can Aunt Dorothy account for that, granting that de Vallanelle's visit at that late hour was but accidental, an unfortunate coincidence? Where did Helen go? Where *could* she have gone at that hour? "And to take the child with her! That very fact," flashes in poor distracted Dorothy, glad to make a point, "that very fact alone would prove her innocent. Do you think—could any man in his sane senses think—that if *that* vile thing were true," pointing with loathing, scorning finger, to that hateful bit of harmless looking paper lying at their feet, "that Helen—that any woman, in such circumstances—would take her child with her; a child, too, not a baby, but a sensible little boy, for all his dreamy, bookish ways, past seven years old. No; the true explanation of what seems a mystery is this—she got a sudden notice of dire distress, sickness, suffering of some kind in your neighbourhood. She did speak to me the other day of relieving a miserably needy but deserving family, in a poor quarter near you. The husband and bread-winner had just died, I think, and starvation stared in the face those he left behind. Poor girl, she brought her English ways here with her, and thought in her fearless single-mindedness she was as safe in Paris as at home in Devonshire. Most likely she got word that the widow and mother was ill, perhaps dying, and with her impulsive good-nature, her warm charitable sympathy, and kind-heartedness, rushed off at once; and as you were from home determined to stay the night, to comfort the afflicted, taking Lion with her, both for company and thinking he might feel lonely to wake up and find her gone. This, I am convinced, is the true solution of all this wretchedness, and I only trust and pray the dear soul has not been too credulous."

"But there was all yesterday and last night," suggests half-believing Lionel; and the woman's heart gives a great bound of terror, though she answers in calm prosaic fashion; she fights with the wild alarm that is growing strong within her—for his sake. It blanches her cheek, and causes her to tremble inwardly, but she maintains control over her voice, and he does not guess the horrible dread with which she is struggling. He does not imagine the fearful pictures rising vivid and ghastly before her mental eye. Pictures lit up by a lurid glare of blood. Pictures, wherein a woman's figure lies stark and stiff in the foreground: a woman with Helen's face, whereon is stamped an awful death agony; and the background whereof is some squalid den, in some noisome purlieu of the shining city of Paris, where she has been decoyed by some false story of distress, robbed, and brutally murdered. But she shuts up these terrible thoughts in her heart. She is brave in her love and pity, and congratulates herself, in the midst of her own misery, at having partly succeeded in turning the current of her nephew's thoughts adrift from the picture of dishonour that he has been gazing on, till he was half mad with grief and rage; and she feels her unselfish efforts at consolation are amply rewarded when he looks in her face, with terribly anxious, sad eyes, but with the wildness died out; when he speaks with eager rapid speech, of the search they must begin to make at once for his darling (unless—blessed thought—they find her at home waiting for them), but speaks rationally, earnestly, reasonably with the fierce uncontrolled passion gone, smouldered away into grey ashes . . . . She induces him to take some food and wine, that he needs so greatly: arguing, when he chafes at the delay, that he must not let his strength fail before he finds his wife . . . . And then, poor courageous, unselfish, weak, frail woman (how self-sacrificing and enduring they are, these fragile, loving women!), goes upstairs to her room, and hastily makes her few preparations to start with her nephew, to leave her home, perhaps but for a day, possibly for many days; all the while the wild horror in her breast gathering strength and life.

And soon, very soon, Lionel Dacre is on his way back to Paris; but now, the miles do not seem so weary, so interminable. The air is not filled with invisible unearthly presences, with weird eerie voices, for the daylight is around him, dull and cheerless though it be; and, above all, Aunt Dorothy is beside him, and holds his hand, and talks sweet words of comfort to his stricken soul. And after all, the warm, actual, human presence, is more consoling than the chilly, vague, indefinite—perhaps imaginary—spirit ones.

CHAPTER V
LA MORT DANS L'ÂME[27]

OCCASIONALLY during our swiftly speeding lives, at rare, infrequent intervals, possibly only once in a life's journey, there are specks and snatches of that fast-fleeing time, but a grain or two of the ever-falling sand from the inexorable old man's hour-glass, that seem to us to stretch out indefinitely in torturing, wearying length, that seem to rival even our hazy, undefined idea of eternity's unendingness. It may be only months, nay, even fewest weeks, that drag out this so terribly; but the time so lived though, let it be long or short, is never forgotten, never becomes faint or blurred in memory's book. And so it is with Lionel Dacre. Four weeks have passed away since he and Miss Templeton set out for Paris on that dim grey November morning.

Four weeks—28 days—672 hours! Great God!—672 hours! Hours in which each sixty minutes seemed a day, and a day an æon of suspenseful misery.

Six hundred and seventy-two hours, during each moment of which he watched unceasingly, with ever lessening hope and ever growing certainty.

With desperation, rage, grief, and horror, alternately contending in his breast, he watched for *her* who came not, who made no sign across that gulf of silence and horrible unknowingness that stretches now, black and void, between those two who had been all the world to each other.

Will the recollection of those terrible hours, think you, ever

---

[27] *La mort dans l'âme*: with a heavy heart, sick at heart.

fade or grow indistinct in the man's mind? No; not if his years emulate those of the patriarchs of old, will these four weeks lose in memory the active, dread suspense and anguish that he then endured. Those dreadful agonised days of watching, waiting for what never came, will go with him through life.

Four weeks; and in that time no tidings of Helen. What an awful mystery would be her extraordinary disappearance but for the one horrible solution. The Marquis de Vallanelle has vanished for the same length of time exactly, and to his whereabouts Lionel Dacre has failed to obtain the smallest clue.

He had placed the matter in the hands of the police,—much as he shrank, with bitter humiliated pride and throbbing pain, from having his sorrows exposed to the stony-hearted, inquisitive stare of an indifferent, sensation-seeking public,—but they had been as successful as himself in finding Helen; perhaps they had not made any very strenuous exertion to discover her; perhaps they, like all the rest of the world who heard the story of the telegram and note, and knew the character of the Marquis de Vallanelle, smiled a little, with pitying contempt, at the man's credulity, and thought the disappearance very satisfactorily accounted for. But Lionel Dacre had been influenced against his own better judgment; against the conviction that else would have forbade his bringing his shame before the world—influenced by Aunt Dorothy's unreasoning, groundless terrors. Were they groundless? were they irrational? he grew to argue in his own breast: other women, as sweet and pure, and confiding as his Helen, had been decoyed from their homes before now, and robbed, and murdered.

And so he bade those officers of the law search for his missing wife; bade them unravel the mystery of her disappearance, provided them with her photograph, had the Morgue visited daily, and all suspected quarters watched closely. Employed a clever detective day and night to seek amongst the purlieus of Paris,—amongst its dens of misery and infamy, where vice and crime stalk hand in hand—for some trace of the supposed murdered woman and her child.

And yet all the time the knowledge grew stronger within him that it was but labour spent in vain. That the Seine would never give up his Helen. That her fair drowned body would never lie on the Morgue's cold horrible slabs. That his wife was lost to him more completely than if death's icy river rolled between them. That the voice that had seemed to call him twice so urgently through that fearful night, was but a creation of his own frenzied fancy.

For a little time he had been swayed by Dorothy Templeton's eager and staunchly-believed-in arguments, but, as each endless day dragged itself with lagging feet to a weary close without any tragedy coming to light that could explain the mystery of disappearance, without any sign from her, of her, whom they sought, what was there for him but to accept Rosalie's narrative and the anonymous communication, as the true explanation of this terrible puzzle?

Helen was gone; that was an undeniable, incontrovertible truth. Gone, without sign, word, or warning. If any dread fate had overtaken her, either by accident or design,—she, an Englishwoman and a lady, accompanied by her son, a boy between seven and eight years old—it *should have* transpired. There were certainly frequent instances of persons vanishing inexplicably, unaccountably, and never again being heard of. But in nine cases out of ten, these were voluntary disappearances for some hidden motive. And at any rate, let the missing one who thus goes suddenly off the path of life hitherto trod, and is seen on it no more, be victim or otherwise, such a one is always alone; above all, he or she is unaccompanied by any child.

And how more than singular would be the coincidence (if as mere coincidence it could be regarded) of the Marquis de Vallanelle's extraordinary unaccounted-for absence.

Mr. Dacre had taken upon himself the task of tracing the destroyer of his peace, the soft-tongued, friendly-mannered, frank-faced murderer (aye, murderer! for is not he, who deliberately and wilfully compasseth the death of a white, innocent, trusting soul, as guilty of slaughter as he who stabs his victim to the heart?), but he had failed miserably. All his enquiries at the stately old hotel in the Faubourg and at "Sans Souci," had ended in equally barren results. The staff or servants in each professed utter ignorance of their master's whereabouts, his intentions, his movements. The story of the coachman's dismissal was repeated, in slightly enlarged edition, by the man himself; but this shed no new light on the subject, but rather, wrapped it in murkier gloom.

The *coupé* was ordered for ten o'clock, he stated, and, by the Marquis's desire, the valet was summoned before they left the Faubourg, and took his place on the box beside him;[28] he thought it a little strange that his master should take his valet with him when he was not going away anywhere, not even for a night; he had not so much as his dressing-case with him; he just stepped into the *coupé* as if to drive to the next street, and then when they got to the street in the Chausée d'Antin, where he (Monsieur Dakare) lived, the Marquis told him, as he was about to remount the box, that he might walk back again, as he (the Marquis) was not returning for some little time, but that there was no use in keeping two men out late, and that Felix could drive him.

He (the coachman) thought this the strangest of all; to send

[28] *Coupé*: an enclosed, four-wheeled, horse-drawn carriage.

away the man whose business was driving and retain the other; but of course it was not for him to make remarks, but to obey; and he set off to walk home, while Felix gathered up the reins with a queer smile on his face. He went straight to bed when he got back, and thought no more of it until he heard in the morning neither the Marquis, nor Felix, nor the carriage had returned all night; then he began to think there must be something in it, something below what appeared on the surface. Felix had been with the Marquis many years, and was quite a confidential servant; he himself had been in his present employment only twelve months.

Such is the unfinished, sketchy outline of the facts of that eventful night that Lionel gleans, and finds he has got no grain, only husks and straw.

The Marquis de Vallanelle is wealthy, very wealthy, and has large estates in Brittany, besides his patrimonial heritage in Auvergne. Distant from each other as are these spots of French soil, the deserted husband visited both, but still failed to track the fugitives; he had felt almost sure that in the wild, solitary remoteness of that stately château, on the picturesque, lonely Breton coast, somewhere between St. Brieux and St. Malo, he should once again behold his wife; that once more, and for the last time, he would look upon the face of the woman he had worshipped with an idolatry almost sinful, an idolatry that placed the creature before the Creator; a weakness that poor erring humanity so often yields to, and is nearly always so miserably, so piteously, but yet we must suppose, deservedly, punished for. The creature discovers its feet of clay, it falls from its pedestal and lies prone in the dust, and we weep, and wail, and wring our hands, and cry aloud in our bitter, searing pain that God is unjust, that He has forgotten us; whereas it is we who have forgotten Him; absorbed so utterly in the weak, frail, mortal flesh and blood, we have ceased to remember the Eternal Father, who formed the perishing creature in His own image, and breathed into his nostrils of dust the life so lovely, so wondrous, so transient.

But neither in Auvergne nor in Brittany did Lionel Dacre behold his wife; neither did he hear aught of her, or him with whom she disappeared. Their flight was wrapped in mystery impenetrable. Rosalie had been questioned again and yet again, by Miss Templeton, who bravely remains at her nephew's side, but her tale was still the same; it was repeated mechanically, with automatic adherence to the same words, like a lesson learned by rote; and at the end of the first week she was missing from the Chausée d'Antin; none knew her whereabouts; nor did Lionel or Miss Templeton try to trace her; the former felt assured that she was a creature of the Marquis's, and that he had ordered her flight; the latter thought the girl was nervous, and alarmed—ignorantly thinking it possible that she might be involved, in some way, in her mistress's strange disappearance, and so fled to avoid imagined dangers. She had always seemed ill at ease, scared almost, when she told her story; her connecting the Marquis with the incomprehensible gulf of mystery, into which her niece had been absorbed, Dorothy Templeton considered only the natural result of her training and order of mind—ill-regulated, imaginative, coarse,—to whom the idea of intrigue and domestic treachery was second nature. Her mistress got a letter which appeared to distress her; the Marquis arrived, of course by an unlucky accident, close on its heels; they spoke together quickly, and, as she chose to fancy, eagerly, in a language she could not comprehend when spoken rapidly; his carriage remained at the door and Helen accepted it, as she had done so often, to drive where that urgent appeal had summoned her.

This was Aunt Dorothy's embodied thought. Rosalie insisted the Marquis accompanied Madame Dacre. Well, even so, to a doubtful neighbourhood, as she felt assured was her brave, impulsive Helen's destination, he had gone with her to the poor home, where she was a ministering angel: if the address of the suffering people, whom she had befriended, could be known, it might explain much now wrapt in deepest gloom. Her darling girl had gone to those unknown creatures, whoever they might be, on her errand of mercy, and while there, or on her return alone, had been in some way entrapped by some tale of greater woe, decoyed in her sweet unsuspicion to some criminal den, and there made away with.

Such is Miss Templeton's reading of the facts of that fatal night; and staunchly she adheres to it, although the passing of each day seems to prove more certainly, more incontrovertibly, how fallacious and improbable is her theory. Each hour brings more and more deadly conviction to the husband, but not so to the aunt; she feels her niece was pure and good and true, and her faith remains unshaken.

That she will never again see Helen with her mortal eyes she feels assured; she even now begins to despair of hearing aught of her miserable fate; but that she is alive and well and deliberately gone from them to dishonour, she casts from her as too loathful a thing to dwell for an instant in the minds of those who had loved and believed in Helen Dacre.

She mourns her niece as dead; dead in the flower of her womanhood, in the pride of her days, in the fulness of her happiness. Dead—by some secret, unknown, awful violence; but even this, grievous as it is, is better than the horror of hatred, contempt and despair, she sees daily growing in her nephew's face. She scorns him, for his want of faith; but yet she pities him profoundly; pities him for the ghastly misery she sees written on his brow, for his ruined life, his wrecked hopes. She tries to offer him consolation, to induce him to accept the melancholy certainty that is her creed, but he turns from her in compassionate contempt.

The *appartement* on the second floor of the Chausée d'Antin still remains the same; the servants who had been hired by the Marquis de Vallanelle, still are at their posts (all but Rosalie, who fled, it was supposed, in a panic), though Lionel Dacre has never again set foot across the threshold. He sent for his own personal belongings on returning to Paris with Aunt Dorothy, but never more entered those rooms in the Rue Philippe, which, to him, are haunted by a more terrible phantom than that supposed to glide and hover where murder has been wrought. The wraith he sees in fancy, wringing its hands and wailing in those deserted chambers, is that of expiring honour, dying truth, faith, love, and loyalty. The ghost of slaughtered happiness and purity there abides; the stain of shame is deeper and more indelible in his mind than the stain of blood.

In a small entresol in a neighbouring street, he and Aunt Dorothy have spent that miserable month.[29]

Christmas is past. Great Heavens! what a Christmas to the broken-hearted alien.

How hideous was his desolation in that great, shining, callous-hearted city. How he hated its beauty and airy lightness; its stately boulevards, brilliant theatres, and radiant cafés; its song and laughter, and luxury; its frivolity and vice; all which flourished so exceeding fairly in those latter days of the Second Empire. Though perhaps unsuspected by that gay, moving, feasting, inconsequent throng, the storm, which wrought such deadly havoc later on, was

---

[29] Entresol: mezzanine between the ground and first floors of a building.

brewing even then. Its first faint murmurings, as yet no louder than an infant's coo, had been heard perchance by ears accustomed to listen for such sounds, though years had yet to pass before the storm would break. Faces in high places were looking grave and even anxious; and *one* who moved in the centre of all, the author of all that glistening white beauty (whose sun had shone with such exceeding brilliance as almost to dazzle those who gazed, the glare and brightness blinding them to the sinister gloom through which that radiance had been reached), looked abroad upon that setting sun with sombre, sad, suffering eye.

Yes, Christmas is past, and the old year dies, and its successor rushes to its inheritance with indecent haste, making no even hypocritical pretence of mourning. Why should it? Why should any mourn for aught? Life and Death is the law of the Universe. They are exchangeable terms. Life means death, and death means life. There can be no life without death, no death without life; they are co-existent and co-equal.

Still another week runs away, the first week of that raw young year, which holds in its youthful bosom such noble aspirations, such sweet hopes, such perfect happiness; and before it completes its terribly brief course, over the graves of how many slaughtered hopes and aspirations will it bend? over how much murdered happiness, happiness that seems now as sure as Heaven, will it crouch repentant?

It is the eighth of January, exactly six weeks and three days since the evening Lionel Dacre started with so tranquil and happy a heart for the South, with his wife's clinging farewell kiss warm upon his lips, with the odour of her flowers, the innocent Devonshire violets and heliotrope, faint and sweet in his nostrils; and now— he shakes the dust of Paris off his feet for ever.

How horribly long ago it seems since that lovely October day when he and his Helen arrived in that city and gazed at its dazzling beauty for the first time; and yet 'tis scarcely three months since those nights, but two in number, when after visiting opera or theatre at the Marquis's urgent insistence, they supped at the Maison Dorée and mingled for a short hour or so in that brilliant restless stream of Parisian life at midnight. He remembers how strange and novel all seemed to their insular ideas; how Helen shrank a little, half in pride, half in timidity, from entering those radiant cafés, thronged with gay loungers from the boulevard; he looks back on all vaguely, as if a mist of time rolled between then and now, a mist of but a few shortest, miserable weeks, as if they were experiences he had gone through in another existence.

And now he leaves Paris alone! with a sick hopeless despair, a despair that holds a bitter, savage hatred and scorn; a maddening sense of deepest, direst wrong at its core, for his sole companion. The wild fury of wrath, the ungovernable surging rage that demanded swift and deadly vengeance on the betrayer who had wrecked his life, with as little compunction as he would crush a fly, is abated. If he and the Marquis de Vallanelle had come face to face at any time or any place within those last few weeks, it would have been a duel to the death between them; Lionel Dacre would have forced the aristocrat to meet him, however the latter might affect to despise and scorn the idea of the architect ("*bourgeois*," as he would doubtless name him) attempting to think that he could wipe out the stain to his honour in the manner reserved for gentlemen. But they had not met; and now the deserted husband feels with a pang of anguish, a passion of contempt, that the betrayer's guilt is as nothing to the betrayed.

She, no longer a girl, but a woman of mature years, had

deliberately renounced her wifehood, her motherhood; had clothed herself of her own free will in a mantle of shame, in garments of dishonour.

The wife who so forgot her marriage vows was ten thousand times more guilty than the man who at least disgraced no child.

If he had a reckoning with either it should be in common justice with the woman who had so coldly and cruelly wronged him; and he has sworn a solemn oath that he "will never look upon her face again."

He will not seek a divorce—on that he is determined. He will not set her free, so that by-and-by, by the force of her sweetness and witchery, she might creep into some good man's heart and home as his *wife*, he all unconscious of her sullied and sinful past,—no, a disgraced woman, a disgraced wife she is, and a disgraced woman, a disgraced wife she shall remain.

But though he has vowed a vow, that never more on earth will he look into that lovely face that was his heaven, that never while life lasts will he listen to those tender tones that were to him like sweetest music, that if even, in the audacity of her shamelessness, she force herself into his presence, and beg and implore forgiveness on her knees, he will be blind and deaf to all entreaties; he will scorn all supplications, that she shall be for ever to him a stranger and an enemy, although she bear his name. Yet withal he will provide for her. He will not leave her to the physical misery to which her sin may lead. By-and-by, sooner or later, when deserted by her lover, she will doubtless want money, and money she shall have; not much, for he has it not to give.

Independent of his profession his little patrimony is but some £230 or £240 a year, but of that she shall have more than half. £50 a year she has of her own—all the small fortune she brought him on her marriage,—£150 with that will make £200 a year; and a woman with management can live very comfortably in quiet obscurity (the only life open to her in the future) on a couple of hundred a year; even be she burdened with a child; the remaining £80 or £90 will do quite well for him on which to drag out a broken and maimed existence. In his early youth he and poverty had been somewhat intimately acquainted; there was a time when £90 a year sure would have seemed comparative wealth and certain ease of mind; now it is quite sufficient to provide him with bread and cheese in some remote seclusion, and this is all he asks from life; his hopes, dreams, ambitions, are over, his life is lived, and now he will but wait for the end, which he prays may come quickly; he would be glad, oh, so glad, to lay down his dishonoured, weary head even now in the quiet shrouding earth. He has no longer a duty, a purpose, an aim in life; nobody wants him, he is not necessary to any living creature; his boy he never even thinks of claiming. She chose to take him with her, to separate and alienate him from his father; and she might keep him, though the law, if he sought its aid, would oblige her to yield him up. The child worships his mother, and is in her hands as clay in the hands of the potter, she can mould him as she pleases; her influence over him is unbounded; doubtless she will now use that influence to turn the son against the father.

The little fellow was fond of his father, a calm tranquil affection, quite unlike the almost ecstatic love he bore his mother; but now he will be taught to distrust, perhaps dislike, that deserted father. He is too young (the innocent dawning mind just beginning to expand and spread its tiny wings a little) to understand anything of his mother's act. To imagine that anything she did could be wrong would be impossible to little Lion; all the world might be in error, father included, but not his mother.

And Lionel Dacre himself, though he tenderly loved his son, yet more for the mother's sake, the boy being his Helen's child, than from any passionate love of offspring. If the child is sent to him he will take him and keep him, and do his duty by him; separating him altogether from his mother, thereby making the boy miserable and probably earning his hatred, especially if, when he was older, he told him the cause of that separation. But if not, he will never seek to see the child again.

* * * * * *

"You'll soon lay that mockery aside," he says in cynical tones, touching with pitying contempt the heavy folds of Aunt Dorothy's sombre black gown, as they stand together in one of the waiting-rooms at the St. Lazare terminus; he is returning by way of Havre and Southampton, he could not bear the other route yet awhile. In ten minutes Mr. Dacre will be on his way to Normandy, *en route* for England, never again to set foot on French soil, and Dorothy Templeton, faithful to this final moment, is seeing the last of him, though sometimes she almost hates him for accepting the only rational solution of her niece's disappearance.

His bitter irony, his sharp, caustic scorn of her credulity hurts her with a pain that is almost physical. But still her pity is stronger that her anger; she has unbounded compassion for the broken-hearted man whose kindly, generous nature has been warped and twisted by this crushing blow; not a sorrow to soften but to sear, and blast, and leave a poisonous trail to the very end of life. And after all, she asks herself silently, as they thus stand together for the last time, can she blame him for his want of faith? does not he only accept what all the world believes? the cruel, scoffing world, that would shriek with derisive laughter at her unwavering trust.

" 'Tis not the custom to mourn with outward and visible sign for the death of a 'soul.' We hoist these woe-trappings but for the dissolution of the frail chemical compound we call the 'body,' " he continues, mockingly.

"The outer sign is but a poor, and ofttimes deceitful, expression of what dwells within; the heaviest sables often cover the gladdest, most shamefully rejoicing hearts. But no matter what my dress may be, Lionel, my heart will go in mourning all its days for my dear dead Helen."

"Not surely if '*Resurgam*' be the watch-word on that mental tombstone?" (with a savage sneer).[30] "And '*Resurgam*' it will be, Aunt Dorothy, as sure as God is in Heaven. Sooner or later, sooner most likely, perhaps before the first gloss of newness is faded from your gown, your dead will rise again; rise from its 'Inferno,' where it has walked in familiar companionship with other shades of vice and evil, and you, even you, credulous, innocent fool though you be, will recognize with shuddering nostrils the faint but damning smell of brimstone. But you are a good woman, Dorothy Templeton, even though you are a fool; you are full of Christian charity, and will take the lost to your home and hearth, if not to your heart, and will urge to repentance and try to wash the foul stain away with your tears. I know how it will be, I can read the future as a book: but however an aunt may weep and wail over a prodigal and receive her back into the fold of her love, crying out with great and bitter cry when she is again deceived, it is not written that a husband must needs rejoice over a wife's dishonour, even though the sinner repents and comes humbly to his feet, when she is cast off by her lover and homeless," (with bitter scathing satire). "And I swear now, by the living God! that nothing will ever induce me

[30] *Resurgam*: I shall rise again, referring to the resurrection of the dead.

to hold communion again with the woman who was my wife. She is dead to me for ever. She and the boy shan't starve: I told you what I mean to do about money as soon as I get to London, and when once that's arranged, all communications will reach me through my lawyers. I'll bury myself far from those who have known me. My profession I abandon, my old life I abjure. That life is virtually lived, and 'tis but a maimed, paralysed existence remains to me. My trust in all things good, and true, and pure is shattered. Even to you, Aunt Dorothy, I'll give no address; you have stood by me and pitied me, and been staunch and faithful, and I am grateful, and thank and bless you; but our paths are ever divided from this hour. I'll cut myself adrift from all connected with the past; if you want to write at any time, write there,"—tendering her a card bearing the address of his legal advisers—"and it will find me, if I am still above ground. But remember, if you write aught of *her*,—unless to tell me of her authenticated death, of which you have positive proof——"

"Ah, Lionel," interrupts Miss Templeton, with swimming eyes, "I shall never need to tell you of *that*, for it has come already, though you are so terribly unbelieving."

It is her last little protest; but he continues unheedingly. "Your letter will remain unnoticed; will be burned unread, when I see its burden. A cleverly bolstered-up lie, an ingenious fabrication may deceive you, but I will give myself no chance of being so influenced. I will hear absolutely nothing. My solicitors will have full instructions to act for me in any contingency.—And now, good-bye, and God bless you, Aunt Dorothy; pray for me, for I am a desolate, despairing man."

And almost before Dorothy Templeton can murmur a tearful blessing and farewell, Lionel Dacre is on his road home to England.

CHAPTER VI

"VENGEANCE IS MINE, SAITH THE LORD"

WHEN Mr. Dacre reaches London he goes straight to Messrs. Lonhed, Suttle and Lonhed, a highly respectable legal firm, who had done business for his father, and who now manage the affairs of the son, whom the senior partners remember as a boy. After regulating money transactions, he commissions them to sell by auction the old house in Devonshire and its contents. Furniture, bric-à-brac, china, books, all indiscriminately to go to the hammer; he retains absolutely nothing; likewise the tiny nest in London is stripped bare and desolate. He never sees either again. He is only anxious for all to be done quickly, so that he may go away unburdened, and bury himself far from that blotted out past.

The evening before he leaves London, and nearly a month after he quit Paris, as he is glancing absently, with wearied, uninterested eyes, over the columns of the *Times*, trying to divert his mind, for even a few minutes, from the brooding sorrow, the corroding shame and hatred that are eating and gnawing away his very heart; those gloomy eyes fall upon a paragraph that make them light with sudden fire of interest and astonishment.

The words that arrest his glance are—

"Sudden death of the Marquis de Vallanelle at a Canadian sleigh chase."

Then follow a few brief words anent the noble French family of which the deceased gentleman was the representative; after which the paragraph goes on to state how the Marquis had come to Montreal some two or three weeks previously; he had been there during the great "Ice Carnival," but had lived quietly, not mixing much in the society of the place, but sometimes joining in the national sports, tobogganing, sleighing, &c. On these occasions, especially when skating, he was always accompanied by a lady, who spoke with a sweet, pure accent, had a graceful, distingué deportment, and was presumably young and beautiful; though the thick veil she invariably wore, tantalisingly shrouded the face, and but for the gleam of brilliant eyes, all was left to the imagination.

She seemed to shrink somewhat from notice; and though bold, daring, and even reckless on the ice, she courted solitude; and if the Marquis were drawn into some gay, brilliant group she remained aloof, skating alone on some distant unfrequented part of the water, till he rejoined her. There was a touch of mystery attaching to her.

She was generally supposed to be an Englishwoman.

Her appearance in Montreal had been simultaneous with that of the Marquis, and she never was seen abroad save in his society.

On the night the tragic event occurred, the marquis had appeared in his usual buoyant health. He and the fair unknown occupied the same sleigh; it was, in fact, a sort of sleighing match or race; and there were numbers of the pretty, picturesque, tinkling, frost-cars flying over the hard white ground, but none more airily delicate than that of the Marquis de Vallanelle.

The bells jangled merrily, the gay, bright voices rang joyously on the still night air, the stars glowed and burned in the distant, blue-black, frosty sky, while all around was fairy-land. Coloured lights gleamed everywhere; swaying from the gaunt, bare tree-branches were lanterns innumerable, of every shape, design, and colour; while each darting sleigh was hung around with multitudes of tiny, glittering, crystal lamps of every variety of tint, fastened by wire so slender as to be invisible, and made to bend and sway, so that when in motion it seemed as if the air was full of living jewels, tossing and leaping round the flying cars. In truth, a pretty sight. But it was soon to me marred by a terrible shadow.

The de Vallanelle sleigh had taken the lead, and had distanced all competitors by some yards, when suddenly, a sharp, wild cry cut through the merry music of bells and laughter; a cry that proceeded from that foremost sleigh, which had come abruptly to a stand-still; and those nearest to it, hastening up alarmed, found the Marquis fallen back heavily, half out of the car, the reins dropped from his rigid fingers, his face of a ghastly grey, and his companion, whose scream had scared them, clinging to him in an attitude of frantic terror. At first it was supposed to be a fit; but a physician who happened to be present, soon ascertained that the Marquis was dead—dead—without any warning—without word or groan, or sigh—dead, while taking his pleasure wildly, unthinkingly, on that stretch of Canadian park-land. The doom of the de Vallanelles had overtaken the last of the race thus early. For it was well known that heart-disease was an hereditary malady in the family.

And so on, in "our own correspondent's" best style, for the rest of the half column, though where he had gathered his facts, stated so boldly, so undoubtedly, in so short a time, seemed little less than a marvel.

But Lionel Dacre reads no more; he throws the paper from him, with a muttered curse. Ay! a curse on the dead. He has no room in his thoughts, in those first few moments, for aught but his own pain. Any doubt that might still have lingered in the most credulous mind must now give place to certainty.

"A lady—an Englishwoman—with sweet, clear tones, a graceful, distingué presence, and brilliant eyes." Are not these Helen's most marked attributes? What matter that they spoke not of those eyes being wondrous violet-blue; of those glorious masses of chestnut hair; of that exquisite white-rose complexion, a pallor as rare as it is beautiful, and as removed from the paleness of delicacy or weakness as it is from the commonplace pink and white, that its refined loveliness vulgarises.

They did not speak of those things because they did not see them; they were concealed by the disguising veil. But Helen's eyes are brilliant; her tones are like music; she is distinguished looking, and she skated magnificently. It had been almost a passion with her in her girlhood, he recollects with savage intensity. Of late years she had had little opportunity of indulging in her favourite exercise, the winters in the south of England had been so mild. But when he first mer her in her distant Yorkshire home amongst the rugged northern fells, the lonely mansion standing on the edge of a wild, desolate moorland, stretching away to those frowning tors, Helen Templeton's chief winter delight was skating. The girl was naturally of a courageous, dauntless disposition, and she attained a proficiency, a wld, daring audacity of skill in this one pursuit, rare among women in those days, when they did not run neck-to-neck with men in all things, whether of business or pleasure, as of late.

When there were still some few occupations to which the odious, illiberal word "masculine" might be applied. When the world was still innocent of lady-jockeys, lecturers, doctors, cricketers; when it had yet to hear of "female trapezists" and football-players! When fashionable ladies had not yet learned to smoke, and when skilled yachtswomen and oarswomen, &c., &c., were not so plentiful as now; even skating, in that barbaric, unenlightened period, had a subtle, delightful flavour of "fastness," that was slightly thrilling. Not that Helen Templeton had been fast; far from it. She was reserved, shy, almost timid, in the presence of strangers; but when alone, or with two or three dear familiar friends, she would adjourn to one of those lonely mountain lakes in the vicinity of her home, some melancholy, frost-bound tarn, and there be as wild, audacious, daring, as the most reckless lady tandem-driver of to-day.

Yes, no link is wanting, thinks the wretched husband, to prove that distinct, nameless, veiled woman to be his wife. And his heart contracts with a great anguish as he recalls the brilliant, joyous, innocent young creature, by whose side he had skated on those grim northern lakes; who, still on the ice, one day when he had spoken looked up confidingly at him, with the trust and unconcealed love of a little child, and, for all answer to that most momentous question, placed her slim hands flutteringly in his. *That* was the girl. *This* is the woman.

And then his thoughts revert to that night scene of sudden, awful death, in the midst of revelry and joy. How terrible it seems; the hand of God had been laid upon the sinner in his sin and lo! he is not any more for ever, though the wickedness he has done must live after him to the end. And the man remembers, with a strange thrill, his own wild prayer for speedy revenge. How swift, and sure, and deadly, had been the answer. How he had craved and thirsted, in the first rush of his rage, to take his enemy's life, to blot him out with his own hand from amongst the living; and had groaned and chafed at his own powerlessness, his inaction. He had done nothing—and yet—

"*Vengeance is mine, I will repay, saith the Lord*," and as he mutters these words, Lionel Dacre shudders with an irrepressible awe, though his heart is exultant within him.

CHAPTER VII

"YEA! BY GOD'S ROOD! I TRUSTED (*HER*) TOO WELL"

THREE or four weeks more roll on in their inexorable course, and March has just made his boisterous bow to a world that greets him with vicarious welcome—a welcome that thinks of the good things his laughing, crying, gentle, younger sister will bring them by-and-by, and, accordingly, is hypocritically civil to the next-of-kin. And, on one of those earliest wild March mornings a letter makes its way to Lionel Dacre, who has shaken the dust of London off his feet, as he did that of Paris, seeking a dwelling remote from the places he has known, and far from those who knew him. One creature in the world he still loves—his only sister, and he went to her in his heart-broken loneliness, and there abides. It is from his solicitors, and contains an enclosure. The note from the firm states that Mrs. Dacre is living, that she has communicated with them, and had forwarded the accompanying letter, entreating them to send it on without delay. No more than this; she has evidently entered into no explanation with them. And he who reads laughs aloud—a laugh horrible to hear,—as he holds his wife's letter in his hand, looking at it as he might look at a serpent's fang. "She did not lose much time," he murmurs, with biting cynicism. "She makes no pretence of mourning for *him*; and yet, to the most hardened, heartless woman it should have proved a violent shock. It is a pity such tragic endings to illicit love don't occur a little oftener" (with sarcastic irony) "and perhaps Society would be purer than it is, women would think twice before they sacrificed everything for such a brief hey-day of vice. She did not bargain to be left in the lurch so swiftly, so utterly. Lover, husband, means, reputation, all shattered, almost at one blow. But she thinks to repair the evil quickly. She flies from his dead body, back to him she has renounced with unblushing effrontery. *I* am to be tricked, duped, cheated, into opening my arms to the prodigal. There is an indecent haste about it that revolts one. She might have waited a little before trying to thrust herself back on me, for, of course, that's the burden of this" (contemptuously flicking the missive he still holds); "but she miscalculates him with whom she has to deal."

And that letter is returned, with the seal unbroken, to the office of Messrs. Lonhed & Suttle.

A week later he receives another communication from these men of law, saying that his wife is in England, has been at their chambers, accompanied by her aunt, Miss Templeton, that her entreaties for his (their client's) address have been most painfully urgent, that she actually went down on her knees in their private office, imploring them to tell her where she would find her husband, that she spoke confusedly, incoherently, but terribly earnestly, and with much weeping, of the horrible mistake there was, of the frightful series of most disastrous coincidences of which she was the unhappy victim, the hideous plot that had been hatched to work her ruin, but that she was guiltless, had suffered fearfully, had been ill unto death, but could explain everything if her husband would but see her, would but read her written statements. She worked herself into a convulsive state of violent distress, moaning and sobbing hysterically" (continued the junior partner, who is Mr. Dacre's correspondent). "Never has our dry-as-dust prosaic office been the scene of such apparent misery. Miss Templeton warmly upheld and supported Mrs. Dacre all through the trying interview. She evidently believes your wife implicitly. When at length we had, according to your strict instructions—I must confess on my part reluctantly—still to withhold your address, she besought us, as if she pleaded for a life, to send you the accompanying letter, with a few lines from ourselves, 'conjuring you to read it in the name of God.' These were her very words, and I must say I pitied the poor lady profoundly. Of course I know no actual fact of the case, as you did not choose to confide unreservedly in us; but, going by my own judgment, I should say she was more sinned against than sinning. She even entreated me, if I could spare the time, to bring you the enclosed letter myself, and make an effort by word of mouth to move you from your stern resolve; and I should have tried to comply with her request but that great press of urgent business forbids my absence from London just now, even for a day or two. But I trust you will reconsider your determination, and at least read what she has written. We have endeavoured to explain all the monetary arrangements you have made for her future maintenance to Mrs. Dacre, and her liberty to keep the boy (who still remains in France) or not, as she chooses. But she listens to nothing, seems to scorn all mention of money, and only craves to see you, to hear from you. If I may venture to advise in so delicate a matter, I would say, give her the opportunity of explanation that she seeks so persistently, so unlike a guilty woman, and doubtless it will be for both your happiness in the years to come. Trusting you will forgive disobeyed orders in the matter of forwarding letters, &c., &c."

* * * * * *

"What fools men are, contemptible fools, where a beautiful woman, who has done them no ill, is concerned," mutters Lionel Dacre, when he has finished that long and somewhat unlawyer-like letter (unlawyer-like, in an interested warmth and earnest vigour of expression, not strictly professional) of young Tom Lonhed, a man still under thirty, and a junior partner in that highly respectable, long-established firm of solicitors. "But wait until it is their own turn to be wronged, deceived, their lives cursed and blasted, by one who seemed fair and good as an angel, and they'll be as hard, as unforgiving, as immovable as myself. The young fellow is quite ready to be the champion of her who dares to try and thrust herself into my presence, and is inclined to regard me as the transgressor. He is caught by the glamour of those lovely, pleading eyes, those sweet, pathetic tones, and does not know, could not believe, that the heart is as false as Hell. Need I blame him, when I, drivelling idiot that I was, never guessed, never dreamed, of the rottenness in that heart till it declared itself openly, without thinnest effort at disguise."

And then he sat down and wrote a few brief, almost peremptory, lines to the head of the firm, old Mr. Lonhed, who was not likely to be swayed by appealing eyes or persuasive voices. He returned his wife's letter, unopened, and did not "beg" this time, but "desired" that no more from the same source should be forwarded to him. Again, reiterating in stern, decisive form his solemn injunctions as to concealment of his address. Alluding to nothing in young Lonhed's letter but the one fact of his wife being in London; and saying, in conclusion, that he should be glad if the money transactions were arranged as speedily as might be, that that was the only real affair at issue, and he wished the matter to be done with as soon as possible, and to hear no more of it, to try to forget the past, if he could.

* * * * * *

It was a harsh, cruel letter,—cruel, that is, to her whom it concerned; but the man was stung to madness, disgusted at the gross cupidity, the audacious importunity (as he considers it) of her who bears his name. How the woman's whole nature is changed with her guilt, devoid of all shame, blunted, glaringly unfeeling.

She—the woman who was his wife, was in Canada with her lover (of that fact he has not the faintest, lingering doubt—how can he?), was at his side when he was struck by the hand of an indignant God, and yet, after that terrible experience, flies back to England as fast as steam can bring her, to try to retrieve what she has lost, to force herself once more into the arms of the man she has outraged, not content with the adequate provision he has made for her. She who, by her own sinful act, has forfeited all claim upon him for ever, she seeks to recover all. Ignorant of his changed life, his abandoned profession, she struggles shamelessly to step into the place she left. And though the wife of a clever rising architect may be in a vastly inferior position as compared to that of the mistress of a marquis, yet 'tis better than obscurity with a stained reputation, and is worth making a strong effort to regain before (as she may very likely calculate) her temporary breach of morality's illiberal, conservative laws, becomes generally known amongst their English friends.

Can we wonder, with these bitterest thoughts crowding and running riot in his brain, that Lionel Dacre's letter was harsh?

But, in spite of the prohibition conveyed in this communication, a few days later young Lonhed, without consulting his father or old Mr. Suttle, himself is the bearer of still another letter from Mrs. Dacre to her relentless husband. He flushes and stammers a little, and offers as his only excuse for almost an unwarrantable intrusion on his client's jealously guarded privacy, the plea of her agonised insistence.

"She implored me for the love of God, in the name of all I hold most sacred, to come to you myself, to bring you this letter, and not to leave your presence till I had induced you to read it. I trust you will forgive me, Mr. Dacre, for taking independent action in such a case, but it is a terrible thing to see a woman, and such a woman as your wife, in so sore a strait. If ever 'truth' shone in a woman's face and spoke in her voice, it is in hers. That she is guiltless of actual wrong I would stake my soul. She feels too much to be anything but innocent."

"Ah! Mr. Lonhed, you have not bought your experience in so bitter a school as I have. When you do, you'll learn that a woman seems exactly the reverse of what she is. She appears to feel exactly opposite of what her real sentiments are. Deceit is the breath of her nostrils, hypocrisy her darling sin. I regret that you took this trouble; a third party, however well intentioned, who does not know the facts of the case, can be no umpire between husband and wife whom deadliest wrong has separated. And even were they as thoroughly known as in my own breast, I could brook no interference in such a matter" (with a haughty frown). "Your father is in full possession of all the details of my miserable story; I confided in him utterly, and he does not seek to induce me to reconsider my resolve; but considers I am acting with generosity and forbearance."

"All I seek as her messenger," breaks in the younger man, impulsively, "all she entreats, in anguished supplication, is, that you give her a chance, an opportunity of explanation. She does not want to 'force herself upon you in any way,' she says, with proud resignation; she only wants to be cleared in your sight, from all imputation of evil. 'As I stand before God, I am an innocent woman!' were almost her last words to me, and they are ringing in my ears yet. Distress is killing her, Mr. Dacre; the vilest prisoner at the bar has the opportunity of pleading his own cause, or rather being eloquently pleaded for; and you will refuse this privilege to your wife, the mother of your child? 'When he reads that letter, if he can, or will, believe me guilty, I can only bow my head and submit,' she said when——"

"Yes," interrupts Mr. Dacre, excitedly, losing the cold dignity of manner that has been his throughout the early part of this interview. "Give myself the chance of being once again cheated, deceived, hoodwinked. No, Mr. Lonhed, for ten long years I was blind to my wife's real nature and character. I was a besotted fool, and thought her best, noblest, purest among women, and true to the heart's core. The result has shown how terribly my trust was misplaced. Yea, by God's rood, I trusted her too well. Possibly—I make no charge to the contrary—her life was all it ought to be, all it appeared to me to be, through those years; but, when the time was ripe, and the hour came, and with it the tempter, the woman was not wanting; it required but a touch, and the fabric of purity and truth I had credulously thought so unassailable crumbled into dust and ashes. No, Mr. Lonhed, henceforth and for ever, my wife is nothing to me. Her own heart knows, let her struggle as she may to achieve rehabilitation, how just and righteous is my determination. Take back that letter—or no—give it to me—it is better thus."

And he tosses it on the dancing flames of the fire, near which he stands, and watches it crackle and blaze up fiercely; the familiar characters standing out so clearly, for a moment, and then—it is all black nothingness. The form still intact, a faint tracery as of letters still perceptible, but only the ghost of the thing that was. And the men, as they stand and gaze at it silently for a brief minute, each thinks, though differently, that it symbolises the writer.

The fair, white message he has cast on the flames, seems to Lionel Dacre like the woman he had believed was fair within and without; and lo! the hot breath of passion and evil comes and shrivels it up, and it is black and soulless for evermore. While the man who has made this journey for her sake, sacrificing business and convenience to her wild entreaties, and who has failed so miserably in his mission, thinks also, that simulacrum of the letter, that waves and floats still in the grate, that a breath would break and scatter, in unrecognisable atoms, to the winds of heaven, is like the hopes in the heart of the writer when that message was penned. They were clear, and strong, and living, when those words, that the flames ate so greedily, were written. Now (when she knows—when he tells her—he will have to tell her—of that letter's cruel grave), they will be like those smoke-curled particles, black, dead, unreal, void, and substanceless.

And then an indignation that will not be repressed, rises in his breast against the man who stands there with a cold smile of scorn on his lips, that are yet pallid from intense feeling.

"Well, Mr. Dacre, you have acted as seems best to you, according to your lights; I only hope those lights are reliable ones, and not a Will-o'-the-wisp; that you will not live to repent bitterly this day's act, which seems to me, forgive my saying so, unnecessarily cruel. It could have done you no possible harm to read the letter, and your refusal to do so appears to me ungenerous. Of course, you are much the best judge of your own affairs, and are doubtless right in your determination; but you might have been less hard. I have to offer many apologies for my intrusion and foolish zeal in a matter in which I have no possible concern. I shan't err again in the same way, believe me. And now I beg to wish you good morning."

And without waiting for rest or refreshment, after travelling all night, Tom Lonhed, who, lawyer though he is, has not yet become ossified, is still capable of fresh, strong, wholesome feeling, and does not look on men and women as mere mechanical puppets, to be pulled this way and that by legal strings, seizes his hat, and walks straight out of the house, feeling crestfallen, angry, and disappointed. While the man who remains behind listens to his departure in frowning gloom.

"How dare any man presume to dictate to me in such a matter! The fellow's in love with her himself," he mutters, savagely; and yet, for the first time, a faint arrow of doubt, so faint as to be scarcely distinguishable, pierces him through the joints of that armour of certainty which has been hitherto impregnable. "Was he right, perfectly right, in refusing all attempts at explanation? Pshaw! Explanation; the word is an insult in such a conjunction." And that little pin-prick frets for an hour or so, but is gone before the day is dead.

CHAPTER VIII
FUGIT HORA[31]

LIONEL Dacre is troubled by no more letters or embassies from his wife. After a week or two, a practical business letter comes from old Mr. Lonhed, stating that Mrs. Dacre had called at their office, once since his son's return from a personal interview with their client; that what was then communicated to her as the result of that interview, had caused her to assume a proud indignant reserve of manner, somewhat trying. She had absolutely refused to listen to any particulars with regard to the arrangements made for her future maintenance, declaring she would never touch a farthing of money thus tendered. She had £50 a year of her own, she said, and she and her boy would live upon it or starve—ten thousand times rather starve—than be indebted for support to the man who was her husband, and who had chosen to brand her with the stamp of infamy. "Some such exaggerated expressions were used," continues the old solicitor, in retrospective condemnation of what he considers irrational, bad taste, &c.; his unemotional phlegmatic temperament having no sympathy with strongly displayed feeling. "However, we managed to inform her, that an account was opened in her name at the National & Provincial Bank of England; that £150 a year would be placed there to her credit, in quarterly instalments, and that, she would have simply to draw the money by signed cheque, when or as she chose."

* * * * * *

For a month or two Mr. Dacre hears no more. Then he gets a

---

31 *Fugit hora*: time flies.

note from "Lincoln's Inn," stating that no application has been made at the bank for the money, now more than two months lying there, and are they to continue to pay in the instalments? "Certainly," is the brief response wired in reply. Mr. Dacre feels this delay to make good the claim is but a ruse, and he is on his guard. Inviolable secrecy has been kept as to his place of abode, but still, he knows not what the next move may be.

* * * * * *

When more than a year has passed away, and he is informed that still the money, though accumulating, remains untouched, unclaimed; that arrow of doubt, that pricked him faintly on the day of Tom Lonhed's visit, again pierces, more keenly this time, and does not go in a day, but abides, though he tries to shake it off, and defies it. An uneasy inward questioning, as to whether he was too inflexible, too harsh, in adhering so fixedly to his resolution,—not that he admits for a moment that he could by any possibility have been wrong or even too hasty, in his judgment—of hearing nothing, troubles him occasionally; and the time passes on now with racing feet. Can it be three, four, five years since the sun of his life went down? Since he became a prematurely old and broken man; broken, that is, not so much as to health of body, as of mind; shorn of career, social and domestic joys, ambitions, pride of offspring, interests, hope, happiness, all at one fell blow.

Yes, five years! and in all that time, the money still accumulating in that London bank, remained unclaimed. Each quarter, to the day, the regular sum had been paid in, and each quarter the same news met the depositor, that no claim had been advanced for any portion of the amount lying there.

What a grievous thing it seems, to the business minds of Messrs. Lonhed, Suttle & Lonhed, for the money to be thus wasted, bringing in nothing, bearing no interest, lying at a dead loss; when it might have been turned over, and almost doubled itself in the time. Not that these worthy lawyers are men to advise anything like speculation, but safe, snug investments are their delight. And even three per cent. (miserable as it is, and tantalising, though provokingly safe), would surely be better—more righteous, as it seems to their financially constructed minds—than wickedly letting good money lie idle.

The sum is small, as sums of money are counted when investment is spoken of; but even £750 will yield a profit if properly handled, and the amount has now reached this figure. And there it is, added to each year, but not increasing itself by so much as a penny. So they make strong representations to their client, of the insane folly of continuing to place money where it can do no possible good to any creature; and he denying himself for the purpose, and to what avail? And he, seeing at length the wisdom of their oft-repeated suggestions, or at least, choosing now to act upon them, desires that no more payments be made into the bank, until some inquiries have been instituted, to discover, if possible, why no claim has been advanced for the deposits.

In accordance with Lionel Dacre's express wish, a letter from the firm of Messrs. Lonhed & Suttle is addressed to Mis Templeton. Three months go by, without any reply being received. They write again; in a few days the letter is returned, from the chief Parisian office, with an official statement from the small village post office at G——, to the effect, that the lady to whom the letter is addressed is no longer living. There is a sudden pull up. How are they to obtain information of her, for whom that money has vainly accumulated, if not through this channel? Perhaps, she, too, takes rank amongst the dead, and if so, the husband ought to be made aware of his release. They propose to make personal inquiries at Miss Templeton's late French address, to which their client accedes, somewhat reluctantly. If she is living, it will seem as if he wished to hear of her; and though deep down in his heart, there is an intense, almost unconquerable desire, to ascertain a something of what fate has befallen the woman he once loved so well, the child who did him no wrong, save in never seeking through the years to see his father's face. Yet the very consciousness of this unworthy feeling, as he deems it, causes him to shrink from making the effort, to gain what he longs to know. But here, it is urged upon him, and he does not refuse consent. So the legal firm sends a reliable emissary, desiring him to ascertain all he can.

But the "all" proves of scantiest proportions. Mr. Blake, the elderly confidential clerk entrusted with this somewhat delicate mission, goes straight to that pretty cottage *ornée*, outside the sleepy little village of G——, where Miss Templeton dwelt in peaceful solitude so many years. He finds it occupied by a happy, boisterous, overflowing family; dogs and children race emulatively in that garden that had been Dorothy Templeton's pride and joy; their merry shouts and barks fill the air; gay, laughing, youthful faces look from those jasmine-wreathed casements which had so long framed the patient, pathetic face of the deformed English woman: young, ardent, buoyant life surges, where calm, retrospective age, lived out its last saddened lonely years. Their tenancy is but a late one, two parties having previously occupied the house, in the interval which has elapsed since Miss Templeton's death. So, even her name conveys no meaning to their ears. Dorothy Templeton is unknown here; and Mr. Blake must go elsewhere if he wants to gain the smallest grains of information. He retraces his steps to the village; but even here, all he can gather is of the meagrest. For nearly a year after Miss Templeton's return from her sudden journey to England, now five years ago, a lady and her little boy lived with her at "La Verte" (the name of cottage). Yes, they believed the lady was a relative, but they were not exactly sure; she kept almost always indoors, and never went about in the village, or made friends with the people. So unlike Miss Templeton, who never was at rest, blessed saint, unless she was doing good to some poor creature. Then the strange lady went away taking the child with her. It might have been to England, or it might have been to Germany, they could not tell, and things went on the same as before; but Miss Templeton seemed to droop a little. She had never seemed quite the same since that journey to England. And then, there came terrible news, the bank in which she had all her money invested, broke, and everything was swept away from her. She was actually beggared at a blow. And this was not the worst, but being a shareholder, she was partly liable. This preyed upon her fearfully. Her sense of honour was so keen, that she felt everything she stood possessed of, her few valuables, plate, trinkets, &c., her furniture, her very clothes even, were no longer her own, but belonged to others. She sank altogether under the shock of this trouble; she had not strength to bear up, and in less than three months from the date of the bank's failure, she was dead.

They did not think (these honest villagers), when questioned closely with subtle skill by the cautious Mr. Blake, that it was for herself the dear lady fretted so at the loss of the money; though when all is said and done, it is a terrible thing to lose one's all, swallowed up by those great greedy banks; and surely, a corner under the thatch, or a hole in the floor, under one's bed, is safer, and better, than letting it out of one's own keeping; but Miss Templeton knew that her time would not be long, and she had friends who would not let her want. The reason she grieved so was, partly at the wrong and misery of the whole thing, in which she was unconsciously involved; and especially at not being able to leave the money, she had always thought was her own for ever, to some one dear to her; it might have been the lady who was with her for that year, but they could not say certainly. All they knew was through the servants; and the French maid knew nothing of her mistress's private affairs or sentiments; and the Englishwoman scarcely spoke. She was always silent, reserved, distant, in her manner; so unlike the sweet lady herself; but Mademoiselle Templeton—Heaven rest her gentle spirit—was a woman in ten thousand.

About a month before her death, the lady who had been with her before, came to nurse her, and remained with her to the end. They never heard this lady's name, she was spoken of by the servants as "Madame Helen," they believed she was a widow. When she walked out, which was seldom, she always went through the lonely lanes, and never spoke to anybody; even the doctor, who was in daily attendance on Miss Templeton, saw little of her, and knew no more than they; she was a relative, they felt assured, a cousin, or a niece, or even a sister, perhaps, of half-blood. She seemed grave, and proud, and sad. She looked very ill, as if she was either in bad health, or had some very great grief; and they felt certain she would not long survive the friend she mourned.

After the funeral, everything was sold, by the dead lady's express desire, and the amount realised was forwarded to the Committee, who were winding up the broken threads of the rotten bank, at whose false doors this good woman's death might be laid, to divide between a few of the poor creatures who had lost—been robbed as she considered it, unconsciously by herself and many, consciously by a guilty few, of—their all. Then "La Verte" was advertised to be let for the first time for more than fifty years, and the English lady and the English servant went away together. That was now nearly three years ago, and they had heard nothing of either since. Judging by the lady's looks, they'd say, it was but a chance whether she was still living.

The little boy? No, they knew nothing whatever of him. He did not return with the lady when she came to Miss Templeton's death-bed. The year he lived at the cottage he never went out beyond the gardens alone. The few times he came to the village—and they were but few—he was either with Miss Templeton herself, or, the English maid; he seemed shy and thoughtful. They believed he and the strange lady used to take long country walks together; but the lady always looked sad, and the boy never laughed, or shouted, or was merry, like other children.

These somewhat meagre barren facts are all that Mr. Blake's clever, astute questioning can extract from these simple rustics. An interview with the doctor who had attended Miss Templeton yields no additional information, save that he inclines to the opinion that Germany was the English lady's destination, as he heard she took tickets for Cologne.

Miss Templeton was beggared, is dead; and of Mrs. Dacre there is no trace. This is the net result of his endeavours, and Mr. Blake returns to Lincoln's Inn, crestfallen and humiliated.

* * * * * *

Apparently it is written, that Lionel Dacre is not to hear aught of her whom he has repudiated, while the past of grievous wrong, of grievous error, which is it? is still fresh, still capable of being atoned for.

* * * * * *

By-and-by perhaps, when it has become a grey, gaunt, dust-laden skeleton, fleshless from the weight of years under which it has lain; when it is too late for any emotion, however strong and earnest, to avail him or her aught, but a profound peace on the one side, and a wild unavailing regret on the other; then, but not before, may Lionel Dacre possibly once again hear of her whose brilliant noon of life was merged in his.

SECOND PERIOD
THE LONE CLIFF HOUSE

CHAPTER I
COMING IN WITH THE TIDE

"Fair was she to behold, that maiden of seventeen summers."

IT is such a lonely house, perched away up there so high in mid air, almost on the verge of the cliff, with no other human habitation near, and no sound to break the silence save the eternal plash, plash of the waves, heard faintly from below, and the shrill screaming of the gulls as they circle round it before swooping out again to sea. And the girl who sits on the huge boulder that projects from the face of the cliff a few feet below its surface, with her hands clasped behind her head, leaning back against an angle of the rock, gazing dreamily seawards, seems in perfect harmony with the scene. She is very fair to look upon, with a wild, picturesque beauty of both face and attitude, that is in complete unison with her surroundings. Her large luminous eyes have caught the reflection of the waters that girt her home—deep, dark, vivid blue, almost startling, as they shine out at one from between those thick, black curling lashes, so intense is their sapphire radiance. Her tawny, shining hair looks as if some errant sunbeams had become entangled in its meshes, and were ever after playing hide-and-seek in their efforts to escape. It is caught back carelessly from the face, and hangs in rich profusion on her shoulders. Two crimson roses bloom on her clear brown cheeks, and the small, perfect teeth gleam brilliantly 'twixt the full pomegranate lips. She has not changed her position for an hour or more, lazily dreaming away the summer morning, having soon after breakfast come out to her favourite rock, which she and her little sister call the Throne.

That smiling, treacherous sea! Who could think to look at it now that but a few hours before, in the darkness of the night, when all life seems so helpless, it had lashed itself into a white-heat fury, its waves rushing in with angry elevated crests, like serpents about to spring, while the abysmal troughs between had become for many a shrinking soul "the valley of the shadow." Many a good ship had sailed into that night's darkness and death, leaving no trace behind, and to-day it tells naught of the tragedies so lately enacted beneath its gleaming surface.

There had been rather a bad wreck on that part of the coast, a mile or two to the left of the lone house on the cliff, but the recumbent figure on the rocks had no special interest in it; the only two belonging to her are well and safe, and she looks down with satisfaction at her own pretty little boat, lying high and dry upon the beach, where it had escaped uninjured last night's storm.

* * * * * *

The owner of the boat at last falls soundly asleep, quite a shameful proceeding in the lovely early day; but the storm kept her awake last night, and the air is so balmy and the sun so warm. And another hour slips swiftly away. It is nearly twelve o'clock when she starts suddenly, looks about with a slightly bewildered expression, and shivers. A great change in the day has taken place during her brief hour's slumber. The soft white billowy clouds that had refreshingly broken the blue monotony of sky have drawn nearer together, and grown larger and denser, the sun is obscured, a brisk, somewhat chill breeze has arisen, and wails round the distant headlands with a dismal moaning sound, while the now grey gloomy waters are heaving and tossing with a faint reflection of their last night's fierce wrath.

The day has grown decidedly disagreeable, thinks the girl, as she rises with another pronounced shiver. Sleeping has chilled her, the friendly sun having withdrawn his ardent rays, and even in her nest in the great cliff wall that vigorous breeze makes its presence unpleasantly felt. She stretches herself and yawns prodigiously, picks up her book and hat preparatory to retreating within doors, and then takes a look at the sea. The tide has turned while she slept, and is coming in rapidly. As she idly glances with no purpose in her gaze, her eyes are suddenly arrested and distend widely. What is that? Something small and black, bobbing up and down with a strangely jerky motion, still far out to sea, but seemingly coming in with the tide. She gazes at it long and earnestly, but can make nothing of it. It is certainly not a boat, and yet seems to have no volition of its own. With a sudden thought she springs up to the top of the cliff and disappears within the house, reappearing almost immediately carrying a powerful glass, with which she eagerly scans the distant object.[32]

"It is a man!" breaks almost instantly from her lips; "but that's not swimming," she continues. "He looks as if he were fastened to something. Oh, I wonder, is he dead?"

She now notices that, although coming in with the tide, it appears to be approaching from the left, and will most probably be borne along by the strong outer current, combined with the fresh south-westerly breeze now blowing, past the little natural harbour, and drift in, God knows where, lower down the coast; to certain death, if not already dead, and in any case to be dashed to pieces

---

[32] Glass: spyglass, a small telescope.

against those terrible cliffs. She again looks long at that distant floating atom of humanity.

"If I could only know whether he is alive or dead," she mutters, and then glances down at her boat so snugly at rest below. "At any rate I'll try," she cries, closing in the glass with a snap.

A narrow, winding, zigzag path, close to where she has been sitting, leads straight down to the beach. Down this she races at headlong speed, her slender feet flying over the ground, her bright hair streaming on the wind. Reaching the shore it is but the work of a moment to unfasten the boat from its moorings, push it into the water, leap in and be off. All fair and easy so far, but no farther. To row and to endeavour to make rapid progress against a swiftly inrushing tide, with a strong breeze blowing in your teeth into the bargain, is not the most facile task in the world. But the girl is a splendid oarswoman; she pulls with a will, and her supple, lissom figure shows to magnificent advantage as she bends to her oars, rowing with a long, steady, clean stroke.

When more than half-way out she rests on her oars for a moment or two. She is very warm now, and a little breathless from the exertion. She flings off the shawl that she had caught up when she rushed to the house for the glass, and taking up the latter, which she has brought with her, again eagerly scrutinises the object for which she is making. She can now plainly distinguish that the man is lashed to a spar, or some remains most probably of a wreck, of which he has been a victim. The figure seems to be perfectly void of life or motion, drifting helplessly as the waves list, and the girl's heart gives a great throb of something akin to fear, as she reflects that more than likely she is gradually coming face to face with death.

However, she holds bravely on, rowing now more swiftly than ever, and keeping steadily to the right, so as to intercept the body in its eastward course. This makes her task much more difficult, and she feels very anxious as to being able to cross its path at the right moment, for it is drifting rapidly now, the wind being stronger, and if she misses it she may have a long chase, and very possibly a hopeless one.

* * * * * *

Nearer and nearer they approach each other: the eager, striving girl, so intensely living, and that motionless, death-like form of the unknown man. And now he is sweeping past the boat, and with a little inarticulate cry, induced by her swift, half-terrified glance at the pallid drawn face, when she sees a faint, muscular twitching about the mouth and eyes, that tells her in one glad flash that her effort has not been fruitless, that the poor, helpless, floating waif is not dead, the courageous creature leans well over the boat's side, and stretches out her hand to catch the long loose end of the rope that lashes man and spar together. She just misses it by a hand's-breadth, and with the jerk she gives in her straining effort to reach it, the little boat, being so weighed to one side, capsizes, and the brave, energetic girl disappears beneath the swirling, foaming waters.

But in a moment she has risen to the surface, panting, blinded, deafened by her sudden plunge into the rushing waves, and half choked by the water she has swallowed; and with one hand tries to clear her eyes, pushing back the long, streaming hair, its yellow beauty drenched, and tangled with seaweed, which impedes her vision, while with the other she keeps herself afloat. She is very pale, and somewhat scared-looking; the start of being suddenly engulfed in those deep, tossing waters, the alarm of finding her boat, hopelessly unattainable, already many yards stretching between them, would be enough to make a tolerably stout feminine heart quail a little. But this child of the cliffs has a dauntless, unselfish spirit; she is not going to give up, without another struggle, what she had so nearly attained; she now knows that a life is dependent on her powers to save. Of course, if the man had been dead, as she had felt almost sure, why then she would think of herself, and make for shore at once; but she saw those quivering muscles that betrayed the lingering life, and she will make a desperate effort to save that helpless, unknown creature, that drifting human item, from the awful fate of being crushed and battered beyond all recognition on those terrible cliffs lower down the coast, where he is sure eventually to drift. So, with a skilful, rapid movement she manages to kick off her shoes, and, unloosing the bodice of her dress, so as to give herself as free play as possible, she strikes out boldly in pursuit.

She swims excellently well, being nearly as much at home in the water as on dry ground. But she is fighting against long odds; fully dressed as she is, her progress is slow and difficult, her breath comes in quick, short gasps. She will soon grow exhausted thus. Robust as the girl is both by nature and training, yet she is not vigorous enough to battle long with those contending waves; she feels her strength going, and her heart contracts with a sharp, wild pang of fear, almost despair. What if she is going to meet the fate she seeks to save that other from? If she grows unconscious the waves will do with her what they list; but even with this awful thought she will not yield. Not yet. Once more she will try. Remaining motionless for a moment or two, she draws one or two deep, full breaths, and then, with a swift, sharp glance at the object she is slowly gaining on, she dives beneath the angry, tossing surface into the calm, still water below, and, after a few seconds, comes up breathless. Twice she repeats this manoeuvre, and the second time rises with great joy and thanksgiving in her heart, for she is abreast with that quiet, stirless form, and she snatches the end of rope that had before eluded her, and, keeping herself afloat by treading water, she firmly binds it round one of her wrists, feeling that it is best not to trust to merely her grasp, as before they quite get in she may grow weak from fatigue; and then she turns her face shorewards, exhausted, but so thankful, her task being now comparatively easy. For a few minutes, till she gets well within that strong outer current that sweeps all things eastwards, till she gets within those protecting giant arms of the little natural harbour, she has to be very careful, and use all her remaining strength to direct her course aright. But once in the safety of their shelter, she feels secure as a babe in its mother's arms, and weary and half unconscious, she turns over on her back, and floats slowly in with her strange burden in tow.

An odd, weird scene rather it makes. The sun has burst forth again through a jagged fissure in the now angry clouds, the dazzling light, so condensed, as it were, seems to gleam with a fierce, boding radiance; the tossing waters, sullen, sombre, menacing, lit by that one broad streak of blinding glare, an illuminated path that seems to stretch out across a mystic, rayless ocean; the stern, frowning cliffs, rearing their mighty granite masses skywards, the strip of soft, golden sand at their base; the lonely house perched up aloft, and in the foreground the young, beautiful girl, in her pale blue gown, with streaming yellow hair glittering in the sun, her face turned heavenwards, and eyes, blue as those heavens, as seen through the narrow rift in the dusky cloud-curtain, gazing dreamily upwards, "floating—floating on," as if wrapped in some strange, solemn, calm; and that ghastly, motionless form, that looks so horribly like death, gliding silently in her wake. Yes, not a bad subject for an artist's pencil.

And now they reach the shore, and the exhausted, half-dazed girl is roused to things of earth by the voice of her dear old nurse who, with her fellow-servant from the house above, a sturdy Cornish girl, remarkable for her strength of body, awaits her beloved young mistress. Her old eyes have, through a strong glass, watched with terror and dismay the foregoing alarming scene, and she now greets her darling with tears, and reproaches, kisses, and blessings, all in one breath. And in a moment or two, when the stout Nan has hauled in the stranger, and unlashing him from the spar, opens coat and waistcoat, and laying her hand upon his heart, declares triumphantly he lives, the old woman breaks forth—

"Ah, Miss Ula, Miss Ula, you're the fearless, brave bit lassie, and the great, gude God will love you, and bless you, my bairn, for you've saved that puir braw laddie the day from a frightfu' death.[33] You've saved a life, my bonnie lass, an' the angels will keep and guard you for ever and ever. Oh, my hairt is proud and glad this day!"

And she whom they call Ula kisses the agitated old creature, and glances at the "braw laddie," as her nurse dubs him, her tongue returning, in its excitement, to its native Scotch. Yes, he is "braw," a tall, broad-shouldered man, with long, straight limbs, a crown of dark, curly hair surmounting the now ashen face, and broad, intellectual brow, a dark moustache, and soft, curly beard, shading the handsomely cut mouth. Yes, he is "braw," thinks the girl, as with weary, halting steps she tries to make her way up the zig-zag path. Her progress is slow, and she is shivering violently, in spite of the heap of shawls and blankets old Bab has wrapped around her, and the brandy she has insisted on her swallowing. Nan Penlyon wanted to carry her to the top, and then come back to see to the stranger; but Ula will not hear of their minding her, and after that one long glance at the unknown, in which she sees the closed lids

[33] Braw: fine, good-looking.

quiver and open, disclosing great, dark eyes, that gaze vacantly for a moment, and then close again, she stumbles off, leaving the women to revive the creature nearly buffeted to death by the cruel, hungry sea.

Yes, he is "braw," she thinks again, when more than half-way to the top she stops a moment to rest; then, after a pause, "Who is he?" that still nameless "he." Was it ordered that she should save his life, that their paths of life should cross? And then comes into her mind, like a sudden savage stab, the dismal prophetic distich which she has heard so often, "Save a stranger from the sea, and he'll turn your enemy," and she shivers more violently than ever as she continues her toilsome way up to the house. But a warmth remains round her heart that will not be dispelled. She has saved a life, thank God, thank God!

What a mystery it seems; a life in the world, perhaps a great and good life, that would have gone out for ever only for her, and the angels will now always guard her and keep her, old Bab says,—they all say so about here—and even if nothing else should ever happen in her life, remarkable, or mysterious, or eventful, she will always have the memory of this day, and will feel that she has not lived in vain.

So the girl, at once dreamy and dauntless, imaginative and energetic, ardent, unselfish, enthusiastic, with a strong vein of idealism in her highly-strung, poetic nature, pauses again on the threshold of her home, and, with clasped hands and upraised, introspective eyes, murmurs, "Yes, I have saved a life, a strong man's life—*I*, Ula Ferguson, only a girl, unaided, alone. I can never feel quite the same again, I think; never so inconsequent, so childish; it seems as if there was a deeper meaning in all things. 'I thank Thee, O God, for letting me be of some use in the world.' "

And then, in a different tone, while a faint smile creeps round the chill, pale lips, "My father will be so pleased, so proud; and darling old Eff, how mystified she will be, she'll think all her fairy stories and legends have come true at once, only it's the other way, the lady saves the knight, and not the knight the lady—and," with a deep-drawn breath, "I wonder, oh, I wonder, what the future hides!" And she vanishes within doors, while the women, far down on the beach, fan the flickering life that had sunk so low, and by-and-by laboriously toil up the steep, winding cliff path, supporting the erst powerful man, now weak as a little child; at least, Nan Penlyon's brawny arms do serviceable work, as old Barbara is little help; and all is quiet once more on that little strip of sand under the mighty rugged cliffs of Penmaerwyn.

CHAPTER II

HONOUR *VERSUS* INCLINATION

FOR a week and more the stranger lies between life and death in the pretty spare bed-chamber of the lone Cliff House, and the doctor from the village of Penmaer, a mile away, a skilful physician, comes and goes many times.

His patient was sorely bruised and buffeted in his long contest through the dark night with the swirling terrible waters that lash that wild, iron-bound Cornish coast in time of storm. He had been many hours immersed; after the awful wreck of which he was a victim, he had been carried far out to sea with the receding tide, and he lies for days weak and helpless as a young child, half unconscious and haunted by one strange vision that always repeats itself in the same form, and though it sometimes soothes him, yet it puzzles the poor weak faculties to try to understand. He fancies he is miles down below the surface of the sea, and yet the water is blue and translucent; his hand is held by a lovely mystical creature that he feels must be the fabled mermaid of superstition, a creature with a beautiful woman's face, streaming yellow hair, and the long twining scaly tail of greenish blue that writhes and stretches far behind, and she is drawing him gently but irresistibly on and on where he knows not, but he must needs follow, he has no choice. And by and bye he longs to follow, and would not desist even if she bade him. And then suddenly they meet a great darkness, and he no longer feels the guiding hand, and though he sees a faint light across the darkness, yet the vision fades ere he can reach it, only to repeat itself in similar fashion a few hours later. It is really partly a phantasmagoria of what actually occurred. Once or twice, as they floated shorewards, the dark eyes had unclosed with non-comprehension in their dim misty gaze, and hazily seeing the sky and water and the floating girl-face framed in those lovely tawny tresses, the poor dazed brain had conceived this odd and singular idea, transforming poor Ula's innocent pretty blue gown into a snaky tail.

But after a while the weakness and the fancies alike vanish, his youth and strength carry him through, and in less than a fortnight he sees the dream-face which has haunted him so pertinaciously. All mists of memory are dissolved; he recollects in a flash of instant, almost mysterious remembrance, the circumstances of his rescue, as he had not been so unconscious as he seemed; his body had been locked in death-like motionlessness, but his spirit had not reached the blank of complete insensibility, a vague, dreamy fantastic consciousness had remained to him, an unreal visionary state, not unlike the gradual fading of the senses that accompanies a frozen death; and he recognizes the girl who so nobly and bravely saved his life at the imminent risk of her own, and his heart gives a great bound of intensest undying gratitude and admiration, coupled with a great pervading wonder at her extreme youthfulness and girlish, modest simplicity. How daring and enduring and fearless she had proved herself, nobly unselfish and heroic, that young, beautiful, blushing thing who seems so shy and nervous in his presence.

And will that moment ever fade in Ula's memory, when he, the man whose life she had saved, suddenly stood before her on that great rugged boulder they call "the Throne," that giant rock that projects from the face of the frowning, unscalable cliff, almost directly at the back of the house, and on which she lounged in idle dreaminess that morning when the distant *something* was coming in with the tide.

The first freshness of the early day was around them as they stood opposite to each other for the first time, when he caught the girl's hand impulsively, and tried to pour out in a few vigorous, never-to-be-forgotten words, a portion of the intense living, immeasurable gratitude that lay so deep, so almost unutterable in his breast. His heart rushed forth in speechless thanksgiving for the precious gift of life. He had bidden it farewell in anguished desperation, hopeless of rescue; he had closed his eyes for ever, he supposed, on this lovely world; and now he is again looking up into God's wide heavens, again walking the earth with the free, vigorous step of youth and recovered strength. To live, to breathe, on such a morning is joy unutterable, and who under God has given him this great gift? And thinking thus he turned and beheld the girl to whom he owed all. With a few rapid strides he is at her side and holds her hands in his, and there, with the blue Atlantic stretching away from their feet far below, with Tintagel and its ruined castle surrounded by its halo of traditional romance, its lovely legend of bygone love and chivalry in the dim far distance, and those grey and mighty cliffs near at hand, he speaks words which never till the latest day of her life,—be that life long or short—will grow dim or faint in Ula Ferguson'a memory, that will never cease to throb with the vivid life which glowed in them when uttered. Could she ever in her whole life again feel so intensely happy and proud, and sweetly shame-faced as at that moment, she thought, after he had left her and she remained alone a little while to recover her composure before returning to the house to breakfast, to battle with the emotional tears that blurred her vision and produced a choking sensation in her throat, to still the trembling which thrilled her robust young frame?

* * * * * *

But it is already a whole week ago since she wonderingly asked herself this question, and even now, vaguely, indefinitely, instinctively, she feels that there are words which might be uttered by the same speaker that would cause her to experience the same emotions, only in a still stronger ratio.

*   *   *   *   *   *

Yes, another week has come to its close and still Geoffrey Graham—which the Cliff House people have learned is the stranger's name—lingers on in that wild sea-girt home. He is quite his own strong self again, and of that terrible night there are no traces save in his wounded arm, which still rests interestingly in a sling. These three weeks complete rest and repose in the lone Cliff House have invigorated him wonderfully, coupled with pure bracing air, fresh from the wide Atlantic. And the week that has elapsed since he left his room, he has spent almost altogether out of doors, drinking in deep life-giving draughts of that best of all tonics. As he tells Ula in one of their long talks, for they have grown very friendly now, dangerously friendly perhaps, he feels a changed man from what he was before that awful night. He had been feeling sadly jaded and exhausted previous to taking that holiday, of which he stood so much in need, and had only consented to take it at his mother's earnest request. He has been working hard for years, he says, almost without rest or cessation from toil, striving to make a better position for himself and her whom he appears to love so fondly. He is a civil engineer, and feels that he has it in him to make his mark in the world if but favoured with opportunity. So he has worked on perseveringly, studying much in the intervals of labour, to fit himself for any higher branch in his calling to which he may attain by-and-by, and hoping a great deal. And within the past year fortune has smiled more favourably on him;

a certain branch line of rail of importance, and embracing many difficulties, the construction of which had been placed entirely in his hands, he had managed very skilfully and had been complimented thereon. Since then his hands have been full of work, and, as he tells Ula with a flushing brow, he hopes the day may soon dawn in which he will be famous in his profession. Not for his own sake, he makes haste to add, but for his dear mother's, whom he yearningly longs to see in the position she should occupy.

The relationship has a peculiar interest for the girl, as she passionately loved her own mother during the very few years of earliest childhood which she was spared to her, but that dear mother died when her little sister Effie was but three months old, and she herself had not quite completed her sixth year.

* * * * * *

And what are Geoffrey Graham's thoughts as he slowly wends his way to the distant village, his destination being the rural post-office, where he guesses that a letter may be awaiting him? They are not all pleasant, if one may judge by the shadow which rests on his brow. He is engaged in a sort of mental conflict; conscience whispers to him that he ought to be gone; that it is but a sorry return for the infinite good he has received, to remain on in that lone house, now that he has recovered and that its master is still absent. For the past two or three days he thinks he has read uneasiness and dissatisfaction in old Bab's face and manner, and that troublesome inward monitor tells him she is right. His young chatelaine is *so* young, and frank, and guileless, she is sweet and friendly and familiar with the stranger, she and her quaint, precocious little sister taking long strolls with him along the cliffs in perfect faith and good fellowship. She is not to blame, if there was any one to make remarks; he, and he alone, would deserve censure. He felt he had no business to remain longer in that household of women; but he tried to stifle conscience with the lame excuse even to himself, that it would be ungrateful to leave till he had expressed in person to Ula's father his undying and immeasurable gratitude; also trying to comfort himself with the reflection that there are no prying neighbours to circulate ill-natured gossip. The village he is bound for is a good mile distant from the Cliff House, and the nearest town of any importance is Bodmin, nearly six miles off; in fact there is no habitation of any kind near the lone house on the cliff save the coastguard station, full half-a-mile away to the left.

But by the time he has reached the village, his nobler, higher nature has asserted itself, and he has determined, no matter what the effort may cost him (and he does not disguise from himself for a moment that it will be a great wrench), to leave Penmaerwyn and Ula Ferguson the following Monday. This is Saturday, so he cannot well go sooner. He will come back, most certainly he will; the girl holds him with magnetic chains; but he will go for the present; perhaps in a week or two her father will have returned.

The letter which he anticipated finding is waiting for him. He has written several times to his mother, the first two or three from his bed, and she, poor, loving soul, has not failed to write regularly every day since she heard of the accident. She would have flown to her darling's bedside, to nurse him as only a mother can, had not cruel fate forbidden it. The very morning that her beloved son was drifting in helplessly to Ula's feet, she had slipped down a couple of stairs and sprained her foot rather badly, which has since kept her a close prisoner to her sofa. Her heart waxed sore within her, but she was fain to be content with that cold, unsatisfactory medium of pen and paper. How barren and unsympathetic it seems, when we long, with intensity unspeakable, for the grasp of the hand that held the pen, or for one look into the eyes we love so well, that gazed on this bit of white paper we hold in our hands, as they traced the characters thereon. Ah! even so; and how much stronger and overpowering is this feeling upon us, when we gaze on the dear familiar writing of a beloved one laid to her rest! We feel indeed then, that we would sacrifice almost anything for

> "The touch of a vanished hand,
> The sound of a voice that is still."[34]

Geoffrey Graham takes his letter into a sweet clover meadow, outside the village, to read it in *al fresco* enjoyment. There is in the air a delicious scent of new-mown hay, and he throws himself down at the side of a noisy, babbling little brook, that the villagers dignify by the name of river, which is making its way to the sea, a mile off, with as much fuss as possible. Everything is very sweet and peaceful round him this waning August afternoon, and he prepares to enjoy his mother's letter. As usual, it breathes love throughout, and delighted tender congratulation on his rapid recovery, urging him in terms of strong affection not to dream of lessening his proposed holiday by as much as one day on her account, as she is quite easy and happy about him now (poor, unselfish fibber, when she is absolutely hungering for one glimpse of her boy's face). And she argues that if he feels unequal to carry out the original plan of his summer trip, he cannot do better than remain where he is, from what she has gathered from the doctor—who had first written, indeed telegraphed and then written, to appraise her of his safety, at Geoffrey's whispered request, dreading the terrible effect upon her of the newspaper account of the

[34] From the poem 'Break, Break, Break' by Alfred, Lord Tennyson.

calamity,—and also from himself, besides what little information she has been able to glean since, she imagines that Penmaerwyn must be about one of the most salubrious and health-restoring spots in the kingdom.

The plan of the two months' summer holiday which she alludes to, had been crushed at the very outset. The young man had elected to commence it by a coasting expedition. Living as he did in one of the northern counties, he longed to see the southern and western shores, so he took a passage in a small excursion coasting steamer, which would eventually land him gently at Dover, after having had a few days' pleasant rest at sea, which would be particularly acceptable just then. After landing, his intention had been to run over to Paris for a week or two, where he had friends, and then on to Switzerland to do some Alpine climbing. But—*l'homme propose*—that poor little steamer was doomed to destruction.[35] Caught in a swift and sudden storm, in the blackness of the night, she had been mercilessly dashed on those giant Cornish rocks, and her joyous, eager, living freight of pleasure-seekers were either drowned in the horrors of the thick darkness, or pitilessly torn and beaten to death in their frantic efforts to get a footing on that terrible coast. Only two besides Graham had fought successfully against such fearful odds, whilst all the rest of that gay, unthinking crowd had been suddenly summoned to yield up their lives in the midst of that awful warring of the elements. Will the remembrance of that terrible night ever pale in any of these three survivors' memories?

Thus his mother, poor, loving, unsuspecting soul, does her best to undermine the good resolution which he has found it so difficult to make; but she never for a moment imagines that he

[35] As in *l'homme propose, dieu dispose*: man proposes, god disposes.

can be in any danger of the kind that threatens him. Her worst fear now is that he will not be properly taken care of, as to meals, etc., in such an out-of-the-way place, and with these, as she chooses to fancy them, humble fisher folk. Not that any one has wilfully deceived her on this point, but from the slight allusion made to them by the doctor in his formal communications, and also her son's description of the peculiar situation of the house, and the girl's strange familiarity with arts almost unknown among gentlewomen when she was young, besides the proofs given of her physical strength, etc., had all conspired to lead her to the conclusion that they were but "toilers of the sea," to be thanked in coin and nothing more. She did not guess (how could she?) that the tawny hair of a Venus Aphrodite was entangling her son's affections in its meshes, that Calypso's fairy grotto was not more enchanted ground to Ulysees than that lone Cliff House to Geoffrey Graham.

But, to do him justice, though his resolve wavers for just a little after reading her letter, yet as he strays slowly shorewards in the gloaming he determines to write her word this evening that he is leaving on Monday, and to ask her not to write again till she hears from him in Paris, where he will spend a portion of the month which he still has before him.

CHAPTER III

A SINGULAR DREAM

AS he approaches the Cliff House, Geoffrey becomes aware of some change having taken place in his absence. His ears are saluted by an unfamiliar sound to him in that region, the vehement barking of a dog; and on coming nearer, he beholds a rough and shaggy terrier of warlike aspect keeping obtrusive guard by the house-door. He has scented the stranger afar off, and thus incontinently defies him. He stands in the middle of the entrance, as if challenging the intruder to come farther if he dare; but quite suddenly "a change comes o'er the spirit of his dream," perhaps his memory has been jogged, and he recollects that a visitor is expected; or more likely, a word of censure and admonition has reached him through the open parlour door, for he retreats on one side with an expostulatory growl.[36] Geoffrey's olfactories are also greeted as he crosses the threshold with the welcome and familiar incense of tobacco, a sure test that the masculine element exists within, and on entering the pretty low-ceilinged sitting-room, a tall old man, putting Effie tenderly down from his knee, rises from the deep embrasure of the window-seat to greet him.

Effie has been giving him a full, true, and particular account of the stranger sojourning within his gates: how he came, how he looks, what he says, and what he does,—details not vouchsafed by Ula; but on Mr. Ferguson's asking the very natural question, "Is he young?" he is solemnly assured by Effie, "Oh, no! he has a beard

[36] Based on a line from 'The Dream' by Lord Byron: "A change comes o'er the spirit of my dream".

down to that,"—indicating with a tiny finger, an improvised spot on her pinafore, plainly showing that in her infantile mind beards and youth are quite incompatible.

The light has grown very dusk when these two men stand opposite each other under the same roof, face to face, and grasp each other's hands: they each see the other but very indistinctly; they each try to penetrate the gloom which surrounds them, but fail. But Mr. Ferguson sees quite enough to know that the stranger resting at his hearth during his absence, is a young and handsome man, and he is conscious of a pang of self-reproach, as he thinks of his Ula being alone and unprotected, and subject to the very influence from which he has tried most to guard her. Geoffrey sees only a tall, slight, bent old man, with snow-white hair and beard. They sit down and begin to converse, and soon, wonderfully soon, their talk flows pleasantly, almost familiarly. They each take a vivid interest in subjects outside the common range, subjects of a loftier order than form the basis of ordinary conversation, and they each soon discover that the other is a refined intellectual man of cultivated mind. They dovetail, so to speak, these men, if one may be pardoned the expression. There is a strange similarity in their views on many things. They are "congenial," that is the true word, and the only stable foundation on which real liking and friendship can be built.

They sit on talking, these two, in the gloaming, and the shadows fall around them, wrapping them in deeper gloom. Effie, who has climbed to her perch again, is cuddled in Mr. Ferguson's arms, and has fallen asleep with her head on his breast. Ula's voice can be heard faintly in the distance, on household cares intent; and all around that lone house on the cliffs is very still and hushed; the murmurous, monotonous lapping of the never-resting waters only serving to increase the feeling of rest and repose. And Geoffrey Graham feels the external calm enter his breast and take up its abode there. He feels, he knows not why, happier and more peaceful than he has done for a long time; and yet withal he is conscious of a strange all-pervading feeling of wonder, almost unreality, underlying it. He catches himself, as it were, searching mentally for some missing link. Some undefined sense of connection between a long dead past and this present is strongly upon him.

Geoffrey is not in general fanciful or imaginative, indeed he rather prides himself on being quite the reverse, and his experiencing so uncommon a feeling in so marked a degree, strikes him as being at least peculiar.

* * * * * *

The next day is Sunday, and a very sweet and peaceful Sunday it seems to Graham as passed in Penmaerwyn. He and the Fergusons walk to church through the fields, morning and evening. As they return from the latter service through the sweet summer dusk, a warm vaporous dimness, quite distinct from darkness, that lends a sort of uncertainty and enchantment to all things—

> "Till now the doubtful dusk revealed
> The knolls once more, where couched at ease
> The white kine glimmer'd, and the trees
> Laid their dark arms about the field."[37]

> "The cool delicious meadows of the night,"[38]

---

[37] From *In Memoriam* by Alfred, Lord Tennyson.

[38] From 'A Life-Drama' by Alexander Smith.

" 'Twixt dew and bird
So sweet a silence ministered
God seemed to use it for a word"[39]—

these and other lines from her favourite poets keep running through Ula's mind. She feels very strangely happy, as they continue their way through the perfumed gloom, while soft shadowed creatures of the night and silence float dimly, dumbly by on the still air, and human voices sound too clear and resonant, if raised to their normal key, in the evening hush in which nature has wrapped herself, and involuntarily take a lower key.

She and Graham and Effie are in front, Mr. Ferguson having fallen behind with Dr. Wenvoe. The little girl has been, and is, thinking busily. She is a strange little creature, with an eerie fantastic nature; a small delicate, fragile child, seeming much younger than her eleven years. She is the spoiled darling of the old man. She has been very favourably impressed by the stranger, which is quite wonderful and highly complimentary, though Geoffrey may not properly appreciate the fact, for Effie is a small autocrat, and it is difficult to propitiate her. She has hitherto proved herself decidedly elusive, but now she makes a new departure in Geoff Graham's favour. She took covert peeps at him during the service as he sat or stood by her side, and in turn compared him favourably with both Lancelot and Arthur. Indeed, these traditional personages were somewhat crowded out towards the end of Effie's musings, and "Geoffrey Graham, gentleman," as she harmoniously alliteratised him, took the field without a rival. He combined the best points of each, she reflected, with precocious criticism, glancing at Geoffrey's grand proportions. Arthur wasn't a bit taller, she was sure; didn't he

[39] From 'A Vision of Poets' by Elizabeth Barrett Browning.

(Geoff) tower over the other men round him in the little church?—and Lancelot could not have looked any braver or handsomer.

On that poetic coast, among the cultured, even children measure male perfection against these lofty legendary standards. Now as she springs along with gnome-like measure at Ula's side, the strange odd child, with the solemn questioning dark eyes—eyes singularly like Graham's own, as both Ula and her father have noticed with a little surprise,—her mind flies off at another tangent, and she blurts out suddenly one of her eerie startling questions:

"Is *he* 'the secret of the sea?' " she asks, nodding her head at Graham and staring at him with grave contemplation.

Her bizarre thoughts have darted off in a direction, widely apart from Arthur and his stately knights, to a weird sombre tale which she has read somewhere, a story with this (to her visionary, elfish mind) impressively attractive title, in which something or some one was given up by the sea, wrested from its very heart, by which some awful hidden secret was discovered, and brought woe and desolation in its train.

"Why, you small fay, what do you mean?" exclaims Geoffrey wonderingly. "Do you think *I* am an embodied secret? Well, it is an original idea at any rate. There are few lives that don't hold a secret of some kind in their depths, I believe," and his face darkens suddenly, while the bantering tone dies out of his voice, changes, which the girl at his side is quick to perceive. "But I am not personally acquainted with a 'secret' that walks about on two legs; it would be rather a novel kind of one." And then he changes the conversation to a more sprightly theme; but Ula's bright gaiety is gone. She is almost silent for the rest of the way, answering in monosyllables, while a dreamy saddened look dwells in the great luminous eyes.

Those strange words of her quaint little sister have robbed her temporarily of her delight in all things. The prophetic couplet that had struck her almost like a blow, the day she had saved the man's life who now walks at her side, again rushes to her mind. Is that dreary, miserable distich true? Is she fated to discover its truth? Does a doom of unhappiness, or mystery, always overshadow those who stand in the same relation to each other as she and the stranger? Was she but working out unconsciously a predestined doom, that day when she rowed out to meet that distant, floating, helpless waif? Was he to bring sorrow to that peaceful home, that tranquil little household on the wild Cornish cliff? And how?

These are the questions that torment her brain. Then Effie spoke of a "secret." What secret in the life of him given up by the sea at their doors—supposing he had one—could possibly affect them? Thank God! they have no secrets. How silly it is of her to be influenced or impressed for a moment by the wild nonsense talk of her uncannily imaginative junior, she reflects, with a touch of scorn for herself; and yet she cannot shake off the unpleasant feeling, though she tries to listen to and interest herself in Graham's talk with Effie. The child has come out of her meditative fit, and is full of chatter: chatter which Geoffrey is constrained to respond to, seeing that Ula has sunk into silence. But the girl finds her mind irresistibly drawn off from the present, and vaguely diving into the unknown future. And mingled with these struggling efforts to read that so oft blessedly sealed book are some of Effie's thoughts of a few minutes since. The stranger she saved from those cruel waters is already, perhaps half-unconsciously to the girl herself, the impersonation, the materialised presentment of those misty poetic mind-heroes whom she has dwelt amongst in imagination. And though these flattering comparisons between stalwart nineteenth century flesh and blood, and legendary perfection, can do the quaint little girl no possible harm, they may prove somewhat dangerous musings for the elder.

* * * * * *

And now they have left behind them the sweet summer dusk, and perhaps the fancies it engenders and the mysteries it seems to hold in its shadowed bosom, and have merged into the lights and home and supper. And Ula involuntarily sighs. Are things only nice and attractive, she wonders, when they are vague, unreal, imaginary, dim with the shades of shadowland upon them? Would everything, if illuminated by a flaring torch—the torch of truth and reality—shrivel up, and become shorn of its interest and suggestiveness? Is it only as long as a subject, or a person, is but dimly understood, while a touch of mystery is clinging about it or him, that an interest attaches to either? And then she looks across at Geoffrey instinctively, and meets his earnest gaze fixed upon her, and colours vividly at her own thought, even more than at his glance. *There* is one who is surrounded by no mystery, and yet the interest is not wanting; and even were there mystery, and it was solved, why the interest—ah, Ula! more than interest we fear—would be stronger than ever.

"So Fanshawe has returned; have you seen her?" This remark Mr. Ferguson addresses to Ula, as he helps his guest to a tempting little sole cutlet.

"No," in lively, eager response, mysteries, metaphysical speculation, etc., alike incontinently forgotten.

"They arrived on Thursday, and he walked over yesterday afternoon, but saw nobody. Eff and I had gone shrimping, and Mr. Graham had gone to Penmaer for his letters."

And he, listening, wonders, was it only yesterday that he lay in that distant clover meadow, reading his mother's letter, and coming to the stern, hard-won resolve of self-banishment? The circumstances that made that line of action desirable, nay positively absolute, do not now exist. He remembers the delicious feeling of reprieve that stole over him last evening when he became aware of the master's return. And yet now the thought strikes him, bringing with it a sort of mental chill,—what earthly excuse has he for remaining on? He is quite recovered, his appetite is prodigious, and constantly making him feel hot shame at the inroads he perpetrates on his host's larder; he wears no longer an interesting invalidish pallor, but has grown detestably healthy-looking, tanned and vigorous; and as for this rubbishy, humbugging sling—— No, he must go; that is the long and the short of it; perhaps not to-morrow, as he had heroically determined, but the day——

And then his thoughts come back to the talk going on around him. "Yes, you'd better go to-morrow," Mr. Ferguson is saying, and he almost starts, it is so curiously apropos to his momentary reflections, but it is to Ula he is speaking. "It would be only a proper attention; in fact, not to do so would be a breach of propriety, after our long intimacy with her husband; of course it would be against all rule for her to call first."

"And must I go alone? Won't you come? Do, dear," entreatingly.

"No, child, you know I never visit; as long as Fanshawe was a bachelor, it was all one to me whether I smoked my pipe in his house or my own, but I should feel quite out of my element in a fine lady's drawing-room."

"Perhaps she's not a fine lady," hazards Ula, meditatively. "I'm sure I trust she's not. How could I ever get on with her, if she were? How should I even have courage to call, and alone too?" looking almost scared at the prospect. "I wish Alice could go in my place.

She would be delighted, and would acquit herself decently. Lucky girl! when she calls, she'll have her grandmother to back her up!" in enviously disconsolate tones.

"Aye!" laughs Mr. Ferguson, "and as we all know, would gladly dispense with the old lady's company; Miss Alice Wenvoe has no qualms as to her fitness for all possible emergencies. I am sorry, Ula, my pet, that I cannot endow you with a grandmother, ready made to order, who would take my little girl a visiting; but you must learn to be self-reliant. However, if you are so appalled at the idea of calling on our friend's wife alone, doubtless Mr. Graham will have no objection to accompanying you, eh?" turning to Geoff with a smile. "What do you say? A lovely and fashionable bride is not an everyday sight in this quiet corner of the earth, I assure you. Will you take the goods the gods provide you?"

"Willingly, sir." laughs the other, delighted with the proposition that would give him an undisturbed *tête-à-tête* walk with Ula, perhaps their last. "I plead guilty to a small curiosity to see the new importation, feeling already something like a native; I am quite at Miss Ferguson's disposal, whenever she——"

"And mayn't I too go, Pops?" in loud vociferous interruption from Effie, who has been amusing herself feeding Mr. Ferguson's faithful rough terrier Dusty—who barked defiance at Geoff last night—and the kitten, her special property, off the same plate; and being highly entertained at the spit-fire efforts of the fiendish little feline to drive off the enemy and claim all herself. Her growls, her splutterings, her trying to spread her tiny form over the plate, sometimes planting her whole four small paws therein, with shocking want of breeding; and her systematic scratchings of the canine nose, which we suppose has got indurated from long habit, as the insulted Dusty scarcely winces. He is wonderfully long-suffering, being a dog not easily ruffled, or put out; he has a lofty calm of disposition, very trying to the aggravator, for it seems like contempt; he never retaliates in kind, as an ordinary, vulgar, low-minded dog might, but he has been known on occasions, when Mam'selle Puss's conduct has become utterly outrageous, to catch up the offender by the skin of the neck, and gravely and deliberately carry her out of the room, sometimes only depositing her on the mat outside, with an admonishing growl, and quietly shutting the door in her face; sometimes, if she has been extra naughty, carrying her to the remote regions of kitchen, scullery, garden. Once it is on record that he actually shut her into the coal-vault, and little Puss cried herself hoarse before she was released.

"That would be storming the citadel in earnest," responds Mr. Ferguson. "I fear, witch, you might be considered an intrusion."

But Effie is persistent, and as usual gains her point, much to Mr. Graham's chagrin. And then Ula betakes herself to the next room, whence the others follow her, and drawing a violin from its case, she, and the little girl who accompanies her on the piano, embark on a plaintively sweet, sacred duet. It is a very simple one, as far as the piano part is concerned, but the violinist has plenty to do, and does it well. She handles the instrument lovingly, confidently; her eyes shine like stars, but with an abstracted visionary light in their luminous depths. She is almost unconscious of her audience, the music is in her soul, and she is in the music.

After the duet is finished, and Effie subsides from her prominent position, her sister plays selections from Berlioz's glorious "Te Deum," and grandly solemn "Messe des Morts," in a thoroughly masterly and efficient manner. The girl has the instincts of a true musician, and cares for only what is really good. Quite suddenly she ceases, places the violin in its case, while Geoffrey breaks forth with expressions of gratitude, wonder, delight. She looks at him with a dreamy, abstracted gaze, pale with intensity of feeling, her lips tremulous, her whole being vibrating with emotion, and before he is through three sentences, she slips quietly from the room. But he is not offended; he knows that the spell of the music is upon her, and that she instinctively seeks silence and solitude.

"And what do you think of my little girl's music?" asks the old man after a long pause, breathing a heavy sigh as he speaks; and Geoffrey starts, the silence has been so complete, unbroken, since that sudden cessation of the violin's voice, that he has forgotten he is not alone, and has been dreaming. Somehow that strange impression has been again upon him as of some indefinite link between now and the forgotten misty past. What it is he cannot say, but it is there; some vague, indistinct recollection, that seems in some way blended with the sound of the violin, and voices of long ago.

"Your daughter is a genius, sir," he exclaims enthusiastically. "I could scarcely have imagined it; so young a girl, and with, as I presume, so few opportunities for developing musical talent in this lonely spot, to have attained such excellence! But doubtless the talent is hereditary; you are a musician, perhaps?"

"Oh, the child was fairly well taught in her Plymouth school; don't give her too much credit. But the lassie has a gift, I fancy; and I sometimes think that perhaps it ought to be cultivated. And yet '*Cui bono*?' " with a weary sigh.[40] "She won't need to fiddle for her bread. I hold myself responsible for having inoculated her with her craze for the violin; I used to play long ago, and taught the child it and her alphabet together. I never touch it now, but my

[40] *Cui bono?*: to whom is it a benefit?

old violin has passed into better hands, as the pupil has far excelled the master." And he sighs again.

Then the men drift into a languid musical controversy, which lasts until it is time to say goodnight; and Geoffrey Graham's last conscious thought is—how he can possibly force himself to leave this house, where his heart seems to have found greater rest and at the same time a sweet unrest. A soothing calm has descended on his spirit, that he has not previously known; it is as if he had found some haven for which he has long been unconsciously seeking; and he feels a sharp twinge of self-reproach, as he thinks of his loving, distant mother, from whose tender thoughts he is never one moment absent. Such reflections seem a sort of disloyalty and treachery to her; and then he falls asleep, and dreams a strange dream. He dreams of Ula (they are out upon the cliffs together), looking as she did while she played; the luminous eyes rapt and visionary, the whole face quivering with exalted emotion, which, as he looks, changes to love! Soft, warm, human love; the eyes lose their distant dreamy outlook, and turn on him with tender shyness. And he—his heart in dreamland, is overflowing with passionate love for this child of the cliffs; he will reach her side, and speak those words that will bind them to each other for ever. And as he so determines—lo, an obstacle, an insurmountable obstacle rises between them. He knows not what it is; but it seems to shadow all the earth with its brooding darkness, and gradually shuts out from view the girl crouching on the other side. The last glimpse of her reveals a face white and anguish-stricken; grief and horror look from the great dilated eyes, and then—she is gone! And through the gloom in which he is enveloped, he sees outstretched, *a hand*—a delicate, aged woman's hand, a hand that seems familiar. Ah! he recognises a ring upon it worn by his mother! But the hand does not beckon, it points menacingly; and with a weird, ghastly feeling of probing some awful, hidden mystery, he turns slowly, at the bidding of that ghostly, directing finger. And then, as he looks, all fear of any terrible revelation dies away in his breast. He sees but a stretch of sunlit road, and along it is coming a man he seems to recognize. Yes, it is Mr. Ferguson, who sings softly as he walks, and is unconscious of that shadowy pointing hand.

At this juncture the dreamer wakes, but the vision of the night remains with him, and banishes further sleep.

What an unaccountable dream it was, with all the startling incongruities and inconsistencies of dreams in general, but still strangely vivid and realistic. Was it in any way prophetic? he finds himself questioning, with a dull throb at his heart, and a dim unfamiliar sense of impending trouble.

CHAPTER IV

A RECOGNITION

NEXT day, somewhere between three and four o'clock, the little party from the Cliff House start to make that visit of ceremony which, to Ula, is fraught with some perturbation of spirit. She is fluttered and nervous at this, her first state visit as a grown-up young lady; and to a bride! This fact makes the ordeal more alarming; and she would be ashamed to confess, even to herself, what an immense relief and support Graham's companionship affords her. It is scarcely more than half-a-mile to the coastguard station, but they lengthen it out as much as possible: Ula, from the ignoble desire to put off the evil moment of entering the stranger's presence; Geoffrey, from a wish to protract, as long as he may, this, perhaps his last walk with the girl.

Effie is the only one of the three anxious to reach her destination; her curiosity and interest in the new-comer being quite as strong as Ula's and not tempered with the nervous shyness of her elder. Their talk is chiefly of music, as they saunter slowly on over the cliffs, and Ula confides to her new friend how she has hoped and dreamed that she may some day study art properly, in a foreign conservatoire. "I should dearly love to attend the 'Conservatoire' in Paris," she says; "but that, I fear, will never be; it would be very expensive, I suppose, but it's not altogether that," pausing.

"Your father would not part with you, to let you go so far away," suggests Graham.

"Oh! we shouldn't part in any case," smiling. "Wherever I went, he'd come too; but he would never go to Paris, he hates it so; I don't think anything in the world would induce him to live there.

But I believe there is a very good conservatoire at Geneva, or then we might go somewhere in Germany."

And then, as they talk, and grow more and more confidential, Geoffrey tells her, what he has not before mentioned, that for several years his mother, who has musical talent, gave lessons.

"The dear mother had a struggle for it, poor soul, when I was a good-for-nothing youngster; but, thank God, for the last eight or ten years I have worked for both. She loves music passionately; how enchanted she would be with yours, *en parenthèse*, and she always declared that it never was a trouble to her to teach, unless she had the misfortune to meet a very dull pupil.[41] Some, who owed all their musical instruction to her, turned out very credibly indeed. There is one young lady, an especial pet of hers, who was her first pupil, and almost her last by the way, a wild, merry, romping girl; they became fast friends, and though it is nearly nine years now since they met, they correspond frequently. She has, I believe, quite distinguished herself amongst London musical amateurs; and the last we heard of her was that she was about to be married,—a love match, though the man is old enough to be her father, and her future life will be, I take it, obscure rather than brilliant. But all this seems very irrelevant; what I was about to say is, that my mother studied at the Geneva Conservatoire for a year or so, and thought the training excellent."

"And did she go away from her home all alone?" questions Ula, much interested.

"No, I was with her," answers Graham, without reflection.

"*You*," repeats the girl, in some surprise. "Why, I thought it was when she was quite young, before she was married."

[41] *En parenthèse*: in parenthesis.

"No," he responds, somewhat constrainedly. "Circumstances arose in after life, that made her wish to improve her music, and—ah! here we are."

With a relieved air, as, turning a sharp curve in the Cliff road they came suddenly on the small coastguard station, with the officer's pretty dwelling showing to charming advantage in that wild spot. It is strongly built, quaint, roomy, and low, with a Swiss flavouring in its architecture; decidedly picturesque, a delightful verandah running right round it. It stands slightly higher than the men's quarters, and commands a noble sweep of never-resting ocean, besides looking away inland towards Bodmin; a stretch of green, undulating hills, where the wild flowers grow in rare profusion, rest the eye, if weary gazing on the heaving waters, and a little of the green has been caught and caged, for, besides quite an ambitious flower-garden, Mrs. Fanshawe has actually a small but perfect tennis-lawn.

"Tennis!" murmurs Ula, glancing compassionately at the netting, and a racket or two thrown about, "whom does she expect to get to play here at the end of the world? unless she's strong-minded enough to look forward to dummy games with her husband."

"Why, she'll have you and Effie, of course, and your friend Miss Wenvoe, and perhaps a young lady or two from Bodmin, and a couple of curates to weigh down the scale and infuse the proper amount of animation."

And then they ring, and the neat, bright maid-servant who opens the door, says Mrs. Fanshawe is at home, and in the drawing-room alone. She precedes them, and announces "Miss Ferguson" simply, and Ula advances into the pretty, artistic, modern room somewhat diffidently, her guard in the rear. At first the room seems quite empty, is, in fact, empty; but just as the girl glances about a little wondering, a figure comes swiftly, impetuously through one of the three windows, which all open upon the verandah and look out upon the sea, the drawing-room being on the opposite side of the house, and concealed from any one approaching in orthodox fashion by the hall-door.

"Miss Ferguson, how good of you—I am delighted to know you—I have heard so much of you all from my husband."

In warm, impulsive greeting from the hostess, catching both her visitor's hands unceremoniously, and looking into her face with friendly, laughing, honest eyes; then, in the act of turning to accord Effie an equally warm welcome, she glances enquiringly at Graham, whom she has not yet regarded. He is looking steadily at her, with puzzled recognition in his eyes; but the moment she turns her full face towards him there is a simultaneous exclamation from both—

"Madge!" "Geoff!"

They cry, in tones of astonished, pleased surprise, and then their hands meet, and the sisters look on in dumb amaze at this unexpected encounter of evidently old friends.

"How do you come here?" questions she whom he calls Madge. "Am I dreaming? or is it Geoff Graham again after all these years? And yet I think I'd know you anywhere, in spire of that wonderful beard," caressing her own soft, round chin with pretty, roguish grace.

"And to think that *you* are the Mrs. Fanshawe I have been speculating about; how contemptibly small the world is! I come to gaze on a young, beautiful, and fashionable bride, and find—my old chum, Madge Harefield!"

"Who is neither young, beautiful, nor fashionable. Thanks, old friend, for a very graceful little compliment," laughs Mrs. Fanshawe, merrily. "But, you bad, naughty boy, your dear mother knew my new name that was to be almost as soon as I knew it myself," with a bright blush.

"Yes, of course I heard it, but it slipped my stupid memory."

And then Ula, who had been feeling a little mystified, and also, with her over-sensitive nature, slightly *de trop*, is included in the talk that flows so swiftly and easily[42]—and why not, for have they not an infinity of subjects to discuss?—and she very soon discovers that this bonnie, brown-eyed bride, with the frank, laughing, kindly face, is the identical "merry, romping girl," his mother's pupil, that accidental allusion was made to by Geoff Graham on their way thither. What a strange coincidence it is! and she listens eagerly to their talk, their reminiscences of bygone days; the constant references to Mrs. Graham, the woman in whom already the girl feels so indescribable an interest, whom she longs to know; and as she hearkens she glances about her. The house she is very familiar with, but not since it put on its best smiles to welcome its new mistress. How pretty this room has been made to look, with its carved dado, and deep red walls flecked with gold; the bright, Dutch-tiled grate, with brass dogs and fender; the high carved mantelpiece, with niches on which stand oriental jars; the rich-toned amber hangings; the soft, low lounging chairs, the Chippendale tables and cabinets; the flowers, and photographs, and china, scattered here and there with artistic carelessness and profusion. The tints may be a little deep and warm for summer, Ula thinks; but after all, the room is so deliciously cool and shadowy, with its three French windows opening on to the verandah that looks straight away over the tossing blue waters; and then there are cool, green, flowering plants peeping in at one from it, and the hearth is a bank of green and white,—very simple white, only ox-eyed daisies growing in their native sod, but yet pleasantly refreshing to the

[42] *De trop*: unnecessary, unwanted, superfluous.

eye; and altogether, Ula concludes, it is certainly the prettiest room she has yet seen (poor child, her experience has been painfully limited), and a very becoming framework for the living picture that reigns therein.

Mrs. Fanshawe wears a soft, cream, Indian silk tea-gown, with a lovely dusky-red rose nestling under her chin; her glossy, dark hair is piled high on her head, and kept in place by a golden arrow; the slender feet are cased in cherry-red slippers, embroidered in gold; on the round white arms are fairy-like golden bangles of exquisitely delicate Indian workmanship; while on the balcony, which she has just left, may be seen a huge, red, Japanese umbrella, and a low bamboo chair with amber satin cushions. All is harmonious, and adapted to the brunette comeliness of the mistress. She is no beauty, Madge Fanshawe; but that creamy skin, those damask cheeks, those big, laughing, brown eyes, the small, white teeth, and quantities of silky, dark hair, and, above all, the bright, frank expression of honest kindliness, the genuineness and sincerity that shine from that pleasant face, do much to make one forget the over-full lips, the too chubby cheeks, the almost snub nose. Though she looks so young and girlish, thanks partly to this very unclassical "chubbiness," she is actually seven-and-twenty; but Ula does not suspect the more than nine years' gap between them.

Captain Fanshawe, a fine, handsome man, not yet quite fifty, soon joins them, and is very pleased to make acquaintance with his wife's old friend, besides being duly impressed by the singular coincidence that the old friend should have happened to be the flotsam and jetsam saved from the sea by his young favourite, Ula.

While they are talking, the vicar of St. Olave's, a handsome, shaven, celibate high-priest of the most advanced Ritualistic school, is announced, and enters, followed by his interesting-looking curate;

they generally visit thus is dual fashion, to make the ceremony more impressive, and have lost but little time in coming to welcome this new member of their flock. Captain Fanshawe and his men always attend St. Olave's, but it is chiefly on the feminine element in his congregation that the Rev. St. Leger Stewart depends for his popularity. They are his bulwark and defence; fighting behind them, he brings down the few recalcitrant males who make a weak struggle against ultra "Anglicanism." "Once gain over the women, and the field is won," is his favourite axiom, and is he not right?

Not that Captain Fanshawe is amongst the disaffected. He is an easy-going man, and does not trouble himself much about vexed questions of formula. He says his prayers to his God honestly and faithfully in St. Olave's ornate little home of ritual, and this to him is sufficient. But this is a neutral state of mind highly unsatisfactory to the Rev. St. Leger; he desires partisanship warm and eager, and this the women yield in rare abundance. Besides, has he not heard that Mrs. Fanshawe has a fortune, not a large one but still a fortune, over which she has complete control? and has not unworthy "mammon" been a potent factor in the glorification of that exquisite little Cornish temple nestling on the confines of the village of Penmaer?[43] And so the *raison dêtre* of this prompt pastoral call at the hitherto somewhat neglected coastguard station.

Madame is not an "acrostic," as Effie artlessly suggested on not seeing her at church the day before, and receives the clergy sweetly, though she chafes inwardly at this untoward interruption of her delightfully commenced renewal of intimacy with her old friend Geoff Graham. They had just embarked on a delicious dualogue in which "Do you remember?" took a prominent part, with Ula

[43] Mammon: a biblical term for money, riches, material wealth.

and the adoring bridegroom as charmed listeners. But after all, she is not to be altogether disappointed of a little confidential talk with her quondam chum; for just as the conversation has taken an uncongenial and parochial turn under the influence of the clerical visitors, Alice Wenvoe and her grandmother are announced, and Mrs. Fanshawe feels that considering the benighted wilderness she has come to, she is holding quite a levee in her pretty drawing-room. She insists on all remaining for afternoon tea; it is just time for it, and it is always such a social unconventional gathering, she declares, and she wants to feel very friendly with these her few nearest neighbours in those lonely wilds, so they must not refuse. And they do not, but feel rather pleased to stay; there is not much spontaneous hospitality or sociability in the neighbourhood, and even the clergy are not quite contemptuous of that pleasant tea-drinking in the cool, shadowed room, perfumed with the sweet breath of flowers, and musical with the murmurous, monotonous lapping of the waters beyond its windows, which brings a soothing feeling of rest and calm.

And now Mrs. Fanshawe has the opportunity she desires; seating herself at the pretty fantastic Indian tea-table that the maid has wheeled forward, she signs to Geoffrey to come to her aid as lieutenant-in-chief to assist her in dispensing the cup that cheers.

The vicar is engaged in an animated discussion with Captain Fanshawe and old Mrs. Wenvoe; while Alice, her granddaughter, and Ula's only real intimate girl friend in Penmaerwyn, is quite happy *pro tem.*, having secured the undivided attention of the curate, the Rev. Mark Temple, who was slightly attracted by her Dresden-china prettiness on first acquaintance, though that attraction has since palled.[44] Ula is alone silent, but she does not want to talk. She is

[44] *Pro tem.*: abbreviation of *pro tempore*, meaning 'for the time being'.

seated near her hostess, and though not close enough to overhear her conversation with Graham, yet she is content to look on and think how strange and pleasant it all is. As she thus reflects while she tranquilly sips her tea, she notices, with a stab of self-reproach at her own engrossment and carelessness, that Effie is not in the room. Where has she gone? She must have slipped out when the Wenvoes came in. How rude and naughty of her! what will Mrs. Fanshawe think of such ill-breeding? for though the child was at home enough there when Captain Fanshawe reigned alone, yet now, with a new mistress, it ought to seem like a strange house. And to set off on a voyage of exploration! And Ula's cheeks burn, as she glances guiltily at her hostess as if she herself were the offender, and then uneasily at the door by which the culprit must return. But Mrs. Fanshawe is serenely unconscious or indifferent; she is talking quickly and eagerly to Graham, and soon Ula is included in the conversation and forgets her sister's misconduct.

And by-and-by, when they are all standing up, preparatory to taking their departure, she has the satisfaction of seeing the delinquent steal quietly in through one of the windows from the verandah, and congratulates herself secretly with the thought that it will appear as if the child, wearied with the grown-up talk, had stolen out on the balcony for a little variety.

The fact really is that no one has noticed the little girl's absence, and no one notices her return save Captain Fanshawe, with whom she is a favourite, and who now stealthily supplies her with cake and fruit from the table, on hearing her shamed and whispered confession that she had had no tea, having followed the "snow-ball" cat out of the room in amazed admiration. Such is Effie's terse, graphic description of Mrs. Fanshawe's lovely Persian pet feline, a marvel of white fluffiness and an innovation.

Ula notices that the child looks somewhat excited and important, as if brimful of something and wanting to run over, but held in check by the presence of strangers. And she devoutly hopes that she will at least have the grace to hold her tongue, and not add to her misdemeanours by blurting out something that she seems to have discovered anent her hostess's household.

Presently they all leave together, and though the clergy soon strike off across the fields, Alice and her grandmother continue with the Cliff House party, though it is a longer way round; but old Mrs. Wenvoe is very active, and dearly loves a gossip, and now she is tingling with quite a pleasant, legitimate, invigorating, and thoroughly good-natured curiosity. An interesting stranger has come (or rather has drifted) into their midst in a thoroughly interesting manner; and now a charming young bride has come amongst them, and these two foreign elements discover themselves to be old friends, and feel equal surprise at each other's presence; and deep down in the old lady's heart, it must be acknowledged, there is a faint suspicion that these two were perhaps more than friends in the old days, and this thought invests them with a greater interest in her eyes. So, instead of turning off by the fields with the clergymen, she keeps on along the coast, somewhat to Alice's chagrin, who looks regretfully after her curate, watching the two tall clerical figures diminish in the distance; while Effie remains wrathfully silent, looking unutterable things at dear, chatty Mrs. Wenvoe.

The spoiled child is expiring with impatience to detail her pilfered knowledge of the Fanshawe *ménage*, and bitterly resents aught that enforces dumbness on her part;[45] for knowing the child

[45] *Ménage*: household.

so well, and reading her face as she would a book, Ula has mutely laid an embargo of silence on her; she has no curiosity whatever as to Effie's news, she knows from long experience what her grand communications are apt to be, and values them accordingly.

CHAPTER V
FRAU BENGHAUS

AT last the Cliff House is reached, and the Wenvoes depart, after a few minutes' talk with Mr. Ferguson, who is smoking his pipe outside, and who asks them to remain for tea; but as they all have just partaken of this refreshment, they decline and set off home, for to these primitive people Mrs. Fanshawe's five o'clock ante-dinner tea is tea indeed, only taken a little earlier than usual, they having dined at two. Effie executes an impromptu war-dance, suggestive of derision, disdain and delight, and then dashes, *in medias res* fashion, into her subject, before the words, "Well, how do you like her?" addressed mutually to Ula and Mr. Graham, are well out of Mr. Ferguson's mouth.[46]

"Oh! Pops, she's so grand, all white and red and yellow, and her room the same. And she and Mr. Graham knew each other always,—think of that! And such a funny, beautiful cat—*you* did not see it, Ula, so you need not say anything, but *I* did,—just like a great snowball, Pops; I followed it out of the room. Well, I know I oughtn't—," with defiant breathlessness, seeing the old man's uplifted hand of disapproval, and hearing Ula's murmur of rebuke,—"but any of you would have done the same if you had seen it, it was *such* a wonder; and no one minded my going. And oh! Ula and Pops, I want to tell you—fancy! she's got a maid, all to her own self, a lady's-maid, you know,"—with an impressive nod, and a manner as if enlightening primeval ignorance,—"who does

---

[46] *In medias res*: in the middle of things, beginning the story partway through rather than at the beginning.

up her hair, and dresses her, and everything, for I asked her," which unwise confidence calls forth a shocked "O, Effie!" from Ula. "I met her on the stairs when I was trying to coax the cat to be friends. She stared at me so queerly she frightened me just at first. 'Who are you?' she said, in such a funny way. I knew at once she must be a foreign woman. 'I knew some one just like you long ago,—the very same eyes,' and then she said something like 'ceiling' and 'mine got,' but I don't know who could have got her ceiling; I am sure no one could carry off a ceiling, and I laughed at her. 'Like and more like,' she cried,—'his very laugh! Is it a ghost after years so long?' And when she said 'ghost' I was going to run away, but she said, 'Don't go, talk to me; tell me who you are.' 'No,' said I, 'but who are you? What's your name?' 'I am Frau Benghaus,' said she—a very ugly name, I think."

"Ah! German," exclaims Mr. Ferguson suddenly, in a strange, sharp tone, and Ula, glancing at him curiously, notes he is pale and strained looking.

"Effie, do be quiet, and don't chatter so. What matter about Mrs. Fanshawe's maid, you can tell us of her at some other time; though, indeed,"—remembering her grievance,—"you ought to know nothing of her. How could you be so ill-bred as to go rambling over the house, questioning people? What will Mrs. Fanshawe think when she hears of your rudeness?"

"Oh, Madge won't mind; she's thoroughly good-natured; I know her of old; we were *bons camarades* in the long-ago.[47] She has no priggish stiffness about her. I venture to say that Effie would be perfectly welcome to explore every nook and cranny in her house," says Geoffrey, speaking for the first time.

---

[47] *Bons camarades*: good friends.

"*Madge!*" echoes Mr. Ferguson, in his turn surprised, glancing interrogatively at his guest. "Are you and Fanshawe's young bride friends, then?"

"Yes, Pops," cuts across the child, constituting herself Graham's mouthpiece. "You couldn't have been minding; I told you they were; they cried 'Madge' and 'Geoff' at one another when they met, and she said she hardly knew him for his beard. You hadn't it always, then?" nodding enquiringly at Graham, who is laughing softly at the little girl's eager excitement and uncheckable loquacity, but, as he reflects, a bride, a foreign serving-woman, and a Persian cat are not articles to be met with every day in Effie's limited world.

She races on again with vehement incoherence, scarcely pausing for breath. "Yes, Pops, you're right—Germany. I asked her where she lived before she came here, and she said, 'London, with Miss Harefield,'—that was Mrs. Fanshawe before she was married. 'And before that, again,' said I, 'for there's no use pretending you're English; I know you're not; you talk so rubbishy like.' " (Here Graham's laugh grows pronouncedly audible, and Ula finds it hard to keep a reproving countenance). " 'No, little Mees, I not an Englishwoman, I am'—and then she stopped and looked strange and sighed, and then she went on, quite hurried, 'before London I lived in Germany; Germany, Germany, always Germany, of course.' And then she sighed again, and I thought her a very funny woman not to like her own country, and that didn't seem like liking it, did it, Pops? 'But when my poor husband died I have to leave it,' " continues the "irrepressible," not waiting for either comment or response. "Perhaps that's the reason she sighed. And then she made me tell her my name, and asked me how old I was, and how old was Ula, and was my mother alive? And I said 'No!; only you, Pops. And she was so surprised I hadn't a brother, a big man brother.

And I said I never had any brother, and didn't think I ever would have one—though, if he was like you, I'd like him very well."

Again nodding sagaciously at Graham, who flushes slightly at her somewhat ambiguous speech, and involuntarily glances at Ula; but she is quite too unconscious to see any second meaning in Effie's careless words, and her innocent young cheek catches no reflection of the colour that momentarily glows on his. "And then she wanted to now what Ula was like, and asked me to describe her, and when I did (I made you as handsome as I could, Uley, dear),"—with an insufferably patronising air, as if trying to assure her listeners that she had made the best of a bad subject, for which Graham feels a strong desire to shake her,—"she asked was she like my mother, and I said I didn't know, and that she was a very silly woman to ask me such stupid questions, when I had just told her that my mother died when I was a baby, and babies don't remember things, at least they may in Germany, but not in England," the repetition of which caustic reply results in a general laugh. "And then she wanted to know was my father handsome? Fancy the idea of old men being handsome! how could they?" with a fine and heartless disregard of the feelings of the single specimen present. "And I said he was all white, hair and beard, and everything and then she took no more interest in him, but asked me about home here, and did I always live in England? And I said, 'You are a very curious woman; you ask too many questions.' And I turned to go away, but she caught me and said she must kiss me for the sake of the person I was so like long ago; but I wouldn't let her, and I told her she was very rude, and that I'd never speak to her again, and that I was very glad I lived in England and not in her country, if the people were all like her. But how could one expect anything from idolaters?"

"O, you dreadful child!" cries Ula, really distressed. "So much for taking you visiting."

"I thought, Pops," continues the "dreadful child," quite unruffled, "that the Germans were like us in their religion, but she is a Catholic, I know, for as I pulled to get away from her, when she tried to kiss me, I caught a tiny little cord round her neck, and out jumped what old Bab calls a —— a —— a 'scalp,' that they believe, you know, is a charm against ——."

" 'Scapular,' I suppose you mean," interjects Ula, trying vainly to look grave and displeased; while Geoffrey, thoroughly enjoying the child's quaint originality, says approvingly:

"By Jove! Miss Ferguson, your sister is a brick, to stand up so defiantly for church and state. You have the courage of your opinions, little Eff, and that's something to be proud of. Always uphold England and the English against all the world. It's the proper thing to do, my child, and though a little braggadocio, yet it wins, perhaps, in the long run.[48] Full of avowed belief in the insular article, open and undisguised contempt for the foreign, is, I believe, our national characteristic, and possibly has placed us where we are, eh, sir?" But Mr. Ferguson only shakes his head, and murmurs something not quite intelligible; and Ula, again noticing how fagged and worn and white he looks, summarily ejects Effie from the room before she can once more embark on her exhaustive (and exhausting) narrative.

"You are worried, dear, by that child's tiresome tongue; are you fatigued or unwell?" walking round to the back of the old man's chair, and laying her hand fondly on his shoulder.

"Only a little weary, love," patting the pretty, brown, slender

[48] Braggadocio: boastful, cocky, arrogantly pretentious.

hand. "I shall be all right when I get a cup of tea; though you good people have revelled in that invigorator, I am still in expectation, you know,"—with a somewhat forced, sad smile.

"How selfish of me!" exclaims Ula, with swift self-blame, "to forget you, father; but it is so unusual an occurrence to have taken tea abroad, afternoon tea at least, that one feels quite to have lost one's bearings."

Graham vanishes to his own room; while Ula, after hastily changing her precious best frock, presides at the master's solitary tea, Effie being still excluded, or rather being once banished, sulks, and refuses positively to leave the kitchen, and old Bab and young Nan's company.

At first Mr. Ferguson is very silent; then he asks a question or two anent the visit just paid, and his friend's new wife; and Ula dilates pleasantly, though not wearisomely. She is delighted to discuss Mrs. Fanshawe, for whom she has conceived a warm, unstinted, almost enthusiastic admiration, as is so often the way with girls for a young, attractive married woman.

"So Graham and she are old friends. What an odd coincidence that they should both turn up here together! Hardly seems like chance, eh, little one? Was it design, think you? But how should a simple child like you know or imagine anything about it? He seemed strangely silent just now."

"They are old friends, but there was no mistake that they were immensely surprised to see each other," looking wonderingly at the old man's thoughtful face. "Besides, dear, how could their meeting be anything but chance, arising from the terrible misfortune of the shipwreck? Wasn't that chance indeed?"

"Ah! I grant you the shipwreck was unpremeditated—but still—but still it is queer and hard to regard as altogether an accidental rencontre; he must have known she was coming here, and the name of the man she was to marry."

"No, indeed, that is what he particularly insisted on, how completely the name had escaped his memory," urges Ula, unconsciously defending the absent from some shadowy, indefinite charge, the nature of which she does not yet guess.

"Well, well, I am an old man, and perhaps too suspicious, and you are a little girl, and most assuredly too credulous. Besides, what is it to us? whether it was an accident or design it affects us not at all. He is a stranger in whom we have no interest, and who to-morrow or the next day will be gone out of our lives for ever."

How these words—apparently spoken carelessly, really chosen with grave deliberation for his darling Ula's good—fall like ice on the girl's heart! She feels as if a numbing, intolerable weight, suddenly pressed her down, down. She gives a little involuntary, noiseless gasp, and then sits quite still and white, shocked and scared at her own emotion. How horribly silly she is! Yes, of course, he will go "out of their lived for ever." What else has she been thinking? People are always meeting and separating, and never seeing each other again, and they think nothing about it—that is, strangers as they are; of course relatives and old friends are very different, they have a right to care. She herself has not minded saying "good-bye" for ever to people. When Alice Wenvoe's only brother married and went to settle abroad for always, nearly two years ago, she thought nothing of it, and she knew him much better than she knows Mr. Graham.

She mechanically hears, as it were, without minding, the remainder of Mr. Ferguson's speech. "And as to her, Fanshawe can look after his wife, I suppose. If there was anything between them long ago, that may not, I trust will not, prevent her making my friend a good wife. But they are all alike, these women—false, fair, treacherous. It would be just like them, to come here a bride to meet a lover. And he, poor beggar, thinking he has won the first fresh love of a girl's heart at forty-nine years old! Faugh! what credulous weak fools men are!"

The latter portion of these uttered thoughts has been murmured quite *sotto voce*;[49] but the first two or three sentences spoken aloud, though falling at the instant on unheeding ears, were really heard, and after a little the meaning penetrates the girl's brain. Her silence has not struck the old man, who has been indulging in his muttered monologue, and when, with an effort, she speaks again, he does not notice that the life and brightness have gone out of her voice.

"Something between them? what do you mean by that, Pops?" using Effie's *nom-de-caresse*, which she seldom does, except at odd times when particularly gay and buoyant.[50] Poor child, is she already wrapping round her that mantle of innocent deceit so familiar to her sex—the decent covering 'neath which they hide their pain, like the Spartan boy of old?

"Oh, perhaps they were sweethearts, you know, in that long ago he speaks of. She may have thrown him over, but he many not be quite cured yet: looks not unlike it, I must say."

"Sweethearts!" and she grows brightly red, and then paler than before, speaking quickly, almost eagerly. "But that is nonsense, dear, how could it be? They have not met for eight or nine years, and she must have been only a child then."

"Not a child at all, but a strapping lassie as old as yourself, pet. Though you, you little inexperienced girl, think her so young, you

[49] *Sotto voce*: in a quiet voice, under the breath.

[50] *Nom-de-caresse*: pet name.

forget that Fanshawe told me the lady he was going to marry, though quite a young women, was turned seven-and-twenty, and that would leave her eighteen nine years ago, older than you by a trifle, and just two years younger than our guest, who informed us last night that he'd be thirty his next birthday."

"Twenty-seven!" she blankly and stupidly repeats; and she had thought that laughing, bonnie, brown-eyed bride twenty at the most. "Old lovers!" why had she not thought of it before? How natural and likely it was! And yet the girl's honesty and innate nobleness of nature rejected the theory the next moment. Their astonishment at meeting was genuine and unaffected, she is sure. And then that girl, that bride, just married to her husband, whom of course she loves, to come deliberately to meet a lover! No, she would never think such a wicked thing as that. He may admire her, he must, he could not help it. He may have loved her in those old days, though she could not care for him; and yet, the girl unconsciously stops to ask herself, "could this be?" A startling proof to herself (if she were not too unused to analyse such matters; too much of a novice, only now entering fearfully and half unconsciously on the threshold of these sweet, vague mysteries) of her own sentiments with regard to this stranger. But she does not consider this, she is thinking only of him and of her—that other woman—and for the first time in her young life a faint doubt of, and antagonism to, one of her own sex, is born incontinently in her mind. Jealousy, the ugly twin brother of love, unacquaintance with whose gloomy, distorted face, leaves a woman's life-story incompletely perfect—perfect, because entirely happy; incomplete, because the real radius of the heart's strength, and depth, and width, cannot be known without applying this crucial test to that inner, mystic circle of being, from which spring all things nearest to heaven in this sad, bad world.

Ula soon determines that she will not believe there is any treachery in it; it was all but a chapter of chances. She, the new-made wife, is true and good; and he had no secret purpose, no motive for managing to get shipwrecked on Penmaerwyn's cruel, unfriendly coast. They met quite accidentally with mutual surprise and pleasure; there was no design in that renewal of old friendship, of that she feels assured. But yet—the rest may be true all the same. They may have been lovers in that dim olden time. Why not? and what is it to her or to any of the inmates of the Cliff House if they were? And as she so concludes her reflections, a cold feeling of depression, of nameless, indefinite sorrow, presses upon her with an actual chill of physical distress.

But by-and-by, when Geoffrey join them at supper, these desolate, unaccountable feelings dissipate themselves unconsciously. His manner is so completely as it was, that Ula cannot fancy there is anything behind. He talks so naturally, so spontaneously, about his pleasure and surprise at meeting his old friend. He dilates with such frankness on the details of their old acquaintance, laughing over reminiscences in which "Madge," as he calls her with affectionate, brotherly familiarity, bore so large a part; dubs her a "brick," a "trump," an "out-and-out good fellow," and other appellations significant of approval and good fellowship, but very far removed surely from sentiment. He alludes, also, to his "beastly stupidity," as he calls it, in having forgotten her name that was to be. He knew vaguely that she was to live in Cornwall, but that was all; his mother was her correspondent, and doubtless he forgot half she told him out of Madge's letters. The last time he was her was more than four years ago in London. She sang at a charity concert, and he was one of the audience. He chatted with her for half-an-hour or so afterwards; she wanted him to go home with her and stay a few days in Bloomsbury Square at the house of her uncle and aunt, with whom she was then living, they having adopted her when her parents died in that northern town where she had been Mrs. Graham's pupil. But he had made arrangements to leave London early the next morning, and could not delay his departure. And so they parted, and that was their only meeting—a chance one—in all those nearly nine years.

Ula cannot resist giving a faintly triumphant little look across at him who styled himself "a suspicious old man;" but in another moment she is inclined to repent it, for almost Geoffrey's very next speech seems to an aroused imagination completely to confirm Mr. Ferguson's words.

"She has asked me to spend the rest of my holiday with her and her husband, and I very gladly consented. I have been feeling the last few days that I ought to be off, that I had no right to trespass on your hospitality any longer, sir. Indeed, I think three weeks is a pretty good spell, and Miss Ferguson has been very kind not to have turned me out," with a little laugh, as he glances curiously at the girl's flushed, downdropt face. "But I should have been very sorry to have gone without seeing you; besides, I looked forward with immense regret to leaving Cornwall," with another quick look at the still drooped face, which has grown paler now, and is that a look of pained compression he sees round the soft, tender mouth? "But now it all fits in nicely; Madge will be glad of a visit from her old friend; Fanshawe—who seems a thorough good fellow—seconded her invitation very cordially, so I shan't feel myself an intruder, as only for your great kindness I should have been inclined to do here. You know I came—uninvited," with another laugh, which he hazards rather experimentally, to see whether it will draw forth any response from the strangely absorbed face opposite to him.

But Ula has not yet had time to recover the sort of stab she felt on hearing the confirmation, as she thinks, of what she had deemed unjust and suspicious; and she has not yet learned to wear Society's all-concealing mask, behind which all emotion and evidence of feeling is strangled at its birth; so she remains silent, absent, grave, and Geoffrey wonders in what he has offended her.

By-and-by she forces herself to be bright and lively again, perhaps a little more so than her wont, dwelling with an easy indifference that is a shade overstrained on the delightful opportunity this chance meeting will give Mr. Graham of renewing an old and pleasant friendship; and how charming for Mrs. Fanshawe to come a stranger to a strange place, and find at her gates an "own familiar friend." They will take such delight in visiting all the places of interest in the neighbourhood together—and there are so many—which being novel to each will complete the charm. There is a small spice of bitterness here, as Geoffrey in the first days of convalescence had made allusion to the excursions they must make, when her father returned, when she should be cicerone, and initiate him into all the mysteries of Tintagel and its immortalised surrounding district.

Mr. Ferguson says but little; he seems thoughtful, *distrait*, and leaves the talk to the young people, who, before they part for the night, are quite on their usual friendly terms, Ula having shaken off her temporary depression, as Graham insisted on planning all the various and delightful little trips they must make during the next few weeks. Fanshawe will of course want to take his wife to see everything there is to be seen round about her home, and surely Miss Ferguson, steeped to the lips in the poetry that hallows the place, even more than the traditions that poetry idealises, will prove a more efficient and sympathetic guide than the honest, unimaginative navy captain.

CHAPTER VI
"THE TIME OF ROSES"

"Love took up the glass of Time, and turned it in his glowing hands,
Every moment lightly shaken ran itself in golden sands."[51]

IN a day or two the Cliff House has lost its guest, but there is such constant intercourse between these two isolated little colonies on the wild lonely coast, that Ula thinks life seems even brighter than when she and Geoff Graham dwelt beneath the same roof. That one week of strangely familiar association was sweet, very; but she now feels almost glad he is gone, when he is still so near. Sentiments had sprung into life in her breast since that visit to the Fanshawes, or rather, sentiments had developed which she but half understood but which she felt instinctively she must guard and hide from observation, especially that of him who had evoked them; and this effort to appear gay, careless, at her ease, during the forty-eight hours or so that elapsed between their return from the visit to the coastguard station and Geoffrey's departure thereto from the Cliff House, oppressed and stifled her.

Since that jealous pang had shot through her heart on hearing the suggestion, that probably Mrs. Fanshawe was an old love of Mr. Graham's, it had dawned upon her, though still but dimly, what her own feelings towards this stranger whom she had saved from the cruel, hungry sea, really were. And the soft brown cheeks burned, and her very heart blushed as she wrung from her own breast, as it were, the secret which she might have hidden from herself a little longer but for this trifling incident. And so these two

---

[51] Lines from 'Locksley Hall' by Alfred, Lord Tennyson.

days were days of pain and pleasure, distress and sweetness curiously intermingled. But now he is gone, and that word, instead of bringing a sense of desolation and sorrow inexpressible, as would be the case if the going were afar off (as she acknowledges now to herself, with face hidden in her hands that seek to cover up the hot shamed cheeks even from the very eyes of her own spirit), conveys rather a feeling of relief. He is gone, so that she is free to sit, and think, and dream of him, without the almost certainty of any moment the voice that vibrates and thrills through her whole being, breaking in on that reverie that enshrines himself, and making her heart beat to suffocation, and her eyes droop in dazed confusion, and her tongue falter as she struggles wildly to talk in the unconstrained, friendly, easy fashion, of one little week ago; and yet he is so near, so reassuringly, consolingly near, not yet "gone out of her life for ever." No, thank Heaven! not yet. That evil day will come, of course, as all sad and unhappy things do, unfailingly; but it is not yet. And even a few weeks, when one is quite young and buoyant, seems quite a goodly time to look forward to, especially when the brief period holds a sweet and trembling happiness in its heart.

The days in passing do not seem to race by with heartless, taunting, terrible swiftness, as they do in after life. A summer's day in youth is quite a long and golden dream of life's delight; in age it is but a snatch of a vanished joy. The night has tumbled on the morning, and the day is dead before one has well awoke to the fact that it has commenced.

Yes, he is gone, and the girl can dream undisturbedly on the "Throne" in the mellow September sunlight. Aye, a dream of him who has come to this rock-bound home to disturb the calm of this fair pure maiden soul. Many an hour she spends on that huge boulder, half sitting, half lying in luxurious idleness, "dreaming dreams and seeing visions," dreams and visions that are surely one of youth's sweet prerogatives.[52] And then, to make these musings more realistic, there is always the entrancing feeling that by-and-by, in an hour or two, or to-morrow at farthest, she will be with him around whom her thoughts centre; she will hear his voice, he will be by her side, and look into her eyes, and touch her hand.

Mr. Ferguson has many qualms during those autumn days. Somehow the whole even tenor of their quiet, uneventful lives seems broken, and he feels as if they could never take up the severed threads again. How long had the pool remained stagnant, but now it is stirred to its very depths. A strange brooding sense of some coming misfortune, disaster, or at least some startling unlooked-for event is ever on him. He feels strained, restless, ill at ease, and cannot account for his own sensations. Geoffrey's friendship is a comfort, a delight to him. Though they were but four or five days under the same roof, yet he missed him sorely when he went. The fact is he had felt strangely, irresistibly drawn to the young man from the first moment they had met. Graham possesses a singular, nameless attraction for him, and but that he felt it was politic for him to be gone and safer for his darling's sake, he would have insisted on his remaining his guest for some time longer; and yet, though he feels thus drawn to the stranger, he is aware that the change in their lives, and the unaccountable nervous tension he is always conscious of, dates from the commencement of that strangely formed acquaintance.

He is anxious and uneasy about Ula. He is keen enough to perceive an undefinable change in the girl, a shadowy something,

52 Biblical reference, eg., Acts 2:17, 'And your young men shall see visions, And your old men shall dream dreams.' (KJV)

faint, indescribable, vague, yet marked enough for loving eyes to note. She has been always fond of dreaming on the rocks, with a volume of her favourite poetry in her hands; now, she dreams even more than of yore, but the book lies closed upon her knee. Her tongue has grown strangely silent, and she moves about the house as one wrapped in blissful reverie. Are not these signs and tokens the very alphabet of that ancient tongue, the letters of which, large, clear, easily decipherable, arrange themselves with mute, mystic, intelligence into the sweet old familiar story that we all read for ourselves at some time, some earlier, some later, during our earthly lives? And who is this man who has thus suddenly thrust himself, as it were, into their secluded home, perhaps to destroy its peace for ever? Who is he? He has fallen as if from the clouds into that nest aloft on the grim Cornish cliffs, and has quietly slid into its ways, and seems happy and at home therein.

During this constant communion between these two lonely dwellings, for Mrs. Fanshawe is very bright and gay and organises numberless pleasant outings, both by sea and land, Effie has plenty of opportunity of cultivating her feloniously begun friendship with Mrs. Fanshawe's German maid. Not that after gratifying her first curiosity, the little girl had any special desire to cement that acquaintance. But Mrs. Benghaus (as the new importation is called in that primitive Cornish district, the good people alike despising and ignoring the unfamiliar, and in their opinion heathenish, "Frau") evinces such a strong, decided fancy, almost affection, for the child, that her egotism (a somewhat pronounced feature in the little girl's general economy) is flattered by it, and she responds, though often very ungraciously, to the woman's strange interest in her small self.

Ula and the German meet of course often, but oddly enough she—the elder, the heroine of such a remarkable late adventure, with the hero still well in the foreground; the lovely, winsome girl whose very face reflects the sunshine of a sweet nature, of a noble, generous heart,—exercises none of this unaccountable attraction for Mrs. Benghaus. She was desirous to see Effie's sister, very, but when once she beheld her, all interest in her died, and centred all the more strongly round the little one. When the girls are at the coastguard station, she will use every art to lure Effie away for half an hour or so to her own private sanctum, and will never tire of questioning and talking to the child about herself, her present life, above all her past; such brief past as the small despot possesses. She tries to win from her her earliest recollections, asks many questions about the mother Effie never knew, about the father, whom the child loves with the whole strength and passion of her odd, fitful, contradictory nature.

Sometimes the little girl's weird precocity, her impish freakiness, her uncanny imaginativeness, or again, her almost infantile simplicity, will seem to grate on the woman, and she will murmur half aloud, "Not like; not one little bit like; and yet how so like in all things else!" With whom is she mentally contrasting and comparing the child?

On the occasion of Mr. Ferguson's one visit to the "Eyrie,"—so Mrs. Fanshawe laughingly named her dwelling at first, and the name seeming not inappropriate, stuck to the house and was used by all,—Mrs. Benghaus managed to have business that took her to the drawing-room before he left; she gazed at him intently for a few moments and seemed strangely disturbed, and from that date she ceased to question Effie; but on the few occasions that she called at the Cliff House, bearing messages from her mistress, or whenever opportunity offered, she appeared to watch the old man with a strange, silent, stealthy watchfulness. Also she tried once or twice ineffectually to substitute Ula for Effie, deposed, as historiographer-in-chief, of their collective past. But the girl had taken an instinctive antipathy to the woman—why, she could not say, as she was rather predisposed to like people,—and gratified her apparent intrusive inquisitiveness not at all.

What a supremely lovely autumn it is! Already September has spent itself, and October is upon the land, and still there is no diminution in the beauty and balminess of the rare and perfect Indian summer that has graciously visited our grateful island. Geoff Graham has heard much of the genial mildness of the Cornish climate, and attributes the glorious aftermath of the year which he is enjoying to the favoured spot he is located in; but the dwellers of these wild western shores could tell a very different tale. Though winter here may lack much of the rigour of its cold, yet it is not the land where it is always afternoon, with a golden atmosphere, radiant skies, and a dreaming earth, and general air of lotus-eating languor and loveliness. This rock-bound coast is familiar with nature in her wildest, fiercest moods, and weather that would make denizens of other districts shrink and turn pale, is stoically accepted and hardly commented on by these sturdy Cornish fisher-folk.

Yet, it is a glorious fading of the year; dying so lingeringly, so lovingly, wrapped in so gracious a mantle that none can see the decaying worm that broods 'neath all. Aye, "that broods 'neath *all!*" The sweetest, youngest, fairest; the most glorious landscape, the loveliest, most fragile flower, the mightiest rocks, the overshadowing hills, the grandest, noblest human creation, that in its wondrous mystery of infinite eternal mind and soul, combined with finite perishing matter, surpasses in perfection all the force and majesty of blind beauteous nature—in all is the fatal canker; and decay and death will come to all things under Heaven, save the souls of men. That foul spirit of decay has no power over the impalpable essence that sits enthroned in each man's breast, and is *the* man in very truth born to eternity, heir to an everlasting kingdom.

But to return to earth and the "glory of this world that passeth away;" it is an exceptionally lovely season this autumn that Geoffrey Graham and Ula Ferguson are spending in such close communion.[53] The girl feels as if she had by chance wandered, like the heroine of one of Hans Christian Andersen's exquisite child tales, into some delicious fairyland, where the sunshine is more radiant, the flowers more faintingly sweet, the songs of the birds a grander, more jubilant chorus of ever-swelling harmony; where all things, even to the grass in the field, are more beautiful and perfect than in this everyday world of ours. The golden autumntide is the brief period in the lives of these two, that will remain with them in memory fresh and green to the end, with a halo of light and love surrounding it, making it a sweet and sacred recollection. And still no word has yet passed between them, interpreting the mute language of look, tone, gesture that expresses so much. They have not yet crossed the shadowy boundary that divides the unspoken from the spoken. They are still within that charmed circle of silence when the mysterious magical sweetness of that wondrous inexplicable action of the human heart that men call "love," is so much more divine and exquisite than when translated into speech. The girl asks for nothing more. She feels and knows she is loved, and that is enough for her, while she is daily with him to whom her heart has gone out.

The very thought of this entrancing, dreamy idyl, this sweetest summer poem that she is living through, finding utterance in ordinary language, would seem to rob the joy of half its rapture.

[53] From Joseph Sutcliffe's reflections on Numbers 11 in *A Commentary on the Old and New Testament.*

When once this trembling gulf of sweetest silence is crossed, no longer will there be that feeling of hugging a secret, hidden, unsuspected happiness to her heart of hearts; a happiness, a joy she hardly comprehends but yet treasures as her dearest possession. So thinks the girl. Not so the man. Half a dozen times within the last few weeks have the pregnant words been hovering on his lips, but he has checked them, and it is principally loyalty to his mother that has thus actuated him. That dear, absent mother has been hitherto his sole object in life, his only love, his friend, his companion, his adviser, his sympathiser. Never was there a greater bond of perfect union and affection between mother and son. They have lived for each other and in each other, with no thought in either breast that the other did not share. The son knows the bitter sorrows and wrongs of his mother's life, and endeavours to make the peace and tranquility and quiet happiness of the present compensate in some measure for that troublous past; while she buried the grief and anguish which at one time threatened to engulf her mind and body, and finds a joy in life, which she had not thought to know again, in the love, and tenderness, and devotion of her beloved son.

*　　*　　*　　*　　*　　*

And now a something has arisen between them—only a girl's slight form; only a girl's sweet face. And yet how potent a barrier sometimes to divide the nearest and dearest! Yes, Mrs. Graham has not the slightest suspicion of the real reason that detains her son in Cornwall. She was thoroughly delighted when she heard of his meeting with her old favourite and pupil, Madge Harefield, and rejoiced to learn of his removal from the humble native home (as she considers it) to Mrs. Fanshawe's charming dwelling.

Since that transition she has had letters both from Geoff and from Madge, and yet, still nothing has been made clear to her. Mrs. Fanshawe speaks enthusiastically of Ula Ferguson, her nearest neighbour on that lonely shore, and her quaint little sister; but in that ardent praise Mrs. Graham sees no glimmer of light, and recognizes not in the girl thus extolled her who saved her son from death, Madge making no direct reference to the fact, feeling certain that her correspondent is in full possession of all particulars, and sundry vague allusions and remarks reveal nothing where there is no idea of the real state of the case. Not that there was any intentional deceit on Geoffrey's part. The mistake originally arose from misconception on her side of Dr. Wenvoe's hurried communication, and Geoff's few lines scrawled from his bed, and she has remained tenacious of her first impression.

And it is this ignorance and unsuspicion on his mother's part which has sealed Graham's lips, when he has yearned with intensest longing to break the spell of dumbness that still stretches between him and Ula. He begins now to feel that he cannot remain more than another week or so in Cornwall. His pleasant lotus-eating time is nearly over, and he must hie back to harness and to that lonely mother, who must miss him so sadly, though with brave unselfishness she admits no such weakness.

Another week and he must say "Good-bye" to Ula Ferguson, to the girl whom he feels to be almost part of his very life. Good-bye! And must he go without speaking? Will loyalty to that absent mother demand such a sacrifice? And yet, to go home to her who has ever made him her chief and only object in life, and tell her with brutal abruptness that he is going to be married; that she is dethroned from the place where she has reigned so long; that during that holiday, while she sat at home in solitude and suffering, pain of body and grievous distress of mind on his account, he had deliberately forsaken her, and given his allegiance to another. No, he shrinks from doing this, although he knows full well that after the first shock of pain, her heart, that true, faithful heart, would go out in generous tenderness to that unknown girl who loves her son, as she trusts and believes in him too thoroughly to think he could choose unworthily. And how much more than worthily he has chosen, he thinks, with all a lover's vivid idealisation. Besides, even without choosing, does not his life belong by right to her who made him a gift of it?

And just while he is still torn with doubt and conflicting desires, unable to make up his mind how to act, Mrs. Fanshawe receives a long letter one morning from her old friend and instructress, which at the same time delights and grieves her. Mrs. Graham is actually coming to Cornwall, she who has not left her home for years, on a self-proposed visit to her dear pupil of olden days, coming now immediately. This is the joyful part. Then comes the sorrow. The lonely, unselfish woman confesses—though at the same time charging her correspondent to secrecy as far as Geoff is concerned—that for a long time past her health has not been satisfactory. For years she has had reason to suspect there was some heart trouble, and now her fears, which never amounted to actual certainty, are confirmed by medical opinion, which declares that there is heart complaint of long standing; that the late grievous anxiety about Geoff, coupled with the jar the system received in the fall, resulting, apparently, only in a badly-sprained ankle, had aggravated the malady, weakening the nerves, and undermining the strength both of mind and body. The disease, though deep-seated, may not necessarily prove fatal for some time, unless under the pressure of severe mental trouble.

She is enjoined to let nothing, if possible, disturb, or fret, or vex her. "And, thank God!" as she continues, "my life is very restful and peaceful of late years, a serene, quiet happiness that I could at one time never have thought to attain to. And all this tranquil joy and gladness of my later life has been given to me by my beloved son; he has been the one great blessing vouchsafed me, that has sweetened the intensely bitter cup of life, which a cruel fate forced me to drink. Only for Geoff, your old music-mistress would have been a mad woman long years ago, Madge, and you, I know, will not laugh at this as a foolish mother's idiotic ravings. You know the boy well enough to have some idea what he is, and how thoroughly he deserves all the praise and all the love his mother can bestow. And so, my dear, I want you, for the sake of our old friendship, to help me to conceal this sorrow from my Geoff. I know how terribly it would distress and grieve him; we are only two in all this wide, careless world, and though, God be thanked, no future shocks can come to me, save the shock of bereavement, which He in His infinite mercy will, I humbly pray and implore, spare me, and did turn aside in a manner truly miraculous within the last few weeks; yet I feel, in spite of the doctors, that the sands are running low, that but a brief portion of life is left to me, conserve myself as I may. But I do not want the last year or two to be embittered and darkened by this brooding shadow ever hovering between myself and my dear son, and when once he knew the truth, it would be a great, grey, unlightable darkness ever in our midst; we should look at it, and talk to one another, as it were, across an open grave; there would be one subject chief and uppermost in each mind, yet always tabooed; our intercourse would grow constrained; in short, the whole happiness of our last day together would be marred, while the knowledge of our coming parting could do Geoff no possible good, and only render him less fitted to pursue the honourable career in which already he has won distinction.

"I have reason to be proud of my boy, Madge; his talents, which are great, are set off by the humbler, nobler virtues of faithfulness, industry, uprightness, steadfastness. He is a thoroughly good man, with a true, tender, loving heart, a gift from heaven for which I never can be sufficiently thankful; and the woman who has the good fortune in the fulness of time to win him for her husband will be to be envied, whoever she may be. My one great sorrow is that I shall not live to see and bless that unknown creature, who will be all in all to my Geoffrey when his mother is but a name, a memory, a reverent, tender, ever-green memory I know and feel; but yet only a shade, an intangible emotion of the brain, no longer a reality."

Then she went on to say, that now the foot having recovered, the doctor recommended immediate change of air, telling her if possible to go where her mind would be interested and amused; and where could she be as happy as at Penmaerwyn? It would be such a real delight to meet her dear Madge again after all those years, though there hardly seemed a break in their intercourse, owing to the regularity of their correspondence, which was such a pleasure to her; and to have Madge and Geoff together would be indeed a happiness, especially after these two months of utter, anxious solitude. This was the one involuntary, yearning cry of that loving faithful heart; the one hint of what those weeks had been to the lonely, suffering woman, who had been called upon to bear within that period—besides acute physical pain, and racking distress of mind about one whom she loved better than herself—the knowledge that her apprehensions were well grounded, that she was doomed shortly to go hence, that her days were almost numbered, and at the very longest but a racing, hurrying year or two dwelt between her and eternity.

But she was a brave woman, if a sad and suffering one, and she determined to make the most of that remaining time. Not that she loved life for its own sake; on the contrary, in the shadowed miserable past she had been strongly tempted to lay down its direful burden, and was only restrained from the impious act by thought of her boy; and now that boy was her sole link to life, and for his sake and the great love she bore him, she would fain live out our brief allotted span. She would conserve with grudging miserliness each moment of the remnant of life left her, guarding herself from all worry and petty cares and annoyances; anything greater she did not fear.

Griefs and shocks and torturing wear and tear of mind had come to her in the long-ago, and had wrought their evil work, which was bearing this bitter fruit, but they could come nigh her no more. The past was dead, and she did not dream that "*Resurgam*" was written on that mental tomb.

THIRD PERIOD

EHEU FUGACES![54]

CHAPTER I

ADOPTION

SUCH is the sad burden of Madge's letter, which she loyally keeps to herself, though her heart is very sorrowful within her, for thinking of her dear old friend of former days. She speaks only of the sprain, and the proposed visit, and Geoff's own letter by the same post tells him as much. It is the first he hears of the fall and its consequences, his mother never having even alluded to her injured foot, fearing to retard his recovery, by making him anxious about her. Geoffrey is grieved to hear of his mother's sufferings, but he is delighted at her coming to Cornwall. His late difficulties vanish as if touched by a magic wand; the hard problem is solved without any act on his part. His mother is coming here, actually here to "The Eyrie," within half a mile of Ula's home. She will see, and know, and love the girl, who is all the world to him, and then all will be easy.

Mrs. Graham expects to arrive two days later than her letter, and Mrs. Fanshawe makes glad preparation for her invalid guest. She, and Geoffrey, and Benghaus, will nurse her dear old friend into better health and spirits; and possibly her gloomy anticipations will yield to the cheering influence of renewed strength. Benghaus is a very skilful sick nurse, as she knows; not that Mrs. Graham will

---

54 *Eheu fugaces!*: from Horace: '*Eheu fugaces, Postume, Postume labuntur anni*', meaning 'Alas, Postomus, Postomus, the fleeting years fly swiftly by'.

want nursing, she trusts, but still, in case of any attack of weakness or suffering, it is consolatory to feel that there is some one in the house who knows much of illness.

But as things will happen with a sort of malicious contrariness, that seems almost to argue the presence of some ever-watchful malign spirit, ready to upset at a touch our "best laid plans," on the morning of the day on which Mrs. Graham is to arrive, when all arrangements for her comfort are satisfactorily concluded, and just as Geoff has started for Plymouth, determined that during the last portion of her long journey his mother shall not be alone, Mrs. Fanshawe receives a telegram from London from her uncle Danvers—whose house has been her home since she lost her parents—summoning her thither at once, and charging her to bring Benghaus with her. Her Aunt is ill, dangerously ill, and the German had proved invaluable when the stricken woman was laid low by a similar attack a year ago.

Madge is dismayed by this message. What is she to do? She feels really grieved for her Aunt whom she loves; but at the same time, she knows that her Uncle George is an alarmist, prone so to exaggerate, as to magnify small troubles into heavy calamities. To leave her home is out of the question; it should be life or death indeed, that would compel such a step now, when her guest, whom she so loves and honours, will be here in a few hours. The very fact of that guest being self-invited, would render her going impossible. It is too terrible a *contretemps*.[55] If it were any one but Mrs. Graham, she would not mind so much, she tells herself; but the woman who has written so pathetic a letter, baring to her her innermost heart, at least with respect to her apprehended approaching death,

[55] *Contretemps*: unforeseen, unfortunate occurrence.

and who is coming here, to try and recruit the waning strength, to fan the feeble flame of life; to come, and to find her—gone! No, it could not be. Yet, to neglect that urgent summons is equally impossible; and so, after much distressful and anxious cogitation, she determines to send Benghaus at once to London; on her arrival, she will immediately ascertain Mrs. Danvers' actual condition, and will telegraph the same to her.

She can trust the woman to give a clear, true statement of the case, and then she will know how to act. If her Aunt is really so very ill, she will hasten to-morrow to her bedside; and in the meantime, Mrs. Graham will have arrived, and she will be able to explain everything to her. At any rate, it is the best that can be made of a very unhappy circumstance, she solaces herself by reflecting, after Benghaus has departed in great haste and confusion, and not very willingly, as she hates London, and was looking forward, with an unaccountable curiosity and interest, to Mrs. Graham's visit.

* * * * * *

Mrs. Graham has been in Cornwall a week, but she has not yet made Ula's acquaintance. For the first few days after her arrival, she was weak and suffering, incapable of anything but taking perfect rest. And Geoffrey was too aggrieved, nay even startled, by the change in his mother's appearance, to think of anything else. How can those few short weeks have so altered her? Surely even a bad sprain with its attended pain, can hardly account for that haggard, aged aspect, he thinks, as he furtively watches the pale, drawn face, a face which you can see at a glance is that of one who has known much sorrow and suffering, who has been heavily tried in the furnace of affliction, but in whom the lamp of a great faith, and trust, and peace, has been kindled.

And Ula, with her sensitive nature, shrinks from the meeting;

that Geoffrey cares for her she now feels flutteringly certain, and she fears his mother may consequently regard her with distrust, and very possibly, dislike. But Ula does not understand, cannot guess, or gauge, the profound depth of unselfishness, the utter self-abnegation of a mother's love. And by-and-by, when is Madge Fanshawe's pretty drawing-room, after being earnestly, eagerly scanned by wistful yearning eyes,—eyes lovely still in themselves, but with such a look of unending sorrow in their violet depths—she finds herself clasped almost convulsively to that mother's breast, she feels, with a great indistinctive throb of delight and wonder, a mysterious intuition, that a woman's love, and that woman a mother, *his* mother, is at last hers. She has always idealised this "mother love;" has longed for it with a sick yearning, has jealously cherished the remembrance of those hazy, baby years, the sweet dim recollection—more an impression than an actual memory—of her own dear mother. But now, in one rapturous moment, she feels as if she had found that, for which all her life she has been longing, a woman's clinging, close embrace; a few murmured words, so few, and so simple, and yet so sufficing to the girl's yearning heart—"My child, God bless you!" . . . Mrs. Graham could say no more in those few moments, her heart was too full for speech.

In these few days of quiet dwelling at "The Eyrie," she has discovered her mistake with regard to her who saved her son from death. She has also learned the secret of her boy's heart, unguessed by him; and she waited with a tremulous, sick expectancy, a shrinking fear, coupled with an impatient eagerness, for that meeting which has now taken place.

Who was this girl who had saved Geoff's life, and had then stolen his heart, and abode there? she asked herself with almost frenzied doubt and anxious solicitude; and then——Ula walked into the room, and all doubt and unrest were at an end for ever. Those wistful, worn eyes scanned the girl's face with one intense searching look, there was a silence, but so momentary, that Ula in her nervousness and flutter, scarcely heeded it; and then, she caught the girl to her breast with a little gasping cry, and those whispered words of blessing and adoption. That one glance had been sufficient; the scrutiny so keen, so eager, in the interests of her beloved son, had been brief, but oh! so satisfying. One look into that true, pure, innocent face, had brought her infinite gladness. She believed in Ula, from the instant she met the gaze of those sweet, earnest eyes, raised in timid appeal to her own—eyes that met yours with so frank and open a regard; the whole soft, expressive face, flushing, paling, quivering with a sort of unconquerable, unexplainable emotion, carried faithfulness, and truth, and tenderness, clearly written upon it.

*　　*　　*　　*　　*　　*

Mrs. Graham feels strangely drawn to the girl, and only feels perfectly happy and content in her presence. Effie too, interests her much. The odd mixture of weird precocity and ultra babyishness, as developed in the younger Miss Ferguson, is refreshingly uncommon. She catches herself also watching the child, and studying her face, with a curious feeling as of renewing acquaintance with a once familiar subject. "I know now what it is," she half-sighs, half-smiles, one day, as they all sit at afternoon tea in Mrs. Fanshawe's drawing-room, and the little one being just opposite Mrs. Graham, she has been regarding her intently. "It's of Geoff, when he was a little fellow, that I am reminded."

"Mother mine, are you not a little foggy?" speaks the young man, gaily. He is very happy, deeply, intensely happy these last few days. His mother, he feels certain, has guessed the truth about his love, and yet, she never has been so fond and adoring of him, Geoff, and never has been so sweet, and familiarly friendly, nay, affectionate with any one, after but four or five days' acquaintance.

"Who reminds you of me, when I was a youngster? Not 'The Shah,' I trust; if so, I must have been somewhat of a curiosity," with an amusing glance of feigned apprehension at the beautiful Persian specimen of the feline tribe, which so excited Effie's wondering admiration on her first visit to Mrs. Fanshawe's, and which now reposes in dignified white fluffiness on the little girl's lap.

"My dearest Geoff, please don't be vain, as if you could ever have been as lovely as that perfect cat. No, but Miss Effie is strangely like in my eyes, what you were when quite a little boy."

"Geoff like Eff!" cries Madge, incredulously, and then laughing blithely at her impromptu rhyming. "Well, I have made their names harmonize beautifully, but I should fancy all similarity ends there;" with a slightly mocking glance from Geoff Graham's handsome, bearded, vigorous face, to her small guest's fragile, white, somewhat elfish countenance, with its great solemn weird-looking black eyes.

"I don't say they are like now in the least degree," says Mrs. Graham, still reflectively contemplating the child, "but when Geoff was quite a small boy."

"And a detestable young urchin as a natural consequence!" softly interpolates the person under discussion, with a laugh, and a quick whimsical glance at Ula, who is undisguisedly hanging on Mrs. Graham's words, in her beautiful frank simplicity allowing her face to betray her great interest in the subject.

"When Geoff was quite a small boy," continues Mrs. Graham, unheeding this interruption, "he was very pale and delicate-looking, with a little white, wistful face, and large, serious, questioning, dark eyes, just like our young friend's; he was very fond of books, too, fairy tales," she adds, with a little conciliatory nod and smile at Effie, who is gazing at her with a precociously supercilious stare.

"When you mention the eyes," quoth Madge, again studying deliberately the two faces, "I don't doubt that there is a likeness still."

"I have my own Pops' eyes, doesn't everyone say so, Ula? My own dear Pops' very eyes, and not those of any little strange boy; I don't want to have anything belonging to him," with contemptuous and somewhat incoherent indignation, seemingly not recognising her friend Graham, of whom she is so warm and devoted an ally, in the small boy referred to; or possibly, with a child's fine incapacity, for even imagining the youth of a grown-up person, regarding his boyhood as belonging to some pre-historic period, in which she could have no part.

After a momentary pause, she continues, severely, "You're just like Mrs. Benghaus, 'Frau Benghaus' they ought to call her," looking round on the group, with a glance of scathing reproof; "but the stupid things, they can't say 'Frau'; but you're just like her, Mrs. Graham, she was always saying, when she first came, that I was like, so like, somebody she knew long, long ago, 'his very self,' she said one day, so it must have been a boy or man, or something disagreeable, and I thought it was very rude of her; everybody has his or her own face, and doesn't want any one else's; I'm sure 'The Shah,' here, wouldn't like to be told he was the image of every old rubbishy cat yelling on the walls."

A general and hilarious laugh is the response to the uncanny wisdom, unblushing vanity (terrible vanity, though not intentional, in comparing herself to "The Shah," with his rare charms amongst grimalkins) and undisguised impertinence of this speech.[56] Only

[56] Grimalkins: cats (archaic).

Ula is grave, as she glances quickly and anxiously at Mrs. Graham, fearing she may be offended by her small irrepressible sister's most unruly tongue.

Mrs. Graham then asks, who is Frau Benghaus, who seems to have incurred little Miss Ferguson's displeasure by an impolite reference to a supposed resemblance between her and an unknown somebody of the masculine gender; and for the first time—as Madge has hitherto carefully refrained from any allusion to her maid's absence, or its cause, fearing sensitive Mrs. Graham might think she had timed her visit inopportunely—she hears of Mrs. Danvers' sudden illness, and the German's departure for London on the very day she herself had arrived in Cornwall; Madge now laughingly dilating on her great perplexity that morning, and congratulating herself on having so cleverly solved the difficult problem presented to her. It was such a capital thought to send Benghaus, who wired to her that very night, not to be alarmed—that Mrs. Danvers, though very ill, was not any worse than a year before, when she had nursed her through a similar attack. "Poor dear Auntie!" continues Madge, retrospectively, "I felt awfully sorry for her, but still, it was a great relief to know I need not start for London just then, and I can thoroughly depend on Benghaus; she is a perfect treasure, Mrs. Graham, I only wish you had her double. I should feel so happy to think you had a person like her constantly about you."

"You make me quite anxious to see this paragon of maids, Madge dear," replies Mrs. Graham, with a soft little laugh. "Perhaps I shall be stealing her away from you up to the North; as a rule I don't care for foreign servants, but I think you said she is German?"

"Yes, I believe so, not a very pronounced Teuton in appearance, though; I sometimes fancy she has more the air of a French woman."

"Ah! I detest French serving-women," says Mrs. Graham with a strange energy of expression for one so gentle-natured and mild of speech; and Ula, who has already learned to regard her and all she says and does with loving interest, notices than an odd little shudder accompanies her words, and that the pale face grows paler than before.

CHAPTER II

THE SHADOW IN THE AIR

FOUR or five days later that golden silence that has palpitated with delicious meaning between these two, is broken for evermore, and Ula and Geoff are betrothed lovers.

The confession has been made, with ardent looks and burning words, and passionate intensity of feeling on one side: and on the other—why, another little confession was whispered, in broken sentences, with fluttering breath, and downcast eyes, and furiously blushing cheeks; and all doubt and unrest are at an end for ever. They love each other intensely, and have told their love, and are infinitely content and happy; aye! almost in a state bordering on beatitude. And yet—is fruition ever as rapturously, ecstatically sweet as expectancy? We perpetually live in a vague and distant future, full of indefinite potentialities that if, or when attained, will round and perfect our lives, subduing all unrest and desire, and bringing a great content. But that future never comes, or rather, when the future becomes the present we do not recognize it. We are still looking, straining ahead, gazing away into that misty dimness, over which hangs the entrancing shadow of another veil of years. All we have done is to push the future on a little further, and a little further still. That future holds almost unimagined joys in its mystic bosom, but we never clasp them, we never reach them; they ever elude us, because the "future" always becomes the "present," and loses all the magic of its distant delights. And so we keep pushing and pushing forward that wondrous, intangible future, as we reach each landing-stage of life, until at last that eagerly anticipated time to come lies away at our back, and we see but a grave, and the darkness of the end in front.

But this is wandering somewhat from Ula and Geoff in the first indescribable happiness of their spoken love. No fear that any serpent of discontent, or disillusion, of flatness, or of custom, has yet stolen into their Eden, as that ecstatic betrothal is but three or four hours old. The momentous words were spoken during a pilgrimage to Tintagel, from which they have just returned. Ula is the only representative of the Cliff House family, Effie being rather ailing this day or two, and refusing to leave her "own dear Pops," who has been only once to "The Eyrie" since Madge's advent, and consequently has not yet met Mrs. Graham. But the Fanshawe party was pleasantly augmented by Alice Wenvoe and her genial old grandmother; the harassed, hard-worked doctor, too, for a wonder, joined their holiday-making, and looks decidedly brighter and refreshed for the little change. Also the Rev. Mark Temple, curate of St. Olave's, made one of this small band of pilgrims; earnest, visionary, intense in all he does, he has thrown himself back into that legendary, poetic past all day, and, in spite of his habitual reserve, has proved himself a valuable ally to Ula, in her unanimously elected, but somewhat difficult post of cicerone and general exponent of local tradition.

The fair Alice has been in a condition bordering on beatitude, as she has had the Rev. Mark's society all to herself for a goodly portion of those speeding golden hours, not, we will confess, so much from choice on his part as from necessity, as he would have infinitely preferred Ula's companionship; but she being appropriated by Graham, he naturally fell back on Alice, whom he had been disposed to admire a little before he knew the tawny-haired siren of the cliffs, whose intellectual mind and playful fancy interested and attracted him even more than her witching face. Her intense ardent nature awakes corresponding echoes in his own contemplative, introspective soul, and he sometimes feels that just such a congenial, sympathetic mate would make life almost complete; a twin spirit, to travel with one through this shadowed, mystic valley of life, to belong to oneself, and oneself only, in the great, awful, mysterious "beyond," surely would be a joy unspeakable. But these are only errant thoughts; sweet, hazy imaginings of rare, idle moments; the Rev. Mark Temple's real bride (as yet) is the Church. He is true, devoted, and desperately earnest, a zealous labourer in the Heavenly vineyard, toiling unremittingly and lovingly, with boundless compassion, among the sick, and poor, and sorrowing.

But this little party that returned to "The Eyrie" an hour ago, tired, but happy, is already much reduced. Mark Templeton has gone to a dying bed, than which none can fill more perfectly so sad a duty; intensely sympathetic he, indeed, "comforts the afflicted," and does his earthly best to "bind up the wounds of the broken-hearted."[57] And he who is not so constituted, who is not endowed with that rare and beautiful gift of a ready, perfect sympathy, has little business to go amongst the suffering and the sorrowing; as he only excites sore and irritated feeling, where he should solace and soothe, and creates a greater void in the mourner's breast, by the absence of what the grieving one instinctively years for. Captain Fanshawe has gone amongst his men, as is his evening custom; and Dr. Wenvoe, poor, hard-worked man, has been summoned to a distant patient; Geoffrey has also departed, by preconcerted arrangement with Ula, to see Mr. Ferguson and explain all before she makes her appearance at home.

Ula, meanwhile, is in a restless, emotional state; a feeling of tremulous exaltation, mingled with a strange, newborn sense of

---

[57] Based on 2 Corinthians 1:4; from Isaiah 61:1.

mystery and sorrow brooding somewhere in the air around, as if she were on the brink of some imagined discovery that would steal away her gladness; a feeling of unreality—as if all her life has been a dream, and that now was coming the moment of awakening—weights upon her dimly; and yet above, and round, and through all this strange discordant undertone, that is breathing ominously, as it were, a chill, fateful whisper through her highly-strung system, there is the throbbing of a great delirious joy; a joy and ecstasy that must find some vent; the intense, impassioned nature is strained to a point of nervous tension that must have an utterance, and so, unnoticed by the others, she slips from the room. They won't miss her; Madge and Alice have just embarked on a delightfully animated discussion anent London; its fascination and fashions, a subject of inexhaustible interest to the doctor's daughter, who expects to be enlightened by her hostess as to all the new crazes, whether of millinery or manners; while the two elder ladies are having a snug *causerie* by the fire.[58] But the dialogue soon becomes a little more than a monologue, as Mrs. Graham is feeling singularly weak and wearied, though she does not say so to Madge, fearing to distress her; she has done a little too much, and is not equal to more than to lie back in her low chair and listen to Mrs. Wenvoe's cheery, fluent chat; but it is sympathetic listening, as the garrulous old woman has hit upon her favourite topic, one that she never tires of, and that has for its subject her son, the clever, un-appreciated, hard-working village doctor. If ever the old lady is eloquent, it is when this theme inspires her, and surely it is one that awakes strong and responsive echoes in her hearer's breast; and in a soft, dreamy state of partly weakness, partly tranquil happiness, Mrs. Graham

---

[58] *Causerie*: informal conversation.

hears a son extolled by worshipping mother lips, and thinking of her own son, sees naught ridiculous, naught worthy of contemptuous scorn or pity, as might a scoffing world, in the half-pathetic fact that the child thus loved and idealised is a rugged, worn, disappointed man, not far from fifty years old, a man on whom the world has mostly turned a frowning face, who has been struggling more or less all through life against an adverse and perverse fate, and, though generally worsted in the fray, has maintained throughout a dogged front of patient endurance.

To the drawing-room on the other side of the artistic little hall, Ula bends her steps, she softly closes the door behind her, and then pouncing on her violin—which is more often of late at "The Eyrie" than at her own home—she dashes through a "Liebeslied" of Brahms's; the thrilling passionate gladness within must find a vent, and is it not the very spirit of joy itself, this music that she plays with such masterly command of the instrument she so loves?[59] But then, as suddenly her mood changes, and she glides into a mournful "Andante" of Beethoven's, the other strange feeling, of an underlying brooding shadow somewhere, again seizes her, it must also have expression, and finds it thus in a mode of utterance so much more full and congenial to the girl than any speech.[60] What a wail of mystic unknown trouble breathes through these long slow strains!

Mrs. Graham, resting in the dining-room, let her attention wander from Mrs. Wenvoe, when those first glad musical sounds had softly reached her and had longed to follow the girl and clasp her to her heart; she loved the child's music, marvelling at its

[59] Liebeslied: love song.

[60] Andante: piece of music in andante (moderately slow) tempo.

excellence; she had guessed what had taken place within the last few hours, reading their secret on the two faces that now form her world, love being the key by which she translates this sweetest cipher. But now, as she hearkens to these sad lingering notes, which sigh softly through the house, an unaccountable depression seizes her, she shivers, and looks round on the bright cheerful room; it seems as if some unseen mysterious presence had glided in amongst them, banishing peace and gladness; as if some dim undefinable shadow of coming ill had cast its brooding impalpable shape over the house and its inmates; and then she inwardly chides herself for indulging in absurd fancies, and turns once more to gossipy old Mrs. Wenvoe, who is unconscious, as are the others, of any change in the mental atmosphere.

And soon those wailing strains cease, and Ula catches up her hat, which she had tossed down on a sofa when she came in an hour or so ago, and a soft muffling shawl of Madge's which lies across her favourite bamboo chair, and passing through one of the windows opening on to the verandah she runs swiftly down the short flight of steps leading to the miniature lawn or tennis ground, and thence makes her way to the cliff road, with the half-formed idea of wandering a little way towards home to meet Geoffrey; he is a good while gone, and ought soon to return now.

Really, the strange excited restlessness is so strong upon her that she cannot remain still; her music, instead of soothing as is its wont, seems rather to have intensified the sort of nervous dread that has laid hold of her, almost to the exclusion of that thrilling joy which spoke in the "Liebeslied." The free unfettered feeling of being out of doors is quite a relief at first; somehow that indefinite troublous shadow, that had seemed to hover close and menacingly those last few minutes, is lightened. Is she leaving it behind her?

she thinks, with a queer little superstitious thrill, as she involuntarily looks back over her shoulder at the house she has just left. The sky is clear and serene, the moon has risen, a great deeply-golden disc, as yet but a little way above the horizon, still diffusing a magic mellow radiance; but—is it smoke or fancy? or could it be a cloud?—and yet how strange a shape—just over "The Eyrie" hangs, so close as to appear almost to touch it, a singular brooding vapour, an odd sudden shadow on the lovely evening sky; and Ula, with a quick catch in her breath, walks rapidly on till she reaches the curve, which reveals to her her own home, lying away there in the soft misty distance. A sort of dusky haze seems to spread around and envelop its neighbourhood, that she cannot quite understand, when the night is so clear, and all the wide expanse of heaven over the heaving waters so perfectly unflecked by cloud or mist of any kind; but at any rate it has not the ominous look, the strange human-like form of the mysterious cloud above "The Eyrie." And then she laughs a little at her own folly, in attaching any value to the chance shape of those wreathy mists; doubtless fine as it appears, they are near a change, and these are the advance guard of the coming storm squadron.

CHAPTER III
ON THE TITLE-PAGE

"So!
Another chapter read, with doubtful hand
I turn the page; with doubtful eye I scan
The heading of the next."[61]

WHEN Geoffrey reached the Cliff House an hour ago, he was told by old Barbara Jephson, Mr. Ferguson's housekeeper; and nurse, duenna, friend, almost mother to the girls, that Miss Effie had been very ailing and strange in herself all day. "Most trying, sir, was the dear bairn," she continued, "complaining and fretful, and taking all sorts of queer fancies and crazes into her head. Try as we would, we could not do a mortal thing that would please her, or if she was content for a moment, she was off the next about something else. It's seldom enough, Heaven knows, poor Dr. Wenvoe takes a bit of pleasuring, and it seems wicked like to begrudge it to him, but it is a little contrairy that he should be away just when he's wanted maist. And the puir fractious lassie would bide no place but on the master's knee, with her head on his breast, and holding him tight with her burning mites of hands. And then this evening she fell to talking so odd, I'm sure it hurt the maister sair, as well as skeered him. It was all about her mither, the mither the dear we bit lass never kenned. She asked the strangest questions, the master did not know how to answer; little she knew, puir lamb, what she was saying, or how she was trying him." And the garrulous kindly old woman paused and sighed, while a tear trickled down her wrinkled cheek.

---

[61] Lines from *The First Violin* by Jessie Fothergill.

"Any by-and-by she fell to talking in the wildest way, it made a body's flesh creep to hear her. 'I saw her last night,' she said, after a little, so sudden and quiet like, as if she knew, and that there could be no mistake, that we both—the master and I—amaist jumped with the start of her weird words. 'Yes, I saw her out there,' she went on, pointing through the window, sir, with sich a solemn weenie finger. 'It was the middle of the night, and everyone else was asleep, and I got up to look at the moon, and I saw her waiting just there, and I knew at once it was mither; and I think she was looking for me, Pops, for when she saw me she beckoned, but I shook my head, and said quite soft and easy, 'No, I'm going to stay with Pops, I won't leave him as you did'; and though I whispered it at the window, and she was far away out there on the cliffs, yet I think she heard, for she bowed her head so sad, and I heard a great sob as if it came from far, far distant, and then she was gone, and I went back to bed.' Of course it was only a dream, though the darling bairnie thought it was all real, or she fancied the whole thing as she spoke, for she did seem off her head a bit; but it gave the master and me a sair turn. About an hour ago the puir lassie fell asleep at last, just wore out, in the deep window-seat in the dining-room. We didn't dare to touch her, but just covered her up warm, and then the master started for Penmaer for Dr. Wenvoe's. I trust in the Lord he'll catch him."

And then Geoffrey mentioned the unlucky fact of the doctor being already summoned to a patient living three miles off.

"The master may get something from the assistant," murmurs the old woman, anxiously, "but I don't think he trusts him much, it's little they ken them laddies, the maist of them, but if it was even midnight when the doctor gets back, he'll be sure to come over, he's so fond of my darling Miss Effie."

Then Mrs. Jephson asked Geoffrey would he come in and wait for her master, or walk to meet him. He hesitated for a moment. To go back without seeing Mr. Ferguson, he feels would be savagely unkind, when he is so troubled about the little one, though he feels at the same time, to speak of what he so joyously came to tell, is hardly possible just at present. He decided to wait for Mr. Ferguson instead of going to meet him. Someway his thoughts had been so happy and restful out in the sweet hazy dimness of the October evening, that he does not care to encounter it again, till he can shake off the unpleasant feeling of a nameless apprehension, that seems to be hovering as it were ghost-like in the air around him. There is a lamp turned low in the dining-room, where the child lies asleep. With finger on her lip Bab leads the way past the door, then she stops, and asks him in a whisper, shall she put lights in the drawing-room, or will he wait in the master's study?—a big name for a little room at the end of the passage, which Mr. Ferguson has appropriated for his own special use, and calls his den, and in which there is also a lamp turned low.

Geoffrey chooses the study. He has been in the room a few times already, though never alone, he and Mr. Ferguson having adjourned there occasionally for a smoke, when the weather did not permit their sallying out of doors. Here, the old man keeps his "specimens." He is an amateur naturalist, and these are the results of periodical aimless wanderings which now extend over many years, and which have been rather an excuse for a strange unconquerable restlessness, an anodyne for almost unbearable attacks of fearful depression, than real scientific explorations; still they have borne fruit, and geology and botany, as well as natural history are fairly represented in these small glass cases, and neatly arranged drawers, where everything is so carefully classified and labelled.

Quite an enterprising little collection, thinks Geoffrey, as he pokes about absent-mindedly, trying to put away the time, as somehow he cannot bring himself to sit down to think. He has seen them all before, and feels no absorbing interest in their contemplation, not being one of the guild of naturalists; yet now he gazes, with prolonged and steady glare, at sundry alarming-looking beetles, and pretentious garish moths, who have done their deceitful best to pass themselves off as their refined patrician relatives—the butterflies—as if he were an enthusiastic member of the craft; even going the length of taking up a magnifier to stare pertinaciously at a monstrous and evil-looking centipede, whose extraordinary multiplicity of legs is alone quite sufficient to explain his very low place in the moral and intellectual standard.

But soon he straightens his back, which has begun to ache a little, peering at those poor little transfixed beasts (each, or any of which, if only sufficiently enlarged, would be much more terrifying in physical aspect than any existing animal on earth), and he makes for the books. One wall of this small private room of Mr. Ferguson's is completely lined with books; from floor to ceiling they reach, shelf after shelf; not a very great library of course, the space is limited, but still, not a bad little collection to find out on this projecting cliff, at the very end of the world.

Somewhat a heterogeneous gathering too, Darwin and Huxley, side by side with Carlyle and Ruskin, John Stuart Mill, Herbert Spencer, Kant, &c., leaning up lovingly against the simple child-like faith of him who wrote "Old Red Sandstone,"[62] against sweet sylvan Richard Jeffries, and still more disturbing the pure spiritual atmosphere surrounding him, whose great, and lovely, full,

[62] Hugh Miller was the author of *The Old Red Sandstone.*

and eager life was worked out at the loved "Eversley" parsonage.[63]

The thinkers and dreamers, the workers and idealists, are here, in affectionate juxtaposition. Fiction, too, that modern fungus of giant growth, has a corner to itself, but only the very best has found entrance here.

Geoffrey is just about to extract a volume from this latter selection; he wants to try to distract his mind, if he can, from the sudden oppressive sense of brooding apprehension, amounting almost to dread, that has come upon him, and that is as strange as it is novel; but as his hand reached for it, his eye, which has been wandering over the whole wall of books, is caught by a massive volume, the title of which happens to be in large gilt letters on a dark ground, else he could not have read it, it is up so high, stowed away on the very top shelf.

Why is it up there amidst the dust and gloom? he thinks at first, with almost a touch of irrational indignation, and the next moment, wonders why it is there at all. It is a celebrated and costly work on "Architecture and Design," about five-and-twenty years old, costly, owing to the numerous beautifully executed plates with which it is enriched. Graham has never seen it, though he has often wished to do so, for though not actually bearing on his own *métier*, yet it is as it were, next of kin, and holds much interest for him, engineering and architecture being surely almost twins.[64] But what possible meaning or interest can it have for a naturalist, the man whose only two themes in which he appears to have a learned interest, apart from his amateur calling, are music and metaphysics? What does he know of, or care for, construction or designing?

---

63 Charles Kingsley, author of *The Water Babies*, was rector of Eversley.

64 *Métier*: profession.

There are no steps in the room, these upper-shelf books are evidently not much in demand. A chair will not reach them, even with Geoffrey's goodly inches, so he looks around for something else, and finds behind the door a strong plain box, or small pacing-case. Just the very thing! This and the chair combined raise him quite enough, and as his hand closes on the coveted volume, he feels a thrill of pleasure; the enthusiasm of his profession returns with a rush, that has been slightly in abeyance these last few weeks. For a few moments Ula fades ever so little from the foremost place in his thoughts, and it is more the successful, ambitious engineer, that steps down from that elevated chair than even the triumphant lover. He has long desired to possess this book, but as yet, owing to its costliness, has hardly felt himself justified in its purchase; and now he is not a little surprised to find it here in this obscure cliff home. He carries it to the table that holds the lamp, and draws forward a chair; the book is large and heavy, and he is determined comfortably to enjoy the prize he has found.

"I'll get Ferguson to lend it to me," he thinks, as he turns up the lamp. And then he opens it, and naturally opens the title-page. But what is the meaning of that terrible start—that incoherent, wild exclamation—that sudden flush that dies away into a grey, ghastly pallor? Why those clenched hands, those fixed eyes that glare upon that innocent title-page, while a look of amazed horror or frenzy, coupled with a distracted non-comprehension, spreads and deepens on the vigorous, handsome face? What is it that has caused this startling transformation?

Let us look over his shoulder, and see what has thus transfixed him. Only two or three words of writing above the printed title of the volume: only a man's name, and a date just four-and-twenty years old:—

"LIONEL HARTLEY DACRE,
August, 1863."

* * * * * *

What memories, what associations are linked with this name that affect the strong man thus—that cause that muscular powerful frame to tremble like a woman's? How long he sits there—silent, stirless, as one turned to stone, while a strange, shocked, despair grows in those dark, haggard eyes—he knows not. Then suddenly, with a frantic, desperate gesture, as if throwing off some invisible noxious thing that threatened to coil its deadly python folds around his spirit, he starts to his feet, his limbs still tremulous, his cheek still blanched, but with a stern, determined look of fixed resolve on the changed face.

"No, such horror couldn't be! I will not—cannot believe it—it is too monstrous! But he shall tell me how he came by this: he must have known *him*. Where—how—when? He must—he shall tell me all. And to think that *I* should have found it! That *I* should have come here—been driven here—to—my God! is it fate? is it—could it be?——"

A look of anguish again creeping into the eyes as he appears to wrestle once more with some horrible doubt or suspicion.

"Ah!" with a quick catch in the breath, as turning his head he sees, through the uncurtained window at the end of the room which looks out upon the cliffs, and through which the moonlight is now pouring brilliantly, Mr. Ferguson's figure advancing rapidly by the path leading from Penmaer.

"Even now, without an instant's delay!" he mutters with pallid lips, and with a swift movement he catches up the ponderous book that seems to have held so horrible a secret for him, and is out into the moonlight, hatless, striding towards that approaching form, in a flash.

* * * * * *

When Mr. Ferguson recognizes Graham hastening to meet him with such strange, eager, swiftness, without a hat, wild, excited, unlike himself, he gives an inarticulate cry of dismay, a cold fear grasps his heart and arrests his steps.

"The child?" he gasps; "what of her?—she's worse? tell me quickly—my darling, my Effie!" and there is a sickening interrogation in his worn eyes. Geoffrey looks at him blankly as he stops in front of him, with the book thrust out between his trembling hands, then, after an instant's pause, "The child's all right, as you left her," he answers almost brutally. He has forgotten all about poor Effie and her illness, and resents the intrusion of any subject save that which has absorbed his very being.

"Whose name is that? In the name of God, tell me at once, and tell me truly," he then cries, pushing the book, open at the title-page, into Mr. Ferguson's very face. The moonlight is clear and bright; no difficulty in deciphering anything held close by those pure pale rays. Mr. Ferguson gives a hurried, surprised glance at Graham, and then at the page, "Why mine, of course," he answers impulsively, without hesitation or recollection.

In the first wild rush of gigantic relief about the child—the inexpressible reaction from the terrible panic of apprehension that had seized him when he saw Graham flying to meet him—he is utterly oblivious of all else; and the only feeling he is conscious of in the first moment of this supreme hour in these two men's lives, is a slight gentle amazement at being asked, whose is his own name? But this mental attitude is of short duration. The words are hardly uttered when he would fain recall them for ever.

"Yours! yours!" repeats Geoffrey, in dazed, frenzied utterance, with a ring of rage and despair in the hoarse, broken tones, as he staggers back from the old man, on whose grey, quivering, strangely-moved face, he gazes with wild, shocked, half-maddened eyes. "I felt it was so, though I tried to fight against the horror of it," he mutters dully to himself. "You are Lionel Hartley Dacre!" and there is a touch of indignant, terrible contempt, almost amounting to loathing, in the harsh, changed accents, as he pronounces the name. "Then, if that is so, may the great and merciful Father help and pity me and forgive you, for you have a terrible account to answer for! You were not content with the desolation, the blight, the infinite wrong and wickedness you wrought in the past; you were not satisfied with the destruction, the remorseless, deliberate wrecking of one life—the life that should have been most sacred to you—with the cruel, diabolical wronging of the purest, truest, loveliest soul on earth, but you must needs after all those years—oh, my God! all those bitter years!—when you were as one dead—start into life again to blight and wreck two other lives, also innocent of wrong towards you. That name—that fatal name!"—spurning with his foot the book that had fallen to the ground in the first rush of horrible confirmation of his worst fears; "it is accursed. But though others were more than justified in abjuring it for ever, you had no right to cast it off and masquerade in this cruel, deceptive disguise, that lulled one to a false security. Ah! but fool that I am!—the disguise served as a cloak for the evil that has led to this hideous——"

"Stay*! I say stay!*" Is it the old man who speaks? The voice is harsh, discordant, utterly unlike his usual gentle, somewhat mournful accents; but it is not this which strikes one so much, as the strange, new tone of command, mingled with a fierce, consuming eagerness.

He has been struggling for utterance, and at last speech has burst from those working lips, speech that involuntarily arrests those wild words of invective on Graham's lips, and compels him to pause and look at the face confronting him. It is ashen-hued and strangely convulsed, the hollow eyes, dark as the young man's own, burning with a singular intense light; but surely not the lurid fires lit by the fear of discovery of secret sin, not the light of rage or apprehension, but more the inward glowing of a conscious innocence, of a clear conscience that is suddenly reminded of a great and grievous wrong that has been done it in the past; yes, the whole quivering face seems suddenly to express to Graham's heated fancy a noble, sorrowing rectitude, a shadowed yet stainless honour. "Here is no guile, but grief," seems to say that agitated face, and his heart grows less fiercely hard to the old man.

"Stay!" repeats the harsh, changed voice again, while the devouring eagerness now dominates the tone of command, and no longer to be repressed, animates the man's whole being. "Who are *you*? Who are you, I say, who dares to speak of the past—*my* past—with a tone of knowledge and judgment, who ventures to censure *me*? *Who* are you?" again he reiterates, and the eager wild impatience, now almost awful, seems to leap forth from him, a sentient, separate thing! "Answer! and answer truly, as you will have to answer before the throne of God!"

Where are the mildness and meekness, which are the chief characteristics of the man? Never before has Graham caught a glimpse of that chord of passion that lies hidden in this sad, silent heart.

"Who am I?" and there is an accent of supreme self-pity, with a tinge of scorn, in Geoffrey's voice, as he makes reply to this adjuration. "Do you not know? Can you not guess? I am your thrice miserable son! The child whom you have ignored and virtually disowned."

An astonished, choking cry, almost a groan, breaks from the old man; but Geoffrey goes on unheeding. "Yes, disowned through life; for think you when she, an angel, a saint, aye! a saint and martyr, was repudiated, that *I* would——"

"*You my son! You*—my little Lion! It couldn't be. No, you mock me, and it is cruel—cruel. Lion, the little boy I loved so well—that *she* idolised. *You*?"

What a strange, heart-moving pathos there is in those vibrating, broken words; what a singular conflict is expressed in the doubting, half-believing, half-incredulous accents. An eager, yearning hunger that it should be even as the other says, contending with a horrible fear of being duped, deluded.

"*You* my son! how could it be?" he continues, in dreamy, quavering tones. "He was little Lion Dacre, and you are Geoffrey Graham. And yet the eyes—the eyes are like," peering with a sick, pitiful craving into the strong man's face. "And somehow I have felt all along since that first time I saw you as if—— I don't know what I have thought—could it be?—Lion, a little, little fellow, a weak, fragile child, and now—my son, a clever, powerful, handsome man. Ah, God, the flight of time! cruel, relentless, remorseless time, that hastens on with mocking, gibing strides, and never returns to give you back one little hour in which to atone for harsh words or harsher judgment, one hour for explanation, for reconciliation. No, Time is the inexorable, unfailing, deathless conqueror of all! Everything must go down before him, and——" Then he stops suddenly in his vague spoken reverie; his speech is incoherent, his wits are a little wandering from the shock he has sustained; he has almost forgotten his auditor. He pulls himself together with an effort, and fixing his eyes on Geoffrey with a sudden, searching austerity, he says slowly—

"Why do you call yourself my son? What is your motive? Do you speak the truth, or are you torturing me with revengeful mockery? I had a little son long ago. 'Lionel Dacre,' he was called. I know not whether he is living or dead."

" 'Lionel Geoffrey Dacre.' Do you forget the second name? The first and last were dropped as being too horrible reminders of a vanished past," interrupts Geoffrey, and his voice rings out now in clear and passionate cadence on the moonlit stillness. "She—whom I will not name here—she who was so horribly, heinously wronged in those by-gone years, but for whom it was reserved till *now* that she should be outraged indeed!" with an accent of scathing, fearful condemnation, and a stern, sweeping gesture towards the house, which utterly bewilders and perplexes poor Mr. Dacre, as we must now call him, who vainly struggles to grasp the meaning of this strange phrase and action. "She scorned to use the name of one who, with such deliberate, persistent cruelty, disowned and repudiated her, purest and most faithful of women! Oh, man! oh, man, you have in truth a heavy charge to your account, if you are indeed my father. And yet you don't seem conscious of your own wrong-doing. You look at me with wondering—I had almost said innocent eyes. I *am* your son, your most unhappy son; but if you only shadowed my youth, you have succeeded in blighting my manhood. Do you know what you have done? Great God!"—in passionate, despairing appeal—"that such a horror can be. That out of all the wide world *she*—and—*I*—should—love each other! If I had only known this frightful secret yesterday, before I spoke—but now——Ula—Ula—my—my—*sister!*"

His voice, though not loud, has a deep, penetrating intensity that seems to cleave the silent air, especially in the slow, shocked utterance of the last few words, charged with such a direful meaning. Then a great, rending sob bursts from the deep chest, and he drops his head in his hands.

There is a few minutes' soundless pause, nothing to break the perfect stillness, save the faint murmur of the waves far away below, and there is a deeper tone in their mystic voices than an hour ago; there is a note of an under-swell, that deep breath of the ocean, that always bodes ill. Then the old man, who has been during these few moments lost in a maze of troubled wonder and dismay, wildly striving to discover the meaning in Geoffrey's strangest words, and on whom it has suddenly burst with a blinding shock—then he breaks forth in weak, faltering tones, but though they tremble, and are scarcely above a whisper, there is a note of astonished relief, triumph, almost ecstasy in the broken accents.

"No! No! No! God for ever be thanked—*No*. Did you?—could you imagine such a monstrous thing? This is what has horrified you. Praise God for all His mercies—no! I may have been wrong, hard, cruel, if you will, but thank Heaven not vile. I am faithful, faithful unto death! Banish those fearful thoughts for ever. I tell you it is—No. Thank the Lord, not a sister—hideous supposition—but a cousin—only a cousin. If you are indeed my son, know that I have no other child than you!"

And with a gasp the old tremulous voice, that has both passion and pathos in its quavering tones ceases; but before Geoffrey can find words to express his wondrous amazement and intense, unspeakable gratitude for the extraordinary news just communicated; before he can ask aught of explanation, both men are startled by a strange, strangled cry close beside them.

While talking, they have insensibly approached somewhat

nearer to the house, and are now scarcely twenty yards from the entrance, standing on the cliff-path sideways to the house, and also to the continuation of the path beyond them; opposite to each other they stand, one facing seaward, the other towards Penmaer, and so engaged as they have been, were not in a position likely to notice any approach, whether from the right or left.

They now turn at the cry, and see Effie about half-way between them and the house, close to the cliff-edge, her face ghastly pale in the moonlight, the eyes staring, dilated, great, black, mystic pools in the white face. For a moment Geoffrey feels sure that she walks in her sleep, and makes a quick movement towards her, her position is so perilous! but the next instant his steps are arrested by her strange words.

"See!" she cries in hushed, awe-struck tones, with shadowy little hand outstretched. "She has come again, and for me! I know it's for me. Tell her I'll come by-and-by, but not yet. I can't leave Pops yet awhile." And there is an agonised pleading in these last words. Both men turn at once in the direction indicated by that tiny, pointing finger, but see nothing, though Geoffrey scans the whole moonlit stretch of cliff with piercing, searching gaze.

And then another cry, but this time a scream, wild, desperate, rings close on his ear, and turning his head in startled swiftness, he is just in time to see Effie vanishing over that terrible cliff-edge. In her terror at her fancied vision, she being only half awake, while the illness that is upon her confused and clogged her senses, she has backed over the edge of the familiar path into the awful void that lies beyond!

CHAPTER IV
SAVED!

GEOFFREY stands for a moment frozen with horror. The next, he is grappling wildly, desperately with Mr. Dacre, who has rushed frenzied to that fearful edge. The old man is frantic, mad for the moment. His brain has reeled under the succession of shocks he has received within the last half-hour, coupled with the grievous anxiety and nervous strain of the day. This last terrible thing is too much; reason totters, and he is unconscious of his acts.

Fiercely, maniacally, with the unnatural strength born of insanity, the weak old man struggles with Geoffrey, almost on the verge of that awful gulf, striving to plunge into its appalling depths; but the wrestle is but brief. In a few seconds the vice-like grasp relaxes, his head falls back. "Thank God, he has fainted!"

Geoffrey, whose powerful muscles are already somewhat strained from the fearful contest, draws him far in on the path and lays him gently down; then swiftly, but with a heart sick unto death, he turns once more to the brink of that ghastly precipice. Just at this point the cliff is especially steep, falling away in a sheer awful descent to the sea. To attempt to stand on the edge and look down into that giddy void is impossible in the present state of his nerves; so he flings himself upon his face as he nears the edge, and then draws himself forward an inch or two.

Ah! now he can see away down to that narrow strip of soft golden sand, misty and unreal in the moonlight, and—oh God! so terribly far below. Any creature going over there would be dead long before reaching the bottom. But—what is that object, three or four yards to the left, some fifteen feet below the surface? Great and merciful Father! it is the child!

He had mistaken the exact spot where she had disappeared. On a flat, smooth rock that slopes out from the face of the cliff at an angle of 45° or less, lies the little girl on her face . . . Oh! what a terrible, sickening slant, what a treacherous, slippery surface, a surface so smooth, an incline so great as to be capable of retaining nothing unless held there. But from a cleft between it and the rock adjoining, upsprings a thick tuft of a sturdy cliff plant, bearing a pinkish, purplish blossom, and almost by a miracle the child's right hand seized this as she fell, and it has stayed her so far . . . How long will those slender roots hold out? How long will those slight but tough stems bear the strain? The weight of her whole body is dependent on that handful of sea-shrub. Thank Heaven, but a light, fragile body, or it must snap at once . . . A few pretty, weak blossoms between a human soul and eternity!

The child's feet project over that shelving rock, but providentially only her feet; that sloping boulder bears her form; but if for an instant her instinctive, rigid grasp of that little insignificant plant be relaxed, over that slippery edge she will shoot like a stone into the abysmal depths below. Her left hand clutches convulsively at nothing. She neither looks up nor down; but God be thanked she is not unconscious! If insensibility steals upon her, her grasp will loosen, and——. No, not unconscious, for then again is that strange little shuddering, gasping cry, like the cry of a wounded bird, which had struck on Geoffrey's ear during those few moments of deadly conflict with the old man, and which had penetrated him with sick terror and anxiety to know its cause.

The child is half petrified, her faculties half benumbed by the hideous, inconceivable horror of her position, and she can only give those queer, fluttering, spasmodic cries which sound but half human. If he only could reassure her so that she could have courage and strength to hold on with all her might and all her senses for a few moments longer! So making a gigantic effort to still the breathless tremulousness of his voice and to speak in his natural, matter-of-course tones, he says softly, not to scare her with the sudden sound of his speech, but quite clearly so as to reach her easily:—(Oh God! the horror with which he utters those first common-place words, dreading the start, that would precipitate her into space!)

"Effie, darling, hold on tight with all your strength for another minute or two. I am coming down to you, pet; don't be a bit frightened, and keep your eyes close shut, dear. Recollect I am coming in a minute!"

And then, satisfied she hears and understands, as she makes a faint movement of her head as if in answer, he springs to his feet. This has taken long to tell, though scarcely three minutes have elapsed since the child went over that terrible edge, and the old man is still blessedly unconscious. Geoffrey dashes into the house.

"Rope! stout rope!—there has been an accident!" he cries, in breathless terseness, and receives the answer he expected from the scared women:—

"Nothing of the kind in the house!"

But he is prepared for this emergency. In an instant he has flown to one of the bed-rooms, and with one swift movement has whisked the sheets off the bed,—happily they are a large and strong pair,—and is out of the house again with a rush, calling to the servants to follow him.

Fortunately Nan Penlyon, with her brawny arms and vigorous, powerful frame, is on the spot. She is of a singularly robust and muscular build for a woman, and her strength is undoubted. Her ruddy, fresh colour is paled now, but otherwise, though startled and anxious, she has not lost her courage or presence of mind; and is ready to do exactly as she is told. In an incredibly short time Geoffrey has firmly knotted the sheets together and twisted them so as to make a strong useful rope of sufficient length. In another moment one end is secured round his waist.

Yes, this brave, good man is actually going down himself over that awful edge! Going to entrust his chances of life to these two ignorant women! Poor old Barbara, though tough and wiry, is not much to rely on; but Nan's wonderful strength he has heard of, and he sees her frame; so he is going to risk it to try to save the life of the little creature, between whom and himself he now knows there is a tie of blood, though what that tie is, he cannot yet quite determine.

Once again he flings himself on his face with a thrill at his heart lest his efforts are in vain. Thank God! the child has been able to hold out. She is still clinging madly, desperately to that tuft of sea-pink; but his shuddering ear fancies it can detect the straining and cracking of those slender rootlets.

"I am coming now, dear," he says, quite softly and encouragingly; and this time the head is slightly raised, and the great beseeching eyes gaze up at him through the moonlight with an agonised, despairing pleading in their half unconscious depths.

Not an instant is to be lost if he hopes to be in time. He has already given a few hurried directions to the horrified women; he now makes them lie down flat some little distance from the edge, and showing Nan a round, smooth rock to keep the sheet-rope over and that will help her much, he lets himself down out of their sight, and soon all Nan's energies, all her very being is concentrated in the one act of grasping at that tightening, swaying rope. How terrible a thing it is to think of Geoffrey Graham (as we must still call him), or any man of his physique—tall, with length of limb and breadth of shoulder, and though without an ounce of superfluous flesh on his bones, yet, from his height and muscular frame, weighing just twelve stone,—dangling at the end of a rope held by a woman!

But sturdy Cornish Nan is very different from her weaker town-bred sister. The hardy fisher-folk blood and endurance and staying power of generations, is in her, as well as her own fine muscular development; and though she has not graduated in our latter-day feminine gymnasiums, she is perhaps more "fit" than are many of our fair cricketers or the young women who practise the long and high jump, etc.

Geoffrey's position is even more perilous than those above, who have not looked over that fearful brink, can imagine. On the rock that bears the child, he could not rest for a moment, the incline is so great, the surface so smooth and polished. At first he could not think *how* he would manage; as to trust both himself and the child together to the rope and Nan's strength, he dare not; not altogether the fear of the extra weight, which is not very much, but in Nan's unpractised hands how might they not be dashed, and bruised, and jerked against the face of the cliff! Whereas if he can remain below he could guide the child's ascent, at least part of the way; and at any rate, even if she did get a knock or two, he would be quite certain of her reaching the top safely. And if *he* has to go down all the way to the bottom! Well, it's very horrible; hideously, awfully horrible. And the strong man's eyes close for a moment in a sick, terrible shrinking. Still he will have saved the child. The child the old man so idolizes, Ula's sister! Ula saved him. It will be a life for a life. And her father—no, *his* father . . . Ah! his thoughts are getting entangled and foggy, and he must keep his mind clear, quite clear, for what he has to do.

Just now when he looked down to encourage Effie before descending, he had noticed what escaped his observation before, that just a foot or two below the child, a few inches to her right, a strange pointed rock projected a little way from the face of the cliff. It was of most peculiar shape, that is if the moonlight, always rather misleading, revealed it clearly—not unlike a miniature house-roof, only more slanting; a sharp, level back-bone or centre, and the two sides falling away evenly and completely.

To get astride this rocky saddle Geoffrey feels is his only chance. Once perched on it, with his knees hugging its sloping sides, and his back pressed hard against the cliff-wall, there would be a foot or two, as well as he can calculate, of his granite steed in front of him. A truly awful position, overhanging those frightful depths below; the faintest slip or overbalancing being fatal. Still, so placed, he would have the advantage of being able to use both his hands. And so determining, he guides the swinging rope a little to one side, and reaches that jutting fragment of cliff, which very much realises his expectations. And now, by stretching out his right hand a little way, he can grasp poor Effie's slender arm, stiff and rigid from her death-like clutch on that stout little plant that has done so bravely its very best to help and save. Though now when released from her clasp it is evident that it, no more than she, could have held out much longer. Many, many of those tough little pink-blossomed stalks slide away down the face of the rock and over the edge, and are gone. While what remains of the tuft that had been so thick and luxuriant falls over, limp and dying; all the rootlets are not torn away as are those others, but the struggle was too great, and their life is slowly ebbing.

The human struggle too was very nearly at an end. Half a minute more, and Geoffrey would have been too late! Unconsciousness was stealing over the child, her muscles were all gradually relaxing, and just as Geoffrey's hand touches hers, with the sense of safety and protection, she slips into perfect oblivion. Unhappy little creature! such an experience would leave an indelible impression on any life; how will it mark and shadow hers?

Geoffrey feels very thankful for her insensibility, for it makes their position much less dangerous, and enables him to perform his terribly perilous, onerous task, with greater confidence and celerity. If the child were conscious, and saw the horror of the situation, she would shrink and tremble, might very possibly plunge and start, and thus would perhaps slay their chances of successful escape. As it is, the little girl is so light and fragile, she is almost like a doll in Geoff's strong arms, and he unfastens the sheet-rope from his own waist, and is about to secure it round her slender body, when it strikes him that, placed as he is, sitting, and not able to rise, having nothing in the world to stand on, he will not be able to guide her ascent even part of the way as he hoped. And she—light as the burden will be to Nan—in this unconscious state, unable to make any attempt to defend herself, may get terribly bruised and scratched, before reaching the top. He ponders for a moment or two, and then with great caution and extreme difficulty, he works himself out of his overcoat, which he happens to be wearing, the night feeling rather chill when he left "The Eyrie." In this he encases the child; it protects her beautifully, extending far below her feet; arms and hands, legs and feet, all are now pretty safe, except her face. All he can do for it, is to knot a large silk handkerchief of his own, folded in three or four across it, leaving it hanging loose over the mouth, so as not to impede the breath; and then he has done his best for her and must trust the rest to Providence.

Having made the rope secure, he shouts, which is the preconcerted signal for Nan to draw up; but before he lets go, he takes the precaution to fasten the end of a little ball of twine, which by a strange, happy chance, he finds in one of his pockets, to the end of the sheet, else, as he thinks, Nan might have let down the rope a dozen times, and failed to hit the exact spot where he is prisoned, and from which he dare not, cannot move. Then, in spite of the terrible danger of his position—the slightest overbalancing to either side meaning hideous, mangled death!—he rises a little way in his rocky saddle, balancing his back against the cliff, and with upraised arms (and upturned eyes, as he dare not for a moment glance below, though at that very instant he fancies he heard the plash of oars apparently proceeding from the little sheltered cove where Ula keeps her boat) guides for a few feet at least the rope and its burden, that is being slowly and carefully hauled in.

How immeasurably, indescribably thankful he feels, when his anxious, straining eyes see it reach the top in safety and disappear from his gaze. Words are quite inadequate to express his gratitude, though still the awful doubt remains whether Nan unaided will be able to lift *him* up to life and safety, or whether, when he is just half way perhaps, there will be a sudden, terrible jerk,—clutch,—slip,—of that weighted rope—and then—an awful sense of falling, rushing into void—and—*nothing*, any more—for ever! But even with this fearful possibility before his solemn outlooking eyes, he can rejoice and give thanks for the deliverance that he has been made the agent of.

The curlews are screaming and circling far out to sea; their wild, melancholy notes, softened by distance,—some with almost a human wail of distress in the mournful cry—seem to him like a chant of sorrow at the coming disaster. Bah! what hysterical fancies! There is a tempest brewing somewhere, beyond these lines of lovely light, stretching away to the horizon, and the storm-birds know it, and shriek and lament as is their wont; or, a still more commonplace reading—they are on their way to their feeding-ground, three or four miles further down the coast, where there are great mud-banks in a sheltered creek, and thus lessen the tedium of their journey by those dismal cries.

How strangely, awfully lonely, it seems here, set against the face of the cliff, though it is but a few feet down, from life, and hope, and love. No sound, no sight, no movement reaches him from the living, save those circling, distant birds; it is as if he were alone, in a new, awful world, holding only sea and sky. Is it not so in the grave? only a few—pathetically few—feet down below that warm, moving human thing, we call "life;" and yet—what a horrible, impassable barrier, set between the surface and those sleeping ones beneath, who hold no link, as he does, that frail little cord in his hand, to connect them with the world of men. No link? Hold they not the imperishable link that joins them, not to earth, but to the eternal heavens, the link of the sleeping, but immortal soul? And as he so thinks with a strange impersonal dreaminess, the link in his hand grows slack, and looking up, he sees the sheet-rope descending. Then with a swift rush back to the terrible actuality of his present position, he makes it secure round him once more, and committing himself to the All Merciful in a breath of fervent, silent prayer, he sways out on the moonlit air, in helpless, piteous dependence on Nan Penlyon's brawny arms.

And in that first moment, as he hangs suspended over that awful gulf, he thinks how mad he has been, not to try to let them know above, that he could have managed to stick on to that rock,—especially by keeping his eyes shut—for half-an-hour or so, while they got help from "The Eyrie." But most likely they could not have heard him, at least to understand properly, as the voice of the sea has gradually increased in volume, and there is a dull, ominous sound in the boom with which it breaks far below, and the deep sucking rush of the backwater. And then—the next moment, all his feelings are condensed into a great gratitude and surprise, as he feels himself drawn quickly and skilfully up the cliff without jerk or slip; and as, with a heart overflowing with infinite thanksgiving, he steps over that fearful edge into life and safety, he sees the reason for his safe and rapid ascent.

Mr. Dacre had recovered from his swoon just in time to see Effie hauled up at the end of that impromptu rope. In one swift rush of thought he remembered all, and flew to the child and ascertained in one intensely suspenseful moment that she breathed, that no bones were broken, that she was apparently uninjured, neither cut nor bruised, save a scratch on the chin, bleeding a little, which she got as she was being drawn up; then in a passion of gratitude and joy, he turned to that rope, and a portion of the singular, unnatural strength, that had animated his half-unconscious conflict with Graham, returned, and his skill assisting Nan's muscles, soon rescued Geoffrey from those ghastly depths. And as the two men clasp hands in speechless emotion, both instinctively drop upon their knees, and bow their heads, in mute, inarticulate prayer and praise.

And thus, father and son are reunited by a bond stronger even than blood—the bond of an undying gratitude. For has not Geoffrey rescued the child, the darling of the old man's heart, from a violent, hideous death, at the imminent risk of his own life?

and besides, has he not saved that old life from self-destruction, in the first paroxysm of a desperate horror? And now the old man has done his best to help to save him; and though plucky Nan may have been the chief agent, yet still, there was the intention, and her efforts were decidedly supplemented by his skill.

CHAPTER V

BURIED IN THE "GREAT LONE LAND"

A LITTLE later, and Effie is in bed, and has fallen into a death-like sleep; so profoundly still and motionless is the usually restless child, that one can only know that she breathes by bending low over the tiny form, which is almost awful in its strange stirlessness and unfamiliar calm. It is the sleep of exhaustion, after the terrific strain on the fragile, nervous frame, of those few horrible, never-to-be-forgotten minutes, of convulsive desperate clutching, on that slanting rock.

Geoffrey gazing at her, finds himself wondering with a pang, will she ever wake again? Somehow it is hard to imagine that marble little face wrapped in such almost weird repose, coming back to everyday life and ways. How much easier to fancy her slipping from sleep into death, without ever even lifting those heavy ebon lashes, that lie in such a thick shadowing fringe on the colourless cheek. But he says nothing of his ill-omened thoughts to Mr. Dacre, who is so rejoiced to find the little creature apparently totally, and marvellously, uninjured, with the exception of a strained and swollen wrist, from that rigid grasp, that he is almost unconscious of her singular quietude, or the ghastly pallor of the small drawn face.

And while they watch by her, in the shadowed room, waiting for Dr. Wenvoe, and after Barbara has gone downstairs to prepare some supper for Geoff, of which he stands somewhat in need after his late exertions, he hears, in a few whispered broken sentences, from Mr. Dacre, the brief life-story of the girls—apparently his daughters, and who are in all things the same to him, as his own children—Ula and Effie Ferguson.

They are the orphan daughters of his only, and dearly-loved sister; that sister to whom allusion was made in an earlier chapter, as being Lionel Dacre's only other earthly tie; and whom, when deserted and abandoned, as he supposed, by his wife, two and twenty years ago, he had joined, and they had wandered away together, into the extreme north of Scotland, as he then desired to put as long a distance as possible, within the kingdom, between his present whereabouts and his former home; and it was into those Northern Highlands young Lonhed had penetrated, with that letter which he saw burnt before his eyes, while a great indignation swelled his heart; that letter which explained the mystery of Helen Dacre's disappearance.

Mr. Dacre's sister was, at that time, a childless widow; but in two or three years she married again in those Scottish wilds; married a captain in the Navy, who was just home from the coast of Africa, where his vessel had been stationed nearly five years. He determined it should be his last cruise but one. Once more he would command his frigate when orders came, and then he would retire. For better than three years, as it happened, after his marriage he was almost altogether at home. Then the orders came, and he was off to Chinese waters, leaving his beloved wife, and his little daughter, just two years old, safe in the protection of her brother, whom he loved as his own, a great affection having sprung up between the men, based on strong mutual respect. But he was not long away this time. Little more than two years elapsed, when he was home again, for good, as he intended. He notified to the Admiralty his desire to retire from the service, and a few months passed happily away, when an urgent request came that he would command a North Pole exploring expedition, to start almost immediately, and to none would the Captainship with greater confidence and security be entrusted, than to himself.

It was a compliment; and besides, was a thing he had long wished for. He had an intense yearning to explore those strange northern seas, and never yet had had the chance. They would be absent but a few months, eight or ten he thought at the most; and so, in spite of his wife's earnest entreaties, he consented to lead the Expedition northwards, into the "Great Lone Land."

Ula was not quite five years old when her father kissed her for the last time; not an age to retain very strong impressions, and he had been home but a few months, having been away more than two years out of her baby life. Six months after the day he started came the sad news to that wild Scottish home, that we was dead. That all who had set out in that northern-bound vessel, commanded by the brave, skilful, faithful officer, Captain Hugh Ferguson, of the Royal Navy, had perished miserably; save two men, who had greater powers of endurance than the others, and were picked up in an insensible, dying condition, from off a floating gigantic iceberg, many, many miles from where the unfortunate vessel had foundered amidst the ice floes.

What terrible sufferings the exploring party had endured before the release came! Bereft of the comfort and shelter of the ship, in that region of fearful, unimaginable cold—except by those who have experienced it—on those trackless ice-fields! One by one had been left behind; awful, frozen figures on those white desolate wastes. Ghastly to imagine their continuing so, unchanged (being petrified), immovable, through the years, perhaps the centuries. They had wandered far from all beaten tracks, all known regions, having lost all guides, in the way of charts, compasses, &c., with the vessel; and consequently might elude discovery for ages. Truly death's very kingdom, and these—its occupants. And so, the noble, good Hugh Ferguson, after trying his best to sustain and cheer the others, through indescribable sufferings, lay himself down at last, on his cold, cold bed, and perchance, is lying there still, looking as he looked in his last hour of life.

On the evening of the day that brought this direful news to the Scottish home, Effie was born, and both mother and child were despaired of, but the infant, though so weakly and fragile, with scarcely a perceptible hold on life, struggled on and lived; the mother lingered for three months, and then went to join him whose body lay on that distant ice-field, her last prayer being to her brother to be a father to her orphan children. But that prayer was not needed. Mr. Dacre's very life was bound up in the two helpless little creatures; they were all in the world he had to live or car for then.

It was during the first two or three years of his sister's second married life that he had instituted those inquiries with regard to his wife which, as we know, resulted in failure, being urged thereto partly by his brother-in-law, as Hugh Ferguson was one of those persons, who finding it almost impossible to think ill of any one, felt that perhaps Mrs. Dacre was an innocent and suffering woman; and partly by that horrible insidious doubt, or remorseful suspicion, that possibly he had been too hasty in his condemnation, too obdurate in his refusal to receive any explanation, that had first pierced him with a momentary sting, after young Lonhed's departure. However, when he inquired he heard nothing. The money was never claimed. He was alone in the world, his wife having chosen to deprive him of his son, so all the pent-up love of his heart was poured out on his orphan nieces; and when a year or so later, they were compelled for the infant's sake to seek a milder, more southern climate, he allowed himself to be known as Mr. Ferguson, the supposed father of the children.

He was glad thus to sink his own identity. His very name was hateful to him; and the children really knew no other father; for though Ula cherished a passionate love for her dead mother—which was really more sentiment than actual recollection—yet of her father, memory held no trace. He went away when she was two years old, and during those few months he was home again, when she was in her fifth year, he was a stranger to her; whereas "Unkie," as her baby tongue dubbed him, was always there, Mr. Dacre having lived with Hugh and his wife since their marriage. So "Unkie" easily glided by-and-by into "Pops," as Effie's earliest speech christened him, and the two names meant the one dear thing—"father," in the eldest child's mind. No one was in the secret, except old Barbara Jephson, who had been in Mrs. Ferguson's service during her first marriage, and had loved her, and followed her to her Northern home. She knew the sad story of her mistress's brother's life, nothing was kept from her, she was faithful and true, and she loved and pitied, and respected him also, and thought it only quite right and natural that the children should be brought up to regard him as their father; he had been really a father to them, devoted and self-sacrificing, and why should he not have a father's love? she argued to herself. And so, the girls had never yet been undeceived.

Mr. Dacre had always intended to tell Ula, when she came of age, he declares now to Geoffrey, with a nervous deprecation of manner, as if excusing himself for the deception, that just escaped bearing most bitter fruit. Yes, when she came of age he would tell her, as there was some small—very small—property of her father's coming to her. But it is much to be doubted whether, if the extraordinary fatality, coincidence, call it what we may, of his son Geoffrey's turning up in the singular manner he did, and the attendant complication of circumstances had not occurred, that he would ever have had the courage to do so. If he could have borne to reveal the truth to the elder girl—and it would have been hard, very hard, to lose the first place in her love and thoughts—how could he have endured that the little one, who was all his own, to whom he had been father, and mother, and everything, whom he has guarded and loved, and watched with fostering, idolatrous care, from her earliest, helpless infancy, and to whom he was all the world; how could he have borne that she should regard him as something like an impostor, as he in his sensitiveness thought he should appear in the child's eyes, some one who had won her passionate affection by a fraud? and that her own real "Pops" was far away in heaven all the time.

Geoffrey listens to the halting, broken tale with intense, wondering interest, while a great, overwhelming joy and thanksgiving surges in his breast. His cousin! Thank God! his cousin. His sweet and lovely cousin, whom he is privileged to love and marry. Does it not seem the very hand of God that has sent him thither? He has found his father and his cousins at one stroke, and his cousins are lonely and desolate, save for that frail old man. Their father was an only child, and so they have no relatives on his side.

How sweet to think that they have only him and his, that his father has been his darling's best and life-long friend. That he has a right to love, and cherish, and protect that beautiful young creature, quite apart from his claims as a lover. Yes, it is all gladness and rejoicing in his heart to-night, mingled with a great astonishment. His attitude of antagonism and passionate, righteous resentment towards his father, which has been his life-companion, and which was so strong and burning an hour or so ago, has fallen away for ever. He has been strangely and instinctively drawn to the old man from the first; the same mysterious attraction, against which the latter struggled, but found irresistible, laid its magnetic touch upon the son. He remembers the singular impression, of which he had been conscious on several occasions, of mentally searching for some link between this late present and the misty past. The mystic affinity of blood had thus declared itself, the puzzle is now solved; and for the first time in his life his mother's wrongs are forgotten, or at least, have grown dim and blurred, and he forgets to think and wonder how the events of the night will affect her.

* * * * * *

It is just ten o'clock before Dr. Wenvoe arrives. He is some time examining the child, and he hardly credits that she could have escaped quite uninjured from the fall; but he soon discovers that there is neither breakage nor dislocation, and as far as he can ascertain, no internal damage, only a few bruises; but what he fears, as he says to Geoffrey downstairs, before the old man joins them, is the shock to the system; the little girl is of a peculiarly nervous, highly-strung temperament, besides having a very fragile body; she was also ailing those few days, evidently sickening for the low fever, so prevalent just then in the village. The fever is harmless enough in itself, still, all combined—and he shakes his head ominously, as Mr. Dacre's step sounds in the hall.

Ten minutes later, as the three men are anxiously discussing the child's fall and its probable consequences, Dr. Wenvoe trying his best to hide his gloomy anticipations from the old man, and just as the latter is dilating, with flushing cheek and kindling eye, on Geoffrey's noble bravery, his ready resource, and wonderful presence of mind, there bursts in upon them, pale and panting, a servant from "The Eyrie." The girl has run all the way, and is so breathless, that for a moment or two she cannot speak to make herself understood, but they see at a glance that something is gravely wrong, and Geoffrey, with a strange, instinctive fore-knowledge, moves towards her, feeling that the message is for him. Then she gasps forth—

"I've come for you, sir; Mrs. Graham, the dear lady, is took as one for death. God forgive me for saying it to scare you, sir, but I am that upset. Mrs. Benghaus got home unexpected an hour ago, and came on the poor, unthinking lady in the dining-room, where she was dozing all alone; and then Benghaus went sudden mad-like, raving and crying, and screeching to be forgiven. Them furriners is little better than savages when all's told. An' me, an' the missus, an' cook, ran in, but she went on jabberin' like one possessed, German, an' French, an' silly English all mixed up together, till one was fairly moidered, an' could make out nothin', only that 'twas about some letter long, long ago, that she did something wrong about, an' made your blessed mother suffer; and there was a Marquis in it, too, that made Benghaus do the wrong, whatever it was; an' then, after lookin' white an' awful, Mrs. Graham clapped her hand over her heart, an'——"

But before the excited creature can get further, Geoffrey has seized his hat, and is striding to the door.

"I am coming with you," cries the doctor, hurrying after him, as he mutters to himself, "I guessed the heart was wrong when I looked at her to-day. That bluish line round the lips, and that peculiar appearance of the pupil generally tell their own tale. But if it's as I think, it's rare, and always fatal. Poor fellow!" compassionately gazing away to Geoffrey's swiftly striding figure much in advance. "It will be a bitter cup for him, and one, I fear, he will be compelled to drink within a very few hours."

*　　*　　*　　*　　*　　*

And the long night falls upon the Cliff House, and the old man watches in terrible distraction of mind—torn by so many agonizing sad and conflicting thoughts—by that marvellously quaint little sleeper. The long night that holds storm and tempest in its angry bosom, and the wild winds rave and shriek about the house in clamorous wrath, and the fierce waters swirl, and lash, and roar, like frantic, leaping creatures, down away there in the darkness; a deafening tumult appears to reign without, and still the little one in that quiet room sleeps the sleep of exhaustion, though occasionally, as the hours glide on toward morning, there are faint murmurs of wandering speech. And still, as the hours speed by, though none think of lying down, Barbara being constantly up-and-down stairs, while Nan remains awake and alert in the kitchen, nobody seems to miss or think of Ula; or if they do, they conclude, as a matter of course, that she has remained at "The Eyrie," owing to Mrs. Graham's sudden seizure.

CHAPTER VI

"NUNC DIMITTIS"[65]

MADGE Fanshawe is in a state of wild alarm and feverish expectation when Dr. Wenvoe arrives, for after all he is the first to enter the house, Geoffrey's heart failing him to cross the threshold when he reached it a few minutes earlier.

Mrs. Graham's condition remains the same, and both Madge and her husband are really frightened. After a slight examination, the doctor scribbles a few lines in pencil, which he begs Captain Fanshawe to allow one of his men to take at once to Bodmin. It is to the best doctor there; for small as the place is, it can boast at least one really clever physician, and a man, as luck would have it, especially skilled in cardiac affections. Also he scratches a line to a chemist for a particular, powerful drug that he does not keep by him, occasion for its use being so rare and exceptional. And then he can do no more. The patient will remain in that trance-like state for hours; in fact, it is a sort of cataleptic sleep, from which it is more than probable she will never regain consciousness without the aid of that intensely potent restorative, and even with its help it is problematical whether she will ever speak again, or whether the spirit will pass from that awfully rigid form—which seems as if it were bound in iron bonds—without a sign.

Before one o'clock the Bodmin doctor arrives with Simpson, the chief coastguard man, who had galloped all the way—and the drug. He and Dr. Wenvoe administer it very cautiously and with

---

65 *Nunc dimittis*: Now lettest thou depart, from the Song of Simeon, a canticle taken from the second chapter of the Gospel of St. Luke.

much difficulty, owing to those rigidly-locked teeth and lips; it is tremendously powerful, and an overdose might prove instantly fatal.

They try all other remedies known to modern medical science (even venturing on the electric current) as likely to restore suspended animation, anything that might possibly bring back life and consciousness for a transient hour before both are drowned for ever in death's dark waters. But that awful iron-locked frame resists all their most strenuous efforts. That cataleptic living death remains unbroken, unchanged through the long hours of the tumultuous night.

The storm raves and rages, but it wakes not these two sleepers at the Cliff House and at "The Eyrie." At last, about seven o'clock, when the wind has fallen, and the sun is sending long slant streaks of red and golden glory over the tossing, leaping, still passionate waters, after the watching, anxious doctors, with much hesitation and grave fears for the result, have given a third dose of that fearfully potent medicine, there are signs that it is taking effect. The limbs relax, the whole frame softens and grows life-like, while a faint warmth diffuses itself through the ice-cold body, the eyeballs revert to their ordinary axes, the stiffened jaws and teeth, so grimly locked, drop slightly apart, a look of life—though swiftly-ebbing life—and rest comes into the still unconscious face, as from the cataleptic trance the patient passes, without waking, into natural, exhausted sleep.

The doctors are now satisfied, and thankful that all has gone so well. They have done all that lay in their power to do. That sleep will last six or eight hours, perhaps more; when the patient wakes she will be conscious, though possibly too weak to speak, but virtually, she will wake only to die. It is a mere question of time; perhaps only a few minutes of breathing, conscious existence, and then the end, softly and gently reached, not as through the iron prison-house of that terrific catalepsy. Perhaps a few hours, possibly a day or two, but this is the outside limit. Stimulants in small portions must be administered frequently during the period of sleep, to prevent that sleep gliding into death; also perfect quiet must be maintained. But these directions are simple and easily followed, and Madge and Geoffrey are loving, faithful watchers. And so the wearied doctors leave; after their long night's vigil they can now do no more. Dr. Wenvoe, of course, will return in a few hours, but the Bodmin physician needs not to come again. On their way to the village they are to go to the Cliff House, as more than an hour ago Nan Penlyon, who had been sent two or three times through the night to make enquiries for Mrs. Graham, came again to ask one of the doctors to come as soon as he could, as Miss Effie was quite delirious and seemed very weak.

And so Geoffrey and Madge keep watch through the bright morning hours, the latter having prevailed on Captain Fanshawe—who had been wandering from room to room, miserable and unhappy through the long night—to lie down for an hour or two. Geoffrey tries to induce Madge to take some rest also, but she will not hear of it. When her dear old friend comes back to that transient gleam of life and consciousness then she will leave mother and son alone together, but not before. And so they sit in the shadowed room, occasionally speaking a few words in whispers, and all is very still and silent round them, save for the lingering traces of the night's storm heard in the voices of the waves, as they rush in excitedly telling of the terrible things they have seen and heard through the darkness, out away beyond that distant sky-line.

And still here, as well as in her own home, no on seems to miss Ula, or wonder at her absence—or rather, as at the Cliff House, they believe she is at "The Eyrie;" here at "The Eyrie" they imagine her safely at home. Madge missed her some time before Benghaus' arrival; she noticed that the girl's hat and her own muffling shawl had vanished from the drawing-room, and she felt sure she had gone home, and that then Effie's illness and accident, which Mrs. Fanshawe had heard of in a few words from Dr. Wenvoe, prevented her from returning, as she would have been sure to do on hearing of Mrs. Graham's fearful attack. And thus the girl's non-appearance in either house is quite satisfactorily accounted for by the inmates.

Dr. Wenvoe returns at twelve, but there is as yet no change; the weary soul is still sunk in its last earthly sleep. But about two o'clock there is a soft flutter over the ashen face, a quiver of the eyelids, a sigh, and then, in another moment, the eyes open and gaze straight into her son's face, who is bending over her, with perfect consciousness in their mournful depths. The white lips move, and the one word, "Geoffrey," is breathed in a whisper so faint as to be only heard by stooping low over the face. Then a look of sweet, restful content gleams in the tired eyes, and they close again slowly; but suddenly, after a moment or two's pause, a convulsive thrill as of fear or agitation passes over the entire frame, there is a struggling effort to sit up, a horrible endeavour to speak, memory has evidently reasserted itself, and that scene before her seizure has returned in full force.

Again that effort so painful, so pathetic, and at last the unconnected words burst out in agonised, unfamiliar tones, "That woman said he—your *father*—Ula—*sister*—my poor Geoff!" And there is a look of frightful appeal in the wild, questioning eyes, imploring to be told—trying so desperately to take the duty of the impotent lips.

And here once more, "in the very hour of death," the loving, selfish, self-abnegating mother-soul declares itself. She thinks not, in this supreme moment, of her own blighted, ruined life, of her sorrows, of her wrongs—wrongs so much more deadly if that hateful thing be true. She thinks only of her boy, her beloved son's happiness, his shock ad terrible disappointment about the girl she knows he loves so passionately.

Those three little words, so loving, simple, tender—"my poor Geoff!"—have an intensity of pathos as thus uttered by the weak, struggling creature, who has already entered "the valley of the Shadow," and will soon be plunged in its thickest darkness, but yet who looks back from that lonely, mystic gloom, with straining, yearning eyes, longing only to pity, and comfort, and help the strong, vigorous man who bends above her full in the clear shining light of life. Such beauteous, perfect selflessness, is surely only reached by parental love.

But Geoffrey is quick to see the superlative intensity of affection that speaks in the broken utterance. It is the shock of that terrible fact that she knows will blight his hopes, that has struck her down. It is of this one thing only that the eager, sunken eyes plead with such passionate muteness to be told. And so, with his strong arm supporting the trembling form, and the weary, dying head upon his broad breast, he softly, but clearly and quickly, tells her the story he has so lately heard, and thanks God dumbly at the same time that he has it in his power thus to make her last earthly moments sweeter and calmer. Though she can speak but a word or two at long intervals, and that hardly more than whispered, she can hear and understand everything, and seems happy, peaceful, and at rest, lying thus encircled by his arms, and listening to the voice that is her sweetest music.

Madge slipped quietly from the room when they began to speak, and for a couple of hours, mother and son are more to each other, and nearer to each other, than they have ever been through life. Geoffrey with wonderful sternness and fortitude, and infinite self-command, stifles and crushes the grief that is tearing his very heart strings, smothers all signs of distress and emotion, and bends his whole energies to solace and soothe these all too-swiftly speeding minutes.

Somewhere about five o'clock, when the sun is sinking rapidly toward the West in the lovely October sky, Mrs. Graham, who has been lying very quietly for some time, with eyes closed, but not sleeping, as is evident from the soft, continuous stroking of Geoff's strong, brown hand, which is trembling clasped between her two white and wasted ones, breathes a few words, apparently in answer to some request of his, that must have been made a while ago, as the voices have been silent in that spacious, pretty room, now, for more than half-an-hour. It is but a very little sentence—"Let him come if he will," but it is enough to tell Geoffrey that the permission he desires is granted. He gently kisses the grey, sunken face, and leaves the room for a few minutes, but soon returns, and takes up his old position; and another half-hour or so glides on, a half-hour of that most precious intercourse, so close, so perfect, so supremely comforting to both, that almost takes the sting from death for one, and will be such a help and solacing memory to the lonely man by-and-by. And then, the woman whispers again, after much else has gone before, in little weak, broken snatches from those pallid lips—"Why doesn't she come? I want to see, and kiss, and bless her."

"Yes, dear, after him," murmurs the son, stooping low over her, so as to hide the extra stab of sharp, fresh pain, that flits across his haggard pitifully-altered face, at her words. Yes, why does she not come? It is what he has been asking himself for hours, while his heart has been growing sorer and sorer; and struggling with the feeling of sorrowful surprise and keen disappointment, there is now rising a sense of resentment.

His mother, whom she appeared to like—nay, to love, lying at the point of death, her time now almost measured by moments. *His* mother—and yet she does not come. What though Effie is ill, a little feverish and wandering; what of that? that should not prevent her coming, even for a brief half-hour. And it is not that they do not know the fatal, terrible nature of the attack. Dr. Wenvoe of course spoke when he went back for his horse last night, and besides, there was proof of their knowledge of dangerous, alarming illness, in the fact of Nan Penlyon being sent two or three times through the night, in the fearful storm, to hear how matters went. That was an unusual occurrence—very, and yet, all those lovely hours of daylight gone, and evening beginning to approach, and no sign from the girl, who he thought would be plunged in almost as great distress as himself, at this sudden, awful sorrow, which had come upon him without the slightest warning.

Then, hearing a distant sound as of an arrival, he stoops down once more and kisses that stricken face, over which the unmistakable grey shadow of the end is already stealing. The yearning eyes seek his with infinite, unquenchable love in their saddest depths, and the weak, faltering voice speaks once more—"It is only for a very little while, my Geoff.—I see now more clearly, as I draw so near the brink, and it is all so good—so good!—Fear has fallen quite away, and I feel only a great rest, a divine content. Don't grieve for me, my dearest." As she sees the great tears well slowly in his eyes, that with all his efforts he cannot force back to their source—"It is well with me, most well.—My only sorrow is leaving you behind, my son,—but the time will seem so short,—till you join me on that shore—that I see already dimly; and in the meantime, my Geoff,—you will be happy, thank God for all His mercy! happy with her,—and I am spared that dreadful grief, that would have robbed Heaven of its joy.—God for ever bless and keep you, my darling!—And that He may give you in the fulness of time, the one great priceless blessing—that has been my very life—a child's love, and devotion, and tender care and sympathy, is the last—and dying prayer—of your passionately loving mother . . . Go now, dear—I would see him alone. Give me the packet—with my own hands; yes—my dying hands . . . But, ah! I need not care now—*she*—'Rosalie'—can tell him—she is sorry for her terrible sin." And in another moment Geoffrey creeps almost blindly from the room, closing the door softly behind him.

* * * * * *

For a few minutes there is unbroken silence in that chamber of the dying, and the face on the pillow grows greyer, the yearning, expectant eyes dull and close, and the worn fingers relax their tight, tremulous grasp of that small roll of manuscript. A look of unconsciousness steals over the face. Is it sleep, or faintness? Surely not death yet awhile? . . . And then just at this juncture the handle of the door communicating with the stairs turns noiselessly, and a man slowly, nervously, steps softly into the room with hesitating movement.

It is he whom we have known as Mr. Ferguson, the white-haired, white-bearded old master of the Cliff House, but whom we must now recognize as Mr. Dacre, the husband of her who lies stretched upon her dying bed . . . The story of these two lives is nearly told—the sad, unhappy drama is almost played out. That trembling, snowy-haired old man, with the deep lines of mental anguish, of an eternal sorrow and remorse graven on his brow—the handsome, hopeful, vigorous Lionel Dacre, not quite forty years old, of the Paris episode. That shrunken, ashen-faced woman on the bed, with premature age, and terrible lifelong grief and wrong written in indelible marks upon her dying face—the bright, beautiful, bewitching Helen Dacre of the same period, who was as good as the angels above her, and yet this—her fate. *Eheu fugaces!* After two and twenty years they meet thus.

*   *   *   *   *   *

And as the old man meets the long, mournful, infinitely reproachful gaze of those violet eyes, he gives a great and exceeding bitter cry, he hears his own voice ringing through the silence—"Helen, forgive! forgive!" And then he is on his knees beside the bed, with head buried in the coverlet, while a voice, like a faint, far echo of those distant years, vibrates near him in halting, broken accents.

"Lionel, my husband—I forgive. I know now, what I never guessed before, the strong and terrible reasons you had for your obduracy. The evidence was *too* convincing—it would have required a perfect faith—to have resisted it," with a pathetic little smile. "A weak—or wavering—spirit would have no chance against it." This was the only little sting of reproach, surely not a very cruel one.

"I thank my God—for allowing me to know—before it was too late for—that sweetest and most divine thing—forgiveness. Though, even without knowing, surely none can come to lie as I lie now, without feeling in their hearts that they freely forgive—all who have ever injured them."

The weak, failing voice dies away in a soundless whisper, and she points with trembling finger to the restorative that Geoffrey has constantly administered, and which, in fact, has kept the ebbing life from going completely out. It gives a new little gleam of transient strength, but on the remainder of that interview between these two—who have been separated for half a lifetime, but who were all the world to each other in the distant years, and who now meet at last "in the hour of death," for one, in the very "Valley of the Shadow"—we will draw a veil; it is too sacred for indifferent or alien eyes.

Nearly an hour has passed away, and Geoffrey, who waits in an adjoining room, has heard the continual murmur of the voices during that time, chiefly the deep yet low-breathed accents of the man's tones. But now, for the last ten minutes, profound silence has reigned beyond that closed door, and Geoffrey's heart beats, and his pulses throb, as with his nerves all one jarring, trembling pain, he strains his ear to catch the faintest whisper of sound, and strains in vain. All this long sixty minutes he has chafed terribly at being shut out from that inner chamber. Although it was principally by his own effort and expressed wish that that interview has taken place, yet it was more from a sense of duty, a feeling that it was right, that he sought to promote it, than actual personal desire, and he is deeply, mournfully jealous, struggle as he will against it, that those last precious moments should be divided with another, even though that other—at least in different circumstances—would have, perhaps, a higher, stronger claim to them than he had. He grudges each minute that he has to stand aside for any one else. Yet the noble, generous heart, though he knew he would feel thus, summoned the old man to that meeting, that is also a parting.

* * * * * *

But how strangely silent it is! Even if his beloved mother has grown too weak for further utterance, that would not prevent *his* speaking, unless—and a horrible sinking, or rather frightened drop of the heart, comes with the thought, and yet it seems so natural a one,—unless she has suddenly fallen asleep, and that he dreads to make stir or movement that might rouse her. He (Geoffrey) cannot bear this soul-sickening suspense longer. It is but a few minutes that he has strained his very being to try to catch the merest breath or echo of life within that room. But it seems to him hours—ages, as if all existence had come to an end, and that he alone remained, living, fearing, waiting, in a soundless void, with that tumultuous heart-throb in his throat, while all around has attained the most blissful state for all created things—the beatific haven of unconsciousness.

In another moment his hand is on the door. He softly turns the handle, and steps swiftly, soundlessly, across the threshold. There is a brief, breathless pause as he stands there, his tall, strong form swaying as if met by a pitiless, powerful blast, and then—a rush of awful agonised sorrow and lament reverberates through the room, which has indeed become the chamber of death! For even as that shadowy hand was outstretched in blessing on the head of him who blighted that lovely, loving life in its joyous, brilliant noon, by want of a patient, perfect faith, that should have rejected aught of circumstantial evidence, however startling, however incontrovertible, in the face of what that life and love had been; rejected all, until those lips had confessed with their own breath that they had been false. But even as that trembling hand lay in sweet, pardoning blessing on the bowed head, while still the words of almost a divine forgiveness hung upon the pale lips, the gentle, patient spirit winged its way to its eternal home, and Helen Dacre had entered into her rest.

But he who kneels there with the dead fingers resting on his white hair realises it not. He is sunk in a trance of rapturous gratitude, of joy ineffable; and when Geoffrey's burst of ungovernable, terrible grief, rouses him somewhat to outer things, he raises his head vaguely, with an ecstatic, visionary look in the dark, sad eyes.

"She has blessed me, even me also," he mutters, and then, half unconsciously, in rapt, tremulous tones he breathes the opening words of the "Nunc Dimittis," with still that far-away look in the old, worn face, and Simeon's song seems in no way irreverent at that moment from those quivering lips.

CHAPTER VII
ABNEGATION

AND still no one speaks of Ula. The old man has forgotten her; forgotten even Effie, in the flood of strange, exalted, overwhelming emotion that has been his for the last hour. And Geoffrey, though he dumbly feels that his intolerable pain is intensified by the girl's persistent, incomprehensible absence, yet he says no word in betrayal of his sore amaze. While Madge, who feels bewildered and mystified, thinks the girl's non-appearance very strange and unaccountable, but feels that perhaps it is much for the best, in the very peculiar and miserable circumstances which she thinks exist, knowing nothing of the real facts of the story, save from the extraordinary, incoherent statement, or rather confession, made by the woman Benghaus, really, by a remarkable coincidence, the Rosalie of the Paris episode.

So Ula's most singular disappearance still remains unexplained, unknown to those who love her so passionately; while the feeling of a dull, grieved resentment grows mutely stronger in Geoffrey's breast as he remembers that *she* asked for the girl, wished for her, and she came not, and now—it is too late!

* * * * * *

But a mile away, at St. Olave's Vicarage, a note came, two or three hours ago, to the Rev. Mark Temple, who resides with the vicar, they being distantly connected,—a blundering, ill-spelt, somewhat incoherent note, from a squalid little fishing village some twelve or fourteen miles down the coast; a wretched little hamlet, consisting of about a dozen poorest cottages, sunk in poverty and wretchedness, that Mark Temple had accidentally heard of last winter, which happened to be an especially severe one, and his first in Cornwall; and though his duty did not lead him a third of the distance, indeed, scarcely took him in that direction at all, still his kindly, pitiful heart soon found it out, and his frequent visits were like gleams of light to the miserable people, to whose temporal, as well as spiritual, needs he ministered as largely as his means would permit. He, in fact, saved them from utter destitution through that terribly harsh season, as they were ignored by the only church in the district, and were distant from the chapel to whose communion they belonged.

But though they were sturdy dissenters, as the Cornish fisher-folk mostly are, and Mark Temple a priest of the most advanced school of modern High Churchism, which is nothing if it is not narrow, still unconsciously the "Comtist" doctrine, religion, one should perhaps say, of "Humanitarianism," was as strong in the man's large-minded, intensely sympathetic nature, as was the Christianity, of whose mysteries he was so earnest and faithful a "minister and steward," and consequently he was "in touch" with these poor starving toilers of an alien creed; weak, suffering, yearning humanity being the link that bound them together.[66] The Rev. St. Leger Stewart, formalist to his finger-tips, with a cold, exclusive, *borné* mind, would have gone amongst them, if compelled, with his highest high-priestly air of patronising, of condescending, clerical unbending, and would have been hated, however munificent his charity.[67] But the Rev. Mark was loved; his active kindliness and sympathy, his friendly, familiar manner, not suggestive of stooping from moral or spiritual pedestals, but of a common

66 Comtist: positivist philosophy of Auguste Comte.

67 *Borné*: narrow.

brotherhood, these traits had won him all hearts among the poor and sorrowing, whether of the very lowly order, like the dwellers in the tiny hamlet at Trevethick, or those of a better class, who forgave him his ritualistic practices and his odd, sacerdotal garments, for the sake of the ardent, genuine, earnest heart that beat beneath them.

The note he got was from an old, superannuated fisherman, the head of the little clan, as it were, which was now in a comparatively flourishing condition, owing to the prolonged and peculiarly lovely summer season, and an enormous take of fish, especially pilchards, in which the industry of that part of the coast chiefly lay.

Old Sam was very roundabout, and there was not much cohesion in his style; but when Mark Temple had mastered the primeval difficulty of deciphering these strange hieroglyphics that was old Sam's very best handwriting, the meaning of his communication was soon grasped, and might be put in a few words.

Early this morning a boat, bearing the name "Guinevere, Penmaerwyn," painted in gold letters on her bright blue bows, drifted in on the Trevethick half-acre of strand. One oar was missing, the other broken in the rowlocks. The smart little craft had evidently received much damage in the night's gale; though she did not actually leak, her stern was nearly stove in where apparently she had gone aground on some sunken rock; and chief item, though mentioned last, as seemingly an afterthought on the part of old Sam, there was a girl lying on the bottom of the boat, not dead, not asleep, not fainting, yet she would not, or could not speak, and looked like one who had seen a spirit and was frozen with the sight. She was wrapped in a big fur cloak, but she could not tell where she came from or who she was, but just looked and shivered and looked again with great eyes that seemed "as if they saw heaven or summut." The "women-folk" got frightened and thought she must be a ghost of one of the grand ladies from the old ruined castle (Tintagel); but he laughed at them and said she was as much flesh and blood as themselves; "the creature was just daft an' moidered, at bein' to sea in that gale, all by hersen in the night's blackness;" and so "Penmaerwyn" being on the boat, he was "minded" to write to the Rev. Mark, as she must belong to somewhere in his "parts," and perhaps at any rate the "parson" would come and have a look at her.

Mark Temple felt at once that the girl was Ula. He was familiar with her pretty, gaily-painted boat, and knew that it was named "Guinevere," after Arthur's unhappy queen. He was at "The Eyrie" this morning, having heard of the sudden shadow that had fallen on the house where all seemed such innocent happiness and gaiety last evening, when he had gone out from amongst them after a long delightful day spent at the picturesque ruins.

When leaving, he had come across Frau Benghaus, walking quickly up and down the little tennis lawn, with clasped hands and agitated mien (since the terrible scene last night she has been like one demented), and he heard her talking to herself with rapid, excited utterance.

"Also *hatte ich doch Recht; der Kleine* that I so loved in the years long ago, and *der Kleine* at the Cliff House have the same father.[68] I said it to the little Mees *à tort et à travers*, but I had the right; *et mon Dieu, comme le temps fuit*, that leetle, leetle boy, now Monsieur Graham![69] *Si beau, si grand. Ach, du lieber Himmel! mais le père est un*

[68] *Hatte ich doch Recht*: I was right after all. *Der Kleine*: the little one.

[69] *À tort et à travers*: without consideration. *Et mon Dieu, comme le temps fuit*: And my God, how time flies.

vieux scélérat; et ce cher ange Madame, who so great against I sinned!"[70]

And then he was out of hearing and walked on somewhat bewildered to the Cliff House, Effie's illness and accident having been mentioned; and old Barbara, who liked him and trusted him as the rest of the world did, said a word or two which, coupled with a few more words from Dr. Wenvoe later on, to whom the old man had confided a portion of his story when the doctor returned for his horse last night, led Mr. Temple to believe that strange, confused trouble lay upon both houses, the nature of which he hardly quite grasped, except the one fact that Madge was still in ignorance of, there being no one to enlighten her but Geoffrey, and he was too much engrossed by his heavy affliction to think of it, and that was, that the master of Cliff House was not the father of the Ferguson girls, as supposed, but only their uncle.

And now, on receipt of old Sam's note, he determines to go at once to Trevethick without communicating with any one. He feels convinced that it is something connected with this strange, sudden trouble that has brought Uls Ferguson in this wild, unaccountable fashion to Trevethick, and that also explains her unusual, extraordinary manner.

When he reaches the hamlet and enters old Sam's cottage, the best of the little colony's swellings, Ula—for it is indeed her very self—who has been lying on an old settle by the fire wrapt in that strange stillness and impenetrable silence, not appearing to notice or take in anything, and yet not asleep, for her eyes are always strained wide open, gives a sudden great start, her eyes lose the distant, unreal look that has been a little scaring to the poor women

---

[70] *Si beau, si grand. Ach, du lieber Himmel! mais le père est un vieux scélérat; et ce cher ange…*: So handsome, so tall. Oh, dear heavens! but the father is an old scoundrel; and the dear angel… (in a mixture of French and German).

who hover in the background, the colour flashes redly to her face and then as sudden retreats, leaving her, if possible, paler than before, while with one swift movement she is off the cumbersome old piece of furniture and across the small room, with both hands outstretched, half in greeting, half in a sort of mute, pathetic pleading for compassion, sympathy, companionship in her sorrow's solitude.

And as he takes the soft brown hands and presses them with warm, almost yearning pity and sympathy, and a touch of even something more than these, though the girl guesses it not, she breaks suddenly into wild, tempestuous, somewhat hysterical weeping, which Mark as well as the fisher-folk audience feel is the very best thing for her.

Mr. Temple was quite right in his surmise. By-and-by, when she is partially composed, Ula confesses everything to him. How she had left "The Eyrie," as we have seen, and came on slowly home in the moonlight, expecting every moment to meet Mr. Graham. When she got nearly to the door she saw him with her father, a little way from the house, talking earnestly and eagerly. They did not see her, and she slipped in unknown to them and went upstairs to her own room (she had heard nothing, of course, of Effie's so much increased illness), the window of which faced in their direction. It was wide open, and she knelt down by it, though not dreaming of trying to hear what they were saying. But all was very still and quiet, and their voices, at least Mr. Graham's, rang out loud and clear on the night air, and Geoffrey's whole speech of accusation, ending with that dreadful, extraordinary thing about their mysterious close relationship, was borne to her startled, horrified ear.

Her father! whom she had always so loved and respected and honoured, to have actually been that sweet, angelic Mrs. Graham's *husband*, and to have gone away from her and married another wife! (the girl's innocence could imagine no guiltier tie). And then the whole loyal, faithful nature rose up in hot revolt and righteous indignation for that second deceived wife, her own darling mother, whose shadowy memory she so clingingly cherished and passionately loved. The nobility and unselfishness of the girl's character here declared itself. It was her dead mother's wrongs first filled her soul with anguish and passionate resentment, not the destruction of her own hopes, the cruel killing of her new-found joy. And her first instinct was to go away at once from him who had so basely duped and cheated that dear long dead soul who was powerless to defend herself, and whose memory her daughter felt in her hot-headed, foolish, yet infinitely lovely youth, it was now left only to her to champion and protect.

And so, acting in wild, unreflecting haste on that maddest moment's decision, she wrapped herself in her big fur cloak, this nineteenth century "Elaine" or "Elsie," or some other of her favourite heroines, equally devoted, self-sacrificing, and unpractical, and consequently a marvellous and beautiful anachronism in these fearfully prosaic, hard-headed latter days,—stole down the stairs and out by the back way, and scudded noiselessly down the zig-zag path to the beach.

Little she knew of the terrible scene being enacted above as she unmoored her pretty boat. She had heard nothing after those wailing strangest words of Geoffrey's that called her "sister!" If she had waited one instant longer by that window she would doubtless have heard, if the weak voice carried so far, the old man's emphatic, eager refutation of that slanderous charge. But her quick young impulse never thought of questioning, or debating, or waiting; she heard, she believed, she acted, all with the same breath as it were;

and hers were the plash of oars, as she launched off incontinently into the great, wide, uncaring world, that Geoffrey heard at that supreme moment when balanced against the cliff wall trying to guide Effie's ascent even a few feet. She had some vague quixotic idea of endeavouring to reach Penzance, or even Falmouth, where she could embark in some outgoing steamer for some place in Germany or Switzerland where they might let her perfect her music in return for English teaching. Poor innocent child, with no thought of passports, or references, or the extraordinary appearance of a strangely attractive young girl abroad without luggage, or friends, or letters of credit. And then she thought if she soon succeeded in making money,—was there ever such pitiful trustfulness, such lack of worldly wisdom, and above all, of the modern hard shrewdness and calculation that chiefly characterises the young women of to-day?—she would write for Effie to come to her. If she died, as was most likely, before she could make a home for the little one, why perhaps it would be best of all; she would go to her dear mother in Heaven, and Effie would never know all this wretchedness, she was too little and too young to understand, and would be happy with others by-and-by.

And the sweet girlish voice quivers and breaks at her self-abnegating picture; and Mark Temple's heart throbs strangely at the girl's despairing unselfishness, an intense yearning tenderness for her creeps through him, and nestles warmly in his breast, and he awakes with a sudden thrill to the knowledge that he loves her. Yes, real, strong, ardent love for this young fascinating creature,—gazing at him with those dangerously sweet appealing eyes, eyes into which few men could look without looking far too often for their peace of mind, trusting herself and her sorrows with such lovely, child-like confidingness into his hands,—surges wildly for a moment or two in the breast of the grave, earnest, spiritually-minded clergyman. For a brief mute instant he yields to the delicious rush of emotion, so new, so overpowering, so incomprehensibly sweet; then two lines flash into his mind that he has read somewhere lately—

"I slept and dreamed that life was beauty;
I woke and found that life was duty."[71]

And with a little shake, as if he had been asleep, he rouses himself to the fact that his plain and simple duty is to bring the girl back to the life, and love, and happiness, which she thinks she has lost, and that will be all the more rapturously sweet and idyllic, for this black abyss of misery and despair into which she has been plunged for those few hours.

Yes, to take her back to her lover, to the man who is shrined in her heart of hearts, and for whom, in her abandonment of sorrow, she scarcely attempts to conceal her intense, passionate affection.

That is his first and chief duty. And if ever from this day a shadow lies upon his life—well, he must only live under it, and find in duty well and faithfully done his greatest happiness and reward. And the memory of this hour or two in old Sam's cottage, will always hold a supreme sweetness for him, as well as a tender abiding sorrow, and also a shadowy intangible feeling as of renunciation.

---

[71] Lines from the poem 'I Slept, and Dreamed That Life Was Beauty' by Ellen Sturgis Hooper.

CHAPTER VIII
"*IN CŒLO QUIES*"[72]

"God's finger touched them and they slept."[73]

LITTLE more remains to be told. In less than twenty-four hours after Mrs. Graham's death, Effie breathes her last, lying on the breast of him whom she still believes to be her father, and clasping Ula's hand, and almost her last words are characteristic of the quaint, odd child's nature: "You know, dear Pops, I would never leave you," she murmurs, "always recollect that; only *she* came all the way from Heaven to beckon me, and I could not let her go back alone. I can't see her now, but I know she is waiting for me somewhere near, and we will go together soon—very soon. It is a long, long way, and we'll be very tired when we get home to Heaven, but we shall have a lovely long rest there. And I'll keep watching for you, Pops, darling, all the time, through the lovely star windows. You'l make haste to come, won't you, dear? Ula has Geoff and won't be lonely; will you, Uley, love? But *I* can't do without you, Pops, in Heaven, any more than here. Remember, I'll be always watching through the windows, now one and now another; there are so many I can have a new one every night; and when you look up at the stars recollect I am always watching and waiting at one of them for you. And don't keep me too long, dear Pops; you ought to be glad to come and rest too. I have often wondered how it is, when we see all those windows of Heaven—as the stars are, I know, no matter what people say—why we never

---

[72] *In cœlo quies*: in heaven there is rest.

[73] Based on a line from *In Memoriam* by Alfred, Lord Tennyson.

see the door that must be so much bigger. But perhaps it is that God feels that either, if we could look through the great wide entrance into Heaven, we'd see such a dazzling glory that it would blind us for all our lives here; or that every one would want to go there at once; and so he lets them see through all the lovely little windows only the beautiful white shining light that is always there. It was very kind of her—to come all that way—to take care of me going back; but I think I'd rather she had let me stay, to go home—with you, Pops."

And the weak little voice dies away into silence; and the faithful little heart, true to its first and only allegiance to the last, beats more and more slowly until the end.

That roll of manuscript which Helen Dacre's dying, trembling hands placed in those of her husband, contained a full and exhaustive statement of that miserable episode in Paris two-and-twenty years ago, signed by herself, Dorothy Templeton, the physician who attended her through her long, almost fatal illness, the professional nurse, the humble, respectable widow under whose cottage roof she lay for so many weary weeks, and one or two neighbours and friends of the latter. She had obtained, preserved, and carried this precious document all these years, never knowing when the chance might come, as it did at last, of placing it in the hands of him who doubted and repudiated her.

It is not necessary to enter into the contents of that paper, with the exception of one or two points not yet explained: one, an addition to the signed paper, giving the reason of the adoption of the name of "Graham."

When Mrs. Dacre found, after young Lonhed's interview with her husband, that all hope of reconciliation, even recognition, from him was hopeless, she returned heart-broken to France with her aunt, Miss Templeton. But after a little while, feeling that she must try to exert herself, at least for her child's sake, she went into Switzerland to Geneva, to study at the Conservatoire there, hoping to make music her means of support.

She lodged in a quiet house close by, kept by an elderly English lady, a childless widow of the name of Graham, who eked out a small yearly income of some £50 or £60 by lodging and boarding pupils at the Conservatoire. The lonely woman grew strangely attached to Helen and her boy, caring, and tending, and loving the child during the many hours his mother was obliged to be absent. The latter had confided to her, as she felt was only her solemn duty to do, her whole sad story, and had met with boundless belief and entire and perfect sympathy.

For nearly two years matters remained thus and the second year of Helen's studentship at the music school,—which she meant to be her last, as she felt herself now fully qualified for anything she would require,—was drawing to its close, when Mrs. Graham fell ill and died after a few weeks' intense suffering.

Helen Dacre was naturally her faithful and devoted nurse. As she had watched by her dear aunt Dorothy's dying bed nearly a year before, with grieving, miserable eyes, so now she watched by this. Her last earthly friend was going from her, and she mourned sincerely. The desolate old woman was intensely grateful and loving; she had not a relative on earth, and she could do what she liked with her own. So, on the one condition that Mrs. Dacre should take the name of "Graham," she left her all she died possessed of: not a great inheritance, but still a good deal to Helen just then,—something to be most thankful for,—the yearly income, which just exactly doubled her own, a houseful of good furniture, &c. As to the condition, she was only too enchanted to accept it.

The name "Dacre" had become hateful to her from its bitter-sweet associations; and besides, she felt as if she had hardly a right to bear it, when her husband chose so cruelly and determinedly to disown her, and, therefore, Helen Dacre ceased to me, and "Mrs. Graham" reigned in her stead.

The other point in that statement of past events which Benghaus was not aware of, was a strange power of apparently seeing the invisible, and divining coming evil, and which helps to prove that the mystical or "hidden inner life," in short, the separate distinct life of the soul, lies not so dormant in certain rare natures, as in that of most of those around us.

When in the Marquis de Vallanelle's carriage being driven, as she believed, in full and perfect good faith, to her dear aunt Dorothy, who was very ill and wanting her, who had sent her an urgent letter, begging her to come to her without delay, a letter *forged* by the guilty Rosalie at the Marquis's bidding, as the weak, wicked creature had also *burned* the few hasty lines which, before starting, Helen scrawled to her husband, and left with the treacherous French girl to post, substituting that which was thrust into his hand at the station. But when she was many miles distant from Paris, on a dark country road, with her sleeping child lying on the seat before her, Helen had a dream, nay, rather a vision, as she declared most strenuously that she did not sleep. But, singularly, that vision did not show her mere physical things, that her fleshy eye could not penetrate, owing to the boundaries of time, space, etc. No! Her vision laid bare to her the hearts of men. She saw into the hidden secrets of their souls, in that strange trance of the spirit. Suddenly, as she sat in that carriage, rolling rapidly through the darkness, the whole monstrous plot, of which she was the unhappy victim, was borne in upon her—she wrote—with a horrible, unnatural force, as if a red-hot iron seared it upon her brain. In one startled, awful moment of revelation, she knew she was not on the right road to Miss Templeton's home. She saw the Marquis de Vallanelle in his true colours,—saw that he was then following her through the night and darkness, and read his diabolical motives,—saw her letter to her husband destroyed by the French girl's treachery, and another substituted,—saw, with wild eyes of frenzy and despair, a black bottomless gulf yawning ever deeper, ever wider, between herself and her Lionel, and, in her agony of mind, she fainted.

How long she remained insensible she could not say, but she was brought to herself by a sharp, strange jerk or jar, followed by a sound of plunging, and the sudden stopping of the vehicle. For a moment or two she understood nothing, then her terrible situation and the extraordinary, mysterious revelation that had been made to her, rushed back vividly to her distracted mind. What had occurred? Was there fresh peril? or could it be that God had answered her dumb prayer for help just before she fainted, and sent some chance of escape?

She listened intently, scarcely breathing, and heard the driver get down with an oath; then more wild plunging on the part of the horses, more oaths on the part of the man, mingled with coaxing, encouraging words, as if urging the struggling creatures to some effort, which seemed unsuccessful; evidently one of the horses had fallen, and could not as yet arise. She then heard the man come back towards the carriage; he lowered one of the windows, and bade her, in rapid speech, not to be alarmed, that it was but a slight accident, and they would be on again in a few minutes. She had the presence of mind to counterfeit a sort of dazed manner, as if just roused from slumber, expressed no fear, only the anxious hope that there might be no long delay, as she was most eager to reach her destination, where she was urgently needed. Scarcely waiting to hear her words, the coachman, who, she noticed, was not the man with whose appearance she was familiar, hurriedly shut up the window, and, taking the lamps from the carriage, brought them forward to see what amount of damage was done. And now, surely, was her opportunity. The night was terribly dark and foggy, but this very obscurity would be her safeguard. Cautiously she lowered the window he had just closed and looked out. Yes, it was as she felt certain: one of the horses had slipped on a sharp stone. Hurt and frightened, the creature made no effort to rise, while the other horse was plunging frantically, and utterly unmanageable. The reins were also broken. She saw the man bending over the fallen horse, swearing horribly. The glare of the lanterns immediately beside him made the surrounding gloom more impenetrable. Yes, now was her opportunity, her heaven-sent opportunity. Surely God in His great mercy had thus answered her mute appeal for help and protection. The tumult and the shrouding darkness will cover her flight, and she felt she had successfully blinded the man by her manner to any thought of her suspicions being aroused; and so thinking, she stealthily turned the handle of the door of the carriage at the off-side of the fallen horse and stooping man, thanking Heaven for an added mercy, they are not locked in. Then, holding the still sleeping child beneath her heavy cloak, she stepped out quickly on the dark road, softly closed the door behind her, and crept swiftly back the way they had come, keeping well within the shadow cast by the carriage.

On and on, with gliding, rapid motion, in spite of being encumbered by the heavy weight of a child seven years old, but desperation lent her almost an unnatural strength. The little fellow woke, but she soothed him by a whispered word, and he uttered not the faintest cry. On and on, unheedful of the thick, close, saturating rain; on and on, till full three hundred yards lay between her and the carriage, from which she had so providentially escaped; then she turned and looked back. Yes, away there through the murky gloom she could see the circle of dull, faint light, where the man bent over the prostrate horse; strange, and split into misty, broken rays it looked through fog, but at that distance she could see no faintest outline of vehicle or any object, much less could she be seen. She was safe! Heaven be praised—safe! The man would not miss her; in a few minutes he would drive on rapidly, to make up for lost time, without coming again to the window, as he had no suspicion, and thought all was right.

But she must not stay on the open road. She felt, that vision revealed to her, that the Marquis was following at a long distance; besides, she must seek some shelter from that drenching rain for the child's sake. There seemed to be no habitation of any kind near, at least nothing could be discerned through that dense fog. She appeared to be on a road with a small, narrow ditch and straggling hedge on each side; but on one side the hedge was very open, and through it she saw large trees looming, as it seemed, quite close. She must only try and reach their shelter and wait for morning. It will be easy to creep through the broken hedge; but first she must leap the ditch. Well, that will be simple enough too; it is narrow, and the child is again asleep and quite quiet. She springs and clears the small space successfully, but as ill fate should have it, twists her leg horribly; she feels her knee must be badly sprained, she can't move save to crawl through the ragged hedgeway with a groan of anguish. After a little she tries would it be possible to reach those sheltering trees but a few yards off? but no, it is hopeless, she has to desist at once, the slightest movement causing her almost to scream with agony.

Just at that moment she hears the carriage rattle off at a tremendous pace. She has no longer the fear of pursuit, but still her position is a terrible one; now perfectly helpless, in the thick darkness of such a night, having not the remotest idea of where she is. She was really, as she ascertained afterwards, on the confines of a village eighteen miles from Paris, nearly twice as far from G——, where her aunt, Miss Templeton, lived, and hardly two miles from the remote little lonely chalet among the hills at H——, which had been purchased by the Marquis a few years before in an assumed name, and where Felix, the crafty valet and confederate, was taking her. Yes, hers was a fearful position. She crept close to that scanty hedge, and there through the long interminable hours of the night—the light is late in coming in November, and it was barely two o'clock when she escaped from the carriage—she crouched in the thick, close, penetrating rain, the raw, insidious, death-smiting fog peculiar to this melancholy month, vainly trying to protect the little delicate child, until at last in her devotion and unselfishness, she removed her heavy warm cloak, her only protection against the weather, and rolled it round and round the boy, who, thus swathed and muffled, escaped unharmed. But was it any wonder, when the simple villagers found her in the morning, that between anguish of body, frenzied distraction of mind, and serious dangerous illness, that had already laid its pitiless grip upon her, the result of that terrible exposure, she was delirious and utterly unable to help herself in any way; talking softly, with little ripples of happy laughter, of long dead scenes, and childhood's friends and fancies?

Throughout that first day she laughed and babbled in the intervals of sleep; but at night her gentle, little harmless wanderings took a deeper and a different tone. Childish memories were no longer in the ascendant, but later impressions rose in their place. Two or three times in the earlier night she called plaintively, piteously on her husband (one of the watchers had been long in England and could understand). But somewhere between three and four in the morning, after a long silence in which she had slept, she suddenly sat up straight in the bed, gazing right before her, through the uncurtained cottage window away into vacancy, perfect consciousness on her brow, in her straining eyes, and in the intense, rapt, hushed tones of her voice as she spoke.

"He is looking for me—seeking, seeking, and he cannot find. I see him, but he is so far—so far—and all is so dark. Come quick, love! I am waiting—sick and weary with waiting!" Then she paused for a moment or two, and suddenly cried out, loudly and eagerly, her eyes dilating strangely, as if they scaled the blank silences of space opposed to their regard, and saw beyond, "Lionel! love! husband! come to me! Life of my life, come quickly!"

Then a strange, weird stillness fell upon the room, and in a moment, out of that sudden eerie silence, stole the far-off whispering tones of a human voice. It was but the echo, as it were, of the faintest breath of sound, but yet clear and distinct—

"*I am coming, darling! coming! coming!*"

And then no more; but the listening, straining figure on the bed seemed content, and lay down and slept, and in the morning she was raving in all the ghastly wild delirium of brain fever, while rheumatic fever had seized her body in its ferocious grasp.

* * * * * *

And it was at that very hour that Lionel Dacre, out on the lonely country road, being driven to Dorothy Templeton's residence at G—— had heard, as he fancied, voices in the darkness; the voices of those long dead, and then from amongst those ghostly echoes rang out the agonised living tones of his wife whom he sought, in those very words we have now read, and he standing up in the swiftly rolling vehicle had quickly sent back the answer, "I am coming, darling! coming, coming!"

This record of a somewhat singular combination of events might be fairly called, "a story of coincidences."

But after all, what is a coincidence? Is not the generally received meaning of the word—a strange chance agreement, or concurrence of incidents? But query, *chance*. May not some of those wonderfully unaccountable, startling coincidences that have place in some lives, be rather the emanation of, or result from, some peculiar order of human will? a will that may exercise its magnetic, incomprehensible power, consciously, or still oftener, unconsciously.

That the very fact, with some rare mental organizations, of allowing the faculties of the mind to be constantly bent in one direction—the mind currents, as it were, always flowing one way—that the dormant, potent magnetism, or mesmerism in these spiritual natures, may influence the life currents of others, and insensibly compel what they are continually dwelling on or desiring, and thus produce what we are pleased to call "coincidences.'

But whether this theory be true or not, if, as we are told, there is no such thing as "chance" in this earthly life of ours, then there are no coincidences, and "destiny" is the shuttle on which our lives are wound.

THE END

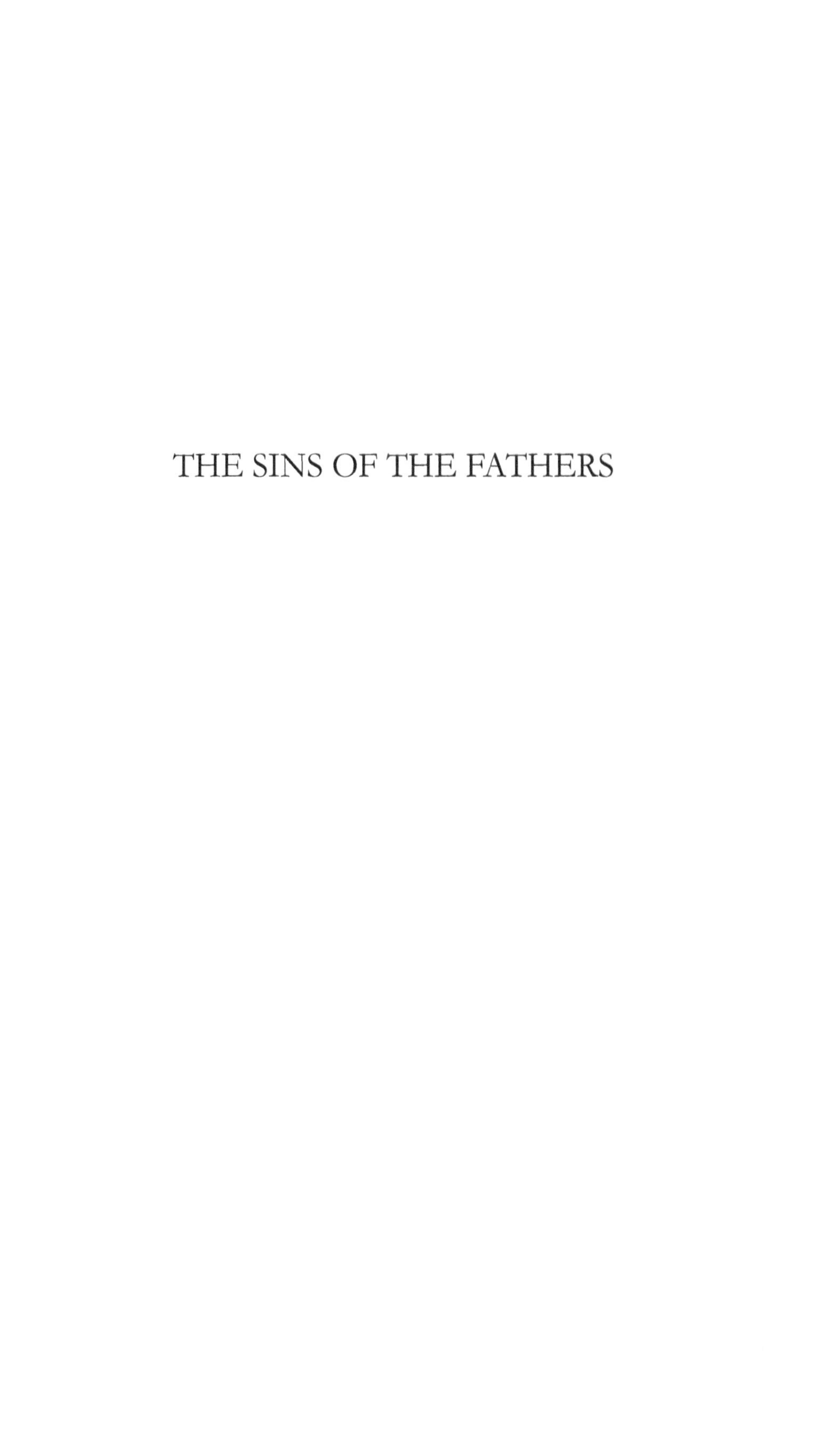

THE SINS OF THE FATHERS

INTRODUCTORY

THE circumstances surrounding the following awful and infinitely pathetic instance of mysterious disappearance do not owe their birth to imagination, are not the outcome of fiction's storehouse, but are actual facts.

Mysterious disappearances are multiplying around us daily, and very frequently defy solution.

The real actors in the following drama may have moved in a somewhat different sphere of life from the occupants of Arden Grange. The details and accessories of this startling record of sorrow, and sin, and mystery, may vary in slight degree from the environment of the actual facts, but all else remains the same, and goes to swell the ever increasing roll of proof that "truth is stranger than fiction."

CHAPTER I
YOUNG MEN AND MAIDENS

IT is a November eve. A wild, stormy November eve; cold, bleak, wintry; neither snow nor rain, but rough, ragged clouds scurrying on before a fierce upper current; a sky that bears on its menacing title-page a clearly-writ prophecy of tempest to come; yet many guests, chiefly young people, are gathered in Arden Grange to keep the mystic All Souls' Night in the good old-fashioned way.

Some of them have come a long distance, and will remain for days, others, who live in the neighbourhood, will disperse to their respective homes after the midnight rites and ceremonies, the trembling, excited, half-laughing, half-fearful efforts to lift ever so little the shrouding veil of the future, to peer the tiniest bit into the great, dim, mysterious "unknown" that lies just beyond the actual and visible around us.

Yes, a goodly company of young folk have met on this November eve, to laugh and make merry; for the master of Arden Grange is a jolly, kindly, country squire of the old school, who loves nothing better than to see young people around him, enjoying the youth that so sadly soon slips away.

The guests, with one or two exceptions, assembled in the early afternoon, determined to have a long and delicious evening of varied enjoyment.

Old-fashioned hours reign at the Grange, the Squire of Arden in no circumstances dining later than five o'clock; and so, it is scarcely more than six, when the musical babble of many gay, sweet voices is heard in the great Arden drawing-rooms.

What long, delightful hours of fun and laughter and innocent young frolic lie before them! Not till eleven, at the earliest, will they commence any of the time-honoured enchantments, the weird strange divinings, peculiarly linked by custom with the night's solemn festival; and all the time between is to be made up of mirth, and music, and pleasure of many kinds.

And so, the really young ones of the party, of whom there is quite a large contingent, indulge in mad, merry games, romping in exuberant glee to their hearts' content. Never has laughter more ecstatic, more saturated with enjoyment, rung out within the walls of the historic old Grange than on this "All Souls' Night," while their elders, the young people who have attained the dignity of manhood and womanhood, dance, recite, act charades, sing, play, and flirt, with equal abandon of delight.

They in no way clash, these two bodies of merry-makers; the suite of four stately drawing-rooms at the Grange, each unfolding from the other, gives plenty of room and to spare for all.

But amongst those grown young people are a few quieter, more thoughtful spirits, who, after an hour or two's participation in the laughter and frolic, grow a little weary of these more volatile amusements, and gather together in the fourth and innermost apartment, and there round the wide old-fashioned hearth sit and beguile the time in much more entrancing fashion, according to their ideas, than do the noisy revellers in the outer rooms.

And soon, the few really elderly and middle-aged people amongst the Squire's guests join them, and by degrees their numbers swell, so that by about half-past eight or nine o'clock, with the exception of the children, who are not yet tired apparently of "Dumb Crambo," "In the Market Place," &c., all are assembled in that inner-room, hearkening to, or telling tales of horror, ghostly legend or ghastly romance, some grimly appropriate, others equally irrelevant to the mysterious night it is.[74]

Among the gay crowd of happy, laughing girls, Mabel Arden, the Squire's niece, is remarkable both for her superior beauty, and for a dreamy, abstracted seriousness in her great, grey eyes. She makes one of the story-telling group, but seemingly half against her will. She shrinks into a corner, and listens as it were under protest; and when the others laugh and exclaim, she only shudders and grows pale.

It needs no words to tell that that tall fine-looking man, with the dark, earnest face, standing in the shadow near her, looks on Mabel's rare beauty in no mere friendly, admiring spirit; no, Hugh Denver's earthly hopes are centred in that gentle girl, with the rapt and visionary eyes.

Several brief, but most unpleasantly uncanny stories have been already told and listened to with much apparent unction and enjoyment, there have been sundry little shudders, and hasty glances over shoulders, and many and various exclamations of astonishment and horror, these being the indispensable accessories and necessary pantomime to properly mount the ghost-telling business; but no one is really seriously impressed save Mabel, and she only grows paler and paler, and sits and says no word, while Hugh stands protectingly, just at her back, darting impatient, angry glances at the eager, unconscious group of young men and maidens.

Another story is at its height, and Captain Armitage, the narrator, who rather prides himself on his powers as a *raconteur*, has reached the thrilling point, the climax of horror, and all these bright girl-faces are turned towards him in pretty breathless interest,

---

[74] Dumb Crambo is a guessing game similar to charades.

and he finds the situation rather pleasant, and wishes to prolong the sequel of this ghastly tale, which owes its origin not to legendary lore or wild superstitions, but to stern history's relentless, cruel, unvarnished facts, being the "walling up alive" of a fair young nun, who had broken no vow but on whom suspicion of heresy had fallen.

But just at this moment a deputation from the younger division rudely bursts in upon the mediæval, inquisitorial atmosphere of the suspense-held circle, with a clamorous petition that some of these sedate elders will come and play hide-and-seek in the west wing.

"It is just the night for it," they declare, vociferously, with energetic volubility, "and just the place." Nowhere can you play such a grand game as in the dear old Grange, where there are such a number of delightfully-unexpected little rooms and passages and quaint, funny staircases leading nowhere. It is just made for it.

But the small pleaders are met with a storm of denial. What foolish children they are. Do they expect everyone to be as great babies as themselves some say; while others declare that they are much too tired, or that it would be much too cold in that uninhabited west wing; while one young lady, an elder sister of two of the delinquents and one of the narrating warrior's most enthralled listeners, asserts with rebuking emphasis that they are very naughty to interrupt Captain Armitage's most interesting story, and that she hopes they will go away and be good, self-effacing children for the rest of the evening.

Just as the youngsters turn away, discomfited, Mabel springs to her feet, with a relieved air, and says that she will go; it will be grand fun—a good game of hide-and-seek to-night; a thousand times better than sitting still listening to such horrors. And although she has actually attained the maturity of nineteen, and is naturally of a rather serious, thoughtful temperament, she marches away at the head of the juvenile band, who one and all declare, from the patriarch of the party, who has reached the venerable age of fourteen, down to the eight-year-old rosy-cheeked urchin, that "Mab is a grand old brick," and that the others deserve, for their selfishness, to be carried off by the "nasty ghosts" they are "so mad about."

Hugh Denver follows through the stately rooms till they reach the outer door, leading on to the corridor, entreating to be allowed to accompany them; but Mabel will not hear of it. It would only render them ridiculous, she asserts; for her, it is only natural that she should go; she often has a good romp with these young cousins and friends when they come to Arden; besides it is her duty to try to amuse the youngsters, when her uncle has no home daughter; and when the children wish to play some of the more boisterous games, such as hare and hounds, hide-and-seek, &c., they generally adjourn to the west wing.

"But they are timid going about this great rambling old house at night by themselves," she continues, "whereas I can find my way through all its quaint and puzzling intricacies blindfold, and I have not a spark of fear," with a bright dauntless smile. "We shan't be away more than half an hour or so, and I hope by then they—" nodding her head in the direction of the distant conclave, "will have satisfied their unhealthy appetites for the horrible." She concludes with a little contemptuous laugh, as she looks up into Hugh's dark face, with those wonderful grey eyes that seem to penetrate and look beyond some mystery that no one else knows anything about. Then she turns, and is gone, joining the impudent children who are waiting for her; and Hugh stands at the door and watches the slender girlish figure as it disappears down the long brilliantly-lighted corridor, with those young things who love her so well crowding round her, and Mab this, and Mab that, comes to his listening ear, in their shrill, clear treble, and the soft musical tones of her voice in gay response.

Then they reach the further end, and turn off to the left, bound for the west wing, and she pauses for just a moment, and wafts a kiss from her dainty finger-tips, while her irrepressible comrades give a shout of triumph; and then all vanish, and Hugh Denver walks back reluctantly to the excited circle in that inner room, whom he looks upon with rather an inimical gaze—though many sweet, bright glances are shot at his interesting handsome face from soft winsome eyes—and finds that the conversation has taken in his absence a somewhat new departure.

CHAPTER II
A FANATIC

CAPTAIN Armitage has finished his mediæval horrors, and Mr. Normal Leslie, a distant cousin of the Ardens—a briefless barrister, who has lately taken to literature, in which he has already made some mark, his short stories, contributed to various magazines, being considered pithy, vigorous, graphic—has plunged into an animated argument with elderly, prejudiced Mr. Burroughs, a country gentleman and neighbour of Squire Arden's, on the late wonderful discoveries in science, and the decided changes that it might be fairly predicted they will effect as time goes on in general life and custom and society; especially dwelling on the suppression of crime and the detection of the criminal by the agency of Nature's mystic, newly-developed forces being summoned to the aid of law and justice.

The old man is fanatically disputatious, and very obstinate; one of those people, who will believe only what they actually see. He is somewhat of a bibliophile, and clever in his cynical way.

He almost lives amongst his books—old, old books; delighting in collecting specimens of editions of obsolete and forgotten works, in unearthing wonderful and ancient manuscripts, of no particular value perhaps, save that they belong to that past which he deifies; while detesting and abhorring all things modern.

He insists with immovable persistence, that the world has steadily retrograded since the Elizabethan age, having then reached its perihelion of intellectual greatness; that the great centre of Divine intelligence, the wondrous mystic spirit of "Thought," that pervades all, and *is* all of life and creation, was then approached more nearly in his opinion by man's finite mental powers than in any after period.

The great modern fetish, *Machinery*, has, he says, absorbed man's best brain power. Into the ever-circling wheels and cogs and cranks, into the mysterious magnetic wires, into all the horror of those roaring, hissing, moving iron creatures, that seem instinct with an insidious demon-like life of their own, he has worked the soul of genius. And is it any wonder that when thus chained earthwards, the Pegasus should have become a very ordinary horse indeed? Capable, certainly, of plenty of good, hard, honest work, but the wings which bore him heavenwards are clipped and will not grow again.

That there is more general knowledge, cleverness, call it what you will, in these latter times, than at any other period of the world's history, he concedes; information is more widely spread, but a universal illumination of pigmy rush-lights is surely dearly bought, at the sacrifice of all the glorious celestial lamps.

Thus, by the hour will old Wyndham Burroughs hold forth.

Certainly, a peculiarly aggravating opponent for Norman Leslie to have tackled, with his many new-fangled and strictly modern notions, his perfect belief in the supreme intellectual standard of his own time, and disbelief in excellence of any other period.

The old man flatly refuses to be convinced by his arguments, sneers at progress, "pish's" and "pshaw's" at the marvellous strides of science in these latter days, declaring energetically, that man is neither happier nor better than he was in the days of what the present presumptuous generation are pleased to call primæval ignorance, despite all these vaunted scientific explorations.

He challenges Leslie to prove his facts; above all the connection between science and crime, or rather, the vanquishing of crime.

But Norman Leslie is not easily worsted; he takes up his cudgels of argument with renewed vigour, and speaks rapidly, earnestly, convincingly, as most of his younger hearers think, for the next ten minutes or so. But he is determined that too much time shall not be spent in the discussion of the dry bones of political economy.

He noticed, while his elderly opponent aired his somewhat singular, and distressingly pessimistic views, that two or three of the younger members of the party have yawned surreptitiously, while a decidedly bored expression shone in more than one pair of lovely eyes, especially in those of a sweet, winsome Irish girl, whose arch and witching ways have made sad havoc in the grave young barrister's heart, though he fears the pretty Kathleen's smiles have a reprehensible catholicity in their undesirable impartiality; and he sighs softly as he watches those lovely, errant eyes turn on Denver—who is unconscious of their glance, his thoughts being with the absent Mabel—with a dreamy dangerous sweetness in their gaze. What would not he (Norman) give for just such a look!

Yet it is given to another, who neither seeks it nor wishes for it; whose thoughts are so engrossed by another woman as to be even unconscious that those witching eyes are turned on him. Is it not ever so in life? he thinks despondently. What we care and crave for, and long, oh, so ardently to possess, is given to another unasked, who values it not one whit, and most likely yearns for quite something else.

A man loves a woman truly and passionately; she cares for him not a straw, and is either, perhaps, unconscious or contemptuous of his affection, while her whole soul, the very meaning of her being, the life of her heart, is given to another man, who does not care for her, has never cared for her, will never care for her—however, poor fool, she may delude herself—who very possibly is serenely unaware of or indifferent to her regard, and who, most probably, in his turn, likes or will like somebody unattainable.

Thus the poor human puppets play at cross-purposes with one another, a blind and cruel Fate pulling the strings.

And then, as he glances at Hugh Denver's absorbed face, he sighs again, this time impatiently and a trifle enviously. Has he not—that unconscious Hugh—everything that women are apt to admire and idealise in the sterner sex?

Nature here has been bountiful of her good gifts, thinks poor Norman, with something like a jealous pang. How goodly to look upon is that tall, manly figure, with the long, lithe limbs and the broad, square shoulders; the dark, interesting face, the face of a student and a thinker, as well as of a brave, good man; a face lit by a pair of wonderfully penetrating intense brown eyes, with a strange magnetic power in them, yet that can look distant and dreamy as now, or passionately tender as a while ago, when talking to Mabel Arden.

And then again how often just such a guise as this will clothe a base, cruel heart, or a frivolous, empty mind. Not that it is so in this case—far, far from it, as Norman knows so well. Hugh Denver is as nobly furnished in heart and brain as in that attractive exterior which appeals to the eye. But it does seem hard, he thinks a little sorely, that externals should go for so much with the greater number; that a man—or still oftener a woman—should, in such countless cases, be valued by his or her looks alone. Liked, admired, loved, scorned, flouted, passed over, as the case may be, according to the outward appearance of that casket in which the soul—which is the real man or woman—is enshrined.

Hugh Denver has a good, true, unselfish heart; but so has be (Norman), and perhaps one even more yearning for love and sympathy. Hugh has a large, intellectual mind; and so has he, with more of a delicate fancy and vivid imagination; and yet (thinking of his own outward man with bitter deprecation and unvarnished cruel distinctness, determined to make the very worst of himself), what eyes could care to dwell on him?—with his slight, insignificant figure, his narrow, contracted chest and stooping shoulders, his small, expressionless blue eyes still further disfigured by odious glasses, lank, nondescript hair, and general pallor and feebleness. So he briefly and contemptuously catalogues his attributes of face and form—ignoring the noble brow and sweet, sensitive mouth—with a brutal unsparing candour that causes him to smile grimly, though he winces at the portrait. Yet, Bah! what contemptible womanish folly it is. Never yet has he been guilty of such absurd weakness; just like some poor, plain girl weighing her chances of partners before a ball; at least, a girl afflicted with that most distressing of all feminine ills—total unattractiveness—the want of that nameless, magic gift, that is so much more potent and enduring than mere beauty.

Beauty may be coldly and carelessly regarded; may in some cases even almost repel, and certainly fades and vanishes; but a woman endowed with that wondrous gift of attraction, or fascination—that really arises from some combined, intangible charm of manner and facial expression—always pleases—the other sex, be it understood . . . The eyes that smile and speak even more than the lips, the look of quick, sweet, bright intelligence and response, the varying light and shade of a face that possesses an expressive mouth and eyes is the real meaning of that word "attractive" as applied to women.

And this is a charm which flies not with the fleeting short-lived youth, but is even more magnetic and alluring in maturer years.

CHAPTER III
FINESSE

BUT to return to Norman Leslie.

He suddenly determines while elderly Mr. Burroughs is cynically refuting his last arguments—heartlessly cutting them up into the mincemeat of ridicule, or, at least, trying his best so to do, though but few present agree with his stubborn, old-world fanaticism—that though he may not be able to win those coveted, prolonged glances of interested admiration, which the witching Kathleen had covertly lavished on the unappreciative Hugh, yet, if he is not greatly mistaken, he will compel her to look at him. Ay! and with eager interest too—and to hang on his words.

Captain Armitage, the glib and self-satisfied story-teller, just retired from public office, won plenty of sweet, bright looks of eager excitement from those glorious, dark blue eyes; and at any rate he can rival him on this ground, specially his own, and not fear defeat.

And so, with partly the ignoble—but only too human—motive of vanquishing and slightly extinguishing the self-complacent, somewhat vapid captain, whom a rather pretty trick of speech has allowed to pose quite picturesquely to-night, and partly, and almost altogether, to win the fascinating Miss O'Hara's sweet, shy, earnest glances, he speaks as follows:—

"Well, ladies and gentlemen, I am rather sorry that Mr. Burroughs has proved so emphatically that his conversion is utterly hopeless and impossible, as I had intended with your permission, to read a slight tale I have just completed, which bears more or less on the subject under discussion, and which has been accepted for one of the Christmas Annuals.

"I have a duplicate copy of the M.S. with me, and I thought it would be specially suitable for to-night's reading, not that the incidents in any way relate to the peculiar customs and superstitions attached to "Hallow Eve," but because the tragic climax of the story took place on this "All Soul's Night" just two years ago."

"Yes,"—as his hearers look slightly mystified and enquiring, "the tale I have written is no fiction, but absolute, authentic fact—fact which occurred in my own family, the chief actor in the drama being my second cousin; and the time—this night two years ago. A peculiarly fitting time, as you will say, for any startling or uncommon manifestation. It was a singular experience, to say the least of it, and I should like some of you to hear it, but as Mr. Burroughs' prejudices against modernism of all kinds are so very pronounced, and as doubtless many think with him," glancing with unconscious, contemptuous compassion on the elders of the party, "I, of course, could not think of intruding it, as——"

But here he is met, as he shrewdly anticipated, by a perfect storm of persuasion, remonstrance, urgent coaxing—

"He must read it."—"It would be too shameful now, after tantalising them to such a degree, to withhold it."—"What matter what some people think?" with unflattering emphasis on the "some."—"Old people are often pig-headed!" whispered very *sotto voce*[75]—"He won't—he can't, he shan't refuse!"—"Dear Mr. Leslie couldn't be so cruel after exciting their curiosity to boiling point," &c., &c.

As for Kathleen O'Hara, she feels quite pleasurably excited!—

---

[75] *Sotto voce*: in a quiet voice, under the breath.

to know a real live author!—how delightful. She has met Leslie on three or four former occasions and never took the slightest notice of him, save what courtesy compelled. She thought him dull and uninteresting; he is naturally of a reserved and somewhat silent temper. She heard that he wrote, certainly, but also the phrase "for the papers," and accordingly felt neither interest nor curiosity—"stupid, dry, political things of course; who cares about them?"

But now to find that he writes fiction—actually stories for Christmas numbers, that are often so wildly delightfully exciting—invests him at once with a charm in her eyes, the charm of novelty. She has never yet known an author and she thinks it a pleasant sensation. And so she is one of the most eager and urgent among the throng.

"Ah! do, Mr. Leslie," she pleads. "Please don't be so heartless as to say a great big horrid 'no.' A story, and yet a real one, that happened on this very night, would be too delicious." This is perhaps a trifle vague, but the tone is so persuasive and the eyes so appealing, that few could resist her. "And I am sure Mr. Burroughs is going to be very good-natured, and not laugh or say mocking things, won't you promise, please?" turning her battery of winning wiles on the old man, who, however case-hardened he may be, is not quite proof against the Irish girl's pretty coaxing ways.

"Don't be afraid, Miss O'Hara, that I shall play the invidious rôle of skeleton at the intellectual feast. A story is always a story, and often a very good thing—a delicacy in literature that I am quite partial to; and Mr. Leslie's tale will doubtless prove most interesting, and then you know——" with a gleam of whimsical humour, or good-natured satire, in his cynical face—"I am not compelled to be a believer. The 'Koran,' the 'Talmud,' the books of the 'Vedas,' are scriptural books of different peoples. I have read all three, but it does not follow that therefore I must enrol myself as a convert to the creed of Islam or Siva. This tale of Mr. Leslie's illustrates, I conclude, his theory advanced so eloquently just now, and that I have combated, namely, that modern science has done, or will produce anything capable of being really a check on crime, or a deterrent to the criminal. I argue that late improvements, discoveries—so called progress—tend rather the other way; and now, though I am prepared to feel interest and admiration in the ingenuity of the illustration, *yet*——"

"Not so much a check on crime in the example I now cite, as a mode possibly, if suspicion strongly attached to any given person, of wringing a confession from him," interrupts Norman.

"Of course, I know this is altogether an individual case, but still I think it is a strong proof that by and by something real and grand may be done, and that advancing science, which is progressing of late with seven-leagued boots, will declare herself an energetic, trustworthy and semi-miraculous agent in the repression or discovery of crime. But, Mr. Burroughs, you say that you are prepared to admire my ingenuity. Pray do not, as there is none in the matter; as I said a few moments ago, perhaps you did not note, that my story is no fiction, but a simple record of actual facts which occurred two years ago.

"With but the necessary alteration of names and localities, and very slight variation of detail, I give these facts now to the world exactly as they took place. I do so without compunction, as the chief actors in the brief drama are already dead. He, whom I call 'John Sutcliffe,' the man who mingled science and law, and who was my second cousin, died more than six months ago—died of a broken heart, if ever man did, absurd as seems the circumstance in conjunction with a lawyer advanced in life. His niece also has died since that tragic All Souls' Night, having never quite recovered the horror of it.

"I have entitled the experience, 'Science *versus* Crime,' " drawing forth the precious manuscript from an inner pocket. "I fear this will tread on your prejudices, sir," with a smile; "but you have promised Miss O'Hara to be very good-natured; and besides, I don't want to contend for a moment that this peculiar form of the subject under discussion could be repeated, unless, indeed, at rarest intervals. But what I do contend is—that as time goes on, and not very far ahead either, science, in some strange new form or forms, will enrol itself as an aid and abettor of the law and righteousness; will prove itself the most efficient of all detectives and suppressors of evil; if not, I say, strong advocate as I am of all things modern, that it lacks its most vital raison d'être.

"If it can execute the guilty one painlessly, instantaneously, by the mere touching of a magnetic button, there must be something radically wrong in the pursuit of science that will fail in these latter days of marvellous enlightenment and progress to make it still more an agent for the extinguishing and steady eradication of the teeming amount of sin and crime that leads to this horrible and unnatural—in a Christian country—deed of violence.

"Let science sweep this old-fashioned evil away as well as it has swept others, instead of trying to do it in an ultra-superfine manner, let it sweep it away by removing the cause. If its first and chief aim is not to make men better than they are, to purify and improve morally our national life, our life as a civilised, religious, cultured community, then I'll agree with you, Mr. Burroughs, and admit that science is a humbug.

"But it won't be so, I feel assured; we are creeping steadily on to better things. The discoveries in science are expanding men's minds and enlarging their sympathies. The good of the human race in the aggregate occupies most of the thought and talent of the day.

"Science may begin her reign as a despotic foe and crusher of evil; her punishments may be rigorous; but she will end by being the angel of peace and mercy in our earth-life. We are gradually pushing on to an organised form of social life—a form that has already been dimly outlined in the far distance by one or two prophetic spirits—a life in which crime and sin, thank God, will be almost unknown quantities. And the beacon lighting us to that glorious 'Arcadia,' that 'Ultima Thule,' of human perfection and civilisation, is—the magic lamp of science!"

And with these words, uttered in impassioned tones, with all the burning fervour of an enthusiast, Norman Leslie opens his manuscript and proceeds to read the following tale.

CHAPTER IV

NORMAN LESLIE'S STORY

"I AM the resurrection and the life, saith the Lord; he that believeth in me, though he were dead, yet shall he live; and whosoever liveth and believeth in me shall never die."

These words are not uttered by an open grave, as the reader will naturally imagine, but by the bedside of one who, when he who spoke them, knelt to pray, still was amongst the living; but the prayers for the dying glide into the prayer for the dead. Arrested in his supplication by a sudden gesture on the part of the attendant physician, the clergyman glances up, and sees that the great change has taken place even as he prayed, and so breathes those wondrously beautiful and solemn words; words so few yet that contain in themselves the whole burden and meaning of our Christian faith, and that ring triumphant, with eternal hope and promise, over each new-made grave.

"Yes, all is over, poor soul—she is at rest at last," reverently speaks the doctor, when the sacred words have died away into silence; and the man who kneels beside the minister of God—and who has raised his head with a look of scared inquiry at the unexpected conclusion to the service for the sick—gives a cry of apparent anguish, followed by a low moan as he buries his face in the coverlet, which his hands clutch convulsively.

Yes, Agatha Hargrave is dead. She has been dying for the last six months—dying of a slow, withering, mysterious malady, which defied the doctor's skill to arrest or even to diagnose. At times, the poor wasted form was racked with intolerable agony; at others, prostrated by a fearful weakness; thus, during these long months the changes rang, and now the end has come and the weary spirit is released from its terrible bondage.

And yet, before the strange fatal sickness fell upon her, Mrs. Hargrave was in perfect health during the whole forty-six years of her life, having scarcely known a day's suffering.

The only two other occupants of the room—that has become in these last few moments a death-chamber—are, a woman who kneels in soft subdued sorrow at the other side of the bed—a woman with a gentle weak face, a face indicative of nervousness and indecision, a cousin of her who lies in her last long sleep—and an elderly man, who stands near the window beside a table covered with scattered legal-looking papers. He had been quietly seated when those words that told so much fell upon his ear, and with a hoarse whispered cry of what sounded like a bitter grief, he rose to his feet and remained standing with his face turned towards the bed. Apparently only the lawyer, the family solicitor whose presence was not unnatural at such a time.—And yet—his face is drawn and grey, as with a great repressed anguish.

After a moment or two his eyes turn upon the down-bent head of him who is supposed to be the chief mourner present—the man whose face is hidden, the husband of the dead woman—and what a strange look of doubt, hate, suspicion, grows in the old man's face as he gazes.

Mr. Sutcliffe is the family lawyer, but he is something else besides.

A dozen years ago, when Agatha Oliphant was about to marry, she had to choose between two suitors—one, John Sutcliffe, the grave, serious, forty-year-old lawyer, who dabbled in science as a recreation, who loved her devotedly and to whom her £800 a year was of little account—the other, young Philip Hargrave, ten years her junior, of no settled profession (though he had studied medicine for a while in Paris), and whose small yearly income of £200 would be very pleasantly augmented by Agatha's dower. She chose the latter.

Faithful, steadfast John Sutcliffe had small chance of success when pitted against gay, handsome, debonair Philip. They married; and through those dozen years of wedded life she never had cause to regret her choice. The world said—while it slightly marvelled—that theirs was a perfect union, and Philip a model husband; and the world, never apt to be too charitable, seemed, in this instance, to judge correctly. Agatha's life appeared all happiness, until that blight of mortal sickness fell upon her and extinguished all earthly joys for ever. And yet, knowing this, why does John Sutcliffe gaze at the prostrate husband with those eyes of questioning suspicion and abhorrence? Are the eyes of love more keen than the eyes that look indifferently? Or do love's eyes think they see what is not there? But ever since the beginning of Agatha's strange illness John Sutcliffe has watched silently, doubtingly, with dread suspicion in his heart, and watches still.

* * * * * *

With the exception of her husband there is no single relative of the dead woman's in England, save Barbara Holland, her first cousin, who kneels by the bedside sobbing softly, and who is also a niece of John Sutcliffe's, though he and the deceased were in no way connected.

Only one near relative in the world had Agatha Hargrave—a dearly-loved twin-brother, of whom no news had come for nearly a year.

Five years ago, Walter Oliphant—then captain in Her Majesty's Service—entered that of the Sultan and sailed for Egypt. He received rapid promotion, saw a good deal of service, was wounded once or twice slightly, and was speaking of returning home on a lengthened furlough, when suddenly all news of him ceased; and for the last few months of her life the great suspense and anxiety about him occasioned the suffering woman much added distress, though still she despaired not of his being restored to them. John Sutcliffe has done all he knows to obtain some tidings of the missing man within these latter months, but has failed as yet; though for this end he had neglected his business, which is great, and his scientific experiments, which he loves, and which are his sole relaxation from the cares and worries of his arduous profession.

Barbara has often asserted that she has a presentiment that Walter is still living and will come back some day unexpectedly, and longs and looks for that coming with mute, pathetic patience, for Walter Oliphant is very dear to the lonely woman. She loves him quite as well as did his sister, though possibly a little differently. Cousin Walter has been the one dream and romance of her grey and colourless life—a dream quite unguessed by anyone, even by him who evoked it.

Her home has been with Agatha for the last three or four years, for when her mother—Agatha's aunt—died, and Barbara was left alone in the world (save for her uncle, John Sutcliffe) Agatha, with her husband's permission, offered her a home with them, which the weak clinging, gentle creature was very happy to accept.

CHAPTER V
"JOHN SUTCLIFFE, I DEFY YOU."

HOW Mr. Sutcliffe craves for the presence of Walter—who would have a right to insist on what he so ardently desires—when half-an-hour later in the library he suggests to the doctor, who has attended Mrs. Hargrave all through her illness, the advisability of holding a *post-mortem* examination. "It would be more satisfactory," he continues, "as the disease was obscure and eluded your efforts to define its exact nature."

Dr. Milsom shakes his head in a somewhat deprecating manner, and glances enquiringly at Mr. Hargrave, who is the chief, indeed the only person to be considered in the matter.

"As Mr. Hargrave wishes, of course," he answers with slow enunciation. "For my own part, I do not see that it is actually necessary, for though the malady baffled me, in as far as regards 'classification,' and some of the symptoms were certainly rather singular and uncommon; still—well—I—I cannot think what purpose would be served by an autopsy, save, of course, always the interests of science."

"Ah! yes, precisely, the interests of science," hastily interpolates Mr. Sutcliffe, glad to catch at the one point that may possibly animate the easy-going, supine, unimaginative doctor to action. "Surely," he argues, eagerly, "in such a cause one ought to make a little sacrifice, even of personal feeling, and——"

"Yes, and in the interests of your vile science, you would desecrate my darling Agatha's poor dead wasted body, with the brutal butchering surgeon's knife," interrupts the bereaved husband, indignantly, starting from the easy-chair in which he had been sunk, apparently absorbed in silent grief.

"No, Dr. Milsom, no, Mr. Sutcliffe, I will consent to no *post-mortem* examination; my dear one will lay her down in her grave perfect as she was in life, with no soil of sacrilegious, prying, scientific hands upon her," (with a baleful look at Sutcliffe) "hands that would not hesitate to cut and hack the quivering nerves of their own dying mother, if by so doing they could add one bare bald item to the gigantic structure of lies they have raised. If I am content I think everyone else may be; how could it comfort or console me, or anyone who loved her, to be told the exact classification to which the disease my poor wife died of belonged?

"What would one medical term do to assuage my sorrow more than another?

"No, Dr. Milsom, I thank you for your past kindness; you did your best to save your patient, and when that was hopeless to mitigate her suffering. You, Mr. Sutcliffe, have made my wife's will (much against your will, I know), and with that ends our connection; I think henceforth we shall be strangers. My poor Agatha liked and respected you, and I respected her prejudices, but there never can be friendship between us, and there is no longer any necessity for assuming it. Old man, and all as you are, you cannot forgive me for being successful, where you failed a dozen years ago, and would injure me if you could, but I defy you, John Sutcliffe!" he hisses in a semi-whisper, with a contemptuous smile on his handsome face, that scarcely looks now, like that of a broken-hearted man, though so grief-struck a moment ago.

"He fears me, he fears me; that is why he wishes all acquaintance to end; he forgot himself for the moment, and dropped the mask; it will be my business to pluck it off altogether and expose the real hideousness of the features that lurk beneath. And yet—I may be wrong, I may be wrong; God forgive me if I am," murmurs Mr. Sutcliffe to himself, though outwardly, he only calmly speaks a few words of apparent ready acquiescence, to Mr. Hargrave's strangely sudden resolve.

* * * * * *

Yes, John Sutcliffe knows what the world does not suspect, what the poor dead wife died in blissful ignorance of—for Philip Hargrave adds a perfect hypocrisy to his other vices. The lawyer knows that the apparent mourner has within the last year conceived a wild, mad infatuation for another woman—a beautiful girl, in a rank inferior to his own, but who is pure and proud, and will never be aught but "wife" to any man. He knows also that nearly a year ago, he himself made Mrs. Hargrave's will, a will in which she left her husband everything she died possessed of unreservedly. And he also knows that the man's life, through those dozen years of marriage, has been very different from what it has appeared to the world and to the trusting woman, who so ardently and faithfully believed in him.

He knows that he has been false, false as hell, all along. He has watched him through those years silently; watched him with rage and hatred in his heart, and yet thankful that by the very power of his deceit the eyes of the woman whom he (John Sutcliffe) so truly loved remained unopened. From the very first he had cause to distrust and doubt Philip Hargrave; young as the latter was when he married Agatha, yet the lawyer had heard from unlikely sources, something of the life he had previously led, that caused him ever after to feel suspicious of the man; but Agatha's happiness was his sole thought, and to have revealed anything to her, would be to have broken her heart, so he only watched, and said no word. And even now he dare not speak out; he can only suspect, with the whole force of his nature, he can only feel morally convinced that Agatha Hargrave was "done to death," as surely as ever woman was; the guilty man's subtlety is great, and must be only met by finer subtlety still, if ever the crime is to be brought home to him.

Another thing which makes the lawyer feel well nigh positive he is right in his horrible imaginings is that quite lately he has had secret enquiries made relative to Philip's life in Paris thirteen years ago, and has ascertained that in his pursuit of medical knowledge there he devoted himself almost altogether to the study of toxicology, to tracing the nature and action of the most deadly, subtle poisons, that simulating by their symptoms various intricate well-known maladies, consequently almost invariably defy detection.

But all these facts John Sutcliffe locks up in his own breast; he can do nothing of himself, and to only one person in the world will he confide utterly, and that is—Walter Oliphant, if fate sends him back to England before it is too late.

CHAPTER VI
BARBARA HAS SCRUPLES

"YES, Barbara, you must do this thing for me. I'll take no denial. Why, what are you afraid of, you timid creature? I'll take all the responsibility on myself; you only act under my desire. And what is it to make such a fuss over? But to speak a few words at my dictation."

"Ah! but such words, uncle," gasped the trembling, frightened woman. "And in such awful circumstances!"

"Nonsense, my dear," rejoins Mr. Sutcliffe, "you loved your cousin Agatha, and surely would do more than this for her; would you not stretch a point to discover whether she came by her death fairly?"

"But what you want to do is like blasphemy both against——"

"Pshaw!" retorts the lawyer, impatiently. "If Walter Oliphant were here, you would not dare, ay or even wish, to deny him this simple service; and don't you think he would urge it even more strenuously than I?"

"Walter would never think such a fearful thing, I am sure, or wish me to do anything so dreadful," sobbed Barbara.

"Wouldn't he? Your cousin, Walter, is not a weak trusting woman, who cannot imagine evil unless she actually sees it."

"But what you want me to do, Uncle John, seems so horrible, so—so supernatural almost," contends the weak creature already yielding, the powerful argument of her absent cousin's approval or disapproval being all convincing.

"One must meet cunning and strategy by sunning and strategy," argues the lawyer, "and if this idea of mine, which I know Walter

Oliphant would commend highly, is a little novel and singular—unlikely to be thought of as a possible mode of detecting crime, why, so much the better."

"But, uncle, if you are wrong in your terrible surmise, as I pray and trust you are? My darling Agatha suffered and died, as we all must when our time comes; but it was the hand of God, not man—it is wicked even to think it; of that I feel assured. But if, as I say, you are wrong, how grievous it may be for you. It may be looked upon as a crime for all we know, and punished accordingly, and those who helped you. What may not——" with a catch of fear in her breath, as she paused in consternation.

"I told you before, Barbara, that I'll take all responsibility on my own shoulders. I'll bear the brunt of my own idea, be it evil or good; and you may be very sure I must feel almost certain, or I'd scarcely take so extreme a measure."

"If you could only get some one else. Oh! why must it be I?" she wails, virtually giving up her invertebrate opposition.

"Dear heaven! It might be her very voice," exclaims John Sutcliffe, with a strange ring of triumph in his tones, but Barbara Holland shrinks.

"No, don't say so, uncle John, it makes it worse, more like mocking the——"

"Now don't get foolish again, Bab; all this argument, and contention, may after all be for no end. If Walter Oliphant, the only person on earth who can insist on what I desire so greatly, does not come home within a reasonable time, or, again, if we find we cannot compel Philip Hargrave's presence at what he doubtless would do much to avoid (though if time passes he will feel secure—secure)—my idea must die still-born. And yet he wouldn't be secure, if it were years instead of months, only we would have no excuse—no excuse—but ingenuity might bring it about in some other way, though nothing so effectual." . . . The last few broken sentences he mutters *sotto voce.* He feels his victory is won over weak, hesitating Barbara Holland, and is satisfied.

This conversation takes place a week after Agatha Hargrave's death, and the day after she has been laid in her lonely grave. Barbara Holland having left Philip Hargrave's house for ever immediately after the funeral, and taken up her residence with her uncle, John Sutcliffe.

Nearly four months pass away in tranquil peace and uneventfulness, save that it is already whispered that the new-made widower may not be very long before he finds consolation; which confirmation of his suspicions makes old Sutcliffe gnash his teeth impotently, and long still more ardently for Walter's return.

CHAPTER VII
NEMESIS

IT has been written "All things come to him who knows how to wait," though for my part I think it might be more truly said, considering the experience of the great mass of mankind, "All things come too late"; but Mr. Sutcliffe is one of the favoured few to whom the quotation is applicable.

It wants just two days of four months since Agatha Hargrave's death, when Colonel Oliphant, unexpected, unannounced, walks into John Sutcliffe's chambers in Lincoln's Inn. He had been taken prisoner by the Arabs, carried into a wild, unknown region, and had been in daily fear of death by torture for nearly a year. Half naked, starved, beaten, made a beast of burden, it was only a wonder how life held out; but at last he made his escape, and after unimaginable difficulties and sufferings, with the terror of recapture ever before him, he at last made his way to the coast, and reached Cairo bereft of all. In his haste to leave a country in which he had suffered so terribly he actually forgot that he had money and effects at Alexandria, where he had been previously stationed; forgot that letters, or communications of some kind, might be awaiting him there; half maddened by his awful experience, his only thought was to get away. So he made his statement to the authorities, was simply provided with all necessaries, and took ship at once for England, where he now arrived, ignorant of all that had happened within the past year.

Ignorant of his beloved twin-sister's long illness and death.

It was just a chance—his regard for that dear sister—that induced him to come straight on landing to John Sutcliffe's chambers rather than to Philip Hargrave's house.

He feared that the shock of seeing hm suddenly, unprepared, after of course believing him dead, might be injurious to Agatha, and now when he walks in, gladly, expectantly, to the lawyer's office, it is to receive a greater shock than any he could have inflicted. There is generally a strange mystic bond of love between twins, and these two were no exception to the rule: a strong and deep affection having existed between them.

At first, Walter Oliphant is utterly crushed and heart-broken by the sad tidings; but by-and-by, when he has heard all John Sutcliffe's story, his heart is more full of vengeance than of grief.

Long and earnest, and explicit in all details, is these men's talk; they converse on into the night, and when they part, it is with a clear and perfect understanding between them. At once, Colonel Oliphant will take action, so long desired by the lawyer. To-morrow, he will apply to the proper quarter for an order for the exhumation of his sister's remains; he has a perfect right to claim it, the circumstances attending her death—as he can now detail them—being decidedly suspicious. He will also see Philip Hargrave, telling him what he has done, but expressing no unfriendly feeling; only saying, that he would feel more satisfied, the doctors having failed to discover the cause of death; that somewhat of a mysterious malady has appeared in their family from time to time, though not in the last two generations, and he wishes to ascertain whether his poor sister has been a victim of it, though perhaps already too long a time has elapsed to allow of any proper autopsy being performed; ending by expressing a hope that Philip will consent to be present, otherwise it might appear strange, and as if there was some ill-feeling between them.

All takes place as they arrange. With little difficulty Colonel Oliphant gets an order for the exhumation of the body, and his interview with Philip Hargrave is satisfactory; though when he suddenly states what he has just been doing, Philip's face grows pale, and he starts strangely; but it is only a momentary weakness. When Walter begs him to be present he immediately consents.

"Though, my dear fellow, I cannot see any possible use in it, only to harrow all our feelings terribly. How can ascertaining the exact name of the malady that killed our dearest Agatha avail or comfort us? We cannot, alas! bring her back to life, and surely it would seem more tender and respectful to her memory to let her rest in peace. But, of course, I suppose you have a better right than even I to say how it will be, and I don't wish to oppose you. If our dear one can be looked upon again by the living without appalling them—which I almost doubt after so long—I will look with you, and support you through the trial."

"Thank you," replies Colonel Oliphant simply. "I am glad you don't refuse, as it might look strange, as if I were acting against your will. I am hungering to see her face once more, even after four months Death has laid his cruel defacing hand upon it. Though I think you are mistaken, in what you anticipate, as to the repulsiveness of the ordeal. I have been with Dr. Milsom, and he is not at all of your opinion; he imagines that there will be very little change. He says my dear sister was so fearfully, so extraordinarily wasted, both by the nature of the malady he supposes, and her intense suffering," (is it fancy, or does Philip Hargrave, wince somewhat at those last words?) "so reduced to almost skin and bone, that the body might remain intact a long time, and present no shocking appearance."

After a little more discussion about that ghastly ceremony of three days hence, they part, and Philip Hargrave mutters to himself:

"Safe! Safe! Four long months, and a week would have been

sufficient to bury that secret for ever. It is that old dotard's doing; what besotted idiocy it is. What can they expect? You may do your worst, John Sutcliffe, I am out of reach of your long-cherished venom. I and my Rita will be happy in spite of you. . . . My sweet! how lovely you are: it is worth going through all for your sake. . . . And yet—how I wish I could evade that! But it would look as if I feared. . . . And yet—how can I look upon her face again! . . . Pshaw! the dead tell no tales, one need fear only the living."

CHAPTER VIII

"BEING DEAD YET SPEAKETH."[76]

THREE days later, on the weird and mystic 'All Souls' Night'—the night when the spirits of the dead are said by superstition to revisit their earthly haunts; when the veil between the known and the unknown hangs peculiarly thin and transparent—on the late afternoon of this November eve the few actors in this strange, brief, but real drama, are assembled for the dread task that lies before them; but what they expect, yet shrink with humanity's natural recoil from looking on, has not arrived. The carpenter is waiting, but the coffin through some unaccountable delay, has not yet arrived from the cemetery. The meeting has been arranged for quite late in the afternoon to suit the convenience of the doctors. But it soon becomes evident that the short daylight will have waned before they can commence their eerie task; and when the ghastly burden is at last carried into their midst, both Dr. Milsom, who is to superintend the autopsy, and the surgeon who is to perform it, declare it will be better to defer till the morrow, as, of course, conducted by artificial light, it cannot be so satisfactory. But Walter Oliphant and John Sutcliffe overrule this proposal, backed by Philip Hargrave, who eagerly urges them to get the wretched business over as quickly as possible.

The doctors positively assert that it will be practically impossible in these circumstances to make as thorough an examination of the remains (supposing them in a state to admit of examination) as Colonel Oliphant desires.

---

[76] Hebrews 11:4 (KJV).

Then John Sutcliffe suggests that if on opening the coffin it is found the autopsy can be proceeded with, why they might just take the first necessary steps and then adjourn it 'till next day, though certainly it would be much better to conclude it to-night if possible.

So it is agreed, and while the carpenter does his part Dr. Milsom and his colleague, with the two young medical students who are to assist, withdraw to a small table in a distant corner, on which stand the necessary surgical instruments, and fortify nature against the coming trying ordeal with reviving brandies and sodas.

John Sutcliffe and Walter Oliphant converse in hushed tones, while Philip Hargrave sits apart, silent, starting at every slightest movement and noise. How strange, and echoing, and ghostlike are the voices as they resound in muffled cadence through the bare lofty room; how eerie those retreating steps slowly descending the distant stairs. It seems, to his excited nervous imagination, as if many lay dead out somewhere in these dusky passages, that are dim and desolate, and suggestive of mystery. As if he, in some terrible isolation, were alone in the world of shadows. Life, and its pleasant, assuring associations, seems to retreat from him, leaving him in that awful loneliness, leaving him surrounded by phantoms—invisible, but that he feels are there, in the air around him—fluttering, rustling, touching him with spirit hands, whispering to him with spirit voices words of dread and fearful meaning. A great, thick horror seems to be pressing him down—down. A nameless terror takes possession of him for a few minutes; then, with a great effort, he tries to rouse himself, to shake himself free of the weird, occult influence that is upon him.

Why did he come? He was a fool to do so. The spell of the horrible night it is, is upon him, he thinks, savagely. He has serious thoughts of even now softly taking his departure, but he feels that he cannot rise from his chair, that some great nervous tremor has him in its grasp, rendering him helpless for the time being. He should be all right, he thinks, if he could only have some of that invigorating stuff those fellows over there are quaffing. And then he looks askance at that long dark object on which the carpenter is still at work, and shudders . . . And now with a sort of wailing creak the concealing lid is off, and Dr. Milsom approaches for a moment, looks within the coffin, and withdraws, with a whispered word to Colonel Oliphant, who comes forward and murmurs in Philip's ear that the moment has come when they two, who were so nearly related to the deceased, are to look upon her face again; and Philip, with a mighty effort, gathers himself together and walks over, and stands at Walter's side, looking down upon that dead face, that is as yet unchanged, save a little yellower, than when last seen by mortal eyes. After a moment or two, he stumbles like a blind man back to his seat, in which he sinks exhausted; while John Sutcliffe, who has unceasingly but furtively watched him, takes his place at Walter's side, as he craves to look once more on those loved features.

For a few minutes they stand thus, in silent contemplation, tears quietly stealing down Colonel Oliphant's bronzed and bearded face, although his hands are clenched as if more in wrath than sorrow, while a slumbering fire burns in John Sutcliffe's watchful eyes.

Then the former turns away with a suppressed groan, and the lawyer alone bends for a moment over that still and awful form, takes a last lingering look at those rigid features, locked in such an eternal repose, and then reverently again covers the face; his hands are trembling, and he is slow in doing this simple act, but no one notices him—the doctors are busy selecting their instruments, and talking in subdued tones, so as not to intrude upon the mourners' grief—and then he too turns away, and Dr. Milsom's voice is heard speaking of the light, which has grown strangely dim this last moment or two. "What has happened to the gas?" he says. "It is going out, and we want light, plenty of light, if we are to do anything."

But, before any one can answer him, in the momentary pause that follows his words, a slight, strange, hollow sound makes itself audible through the large shadowed room; a *sound proceeding from the coffin.*

It is repeated almost instantaneously a little louder than before, a faint grasping cry ending with a moan; then quite clear and distinct, though scarce above a whisper, come the words through the terrible silence fallen upon the room——

"Art thou come, Philip Hargrave?"

* * * * * *

And in the awful pause that ensues upon the ghastly manifestation, there is a rush of sound from the appalled living. One man (the carpenter) has fled from the room, frantic. One of the medical students has fainted, the other, stupefied with terror, clings helplessly to his chair; Dr. Milom and the surgeon have dropped on their knees instinctively, with a great sweat of horror starting on their ashen faces, while the former prays audibly; John Sutcliffe has also fallen on his knees, though his eyes never cease to watch Philip Hargrave, who is paralysed with terror, the body motionless, no attempt to flee, the eyes fixed and glaring fearfully, as they actually protrude from their sockets, the under lip dropped, while a slight foam issues from the mouth; it is, as it were, death gazing upon death! And yet one feels that the man's whole being is concentrated in the one act of listening.

And again those words reverberate through the room, louder this time, and they are Agatha Hargrave's own living tones! "Art thou come to gloat upon thy victim? Thy wife slain by thy hand? All things are revealed to the spirit, and mine returns to the earth to denounce thee. Murderer, confess, ere yet it is too late!"

* * * * * *

That awful voice from the dead ceases, and a wave of icy air seems to rush through the room.

Then Philip Hargrave, who has fallen from his chair, crouching on the floor with the face of a maniac, makes what appears almost a superhuman effort to recapture the reason that has so nearly slipped from him; he staggers to his feet and tries to speak, but his tongue refuses to obey. A mightier effort, and a hoarse fearful utterance at least finds way between those palsied lips.

"I confess—I am guilty! the guiltiest wretch on earth. I confess—I am accursed. I am thy murderer, and may God have mercy on my soul."

And with a ghastly scream he falls insensible to the floor. And when by-and-by he awakes from that stupor, Philip Hargrave is a raving maniac. The words of that confession, made in such weird and terrible circumstances, are the last sane words he speaks, and within a year he ends his sinful days in a madhouse.

* * * * * *

It was hardly worth John Sutcliffe's while to lay his plans so carefully; to elaborate his scheme of vengeance with such almost diabolical skill.

It had not failed, inasmuch as it had wrung the confession from the guilty man's terrified soul, but here the plot of what some might call an unholy revenge ceased; and, yet again, would John Sutcliffe—guessing, feeling, believing as he did—have been justified in letting the criminal go free?

Was he not rather justified, some will say, in using every means—even though these means might not be considered legitimate in a court of law—to entrap that confession, in calling every instrument to his aid to punish such black and fearful guilt?

That marvellous invention of these later days,

The Phonograph

(as the reader will, of course, have guessed ere this) was the detective that Mr. Sutcliffe had summoned to his assistance.

These terrible words we have just listened to are the words that timid, honourable Barbara Holland shrank so fearfully from speaking; but her uncle overruled her; and the words spoken into that little mystic cylinder were carefully stored, and accurately repeated, when the time came, in the very tones of the dead woman's voice, as Barbara Holland's and that of her cousin were startlingly alike.

Thus, the ghastly illusion was made perfect. Thus, the sin of the sinner found him out—and thus, man's wondrous inventiveness, and scientific skill, have added yet another to the powerful agents, drawn from Nature's armoury, in the pursuit and detection of the criminal.

The guilty wretch who seeks to baffle justice, may now sometimes fear another enemy in the magic little instrument, that even leaves the "telegraph" and "telephone" behind; and crime revealed by the "phonograph," may not be an utterly impossible event in the future.

Conclusion of Normal Leslie's Story.

CHAPTER IX
IN THE PICTURE GALLERY

"WE must make the picture gallery our headquarters," Mabel declared, with decision, and all her satellites cried, "Hear, hear!"

This old Grange of the Ardens has been in the family for generations. Built at the time of the Restoration by one Guy Arden, a brave officer and gallant upholder of the Stuarts, it had been tenanted successively by staunch Jacobites, zealous partisans of that unhappy race.

The reason why Mabel proposed the "picture gallery" as their centre was that it abutted on the "West Wing' of the Grange, the part that had undergone no alteration, and stood exactly as it did in the olden days. Here the unexpected little rooms and passages mustered in greatest force. This part was seldom, if ever, used, and abounded in charming hiding places; and here Mabel led her laughing, shouting band of followers.

Every part of the mansion, even to the remote "West Wing," is lit up this "All Souls' Night," but the light is not brilliant, and when they enter that long, lofty, silent gallery, with those seemingly interminable rows of frowning pictures on the walls, only half revealed by the dim religious light, the children involuntarily cease their gay shouts and laughter and draw closer together, the youngest of the five little girls—who in their pretty white frocks relieve the more sombre tints of the sterner sex which prevails in number—saying in tones suggestive of trepidation and inward misgiving:—

"O, Mab dear, we'll never have light enough to play here; don't you think we'd better go back?"

But Mabel only laughed, and called her a "little goose," saying, if they had too much light, they would find each other too easily; and the boys, though they would have gladly voted with little Gracie for more light, felt that it wouldn't do to funk or show the "white feather," when Mab, who was "only a girl," was such a "brave old brick."

And soon they were engaged in such wild merry romps that they forgot to think about the light or where they were. They were enchanted to have Mabel for their leader. She was a "first-rate captain," the boys said. It was she who thought of the most surprising and out-of-the-way places to hide in, and when it was her turn, and they heard the sweet, shrill "Seek," echo through those silent rooms, they set off with the pleasant conviction that Mab would give them some trouble to discover her whereabouts.

What nooks and crannies she did make out, to be sure! And how dusty she got her pretty, gauzy, blue-grey dress in the interests of those noisy young cousins. She looked wondrously fair in that dim light. She had flung a soft, grey, muffling shawl about her shoulders, coming to that cold west wing, and now, with her bright hair loosened from its fastenings and streaming over it, and those marvellous grey eyes, with their long black lashes, looking out of the sweet spiritual face, she seemed, somehow, the impersonation of a summer cloud, and the character for a fancy ball would have suited her admirably. The shimmering, sheeny, blue-grey dress, and the darker grey of the shawl, cloud-like in texture and tint, relieved by the sunshine of the golden rippling hair, all was in accord; and then there was something shadowy, vague, ethereal, about the girl herself.

They had had a good romping, uproarious game of that old-world, but ever delightful, "blind man's buff," varied by the racing, sibilant "puss in the corner," first within the confines of the picture gallery, which had quite rubbed off any little feeling of strangeness or timidity they may have experienced on entering this silent, disused part of the house, and they now raced fearlessly about that uninhabited west wing, their merry shouts startling the sleepy echoes, which woke with a drowsy, displeased growl, at having their territory thus ruthlessly invaded.

And as for ghosts, if any of these somewhat uncomfortable, uncanny tribe amicably shred the solitude of their brethren, the echoes, they fled incontinently before the flood of life that surged through their domain.

After nearly an hour's jubilant, unrestrained play, one or two of the younger rioters were fain to cry, "Hold, enough!"

The little feet were growing tired, the young eyes waxing heavy, but the stronger and more turbulent spirits turned a deaf ear to those wearied ones, until Mabel came to their rescue, saying that they must give up, they had played enough for that evening; once more, though it was not her turn, she would hide, and they would find, and then all would return to the others.

"Agreed," shouted the conquered ones, simultaneously.

"But be sure you don't act shabby, Mab," added Dick, the eldest of the party, "and choose an easy place for the last. Let this 'hide' be the best of all, or we'll cry 'gammon' and not go."[77]

"Oh, never fear," answered Mabel, with her sweet, musical laugh. "I'll give you as much trouble as ever I can; and you ought to be very much obliged to me, you ungrateful boys, giving myself such discomfort for your tiresome sakes. I thought you said I was your captain, and I'm sure good, loyal soldiers never tell

[77] Cry 'gammon': Cry humbug, nonsense.

their officers that if they don't do just what they like they will cry 'gammon,' and not obey."

"Oh, Mab, that's not fair, to catch up a fellow's words so," cried the eldest boy, dancing after her to the door, or rather great arched entrance of that long gallery; but she ran away laughing, calling out,

"Traitor! trying to watch where I am going; I defy you!"

And then they heard her light footsteps in the corridor without, and Dick came back to the others to wait for the sweet, shrill summons that would bid them "Seek!"

They chattered in an undertone, afraid of not hearing Mabel; but "What a row the wind did make, to be sure," grumbled the boys. It had increased much in strength the last half hour, and now wailed, and sobbed, and 'plained round the old house, like despairing spirits clamouring for admission.

It groaned in the wide chimneys, and shrieked through chinks of door and casement with Banshee-like utterance. A wild, tumultuous All Souls' night, and growing wilder as the night advanced.

An imaginative mind might easily fancy the air full of the spirits of the departed—that out there in the darkness, on this night, specially their own, the mighty host of the dead—that multitude that "no man can number"—wrestled and groaned in spiritual pain, calling, pleading, contending with man's selfish unconsciousness and forgetfulness, to be remembered; moaning and shrieking in their despairing anguish at finding themselves completely blotted out from the memories and the hearts where they had fondly hoped and believed they would reign for all time and eternity. Yes, surely this solemn, weird night's darkness is peopled with their mystic, unseen presence. Coming and going, swiftly, sadly, the rush of their spirit wings agitates the air till it seems rent as if with tempest; those eerie sobs and sighs, that seem to fill all nature, throbbing and pulsating out in the black void beyond our windows are the wild lament of those desolate forgotten ones. They ask nothing of us, those pleading, pitiful, sorrowing dead—nought of our time, or wealth, or fame, or comfort; they only crave not to be quite forgotten, and mourn when they find on these yearly visits earthwards that even memory—much less love or yearning—cannot afford them the smallest niche in its cold storehouse.

But this is wandering far from the group of noisy, gay, young revellers gathered in the picture gallery at Arden Grange, impatiently awaiting their captain's call.

"How long Mab is," complains little Gracie, fretfully, she being one of those who had given in and voted for an adjournment.

"So much the better," says Dick, triumphantly, "it will give us all the more fun to find her. Babies, like you and Freddy," glancing contemptuously at these two youngest members of the party, "have no business to come and spoil our sport; getting tired for nothing at all. I'm sure if I were you, Freddy, I'd be ashamed of myself to knock under, when Mab's such a trump."

"But Mab's a big girl, and I'm only a little boy," whimpers Master Freddy, half-crying with crossness and fatigue, and utterly unimpressed by the force of Dick's argument that might have told upon a bigger boy.

"Only a little baby you mean," scoffs Dick. And then all are silent, waiting for Mab's call; but no call comes.

They fidget about impatiently for a few minutes. Why doesn't she shout? What's the use of keeping them waiting so long? Was she playing a trick on them, serving them out for rebellion? Or, can they have missed her call?

No, they have been straining their ears all the time and even the wind could not drown that shrill, sweet cry, which, of course, she would repeat again and again, until she heard her faithful troops coming to release her from captivity.

Then they draw closer together in that long dim gallery; the wind has temporarily lulled—one of those strange sudden pauses that so often occur during the height of a tempest's raging, and seem so inexplicable, when not a leaf appears to stir—as if that wondrous invisible element were gathering up all its forces,—"taking breath"—preparatory to a renewed onslaught.

" 'Tis but the rest of the wind between the flaws that blow."

How terribly silent seems all that part of the house.

A feeling of eeriness and loneliness creeps in among the children, why, they could not say, as they stand waiting for Mabel's strangely delayed summons—a feeling enhanced by the tired Gracie and Freddy setting up a dismal, hopeless, monotonous crying. "Enough to take the heart out of a fellow," as Dick emphatically declares to the rest of the little band, who look on him as their leader, vice Mabel apparently resigned.

"Well, I say, this is a rum go," he says at last, in aggressively cheerful tones and in language more expressive than elegant, feeling himself called on to say something.

"I vote we skedaddle, there's no use in staying here all night. We can holloa when we get outside, and when Mabel finds that we are not coming to look for her, she'll soon come pelting after us."

"I say, Dick," says his cousin Tom, a year younger than himself. "Don't you think that Mab has just paid us out, by going back to the others on the sly? I'll bet you sixpence we'll find her laughing at us in the red drawing-room," as the inner room of the stately suite is called. At this suggestion there is a general stampede; somehow this great, dimly-lit, silent gallery, with the portraits of dead and gone Ardens gazing down with shadowy faces on these their nineteenth century descendants, fill these juveniles with vague fear, now that they are no longer upheld by the conviction of Mabel's neat presence, though what that poor, little, nineteen-year-old girl could save them from they would be puzzled to tell.

Even Dick condescends to run; but when they get out into the corridor, they pause, and the three older boys shout with the full power of their lungs, until that lone, west wing resounds with the girl's name, but—all in vain.

These gloomy echoes throw back the monosyllable—"Mab," but no more; no bright, girlish voice responds to their clamorous appeal.

"It's a beastly shame!" cries Dick, wrathfully. "I never thought that Mab would play one such a shabby trick; it's downright mean, and won't I tell her so."

And then there is a rush of flying feet, through many corridors and passages and stairways, which never slacken till they reach the door of the long drawing-room, which opens on the great corridor, through which they had passed little more than an hour ago, so hilariously, so joyously; now they are breathless, pale-faced, and resentful, while Gracie and Freddy sob convulsively as they bring up the rear at a sharp trot.

But when they rush through the brilliant rooms and, at last, burst into the farthest and smallest of the suite—where the sort of solemn hush that had fallen on the story-telling group, at the conclusion of Norman Leslie's somewhat eerie tale is not quite dispelled, though old Mr. Burroughs, unbelieving as ever, tries to show the supreme folly of attempting to prove future results, of prophesying future general good, from any singular isolated case like the one quoted—no Mabel is to be seen!

"Where is she?" asks Dick, indignantly, looking round with searching, scathing eyes of reproof, intended to annihilate the offender.

Then one and all they tell the story of their wrong to the Squire, all talking together, all more or less incoherent; but the genial old grandfather—who, truth to tell, is delighted at the interruption, having no taste at all for either horrors or scientific marvels, and to whom argument on any subject, save perhaps his pet hobbies, "the Land question, Rights of Landlord and Tenant," &c., is a weariness of the flesh—laughs and rubs his hands gleefully.

Mabel has served them rightly, and punished them for their selfishness in keeping her so long in that cold west wing, and away from all her friends, and they will see her no more to-night, he says. She is just tired of them, and gone right off home to her mother, as she often does, without saying anything to anyone.

"Did she tell you she was going, sir?" asks Hugh Denver, who is standing near, listening with undisguised interest to the children's story.

"No, Mr. Denver, she did not," responds Squire Arden, "but I know the little girl's ways," with a fond smile.

"But surely," remonstrates Hugh, with a grave face, "Miss Arden would not think of venturing out alone, unattended, on such a wild, harsh night as this?"

"Wouldn't she?" laughs the Squire. "You don't know Mabel if you think that. She's a hardy, wild flower is our little Mab, though she looks more like a fragile hot-house blossom. Besides, the 'outing' is not very formidable, somewhere about two hundred yards or so. You know, or perhaps you don't know, that her home—the Arden Dower House—is quite close; you may have noticed this afternoon, when driving out here from the village, a pretty, straggling, many-gabled cottage, about a fifth of a mile from the Grange gates—that's it, and the rear almost abuts on our east wing; so it's but running next door, after all, one might say," with an amused smile. "My poor sister-in-law is a sad invalid, and is scarcely ever able to venture out of doors, and the child gets uneasy about her mother when away from her, and runs off without our ever knowing anything about it. If it's early in the evening she turns up again later on; if not, we see her no more for that night. She's a strange girl, our Mab, not quite like other girls—though a deuced deal better than most," he added, *sotto voce.*

"And you think, Squire, she's gone home, and that we shan't see her again to-night?" says Hugh, slowly.

"Thinking implies a doubt," smiles the old man, who guesses pretty well how matters stand between his favourite niece and this dark, handsome stranger, and is now secretly pleased to watch the clouding over of that thoughtful brow. "I don't think, but I know. To-morrow, however, is my birthday; you see I am fortunate, and am niched in quite comfortably with 'all the Saints.' I ought to feel such rarefied companionship slightly overpowering, but somehow I don't," he said, with his genial, kindly laugh. "And Katharine, my sister-in-law, has promised, if at all equal to it, to make an effort to join us—my family are foolish enough always to make a little *festa* of these recurrent milestones—and if she comes she'll sleep, as she daren't venture out at night, so there'll be no fear of Miss Mabel playing truant when her mother's within sight."

CHAPTER X
HUGH'S REFLECTIONS

HUGH Denver walks to one of the long windows and draws aside the curtain. As it happens, the room looks out on the avenue through which his fearless, little Mabel must, as he thinks, have scudded within the last few minutes, he not being aware of the shorter, more facile rear communication with the Dower House from the east side of the Grange, where a race through some shrubberies skirting the out-offices, stables, &c., of the latter, leads to a little gate in the boundary wall, opening into a paddock belonging to the former, which again opens into the roomy old-fashioned kitchen-garden and orchard of the Dower House, and represents the grounds of the latter, save for a miniature lawn and flower garden in front facing the road.

"How the wind moans and sobs through those grand old trees in the stately avenue," thinks Hugh; "how the topmost branches sway and bend, and wildly toss their heaven-pointing arms as the ruthless air-fiend sweeps on his devastating course." But the night is better in some respects than he thought. There is a wild wrack of clouds overhead, dark and portentous, just over the Grange, as if menacing some evil to the house of Arden, but the outer edges are jagged and broken, and away in the west, still far from the horizon, shines the moon; a real wintry moon, pale, cold, very unsympathetic, but still shedding a chill, white light on the wind-tossed, shivering earth. And as he stands there, realising that Mabel's premature home-going was not such an act of heroism after all—to a country-bred girl that night would seem fine—a slight feeling as of resentment steals into his breast; his heart hardens, ever so little, against the girl whose dreamy, visionary eyes so enslaved him from the first moment he had gazed into their grey luminous depths.

* * * * * *

Six months before this November eve Mabel Arden had just recovered from an attack of low fever, prevalent in the adjoining village, which had much weakened and prostrated her, and the doctor said a change of some kind—to the sea if possible—was absolutely necessary to her perfect restoration to health and strength.

Mabel had stoutly declined to go; her mother not being able to accompany her she would not leave her alone. The doctor was equally determined on his side; at last a compromise was made. It was arranged that Mrs. Arden should be transferred to the Grange, to be her brother-in-law's guest during her daughter's absence, and then Mab consented, very unwillingly, to go on a month's visit to Ilfracombe, to Mrs. Derrick, the Squire's second daughter and the mother of that identical little Gracie and Freddy who led the crying in the picture gallery. But that month lengthened itself out into nearly three. She there met Hugh Denver, a distant cousin of Fred Derrick's, and there the "old, old story was told again," the story eternally old, and yet everlastingly, entrancingly new.

Mrs. Derrick was delighted. Hugh belonged to a good old family—good enough even for an Arden—he was his own master, possessed a handsome estate, and had never yet in all his eight and twenty years cared seriously for a woman.

It was the very thing for Mabel, and though the young people parted after an idyllic two months without anything actually definite being said—there was an unspoken, tacit understanding between them, infinitely more fascinating to them, at least to dreamy young Mab, than any acknowledged, openly avowed engagement—

and Mrs. Derrick felt that her favourite young cousin's future was assured.

And now, when she came to Arden with her husband and children on a visit to her father, intending to spend a month, possibly to remain over Christmas, she brought Hugh a willing captive in her train. He had told Mabel in one of their sweet, stolen confidences at Ilfracombe that he would be in the neighbourhood of her home before long, when he hoped to make acquaintance with her mother and uncle. But stupid, tedious, law-business detained him, an unwilling prisoner in London, until this very week; and now the very night he and Mabel meet again, after nearly four months separation, shyly glad and happy as she appeared to see him, yet she runs off before the evening is half over, voluntarily relinquishing his society, "without rhyme or reason"— as it seems to him, who does not comprehend Mabel's passionate love and solicitude for her frail, suffering mother; first, banishing herself with those tiresome children, which had stung him rather, though on second thoughts he reflected that Mabel perhaps considered it her duty to try to amuse the youngsters, only she need not have stayed away so long—and now vanishing altogether!

He feels hurt, almost mortified, and this is a new experience to Hugh Denver. Hitherto, women have only too palpably sought his regard, glaringly and unblushingly courted his society and notices, requiring but very faint invertebrate encouragement on his part.

Then glancing at the group still gathered round the great fireplace, now laughing and lighthearted again, as they strive to shake off the impression caused by Leslie's weird story, in this very room he thinks there are two or three girls who would be only too glad of his smiles and whispered words; one, whom he had met once or twice before—Kathleen O'Hara, the winsome Irish lassie, with the dark-blue eyes and raven hair, that are indications of her nationality, the girl who exercises over Normal Leslie so great a fascination; and Augusta Dashford, whom he has only met to-night, a tall showy-looking girl, with bold, black eyes, rich colouring, a large, ugly nose, and that extremely unpleasant formation of mouth, where the under-lip projects, giving to the countenance a false, sinister expression; but yet in spite of all, Augusta is good-looking in a loud, flaunting way, and thinks herself a beauty, on the strength of those hard, glittering eyes that she casts with marked emphatic favour on the dark, strikingly handsome face of Mabel's lover. Either of these girls he reflects, and perhaps one or two others among that fair bevy, would be only too enchanted to cling by his side for the whole evening if he exhibited but the faintest desire for their companionship; and so, bitterly thinking, he strolls back to the group and anchors himself by the saucy Kathleen's chair, looking into those sweet arch Irish eyes and listening to those coaxing, bewitching accents that have just enough faintest suspicion of the brogue to mellow and soften the tones, not to mar them. There is a charm about these educated Irish voices; the angles seem somehow rubbed off, and there is a slight contralto softness or depth of tone that is delightful to the ear, after a lengthened course of the sharp, high, unsympathetic accentuation of most English women's voices.

While apparently thus engrossed, Hugh Denver is, in spirit, traversing that lonely avenue full of wind voices; his heart divided between tender protecting love and compassion for the girl who encountered them alone on the one hand, and a sore angry feeling on the other. . . . And Mrs. Derrick moving about the stately rooms, seeing to the well-being of her father's guests (as the Grange unhappily has no mistress) knits her brow and bites her lip with ill-suppressed annoyance, and mutters—"little fool" when she hears of Mabel's "absurd freak of disappearance," as she calls it. "As if aunt Katharine could possibly want her, with Fargus always at hand, who is a devoted creature. And to run away and absent herself to-night, of all nights—how infatuatedly wrong-headed of her! What will Hugh think? It just seems as if she wished to avoid him. What unstable, unreliable creatures girls are; not that I believe really for a moment she has ceased to care for him. She appeared half dumb with joy when he arrived this afternoon, a great ecstasy of gladness shone in her eyes, and seemed to light up her whole serious, dreamy face, and I saw what no one else did, that she passionately kissed the flowers he gave her. Somehow I shuddered a little when I saw they were asphodels; it seems rather an unlucky flower to give, though I was ashamed of myself the next moment for doing so, and attaching any value to such superstitious nonsense. They thought, or knew, nothing of it. Mab fastened a cluster in the bosom of her frock at once—you may have noticed them at dinner—and the rest she put carefully in water. But I am sure Hugh will feel hurt and disappointed, perhaps begin to think that she has got to care for someone else, and I did hope that all would go smoothly." And Mrs. Derrick heaves an impatient, irritated sigh, as she ends her hasty confidential grumble to her husband, who is inclined to make light of the matter, and tells her with a good-natured laugh not to adopt the rôle of a Cassandra—it is eminently unsuited to her and very depressing—ending up with a soft aside that Nature intended all women to be matchmakers, he was sure, they took to the trade so *con amore*.[78]

---

[78] Cassandra: a daughter of Priam and Hecuba who had the gift of prophecy but was fated never to be believed; one who predicts impending disaster. *Con amore*: with devotion, zest.

CHAPTER XI
THE LIGHT STEP ON THE GRAVEL

AND so the remainder of the evening passes pleasantly away, though more quietly than anticipated; somehow, Norman Leslie's singular uncanny story has slightly sobered all these gay young people, and has made them less disposed for frolic and merrymaking.

It was a little after ten when Mabel vanished, and as the hour approaches midnight some of the more elastic, irrepressible spirits, undaunted by the account of that weird incident which took place two years ago that night, or any of the other tales of horror they had shuddered over, proceed to their divinings and innocent incantations, their groping, struggling, futile efforts to grasp and raise ever so little the impenetrable dusky curtain that hangs before all human eyes, for ever shutting out any glimpse, however fleeting, of the mystic, spiritual life that so closely touches on our fleshy one—the life that we are all travelling on to so fast, oh, so fast—to which we must all attain some day very soon, and yet, that is jealously wrapped in such inscrutable, terrible mystery.

Just at this prescient hour the great door of the mansion is set wide open in accordance with an eerie, old-world custom, lingering in maimed fragmentary fashion here and there, a remnant of the ancient superstition that is still, I believe, active and living in some districts of Brittany and other parts of the Continent—where the house door is set open wide during all the hours of darkness of this mystic "All Souls' Night," lights left burning, and food prepared and ready on the table, everything waiting in ghastly expectation of the awful guests, who are supposed to glide into the familiar house during the small hours of this ghostly night, revisiting the spots their mortal feet had oftenest trod.

But woe to those living souls who, daring or forgetful, keep sacrilegious vigil on this unearthly night. Who, not content with the other three hundred and sixty four nights, that are theirs and life's by right, must needs rob the dead of their undivided possession of those brief hours of midnight darkness on this "Hallowed Eve."

Yes, woe to the living intruder, whether by accident or design, who gazes on these phantom guests, who glide in and out at the familiar door and hover by the familiar table, and break the bread or drink the cup in spectral fashion. Their earthly days are numbered, and they will soon go to join that shadowy, unearthly throng.

But this strange belief, which, absurd as it may appear to practical commonsense, has yet a touch of awesomeness and eerie pathos that fascinates one in spite of oneself, reaches not to this pitch of wild superstition in any part of the sober unromantic England of to-day, and the opening of the great hall door at Arden Grange arises from no belief in ghostly visitants; 'tis only conforming to an old custom, the very meaning of which is almost forgotten beneath the weight of years which lie upon it. Just as many old usages and customs are kept up amongst us, the origin of which is completely unknown to those who practise them.

* * * * * *

And so the massive door is set open wide by the butler for a brief space, and all beneath the roof, with one or two elderly rebellious exceptions, assemble in the almost baronial hall, without connecting much idea with the act; the very fact of their doing so showing how corrupted is the old custom.

There is a lull in the storm just at this time, and they all stand about chatting, and laughing, and shivering a little; one or two murmuring at the folly of being expected to comply with an idiotic, senseless custom, just because the Squire has absurd fads and chooses to keep up old-world barbarisms. But these malcontents do their grumblings secretly, and *sotto voce*, and the dear old Squire of Arden and his family never suspect disaffection among the guests.

The moon is brilliant and obscured in sudden, swiftest alternations, as jagged, scrappy fragments of clouds, tinily small but strangely dense, almost black, are flitting in rapid succession over her chill, white face. The shadows thus produced are singular and misleading. One moment the wide space before the great door is all shining brightness, the next it is plunged in gloom, and the next some odd, grotesque shadow, cast by some baby cloudlet is clearly outlined. Looking away down into the great dusky avenue, which reminds one in the day-time of some grand, dim cathedral aisle, is—seen by this light—like gazing into some unknown region of mystery, all seems so unreal and phantasmal.

But after the first moment or two no one looks out; all keep a respectful distance from the door and its draught. Many gather round the two great fireplaces, trying to solace themselves for what they choose to call enforced discomfort, as best they may. Others, despising these sybarites, examine with interest and admiration the fine show of ancient armour, especially the beautiful chain-armour, many specimens of which adorn the walls, besides strange, old-world weapons which were carried by Ardens in the olden time and used right bravely.

Thus employed, talking, laughing, admiring, they do not notice or, at least, pay no heed to a light step on the gravel outside, or a soft, rustling sound as of garments, and are pretty considerably startled when Kathleen O'Hara exclaims, in a delighted yet astonished tone,

"Why, Mab dear, have you come back? I——"

They all turn and gaze at the door as she speaks, and then at the girl, who has stopped so suddenly, staring blankly and stupidly before her.

"Where is she?" she cries, growing pale and half-scared looking.

"She was there this moment, coming in," pointing to the open doorway. "Then the cloud came, and she's gone."

They all stare somewhat unbelievingly into the gloom that has again fallen beyond the great porch; but stay—yes—surely that is a shadow moving through the darkness.

Some press on nearer to the door, one or two actually step through the porch out on to the gravelled drive beyond, but just as they do so, the moon bursts forth again and reveals every branch and twig and stone; but there is no figure within sight in any direction.

For the first moment they look at one another in a soft hush of silence, then they shake off the little spell that has bound them, and laugh and make fun of Kathleen.

She was dreaming. What possessed her to think she saw Mabel? What on earth would bring Mab out at this hour of the night?

"But I *did* see her," breaks out the girl, in vexed, startled accents, eagerly disclaiming the impugnment of being dreaming. "I saw her quite plainly. Do you think I could mistake Mab?" a satirical emphasis in the rich tones. "Why, I even saw the colour of her gown, and thought it so odd that she should be out at that hour without a wrap. She looked very pale and grave, and—and though you laugh and are incredulous, yet you must all have heard the step on the gravel and the rustle as of a dress—you all didn't dream that, I suppose," with a scathing little sneer. The truth is, that pretty Kathleen is frightened and nervous, and consequently a little cross.

The natural superstition that lurks, perhaps unsuspected and dormant but ready at an opportune moment to spring into active life, in most Irish breasts, is stirring strongly in hers. Many of her country's legends and wild weird stories of the "Fetch," &c., are now maddeningly crowding to her mind, and filling her with terror and dismay.[79]

No one is impressed but herself; but then no one else saw, or, as Augusta Dashford maliciously asserts, "fancied" they saw anything.

They are all slightly staggered when she reminds them of the step.

Yes, they certainly heard that, or, at least, something like a step; but they did not notice or think about it, and after all it was doubtless caused—well, not by the wind, for there was not a breath just then, but by some night-bird or other creature of the dark and silence.

"But I saw Mab, I tell you," reiterates the girl, impatiently. "And she looked distressed, and not like herself. Oh, I hope—I hope—that—that—it wasn't her—her *fetch*, and that nothing's going to happen to dear old Mab, for——"

"Kathleen!" cries the Squire, sternly and angrily—he happens to be standing near the excited girl and hears the last sentence or two, though they are muttered in a frightened whisper. "I am surprised at you. I insist on your at once ceasing to talk such nonsense—absurd, vulgar nonsense; indulging in such wild imaginings. You saw nothing, because there was nothing to be seen. I myself was looking straight at the door, and should have seen anything if it was there. I have no patience with such rubbish."

The Squire is really incensed; the very thought that harm could come to his favourite Mabel worries him and makes him extra

---

[79] Fetch: a supernatural double that appears as an omen, usually of one's impending death.

cross with poor Kathleen, who is his eldest son-in-law's young sister, and whom he has known almost from babyhood, and treats like a young granddaughter of his own. She, quenched and a little mortified by the rebuke being administered before so many, cries softly, partly from vexation and partly from nervousness.

"I hope Aunt Katharine is all right," murmurs Mrs. Derrick, uneasily, who cannot help being a little unpleasantly impressed by Kathleen's extreme earnestness and positiveness.

"Constance, my dear," remonstrates the old man, looking at her pityingly and reprovingly, "are you becoming infected by that silly child's fancies?"

"No, of course not," she responds, but there is a slight hesitation in her tones. "But then you know, father, Mab promised to sleep here to-night, and from her not coming back I thought perhaps aunt——"

"If anything were wrong with Katharine, are there not messengers to bring us the ill-tidings?"

"Don't you think, sir," says Hugh Denver, speaking for the first time, though he has followed the foregoing remarks with strained anxiety—not that he is influenced in the slightest degree by Kathleen's fancied vision, he is quite without superstition of any kind; the girl imagined she saw something of course, but the moonlight, with those strange swift changes from light to gloom, is most deceiving, and doubtless she saw some shadow flung by one of the giant trees not so very far away. No; this has no effect upon him; it is the suggestion that Mabel might be in any distress or anxiety that troubles him, and urges him to speak as he does. "Don't you think, sir, that if an enquiry were made at Miss Arden's home, it would be satisfactory to all? It is not so very late, barely twelve, and doubtless it would be an ease to Mrs. Derrick's mind to be assured of her aunt's well-being. I shall gladly be the bearer of any message you might think well to send as an excuse for calling at this——"

"No, Mr. Denver, no, sir, on no account; thank you all the same," quickly interrupts the Squire, and there is a touch of the imperious manner, that his family know so well is a sign with him of inflexible decision. "It should be a very serious matter indeed that would induce me to disturb and startle my poor suffering sister-in-law at this time of night,—certainly not for a foolish child's hysterical fancies."

With a displeased glance at the abashed Kathleen, he adds,—

"Mabel has plenty of emissaries; if she wanted to send here she need be at no loss. The child can't be very helpless, or alone, with three women servants ready to do her bidding; one of them her faithful, devoted old nurse. Believe me, ill news flies fast, and if anything were wrong we should hear only too soon." And he turned away with dignified step to leave the hall, his usual cheery, genial, old face, grave and troubled-looking, as, in spite of himself, a faint anxiety about his sister-in-law remains with him.

Kathleen prepares to follow with the rest, talking softly to Norman Leslie as she goes, who is warmly trying to console and re-assure her, and darts from behind the shelter of his glasses wrathful, indignant glances at the retreating form of the dear unconscious Squire, for his brutality in drawing tears from those lovely eyes. If the truth must be confessed, Norman feels a small shade guilty, and that indirectly he is partly responsible for Miss O'Hara's wild imaginings, as she seemed peculiarly impressed by his story and has been somewhat silent and serious since.

But even he, though her faithful champion, believes it to be completely fancy, as, in spite of his sensational tale-writing, he has no leaning whatever towards the supernatural, and especially scoffs at the old Irish belief in the "Fetch," considering it a particularly objectionable form of superstition.

He has been softly trying to banish from the girl's mind the idea that she saw Mabel or any figure; doubtless her mind was full of her friend, and then some sudden shadow, falling in some peculiar way, resulted in a sort of optical illusion. "Many people more especially those with sensitive, imaginative, highly-strung temperaments, are quite subject to these brain-pictures, Miss O'Hara," he says. "They think of someone, perhaps living, possibly dead, and the chances are ten to one but the person thought of in a moment or so walks quietly into the room, apparently in the flesh, nothing whatever unsubstantial in their get up. The persons accustomed to these little visual derangements grow to think nothing of them, though it must be rather a staggerer when the illusory guest hails from the churchyard! Of course, in excess, these delusions are a very unpleasant and highly dangerous form of nervous disorder; still, I would not attach any importance to a solitary illusion of the kind if I were you; you are a little nervous to-night, and——"

"Remember the awful night it is, Mr. Leslie!" breathes Kathleen, in a low, shuddering whisper. "I am not specially nervous, and it was no optical illusion. I won't contend any longer that it was Mab I saw; that must have been a fancy, a mistake, though I could have sworn it was she; but the face was, I admit, partly in shadow. No, I see now how it is. You know *they*—" (strongly emphasised but vaguely indefinite) "are said to re-visit the earth to-night; it was just twelve o'clock and 'All Souls' night.' It was a spirit I saw, Mr. Leslie! I alone was selected to—Oh! Hark!" she suddenly, wildly exclaims, growing ghastly pale and coming to a standstill, with raised warning finger, while the other hand tremblingly clutches Norman's arm.

"The step again," she gasps, and her words are simultaneously echoed by all present.

The Squire and two or three of the elderly, unimpressed guests, who had made indecorous haste to follow him back to the warmth and comfort, that they felt themselves illused to have been obliged to abandon for even those few minutes, are already out of hearing; but all the rest instantly distinguish, with pale, startled faces, the light, smooth, even step of a few minutes ago. It seems rather louder this time and drawing nearer, as it were; the other somehow appeared to cease at a little distance from the house. They can distinctly hear the crunching of the gravel beneath the light, firm tread, and all gaze spellbound at the door as in a trance of fearful expectation, while Kathleen, whose nerves are wrought to a high pitch of tension, can hardly refrain from screaming aloud.

The next moment a great sigh of relief breathes through the stately hall as a young man—a singularly handsome young man, buttoned up in a great coat—steps briskly into the porch, hesitates a moment or two, as if confused when he sees the group, and then comes in quietly with rather an embarrassed deprecating air, turning quickly off towards the servants' quarters as if he wished to avoid notice.

To nearly all those who are regarding him with interest, mingled with some surprise and gigantic relief, he is completely unknown; even the members of the Arden family who are present do not appear to recognise him.

But suddenly a neighbouring young country squire, who is somewhat in the background, talking earnestly to an exquisite little blonde—a fairy-like *petite* creature, and grand-niece to old Wyndham

Burroughs—to whom Captain Armitage has almost exclusively devoted himself all the evening, much to the chagrin of her present cavalier, calls out lustily, "Hullo! Harman; I say, you've given us a pretty fright. We took you for one of the ghosts who are said to prowl about to-night, you know. What did you do with yourself the first time we heard you? You never hove in sight though the step came quite close. Have you been trying to scare us a bit, eh?"

"I don't understand you, Mr. Loftus," answers the young man thus addressed, flushing slightly under the scrutiny of so many eyes. "I have but this moment reached the house. I went down to the cottage nearly two hours ago to hunt for a couple of leases that the Squire wishes to see on Monday. I have only now returned. I walked fast, as it was late, and saw no one; so I don't even know to what you allude. I did not come by the avenue, certainly, but through the park and bye-path. If I have startled anyone, I much regret it, and beg to apologise," and with a comprehensive bow, that seemed to include all, the young man disappeared in the direction of the housekeeper's room.

CHAPTER XII
THE NEW STEWARD

"I SAY, Loftus," says Fred Derrick, the Squire's son-in-law, "is that old Harman's son? I couldn't imagine who the fellow was. I knew at once from something in his bearing that he wasn't a lackey, and when he spoke I was still more puzzled. The fellow's quite a gentleman; and, by Jove! what a handsome face he has. If he brings his wares to a good market he'll be marrying wealth, and possibly rank also some day or other. These handsome fellows trade on their looks, and make capital of them just as much as our fashionable beauties," he said, with a laugh and a look round on the much dwindled group, now, in fact, reduced to a small knot of men who still linger in the great hall, though the butler has closed the massive oaken door and retired with his lieutenants to his own quarters, and all is as it was before the general adjournment to greet the wandering spirits on the threshold.

"Yes, that's old Harman's son, and a precious scamp, if all the tales are true; though the Squire, dear old man, will believe none of them. Confound the fellow! he contrived to give Miss O'Hara a nice fright, at all events; indeed, to scare us all above a bit, whatever the rascal was up to," mutters young Loftus, a little vexedly.

"And who is old Harman, may I ask?" questions Hugh Denver, languidly, who has been standing close by the two speakers, and has heard the foregoing remarks. "He is not amongst us to-night, is he? And why is his son, when he is here, not with the Squire's other guests?"

"Old Harman is not with us to-night because he happened to have a prior engagement in the churchyard unfortunately, and one that tyrannically detains him," laughs Loftus, somewhat boisterously, but the next moment he checks himself, saying apologetically:

"No, I won't laugh at the poor old fellow; he was a good old chap, and faithful to those whom he served. He was Squire Arden's steward—agent, whatever you may please to call it, Mr. Denver; uncivil people sometimes say 'bailiff,' but it is not a pretty word, and has a slightly unpleasant second meaning." (Squire Loftus evidently prides himself on being a bit of a wag.) "He died some four or five months ago, and the Squire felt as if half of him, I mean the business half, was gone."

"Small blame to him," interpolates Derrick, "when for more than thirty years Harman was his right-hand man."

"Right and left hand, you may say," breaks in Loftus, "in all matters concerning the management of the estate, and as true as steel; in fact, much more devoted to the interests of him whom he served than to his own; if he had looked a little more at home 'Beauty and the Beast' might not run so much in double harness in his present representative. At least, that's not altogether correct; I don't mean to infer that the 'Beast' in the usual acceptation of the term predominates to any prodigious extent there, unless it be the animal of the 'Cat' tribe, that cannot always be trusted."

"You don't mean to say that, Loftus? Mrs. Derrick and I were aware of the old man's death and that the Squire had transferred the stewardship to the son; which somewhat surprised us, as we were under the impression that the young man was doing well, I think in a merchant's office in Bristol."

"Yes, exactly, but nearly two years ago the merchant dispensed with his services. Nothing ever actually came out, I believe; there was just a whisper, a breath, no actual accusation. You see they had a great respect for poor old Harman, he was a Bristol man, and well-known as the Squire's agent, and well thought of; and then the Squire himself, being such a big man about here—you know we're not quite twenty miles from Bristol. So though nothing really got known here at Arden, I happened to hear through a private source more than anyone knows, both of the matter and the fellow's life since. He went to Liverpool after that little affair, ostensibly to a situation. He was in a place for a few months, but he soon left it—lost it, I heard—and he has chiefly lived by betting, I believe, during the last two years; real turf gambling, and not of the most strictly honourable kind either, supplying false tips, &c. I have heard one or two who have lately plunged deeply attribute their being let-in so heavily to treachery on his part, and I have also heard him spoken of as something of a 'leg' rather unreservedly.[80] How he has managed to keep his head above water I don't know. The gambling passion is a perfect mania with him. Before he took up this modest rôle of stewardship he attended every race meeting in the country, and I hear that, as a rule, he lost heavily. Once he had wonderful luck, laid a 'hundred to one' against the 'favourite' or something of that sort, and won a pot of money; but when he had made his pile, £20,000 or some such figure, instead of retiring prudently from the field of action, the horrible, burning thirst was there, as insatiable as ever, and a week or so later he lost, on another racehorse, nearly all he had netted."

"It is hard to say whether the green turf or the green tables exercise the most potent, fatal magnetism on their victims; in either case they are irresistible when once the deadly passion has been contracted," remarks Hugh, meditatively.

[80] Leg: a cheat, usually when gambling on racehorses or cards.

"It's odd, that in each case the verdant colour, symbolical of fresh, raw, innocent youth, should be the fatal tint, eh?" says Derrick, slowly; "but, good heavens, Loftus," he continues, excitedly, "if the fellow leads such a disreputable life as that he's not fit to be——"

"Oh! I suppose he's reformed," resumes Loftus, "or something of that kind since his father's death; it's to be hoped he has. The poor old chap died I think of a broken heart, though no one guessed but myself that he had such sorrow in his life, and I think even he did not know as much as I, but of course, I have not spoken of anything I have heard; no one has asked, so why should I?"

"But my father-in-law should be warned; he should not be allowed to place confidence in such a man. Heaven knows how he may suffer if——"

"Oh! I did try to give the Squire a few hints when I first heard of the agency being placed in Jim Harman's hands, but he would not hear anything; he seemed to have rather a high opinion of the fellow—said he was so greatly pleased with his manner, that he was quite glad he had applied for the agency, and that, though it would be some little time before the young man understood his duties thoroughly, yet that they would work together, and that his old friend's son should always have a strong claim on him. Harman must have been pretty well down on his luck to care to seek such a post, but as I say, he may have reformed; and in any case, if I were you Derrick, I should not be at all uneasy; he can't well touch the Squire in any way, he is too good a business man himself, to allow himself to be cheated in the slightest degree, and the sums that pass through Harman's hands at a time are not sufficiently tempting to stick to his fingers; perhaps he has burnt those same fingers so severely that he has determined to keep them cool and clean for the future. Anyhow, he seems to be tame cat here now. I understand that when he complained of his great loneliness down at the deserted cottage without his dear father's face to make it 'home' for him, the Squire insisted on his taking up his quarters here, and he has lived here now, I believe, for nearly three months, only withdrawing from the reception rooms when there are strangers, as to-night; but in the usual way, when the Squire is alone, or when Mrs. and Miss Arden are here, Adonis dines *en famille*, and doubtless makes himself delightful.[81] The fact of it is when a fellow has a face like that, coupled with a smooth, winning tongue, he may do almost anything short of murder, and it will be forgiven him."

Norman Leslie is not present to appreciate the unhappy truth of this remark, but Hugh Denver, who has been listening with a half-absent interest, makes an almost imperceptible little gesture when Loftus alludes to young Harman's familiarity in the house, and his face clouds heavily.

* * * * * *

They all soon return to the drawing-rooms, where the chilled and somewhat cross elders have been getting warm again and good-humoured over hot, spiced wines, the drinking of which is also a traditional custom attached to this night's proceedings at Arden; but it is one which these disaffected ones regard with a sweet serenity and gentle favour, not extended to outlandish wanderings in cold corridors and halls.

And by-and-by the young people who are staying in the house, the others having taken their departure, being indisposed for any more gaiety, gather round the grand piano in the music

---

[81] *En famille*: with the family.

room and sing sacred songs with praiseworthy persistence; somehow music of a lighter, more secular order grates upon them in their present mood.

Music appropriate to the day that has commenced within the last hour they try first; anthems taken from the epistle for All Saints' Day:—"And I heard the number of them which were sealed."

And again——

"Lo, a great multitude, which no man could number, of all nations, and kindreds, and people, and tongues." And by and by growing more ambitious as the hour grows later they venture on some of the magnificent music of the "Messiah," which they render wonderfully well, especially that divine solo, "I know that my Redeemer liveth," which Kathleen O'Hara sings superbly; she has a rich, powerful, gloriously flexible voice, and Handel's grand aria suits her perfectly.

But splendidly as she does it there is something strange about her as she sings; her eyes have a distant, strained expression, a look of ineffable sadness dwells upon her features, she is very pale, and seems unconscious of those around as she gazes with that wrapt, odd look straight before her. Insensibly as the others watch her, and listen to the solemn words (a portion of the funeral service) that issue from her lips, they shiver a little with a touch of the same feeling that ran through them in the hall.

"Somehow, Kathleen's a bit uncanny to-night, what's come to her? Has she taken to dreaming dreams, and seeing visions?" they ask each other, in subdued whispers.

She almost looks like one who was slightly under the spell of some mesmeric influence, so statuesquely motionless, with that far-away, absorbed look in the dark blue eyes. And when she ceases suddenly, for a moment or two there is unbroken silence in the room; then Kathleen looks wildly round as she exclaims in passionate, piercing tones:

"Oh! why did I sing it? Why did I sing it? I feel as if I had come straight from a grave!" and throwing herself into a low chair she covers her face with her hands, as if to shut out some dreaded sight.

And one or two of her more impressionable hearers, as they look at one another askance, murmur softly that it seems "just as if they had been present at some invisible burial! There seems an actual weight of sorrow and mystery in the air." . . . And they all start most unpleasantly when the girl lifts her head and asks them abruptly, with a deep, awed ring in her mellow voice:

"Was it my own grave I stood beside in spirit just now? What do you think? Oh! tell me. I don't know what's the matter with me to-night. I feel so strange I can't explain it; as if something were trying to tell me something that no one else can see or know—something dreadful—but that I cannot, cannot understand. You know I was the one selected to see that—that spirit to-night, and it's 'All Souls' Night;' and they say—of course you all know—that whoever——"

But at this juncture the Squire walks in amongst them, and there is a sudden hush on the forbidden subject, and soon they all separate for the night, and sleep and silence fall softly upon the old Grange.

CHAPTER XIII
HEARD IN THE SILENCE OF THE NIGHT

AND the wild winds 'plain and clamour round the old house; but not sufficiently fiercely to keep any of those wearied ones from dropping into pleasant slumber.

Even Kathleen, though feeling strained and anxious and somewhat creepy in herself, is exhausted by the very tension on which her nerves have been the last hour or two, and falls at once into profound, dreamless sleep, and all human life is very still and hushed in the great, grey, old Grange.

The rats—which seem to be an heirloom to the House of Arden, as through the years, do what science will for their extermination, they steadily refuse to be banished—may hold high revel, as seemeth to them good, and as is their nightly wont, but no wakeful ears are startled by their pranks and gallops, generally ending up with a free fight, indicated by much spiteful squeaking and scuffling behind the old oaken wainscots.

Though if there were watchers to-night in Arden, it might strike them that the rats were rather more active than usual, not particularly hilarious or pugnacious, but mysteriously, quietly busy.

Odd, strange, dull sounds, and stealthy creaks and movements echo faintly from time to time during the first two or three hours that sleep holds despotic sway, and then all is still and soundless beneath the roof-tree of the old Grange as in Death's very kingdom.

* * * * * *

But by and by, none could after tell at what time, it might be the advanced morning, but still the awful darkness reigns supreme, pre-eminent, two or three of those weary guests—the few who happen to sleep in the east wing of the Grange—start suddenly from their pillows, wide awake—start erect, expectant, with their whole being concentrated in the one act of listening.

Listening for what? For a repetition of the sound that has transformed them in an instant from unconscious, helpless lay-figures to watchful, excited, trembling human souls. But no repetition comes, and they are fain to lie down again and try to think that a dream must have deceived them, and that the awful despairing shriek that seemed to cleave the very house in twain, and yet appeared to proceed from somewhere out there in the thick darkness, beyond the closed and curtained windows—that shriek that pierced their dull ears and penetrated to the very marrow of their bones, must have been but a fancy, a figment of their sleeping brain. The wind has quite lulled, and the silence is profound, unbroken; but one or two of those who have started into such singular, vivid wakefulness are young and timid, and have been listening to most uncanny stories all the evening, so now superstitious horrors take possession of them, and they cower miserably in the darkness, afraid to get up to strike a light, and pull the clothes over their heads and have a thoroughly *mauvais quart d'heure*.[82] Then, after a long time, they fall asleep again, and later on, with the chill November sunshine pouring its reviving, courage-inspiring rays into their bedchambers, and the sweet sound of bells breaking the silence of the early Sabbath morning, their scare of the night seems born of the darkness and the stillness, a very nightmare of the fancy, and they try to think no more of it, as they look out over the winding shrubberies where the lovely arbutus berries already glow red in the sun, over

[82] *Mauvais quart d'heure*: lit. a bad quarter of an hour, an unpleasant but brief experience.

the fine old mulberry and walnut trees intermingled with copper beeches and an occasional lofty elm or two that cluster in rich profusion in the near neighbourhood of this wing of the Grange and act as an effectual screen for the stabling, granaries, &c., into that greenest of green paddocks, where the solitary pony of the Dower House establishment grazes in dignified loneliness, and where the "ruin," that is more or less the boast and pride of Arden, stands grey and desolate in the morning sunshine. It is but a little ruin—but a small fragment of what may have been in dimly distant days a noble castle or fortress, towering in stately strength over those smiling Arden lands, that knew no "Arden" then, or for many centuries later. But when the historical "Guy" of that name, who founded the family and the Grange, purchased these wide-stretching park and pasture lands, the "ruined turret," as it was called, was then as it is now, having apparently, judging from documents describing it, changed in no appreciable degree through the intervening couple of hundred years.

This remnant of some very ancient building consists of but a round, gaunt-looking tower; the walls of massive masonry gape drearily here and there, still showing in places the strange, deep slits in the wall thickness that did duty as windows in that hazy, far-off time, when the grey tower was young and strong. There is also standing a kind of entrance or long passage leading to the turret, the outer portion of which, the walls being low and in wonderful preservation, was utilised some years back by roofing over a space about the size of a fairly large room and putting a fireplace in a niche that seemed just made for it. Then, when shut off from the rest of the ruin, stretching out behind, by a lath and plaster wall—in which a door was left so that visitors could be shown the tower—it made quite a snug little dwelling, and was tenanted by the man who looked after the Dower House orchard, garden, live-stock, &c. But of quite late years, owing to much straitened means, this functionary's duties were so greatly lessened that Mrs. Arden was glad to dispense with his services altogether, thereby reducing her expenses, and what is required to keep her orchard thriving is done by one of her brother-in-law's under-gardeners; so the turret chamber, as it is called, remained untenanted until within the last twelve months, when it has been occupied by an old woman, a pensioner on Mrs. Arden's bounty.

Yes, in presence of that tranquil, peaceful scene, on which that sombre ruin is no blot but rather adds to the picturesqueness, the old-world dreamy stillness and sweetness of the landscape, these Arden guests determine to think no more of what startled them so fearfully, until by-and-by one of their number mentions in a most casual manner at the breakfast table how scared she had been through the night, by what after all she supposes must have been some terribly vivid dream.

Then, those three or four who had been wakened exchanged notes, each detailing at length his or her individual experience, which, when summed up, amounts to exactly the same thing in every case, viz.:—that they had been awakened, by what they felt to be (rather than actually heard with their awake understanding, so the sound ceased with their returned consciousness) a wild, terrible scream; a shriek so awful, so intense in its force of pent-up despairing agony, that it is ringing in their ears still, and now that they know it was no dream, as they began to hope and believe, would so ring through life.

They all agree, even the most practical among them, that there "must be something in it," and something very strange and mysterious. In spite of the painful realism, and hard prosaicality that deals such inglorious death to the idea of romanticism and mysticism of all kinds, in this last and science-ridden quarter of the nineteenth century, there still lingers in most human breasts a taint of superstition,—at least we use this word, which seems vulgar and utterly inexpressive of what we wish to convey, for want of a better. Is not the feeling a shrinking dread—a mortal's dread—of coming suddenly unwarned, unprepared, into contact with any of the awful, immeasurable, unspeakable mysteries that surround us, that hem in our daily life, that are about us, with us, and yet that we can never fathom, can never know, save to know they are, while our mortality lasts? We move amongst them, are of them, in them, part of these great inscrutable mysteries ourselves, but the flesh is the barrier that shuts them out in their awfulness and sublimity, and shuts us safely in. Step out from that poor, weak, yet in this case all-powerful barricade, and we shall be plunged into their weird mightiness, and know all of terror or of joy.

And so small a thing compels each to step out alone to meet those gigantic, overwhelming problems. So small a thing; so short a time.

"Nought but the void between two waves of air, The space between existence and a soul."[83]

Yes, in the pause between our breaths we know all or nothing.

The cry of the soul in its passionate anguish of loneliness and yearning, "Oh God, where art Thou in all that awful space? Where art Thou hid in those infinite realms of air? I cannot see Thee, or hear Thee, yet I feel that Thou art somewhere," is the much more natural cry of a doubting, trembling, human soul striving to

[83] Misquote from *Kenelm Chillingly: His Adventures and Opinions* by Edward Bulwer Lytton; the actual line being '*Less than* the void between two waves of air…'

know, to pierce the terrible envelope of obscurity and uncertainty in which all is wrapped, than any self-satisfied, self-assured asseverations of a serene perfect knowledge of the doings and intentions of the Invisible One.

"There lives more faith in honest doubt,
Believe me, than in half the creeds."[84]

And it is the very feeling which prompts the pitiful cry quoted, that also gives birth to superstitious awe or terror: that thrilled shrinking of the soul from some possible momentary uplifting of some fold of the shrouding, dusky mantle that hangs all round us everywhere, enveloping us in its materialism, effectually screening the life spiritual, that palpitates around unseen, but that every human being is latently conscious of. We long to know, and yet we dread to know, and fear a revelation from the mystic life that we are all travelling on to so swiftly—oh, so swiftly!

Mortality is not to look upon immortality, or things eternal.

The awful secrets of the awful universe, the inscrutable mysteries of life, and death, and soul-life, still lie hid in God, as we have proved through these long, vainly-searching, seeking ages.

But still, all things are possible to the Infinite, and the dreaded, yet craved for, possibility remains, that under singular and unique conditions of temperament, health, or circumstance, humanity may catch a fleeting glimpse "behind the veil," and be either dazzled by the ineffable effulgence, or frozen at the awful blank!

Nothingness and void beyond this life, to know absolutely that all ends in the grave, would be a more terrible knowledge to some than even a surety of sorrow and suffering continued in some unknown state of being; and though to many that perfect peace of

---

[84] Lines from *In Memoriam* by Alfred, Lord Tennyson.

oblivion and unending rest brings the idea of bliss unspeakable, yet the thought of ceasing to "be" any more for ever is generally appalling and antagonistic to man's nature.

But this is wandering far from Arden and the midnight scare.

Kathleen O'Hara, above all, leans to the conviction that that mysterious, fearful cry presages evil to the House of Arden.

But by-and-by, when they appeal to Mrs. Derrick to solve the mystic problem, to probe the meaning and origin of that blood-curdling shriek, she does so in the most commonplace, mystery-slaying manner possible.

"The Grange is not so very distant from the sea, as doubtless some of you are aware," she says, "and frequently, either before or after a storm, the gulls fly inland quite a great distance, and it is well known that the curlew's cry is intensely shrill and piercing at times, with a wild, melancholy wail in it that might be easily mistaken by persons half-awake for a human voice in dire distress."

"But why was it not repeated?" argue the unconvinced.

"Doubtless it was," she retorts, "but all of you, plunged in heavy sleep, only chanced to hear the last weird scream—possibly louder than the preceding ones by the number of the storm-birds being augmented—as they wheeled and circled round the house previous to returning to the far-off coast."

And Hugh Denver smiles—he cannot help it though he has been somewhat impressed by the wild tale of the night, and the cohesiveness of the narrative as detailed by each without previous conference or agreement—as he watches the pretty, eager flushed face of Irish Kathleen, who is only half-satisfied and loth to yield her belief in the supernatural "Banshee"-like character of that awful cry.

CHAPTER XIV

MINE OWN FAMILIAR FRIEND

BUT this apparently trifling incident is soon swept out of their minds by other and more startling intelligence that bursts upon them in rapid and bewildering succession.

They have just finished breakfast and are standing about in desultory fashion, talking idly, in the pretty spacious breakfast-room overlooking the park, previous to separating to prepare for church. Captain Armitage is whispering sweet nonsense into Kathleen's rose-tipped ear in one window, and is being pleasantly scowled at for his pains by another pair standing near, namely, Norman Leslie and Augusta Dashford, Augusta's being a peculiarly malevolent scowl, as Hugh Denver being quite unattainable, she covets the attention of the spruce, debonair captain of the Lancers, and hardly cares to even decently mask her jealous vexation and disappointment to Leslie, who is still more enraged than herself at the way matters are arranging themselves. For has he not overheard that vapid, wily captain asking Kathleen to promise to walk to and from the pretty rural church in dual fashion with himself? He even caught a whispered word or two (confound the fellow's insolence) as to the desirability of taking the stile route, which is lonelier and longer, "instead of herding with the drove of church-goers, like Cook's tourists."

Still Norman, choking his wrath, is endeavouring to appear unconscious and unconcerned, and is somewhat absently addressing conventional inanities at intermittent intervals to his angry, frowning companion, who exercises but little restraint and exhibits her sentiments unreservedly, thereby showing herself of inferior blood and breeding—as is the case, her people being *nouveaux riches*, in fact distressingly new.[85]

As to Hugh, who stands alone and gloomy in a distant window, if he could imagine supplanting his grey-eyed, dreamy, darling Mabel, against whom he feels a wee bit resentful still this morning—she has not turned up yet and it is getting on fast to eleven o'clock; they will soon be starting for church, and she promised last evening that they should walk to, and sit together in that village temple—it certainly would not be Augusta Dashford he would put in her place; she is the type of woman he hates—hates with a hearty, vigorous rancour; whereas the soft, sweet, coaxing Kathleen might steal into a corner of his heart, and there abide, before he was well aware of her fair intrusive presence.

And in truth Miss O'Hara looks fair and bewitching enough this morning to attract and enchain any man who is not very securely and effectually guarded from her fascination by a prior real passion. All her strange nervous impressions and imaginings of last night seem forgotten; she looks bright and sweet as a June morning; the cheering sunshine has frightened away all ghosts and goblins for her, and she is already laughing over her "Banshee" suggestion of a while ago, with the quick, easy, impulsive changeableness of her enthusiastic, impressionable Celtic nature. But, of course, it must be remembered that she was not one of those awakened sleepers; she did not hear the awful, mysterious cry. If she had, no smile would have visited her lips for many a long day to come.

Just at this moment, and as the first notes of the church bell warn her, and other horrified feminine ears, that they will have time

85 *Nouveaux riches*: new money, of a social class whose wealth is newly acquired as opposed to inherited from family.

but for a very scrambled toilette, if they do not immediately repair to their respective adorning shrines, Dickson, the butler, opens the door slowly, and presents a pale, scared face in the opening.

"Sir," he somewhat gasps, looking straight at the Squire, standing erect and stately on the hearthrug, engaged in animated conversation with his son-in-law, Mr. Derrick, and one or two elderly gentlemen staying in the house for some shooting.

"Sir," the man reiterates, breathlessly, "Mr. Harman has been gone and run away; leastways we think it must be that, for his room's empty, and his bed's not been slep' in, an' every mortal thing he had here—which wasn't much if ye come to think of it, he would keep his things at the cottage, an' go back an' forrud for them himself, as if he wouldn't trust nobody; but every little bit of a thing he had is cleared out, portmanteau an' all, an' I've sent to the cottage, bein' in such a scare; but, sir, it's all shut up an' barred, an' no one inside; an', oh, Squire, sir, what'll we do to catch the rascal, whatever?"

And with a strangled gasp Dickson pauses to overtake the breath that has almost escaped him. He has spoken with such incoherent rapidity that no one seems to have a very clear idea of what has happened.

But before he can rush on again, plunging deeper at each word into the mire of confusion, the Squire stops him sternly, with a grave displeasure in his look and tone, coupled with decided bewilderment.

"What are you talking about, Dickson? You must be off your head a little this morning. Even if Mr. Harman should have made a sudden unexpected journey—it must have been quite unexpected" (somewhat *sotto voce*), "as he mentioned nothing to me of his intention yesterday—but even if he has, which I do not at all admit, till proof is given that he is gone, we may be sure that he had a good reason for doing so. And in any case nothing could justify the extraordinary and most culpable manner in which you have just expressed yourself. Pray remember in future, Dickson, that in speaking of young Mr. Harman you are speaking of a friend of mine, and choose your language accordingly."

The dear old Squire has put on his stateliest manner, but his face belies the coolness of his speech. Somehow, a cold misgiving of something gravely wrong is forcing itself upon him.

Dickson is an old and faithful servant, a steady, reliable, sensible man, in whom he has perfect confidence; why then would he seem so strangely agitated if there was nothing more in the transaction than Harman having left Arden without giving due notice of his purposed departure?"

If the young man had received an imperative message summoning him elsewhere, it must have been very late yesterday: in fact, not till the advanced evening, as he saw him and was speaking to him for a few minutes in his study some time after dinner, about seven o'clock, just before he joined his young guests in the drawing-rooms. He mentioned to him then that he wished to look over on the Monday (to-morrow), a certain couple of leases of farms on the estate that his old agent (Harman's father) kept with other documents of a similar nature at the cottage.

And it will be remembered that the reason adduced by Harman to young Squire Loftus as the cause of his putting in so late an appearance at the Grange was that he had had a long hunt at his old home for those aforesaid leases.

But now Dickson, after a deprecatory, yet pregnant pause, continues in an excited though partly restrained manner.

"But, sir, you don't know yet, an' I scarce know how to tell you, I'm that upset an' dumb-foundered with the shock of it all. You could knock me down with a feather, ladies and gentlemen, askin' yer pardin for intrudin' on you all with such a wicked, dreadful tale on this holy Sunday morning. I mean no offence to Mr. Harman, sir," again addressing his ireful, puzzled, tremulous master, who is becoming rapidly incensed at the man's exasperating, roundabout slowness in coming to the point, "but if he ain't the man as has done it, I am blest if any man has done it, bar the fairies."

"Good heavens! Dickson, do you want to drive me mad? What the deuce are you raving about? What has been done or undone? I command you to tell me at once, or to leave the room instantly—instantly, do you hear, sirrah?"

"Yes, sir; certainly, sir, I'll tell you, an' sorry to the heart to have to do so, but the reason I call him a rascal is—an' it's twice too good a name for him—that he's broken open, no, I'm telling lies, but he's opened cool an' clever, with a key, the big iron safe in your study, an' took every bit of the splendid old plate, them grand old pieces what are heirlooms an' the pride of the Ardens."

He looks round on the assembled group for sympathy as he bestows this information.

"Not a solitary piece left, sir; even if he had left us the grand gold drinking cup, with all the lovely stones, it wouldn't be so mortal bad—an' not content with that great treasure, what does the villain do, but break open the silver caskelit (presumably "casket") an' steal all the beautiful jools. It's a clean sweep he's made of all I'm thinkin', an' if there was money in the safe, Squire, we may be dead sure it's gone too."

Squire Arden had sunk into a chair in a state of speechless stupefaction. Many, and various, are the exclamations and questions showered on Dickson from all sides, but he alone is dumb. Fred Derrick especially is wild with indignant rage and excitement, remembering as he does with such fatal clearness the account he heard but a few hours since from young Loftus of this same Harman's character and the Squire's infatuation in his favour and refusal to hear or believe aught ill of him.

How terribly his kindly credulity has been imposed on; how terribly his trust and confidence in, and affection for, the young man have been betrayed!

But now the Squire, with pallid face and trembling lips, has found his voice again—

"Robbed!" he mutters dully, staring blankly before him,—"Robbed and by *him*. The son of that faithful old man, my oldest, best, and truest friend, as well as servant. It's monstrous. The man I have treated almost as a son. I can't—I won't believe it," flushing suddenly, as his voice grows strong and wrathful again; wrath directed against the agitated butler, who, with keenest sympathy in his glance, is anxiously watching the master whom he loves.

"I won't believe it," he reiterates, with fierce emphasis, as if thereby he sought to fight and conquer the horrible certainty that is gradually taking possession of him.

"How dare you come into my presence, fellow, with such a wicked lie upon your lips? How dare you presume to make such an infernally false accusation, without proof of any kind? I am robbed, you say! Heaven knows that's bad enough—terribly bad. Those priceless, historic heirlooms, the boast and glory of Arden—gone. Those magnificent jewel, the heritage of the heir through generations. The actual money loss alone would be prodigious, but their value is really incalculable owing to age and historic association." This last clause he addresses explanatorily to those present. "There has never been a robbery at Arden, wealthy as the place is known to be, in my time, or my father's, and now so bold a sweep. I——"

"But, sir," interrupts Derrick, in frantic, impatient disapproval of what he considers a tendency to irrelevancy and a desire to expatiate on the loss on the part of the old man, rather than to act with lightning speed, "are we not losing valuable time? If Harman's not the man somebody else is; instead of talking here, had not we better secure ourselves of the truth of Dickson's statement and take some immediate steps. If Harman's really gone I must say it looks blackly bad against him—coupled with what one has heard of his character—though we may have some trouble to prove it. Still, Sunday and all as it is, I'll——"

"Fred! I am ashamed of you," roars the Squire. "*Harman*! Are *you* the man? One would be almost as likely as the other. If I am robbed it's by one of his underlings," pointing contemptuously with a trembling finger at Dickson, who has made several attempts to speak this last minute or two, but has been overpowered; but now he breaks forth in eager, indignant refutation of the Squire's charge.

"No, sir; no, by Heaven! I swear it's none as is under me that's done it; they're all as honest as the daylight. Do you think I'd speak so positive like about Mr. Harman if I hadn't good proof to know he's guilty? He's been allus a civil-spoken gentleman to me, though somehow I never did trust him, an' I did hear he was a bad un, though I never thought of anythin' like this, the Lord knows. I have the best of proof; I didn't like to show it too suddint to shock you, sir," glancing apprehensively at the Squire, and drawing some small object from his pocket. "His penknife it is," holding it up for general inspection. "His penknife with his name on it, an' two blades broke short off where he used it to force the caskelit; the key he had for it wouldn't work proper, an' stuck fast in the lock, where it is yet; but he wouldn't be beat, an' used this, an' then left it behind him. I found it where he just dropped it out of his hand in his thievish haste to grab the jools; it was a dark corner, an' he never saw it; an' them two missin' blades will be found as sure as death either in the caskelit or somewhere in the safe, where they jumped in snappin'.—Yes, sir, of course." This to Derrick, who has asked to examine the penknife, the Squire being too dazed at this apparently unanswerable confirmation of the butler's accusation to make any comment. It is a large, handsome. slightly peculiar knife, of green agate, with four blades, two of them (those broken) being remarkably strong, a dainty, unsuspected corkscrew, being neatly packed away among them, as also a convenient buttonhook, a tiny pocket comb, tooth-pick, and indelible-ink-pencil; altogether a rather ingenious useful contrivance and somewhat uncommon, as well as pretty from the green agate and silver mountings. A chased, small plate of the latter bears the owner's name in full:—"James Francis Harman," and the date of a couple of years previous.

"Surely damning evidence, indeed," Hugh Denver murmurs under his moustache.

"And there's something more, sir," continues Dickson, looking at his still silent master. "When I went to his room, thinking to find some traces of him there, I saw, thrown away in a corner, one of his handkerchiefs, and on lookin' close I saw that he must have been tryin' to tie up all the lovely necklaces an' brooches an' things in it, so as to pack 'em away comfortable like in his portmanteau, but I suppose he found it too small to hold the lot an' flung it away in his haste; an' there, held in one corner of the half-tied handkerchief, was this little ring; perhaps you'll take it, ma'am?"—respectfully, almost reverently tendering the small glittering object, which the faithful old servant recognises, to Mrs. Derrick, who is about to pass it on to her father when she glances at it half-mechanically, and utters a faint cry of recognition and distress.

It is her mother's favourite ring; a ring that had always rested upon her hand, that had been in the distant years in fact her "engagement ring," which the loving soul had treasured and worn all her life with an exceeding love, and which had been removed from her hand when dead by her sorrowing husband, who contrary to usual custom would allow none to wear it after his beloved wife, at least during his own lifetime, but deposited it with the Arden jewels, to go with them in the fulness of time, to the bride of the next master of Arden.

This little incident creates a diversion from the somewhat frigid silence which has been growing since Dickson produced his proofs, and which has been induced by the Squire's strange dumbness and dazed, stricken aspect.

But when the poor old man sees again the once beloved familiar little trinket his frozen look breaks up, he melts, as it were, a few thawing tears steal down his wrinkled cheeks, as he murmurs some glad indistinguishable words at having been accidentally left, at least this one little remnant of his precious possessions, and one that has for him such dear and tender associations.

* * * * * *

And now—an excited, confused babble of voices reigns around;—suggestions—surmises—wonderings—condolences—execrations!

"The fellow must have got hold of the keys," says Fred Derrick, "some time or other and taken the impressions in wax, as my father-in-law always keeps them safely under lock and key in a private drawer in his bureau. But doubtless the Squire went to the safe in Harman's presence as confidently as he would in yours or mine—the fellow worked with him I believe in the study—and most likely he mentioned what it contained besides papers; or again the ruffian knew all about it from his father, and came here with deliberate intention.

"What a haul he's made, and what an out-and-out daring, irredeemable blackguard he must be."

"Ay, and what an appalling hypocrite," exclaims Norman Leslie.

"And he's had a start of who knows how many hours," continues Derrick, wildly. He chose his time well; Sunday morning, when one can do so little, and there are so few trains. He may have time to get aboard with his booty, and of course, so accomplished a rascal will melt down all that grand old plate—gold, and silver, and precious stones; that's what he wants—money's worth, not magnificent ornaments, or stately priceless heirlooms—and we shall never be able to trace it. But still I'll do something; to sit down quietly would madden me. I'll make inquiries at Arden, though they're safe to know nothing in the village—we've no stupid blunderer to deal with in Jim Harman, *Chevalier d'Industrie*[86]—and then I'll ride on to Bath, and perhaps be so fortunate as to catch a train for the Clifton and Durdham Down station, I know they run on Sundays at long intervals, and rush into Bristol. In any case I'll telegraph from either Bath or Bristol. All roads lead to London, the best hiding place in the world, I think. He ends abruptly, feeling that from nervous excitement he is somewhat incoherent.

"But then, Derrick, the fellow in his Satanic cleverness, may have made straight for some unlikely, obscure sea-port, not far off, and be even now under weigh, having timed the robbery to suit the sailing," interpolates Leslie.

---

[86] *Chevalier d'Industrie*: a professional thief, a fraud.

"Then I must only telegraph to have them all watched, on the chance of his not having reached one; also for particulars—if I can get them—of persons embarked this morning," shouts Derrick, striding towards the door.

"Doubtless he left Bath by the train that starts at four in the morning—if he went by rail at all, yet, how else?—and now it's getting on for twelve; all those hours to make tracks unsuspected, unobserved."

"How savage it makes one feel. Well, I'm off. Will you come, Hugh? Or you, Leslie? It's better, at any rate, than doing nothing." With a half-reproachful, half-disdainful glance at the Squire, who is hardly yet roused enough from the shock to his feelings, which affects him even more than the great and grievous loss he has sustained, to take a very vivid interest in active measures—active measures to pursue the criminal. What criminal? That young man whom yesterday he regarded as a dear and valued member of his household; who seemed so devoted, so earnest, so good; who was so winning, so respectful, so anxious to please. That young man! Dear old John Harman's son! Why, even for that tried and trusted friend's sake alone, how can he act? How can he prosecute and punish the ill-doer?

The spirit of the dead man seems, to his disordered fancy, to plead for pity and pardon, as he sits there gazing at the sad little ring in abstracted, absorbed distress.

CHAPTER XV
MISSING

BUT before Fred Derrick can grasp the handle of the door, it is softly, hesitatingly turned from the outside, and a woman's agitated face this time appears in the opening. It is Mrs. Parker, the housekeeper at Arden, and she is paler, and more scared-looking even than Dickson when he first presented himself.

She at once addresses her master in trembling, frightened tones—

"Mrs. Fargus is here, sir, sent by Mrs. Arden, to know if Miss Mabel will not run home for a few minutes after church? She is so little used to have her away from home at night that she feels sick and lonesome for a sight of her."

While the woman is mechanically repeating this message every eye is turned upon her in astonished questioning.

The Squire starts to his feet as if galvanised by this new unknown terrible complication or trouble that seems to be overshadowing them; his face is ashen pale, and his eyes glare wildly, uncomprehendingly; at the trembling Parker.

"What's the woman saying? Tell her to speak out," he mutters in a frightened hoarse whisper, while Hugh Denver clutches at a chair near him to steady himself, and stands there with pallid face and tongue cleaving to his mouth, trying to battle with the dreadful swimming in his head.

What was Harman and the robbery compared to this horror?

Then Mrs. Derrick, who is the first to recover herself, speaks with difficulty in slow awed tones—

"What did you say, Parker? That Miss Mabel didn't go home last night?"

"Yes, ma'am," cries the woman, now sobbing outright. "And Mrs. Fargus is come, and how in the name of mercy am I to tell her that Miss Mabel isn't here?"

"For God Almighty's sake," cries the Squire, finding his voice and consciousness, in the strength of his emotion, "keep it from her mother, keep it from her 'till we try to unravel this frightful mystery, or we'll have Katharine's death on our souls."

And with these words he falls back insensible, and for a few moments wild confusion prevails. A new terror creeps in among those startled people. Mrs. Derrick has never before known her father to faint. He, of so vigorous and robust a frame, of so cheerful and equable a temper: what may it not mean? Perhaps a stroke—perhaps worse. This morning's trials may have been too much for him at his age. His poor seventieth birthday was indeed to be celebrated strangely. Was it to be deathday as well as birthday?

But no, thank Heaven! he is coming round—coming slowly to himself again, with the aid of simple restoratives resorted to. It was but a brief lapse into unconsciousness.

The over-wrought mind gave way momentarily beneath the strain put upon it. They must try to keep him very quiet for a while. Perhaps he won't remember everything all at once, even when he gets quite himself again, and they must make a tremendous effort to disguise all signs of agitation before him. Yet how are they to do so with all this dreadful wickedness, followed now by what appears like terrifying mystery, to be cleared up, and that calls for immediate action?

Then they quickly agree to wheel him gently into the next room, which happens to be the library, where he often sits with the newspapers for an hour or two after breakfast. It will seem natural to him to be there, and there will be nothing to remind him of what has occurred; an elderly lady present, a very old and valued friend of the Squire, and a cousin of his late wife, volunteers to accompany him. She can do no good to the agitated council that will have place when she and the Squire are gone, and by going she will leave Mrs. Derrick free to meet the grievous responsibility that has come upon her and her husband, the Squire being unable to give directions or attend to anything.

So it is carried out; and when the door is closed upon them Mrs. Derrick appeals to her husband with scared, haggard eyes.

"Let Fargus come here; would not that be the best way? We must tell her all, and we can hear what she has to say, and she will help us to think what it would be best to tell my poor, miserable aunt."

Fargus soon appears, looking about her with a startled, enquiring gaze. She is a faithful, elderly, Scotch serving-woman, who has followed the fortunes of her beloved mistress, Mrs. Philip Arden, since the latter was a bonnie young lassie of fifteen, who thought not as she rambled on her native hills free and healthy as the sturdy heather which she crushed beneath her blithe young feet, that the day would come, and not so very far distant either, at a time when other women still count themselves in their prime, when she would be a confirmed invalid, suffering much and constantly, comparatively quite poor, and the widow of a bad, cruel, profligate husband. For Katharine Arden is now but forty-three, and these conditions (save the widowhood, which is bliss as compared to wifehood) have been hers for several years. And is there now a last and crowning blow, a sorrow before which all the others of her sad, unhappy life would dwindle, ay, to dwarfish proportions, in store for this lovely, patient, uncomplaining soul?

"Fargus, at what hour last night did your young mistress run home to see her mother?" questions Mrs. Derrick, striving vainly to steady her voice, which will falter.

"Not at any hour, ma'am," answers the woman, looking straight into her interrogator's eyes, with a world of wistful anxiety and uneasy dread in her own.

"We never saw sight or light of Miss Mabel since she left at four o'clock in the afternoon to come up here. My dear mistress was a wee shade better yesterday, poor soul, and she laid her commands on the dear bairn just before she started, not to think of coming home through the evening, as she often does—so foolish, when I'm there—on a cold, wild night like last; and then Miss Mab kissed the mistress, extra warm and serious-like—I thought it was because she was to be the night away—and was gone the next moment. She was more absent and thoughtful in herself all day than I ever saw her, and yet she'd smile sweet and happy now and again, for no reason save in her own mind; and oh! ma'am—sir——" appealing with a wild glance of entreaty from wife to husband. "If she's ill or has met with any accident, poor blessed lassie, won't you tell me? Don't try to keep it back; anything is better than not to know."

"Anything better than *not to know*!" Is not that what they all feel in the dreadful pause that ensues while they try to take in the awful idea that Mabel Arden has disappeared?—disappeared horribly, mysteriously on All Souls' Night, in the midst of her friends and kindred.

"But," cries Mr. Derrick, "Mabel left this house at ten o'clock last night. Did you not say so, Constance?" looking at his wife, who bows her head affirmatively. "And where did she go if not home?"

"Perhaps Miss Arden met with some accident in the avenue," suggests Captain Armitage. "But no, that cannot be; Price—one of the footmen—has been through it twice already this morning; besides she would not go through the avenue but by the paddock gate. "But who *saw* Miss Arden leave the house last night?"

It is Hugh who speaks at last, in a hoarse, broken voice, utterly unlike his own, and there is a dead silence as he says these words; no one responds, but all stare at him blankly.

"It seems generally taken for granted that she went," he continued, "yet no one saw her go."

"But if she were in the house would not she be among us?" says Mrs. Derrick, in dull, dazed tones; it is almost too much for her also, this accumulation of distress.

"No," answers Hugh, "she may have gone to the room she usually occupies when she sleeps here, and been taken ill, and unable to summon assistance, so—"

"That couldn't be," interrupts Mrs. Derrick, "for Miss O'Hara slept there last night," looking across at Kathleen who, now pale and distracted-looking, even more so than last night, is at this moment revolving a horrid idea in her excited brain.

"Or," continues Hugh, speaking with difficulty, she may have had a sudden seizure in some part of that unused West Wing, and been incapable of giving any alarm. I think the children ought to be closely questioned as to how she left them, and where they last lost sight of her; and that the house should be strictly searched at once."

"Denver is right," cried Fred Derrick, who longs to do something, however futile, however hopeless; remaining inactive seems completely acquiescing in one's trouble. And now, of course, he has abandoned all thought of immediate pursuit of Harman, in presence of this so much greater calamity.

*　*　*　*　*　*

The children are therefore had in, and narrowly questioned, which elicits nothing but what we already know; and while their examination is in progress Kathleen creeps round to Mrs. Derrick, and whispers to her earnestly for a few minutes, and soon it spreads among the others that Miss O'Hara has made the frightful suggestion that that appalling shriek, that some of them insist they heard through the night, had something to say to the tragedy of Mabel's disappearance.

Might not she, in some way not easily understood, have discovered Harman in the act of committing that daring wholesale theft, and before she could give a alarm, might not he have silenced her for ever? And that terrible cry was her death shriek.

But though for a moment this horrible thought does impress, almost taking away the breath of those who hear it, yet it is soon found to be untenable. For if Mabel were in the house, where was she from ten o'clock at night till three or four in the morning?

And why should she be wandering at that hour through the lower regions of the house—the study was on the ground floor—after concealing herself so carefully for half-a-dozen hours or so?

And besides, it did not follow that though Harman robbed, he would also *murder*. And what would he have done with his victim's body? Also the cry, that some of them heard, seemed to proceed from somewhere close outside the house, not in it. No, they will search the house—though they feel it is exciting only delusive hopes—they will search the grounds, and then—what are they to do? If Mabel left the house last night, as they will soon prove to a certainty by failing to find her within its walls, where, in the name of Heaven, can she have gone? And what are they to tell her miserable mother?

While they thus take counsel together in shocked and frightened uncertainty, Mrs. fargus has fallen on her knees in a panic of dismayed terror, and rocking herself to and fro wails forth—

"Oh! Miss Mabel, Miss Mabel, what's come to ye, my dearie?—my bairn, the bonnie wee lassie that I nursed in my arms the hour she was born—and it was but a sorrowful hour if this is to be the end. Where have ye gone awa' to, my dearie—gone, and left your puir mither? And her hairt is said and sair this morning—said and sair with missin; you for the one night, for ye're the light of her eyes, dear lass; and now—and now there will be naething left for her but to dee. I didna think ye could forget her. Oh! wae is me—oh! wae is me!"

Thus she moans, quite regardless of those around, and instinctively relapsing slightly into the long-laid-aside accents of her youth.

But while that faithful servant cries aloud in her distress, and afterwards when Hugh Denver follows the others, walking as a man in a dream through that desolate uninhabited "west wing," a horrible thought creeps into his mind—a thought from which he staggers back in a sort of repulsion, and yet that will not be exorcised.

It seems almost a sacrilege for that thought to steal into his mind unawares, but to lurk there, to foster it! He shrinks from himself as if he were guilty of some hidden sin.

And yet he cannot banish it. Are not some of those others, perhaps, at the same moment, thinking the very same thing?

And is it so strange a thought after all?

As the idea dwells with him it grows almost into a conviction, though he would not breathe it to a living mortal.

Perhaps Kathleen O'Hara was right in one sense as to Harman being in some way accountable for Mabel's mysterious disappearance, but in a mode very opposite to murder.

He hates himself for harbouring such an idea, but one must be rational, and after all, the girl is very young and artless, and he, that infamous scoundrel, is wonderfully handsome, and possessed of manners and address quite as good as the men in her own sphere.

"Only her uncle's steward, certainly. A sort of upper servant almost," thinks Hugh, unjust from his fierce pride of birth and ancestry and the wild, furious jealousy roused by the idea, that is taking such firm hold of him. "But—still—well—a sort of spurious gentleman . . . Has been well educated . . . A merchant's clerk, &c. . . . What a brilliant alliance for an Arden!" he thinks, with a savage mental sneer. "But, besides his devilishly beautiful face, the rascal has a winning, plausible tongue, that has deceived even the old and the wise; and women have done such things before, and will do them to the end of time."

What does he mean? What is this compared with what they do?

Women of the very highest aristocracy marry their grooms, labourers on their estates, even the very lackey behind their chair.

Pah! the folly is his to wonder or feel surprised; and above all to have believed in *any woman's constancy.*

* * * * * *

And Mr. Derrick gives vent to somewhat similar sentiments after that miserably useless search through house and grounds. He is less reticent than Hugh, and speaks aloud of his only reasonable, nay, seemingly possible, solution of the mystery—to his wife that is to say—he does not yet breathe a hint to his father-in-law, or any of the others.

"Who can account for a girl's vagaries, her extraordinary freaks and caprices?" he declares with angry energy. "And the fellow, it must be said, has a perfect, almost angelic, face, and like many another silly, credulous woman, poor little Mab doubtless thinks it indicates an angel nature, whereas it seems to me that these marvellously handsome people, whether men or women, generally turn out the worst—the face is no index to the character. God help the child when the awakening comes, as it must, immediately, with such a desperate ruffian and criminal as he has proved himself to be."

And Mrs. Derrick weeps bitter humiliated tears as she remonstrates with him.

"Mab to act so! That dear, pure, noble child," she says, between her sobs. "I wonder at you, Fred, to degrade her so, and she, as we know, so fond of Hugh—secretly engaged to him, as he confessed to me last night. She knew he came with us now, formally to propose for her to her mother and uncle—in fact, Hugh tells me that it was arranged between them that he should do so, though she wished it to be kept quiet till the very last; she's such a shy, shrinking darling, our sweet true-hearted Mabel. They have been corresponding all these months; so you see how utterly, wickedly wrong you are in your horrible suggestion. No, something dreadful has happened to the girl, I feel convinced. What was the meaning of that frightful shriek some of them are so positive about?"

"Rubbish!" ejaculated Derrick, in impatient vexation. "Only absurd nightmare fancies, induced by their goblin tale telling, and Leslie's strange, unpleasant story. Mabel has disappeared, there is no doubt whatever about that. Nothing could happen to her round about Arden, where every one knows her since she was almost a baby."

"And everyone loves her, my poor, dear little cousin," interjects Mrs. Derrick, in a soft, sobbing whisper.

"Her mother's house, too, is just beside us. She has not even to approach the high road to reach it," continues Fred. "No, the poor, misguided creature is gone of her own accord, her own free will, we must suppose; deceived by that hypocritical scoundrel. You speak of Hugh and her engagement to him. I thought as much myself; but do women never break their engagements? You forget that that fellow only appeared here just before she came back from Ilfracombe; since Mab has grown up he has been away almost altogether from Arden. They virtually met as strangers, and they have been all these four months constantly thrown in each other's society—for the Squire treated Harman, I understand, completely as a trusted friend and guest—often possibly alone, in the house, in the gardens, in the wild seclusion of the park, a safe and perfect trysting-place, with none to watch or question their actions, her mother more or less a prisoner in the house, and your dear, noble-hearted, unsuspicious father never dreaming of deceit or treachery. And you may be sure Harman made good use of his opportunities. And now the only thing left to us, is to follow in pursuit. Too much time has been lost already.

"I won't breathe a word to the Squire or her unhappy mother till I get some trace of them and if I fail to do that,—God help the girl—that's all I or anyone can say, when she finds out the real infamous character of the man she has given up everything for.

"We can only then pray and trust he has married her—a fact which I very gravely doubt."

Mrs. Derrick here gives a horrible convulsive start, and glares at her husband with speechless indignant reproach in her eyes.

"Fred!—Mab!"—is all she can gasp out in whispered wild expostulation.

"Mabel has no fortune, unhappily, in her own right; her expectations are all from the Squire—what he would give her on her marriage, provided he approved of that marriage, or at his death," continues Fred, with cruel clearness of reasoning.

"Harman, of course, is aware of all this, and knows he would not benefit a penny by a marriage with Mab; for your father, kind and affable, and unbending as he is to the verge of socialism, is yet at heart intensely proud, and an unequal marriage on the part of an Arden, would, I think, distress him more than anything—and *such* a marriage as the one we are discussing—

"No, Harman took the Squire's measure you may feel certain, and knew exactly what he might expect if he aspired to too much, so he very quietly helped himself to an infinitely larger dowry than any Arden bride could hope to receive, and helped himself possibly to the lady also—without the bride. Doubtless he is quite as dishonourable where women are concerned as with regard to trust and money, and so provided, with laudable foresight, for the contingency of getting tired of his living toy by and by.

"How detestably easy to deceive and dupe a poor, little, ignorant, innocent, loving girl like Mab, a particularly dreamy, unworldly bit of womanhood, with a mock marriage.

"There, my dear, don't cry so. I didn't mean to shock and pain you so terribly. I spoke impetuously, I ought to have been more guarded, I hope and trust I am wrong in my judgment. Constance, my dear, be a brave woman; to whatever height of misery and disaster this sorrow reaches, let us try to meet and fight it boldly for your father's sake, for your aunt's"—that deluded girl's most tried and miserable mother.—"Fancy how much more all this will mean for them, and if we collapse, who is to help and comfort them?"

And Fred Derrick, who has been half beside himself with rage and indignation, as well as grief, rage rendered keener and more ungovernable by bitter maddening humiliation, regrets his biting, half-sarcastic speech, that spoke the truth as he believes it to be—but spoke it cruelly—and soothes his shocked and horrified wife with kind tones and gentle words and earnestly expressed hopes that he is altogether wrong in his most dreadful supposition.

CHAPTER XVI
MEG MORRISON

IN less than an hour Fred Derrick snd Hugh Denver have started for Bristol, and no one goes to church from Arden this All Saints' Day.

A great gloom lies upon the house that was gay last night. The Squire is too ill to appear again, and the white, anxious, strained face of Mrs. Derrick, on whose shoulders falls the whole burden of responsibility of trying to account in some feasible way to her alarmed, mystified aunt for Mabel's absence, seems an actual reproach to the guests, who huddle together in uncomfortable, excited groups and long for the morrow, when they may go away and relieve the stricken family from the misery of being obliged to entertain visitors while bowed down with such heart-crushing trouble; and even though it is Sunday, two or three, who have not a long distance to go, depart at once.

An hour or so after her husband and Hugh have started on their miserable mission, Mrs. Derrick, who has been more impressed than she likes to admit even to herself, by the tale of that fearful night-cry and miss O'Hara's horrible suggestion, steals out, accompanied by one or two of those who heard the shriek and pallid, excited, tremulous Kathleen, saying nothing to anyone of their intention, especially disguising their motive from the servants, and swiftly, cautiously they make their way round to the east wing of the Grange, in which those few, who were so strangely disturbed, slept, and proceed to make a diligent, exhaustive search, throughout all the out-offices belonging to the mansion first, and then amongst those luxuriant, tangled shrubberies, through all the grounds—narrow and restricted rather here, where they adjoin the Dower House, the Grange gardens, lawn, park, &c., stretching away to the south and west—for some solution of that weird problem.

This is the way Mabel Arden must, of necessity, have taken last night if she went home when she disappeared from the picture gallery. Unless, at least, she went by the avenue and high road, which she never did, even in the daytime, as it was much longer and the road very lonely at night.

Under and over everything they look, these four anxious searchers, with wildly beating hearts, and nervous, frightened eyes, not knowing the moment the latter may light on some horrible confirmation of the imaginative Irish girl's frightful suggestion.

But they find absolutely nothing—not even the faintest trace of Mabel's late presence amongst that tangled undergrowth of furze and prickly bushes that abound in this wilder, less cultivated part of the demesne—not so much as a knot of ribbon, or tiniest fragment of that gauzy, blue-grey dress.

If she passed this wing of the Grange she must, as usual, have run through the winding shrubbery path on to the paddock gate. She could never have been crouching amongst those bushes through the hours of darkness, wither waiting for Harman, or—hideous thought—decoyed there to be murdered by him, she having discovered the robbery.

"And yet," Mrs. Derrick argues to herself, "what was that cry, that could not have been fancy when heard by three or four, that seemed to proceed from the near neighbourhood of the east wing of the Grange? If it were the curlews, as she so unhesitatingly and unreflectively asserted when first appealed to, before she knew all this accumulation of mystery and misery that was coming down upon them, why had not other sleepers at Arden been roused? Or, rather, why did the sound apparently only reach the east wing? The birds would have screamed as they wheeled and circled *over* the house, and consequently, there would be no special quarter to which the sound would be confined."

Thus she vexes herself with distracting arguments, as they find themselves brought up short by the paddock boundary wall. They make their way then on to the gate, which is always on the latch, never fastened, and stand looking in across its green width, to the large rambling old garden and orchard, and then away to the straggling, many-gabled cottage or Dower House, with its red chimneys glistening in the sunshine; and Mrs. Derrick gives a strangled sob as she thinks of the lonely, suffering woman within its walls, on whom, although she guesses it not yet, such a terrible blight of sorrow seems to have fallen; terrible whichever way one tries to solve the problem of Mabel's extraordinary disappearance.

For a few hours longer she may be kept in ignorance. For a few hours, perhaps even a day or two, she may be deceived by falsehoods, by the trembling, despairing lie of her child's being detained at the Grange by her uncle's sudden illness—a desperate clutching at a last and likely straw, to stave off the awful moment of revealing the truth to the miserable woman—yes, perhaps for a day or two, as the news of the robbery and her brother-in-law's seizure (purposely dwelt on to account for her child's prolonged absence) has smitten her with greater weakness, and she is obliged to abandon her intention of coming to the Grange to-day as had been arranged—for which reprieve her niece, Constance Derrick, is intensely thankful. Still, two or three days will quickly pass, and if in the meantime they can gain no tidings of Mabel!—

* * * * * *

These are Mr. Derrick's wretched musings as she leans on the gate, looking into that sweet clover meadow, which has not yet put on a wintry aspect, and where the callous, browsing pony seems not to miss the gentle, tender-hearted young mistress, who was wont to bring him his morning treat of apples or sugar.

And as she so leans, a thought strikes her, and she unlatches the gate and passes through, followed at a little distance by the others. She is not going to search the paddock, as there is no place to search, not a tree, or bush, or tiniest shrub to break the green level monotony, or to conceal so much as a rabbit.

No, she bends her steps direct to the left, to the "ruined turret." Not, again, that there is any place of concealment in the old tower, it being much too ruinous, and also occupied, as stated a few pages back; but Mrs. Derrick suddenly remembers the old woman, who has been living in that strange, quaint, old-world dwelling these last ten or eleven months, and determines to question her with regard to that cry heard at Arden, and which ought to have sounded quite as clearly here, as the ruined tower is situated at the end of the paddock nearest to the east-wing windows of the Grange and remotest from the Dower House. Besides, she reflects by some happy chance, the woman might—though she fears it was too late—have seen the girl pass through the gate and across the field to the orchard in the moonlight, or, even better still, Mab might actually have run in to see her for a minute or two, as she has heard was sometimes her kindly custom, if the queer old creature was more ailing than usual.

Who this old woman is who calls herself Meg Morrison, and who is so odd and strange and silent in her ways, Mrs. Derrick, or indeed anyone about Arden, does not know. The story of how she became an inmate of the turret chamber and a pensioner on Mrs. Arden's bounty is as follows:—

Last winter, in the short, dark days just before Christmas, a heavy wagon came rumbling along the high road to Arden village, about four o'clock, when the dusk had already fallen, and everything was wrapped in indistinguishable gloom. It was intensely cold—a black, bitter frost that had begun several days before and lasted for many weeks—severer weather than had been experienced in this part of the country for years.

On came the lumbering, heavy wain, the wagoner, wrapped in greatcoats, crouched half asleep amongst some hay in its most sheltered corner, leaving his steady, plodding, clumsy steeds to their own resources, which were almost as manifold as his own; no fear of their not knowing the way home to supper and to bed.

Then suddenly, when about a quarter of a mile from the Grange, and hardly a hundred yards from the Dower House, there was a jerk, a jolt, a scream of anguish, followed by a long-drawn moan, and the culpably careless driver found that the wheel of his wagon had gone over a wretched old woman who had laid herself down to sleep on the side of the highway, hardly conscious of her act, being stupefied by the intense cold, starvation, and dire fatigue.

That sleep would doubtless have passed into the unwaking sleep of death but for the savage rousing of the wagon wheel,—and so—sorrow, sin, horror, and mystery can be often traced to even a much slighter, more insignificant cause than a stupid carter leaving his horses to their own devices.

As it happened, the wagoner was a labourer on the Arden estate, and the wagon the Squire's property, but instead of bringing on to the Grange the injured old creature, whose leg was badly crushed, the man carried her to the Dower House just beside him to confess the accident and to ask what he should do with her.

Mrs. Arden at first proposed sending her into Bath to the

infirmary in her pony carriage; she would be properly treated and cared for there, and the distance was not great, only four miles—she could be propped up with cushions, &c. But Mabel overruled this; her tender compassionate heart overflowed with pity and sympathy for the poor old woman who was in such desperate straits.

The accident happened at their very doors; they might almost feel themselves vicariously to blame, when it was their (at least, her uncle's) man who had brought such added suffering to the poor, starving, frozen creature.

No, they must take her in and nurse and care for her; she knew her uncle would gladly defray all medical expenses; he would feel it his duty to do so. And when Mrs. Arden in yielding (when did she ever fail to do so to Mabel's wishes?) demurred a little at taking into her house a vagrant off the roadside, of whom they knew nothing, it was then Mabel thought of the "turret chamber," it seemed just the very thing; she would be under their protection but quite away from the house. And so it was carried out.

The wretched old woman suffered horribly for a long time, and was quite helpless, and then she began to mend slowly. She was dreadfully lame, and would be so for the short remainder of her days; and though evidently she had been a tall, powerful woman, judging by her make and build, she had been brought so low by want and misery before the accident that she seemed, when she began to move about again, a miserable, bent, old, weak and feeble creature. The moving was not much, only to a bench outside the turret chamber door, where she would sit in the sunshine for hours, knitting when she could, or else staring straight before her with a strange, brooding, inward look in the dark, sunken, dour eyes. She never spoke, except when compelled to answer a direct question, and then in the briefest manner possible; and when once she was able to get about and help herself a little she would permit no one, at least no servant, to enter her dwelling. Mabel went in and out as she liked, though she seemed to get no great welcome; but the maid who brought her meals from the Dower House always left them on the bench outside, where she found the empty vessels, and never dared, and indeed had no wish to cross the threshold.

Mabel had a fixed conviction that the old woman had met some heavy sorrow or trouble just before the accident, quite apart from her physical misery of being famished with hunger and cold; but she could not induce her to tell her anything. All she would say was that she had been on her way from the South to the neighbourhood of Bath, that she had walked many, many miles, and had not eaten for two days, that she expected to find some people to whom she wanted to make a statement, but it did not matter now, she concluded, with a strange gleam in her eyes.

When found, all she had with her was a small bundle containing a few poor articles of clothing, two or three of which had evidently belonged to a child—a little girl—presumably about six or eight years old; but of this child, whoever she might be, she did not speak. Mabel was the only person who ventured to question her at all; she was so cold, and silent, and hard, and always, as it seemed, brooding gloomily, that everyone else shrank from her; but Mabel's kind, sympathetic nature pitied, and was tenderly compassionate to the lonely, helpless, and as she believed, sorrowing creature, and when she found she could not persuade her to speak of herself, to try to amuse her, she would chat about her own home here at Arden, about her mother, and uncle, cousins, &c., and once or twice the old woman cast off her stony unresponsiveness, and seemed almost interested, her eyes losing the far-off brooding look, and glistening eagerly; she even unbent so far on one occasion as to ask a question or two. It was something relative to Mabel's father—the only member of the family the girl did not care to speak of, and whose name was foreign to her lips. She answered gravely, without expansion, that he had been dead nearly four years. The old woman murmured the word "Dead!" a few times, while her sunken eyes shone with an odd, sinister lustre.

"What was his name?" then she asked, abruptly.

"Why, Arden, of course," responded Mabel, slightly surprised.

"I mean his full name," muttered the old creature, with terse, almost uncivil brevity; but poor little Mab took no offence. She had even then learned the old woman's ways, and answered softly—

"Philip Marmaduke Arden."

"Marmaduke! Marmaduke!" muttered old Meg, several times, with a sort of satisfied intonation in her voice; then—"It is a good name, and ought to have been the name of a good man," she quavered, and then sank into silence, while Mabel's cheek burned hotly for a moment or two at this rather ambiguous speech; not that poor, half-crazed Meg Morrison could know anything of her father. She was only weighing the merits of the name, but her words were unfortunately chosen; for though Mabel was not quite sixteen when her father died, she knew that he was not "good."

Not that she really knew anything of the evil of his life. She was too young then, too young and innocent even now to have any idea of what that life actually was. But though she could dream nothing of the depravity, the real innate wickedness of such an existence, she knew one or two things. She knew that her father had broken her mother's heart and spoilt her life. She knew also that same father had done his best to shame and beggar both wife and child, and that but for her uncle's goodness and generosity they would be now in some obscure humble home, trying to live as best they might, on the interest of her mother's very small fortune, the only source of income which her father had been unable to alienate from them.

Fifteen years younger than his brother the Squire, with several children between them—most of whom had died in infancy—Philip Arden's wife, or widow, had no remotest claim to the Dower House and certain moneys and advantages that went with it; but the Squire of Arden respected and loved, as well as pitied profoundly, his unfortunate sister-in-law, and did what he could to make amends to her for the ill fate that had made her his brother's most unhappy wife.

But to return to Meg Morrison. The foregoing is the story of her accidental habitation of the ruined turret; and she is the old woman to whom Mrs. Derrick now bends her steps, with the hope (a very faint and flickering one it must be said) of hearing something of Mabel's movements last night that might help ever so little to elucidate the mystery of her disappearance. But, as may be imagined, she could hardly have tried more fallow or unlikely ground.

Old Meg is, as usual, seated on the bench in the sunshine. One thick stick is balanced at her side, while on the top of the other her withered, gnarled old hands are tightly clasped, her body bent forward, so that her chin rests on the folded hands, and her eyes stare away into vacancy, with that strange, fixed, inward look on their brooding depths that repels the servants and humble folk that see her, and makes them shiver and say, "She's creepy to look at," and call her "the old witch."

With an effort now she rouses herself when actually addressed, and the eyes, as they turn slowly on Mrs. Derrick's anxious face, burn with a malevolent, sinister light, as the latter thinks for a moment, her nerves being all unstrung and her imagination inclined to run away with her good sense.

But she soon forgets her absurd fancy in trying to make the old woman hear and understand the simple questions she addresses to her. Old Meg is slightly deaf, and seems stupid to-day, and non-comprehending.

At last she takes in the burden of Mrs. Derrick's speech, and answers in her usual brief, uninterested, apathetic manner that she saw the young lady from the Dower House pass yesterday, about four o'clock, going towards "The Grange." She stopped a minute or two to speak to her about her (Meg's) knitting (which same knitting, the old fingers being deft in its production, Mabel managed to get sale for at Bath, and little as it brought her the old creature did not feel quite so dependent when she had a shilling or two of her own earnings). Miss Arden mentioned, she continued, that she should not be coming back that night, as she was going to sleep at the Grange; she then passed through the gate of the paddock into the Arden grounds, and Meg did not see her again. She might have passed back at ten o'clock, or eleven either for that matter, and she would know nothing about it; she went inside at five and shut up the door for the night at six, as she mostly did this weather. Miss Arden had never been in with her so late as ten o'clock; she might have been in at eight, or perhaps even at nine, but that was in the summer time when there was still the daylight. She was most always in bed herself before ten.

When asked about the strange midnight cry, had she heard anything of it, &c., she seemed for a good while not able to understand what was meant, and stared blankly with dull, dazed eyes at Mrs. Derrick, shaking her head many times as if in disapproval of the other's want of cohesion and general tendency to irrelevancy. At last, when the meaning penetrated her addled old brain, she smiled pityingly. What had a cry to do with Miss Arden? She heard no cry, not she; she was "not a fine lady, full of fiddle-faddle fancies," with a touch of contemptuous scorn. When she was in her bed she slept there and did not lie awake to watch "if a poor wounded bird or beast should give a cry or two, perhaps as they lay dying after being half hit the day before by one of them cowardly creatures that call themselves 'men,' who would run over the edge of the earth with fright if they saw a gun only pointed at themselves, and yet went about popping at innocent, helpless things that never did them no harm, and cannot revenge themselves, just for the wicked pleasure of hurting something that can't hit back again. And they call is 'sport,' ugh!"

The old woman works herself up to almost a pitch of violent eloquence, for her, on this subject that she seems to nurse a resentful wrath with regard to, and which is the only one since her tenancy of the turret chamber that has incited her to anything like animated speech. She continues muttering for some time unintelligibly, but with a dark fire in her sunken eyes, and an angry continuous movement of the wrinkled old hands.

And Mrs. Derrick, seeing that nothing more is to be got from her (the poor old creature is half-witted, she thinks parenthetically), turns away with a sigh. That suggestion of the crazed old woman's is not to be despised after all; it is a more rational solution possibly of that weird cry heard at Arden than her own about the curlews, and would account for the scream only reaching to the east wing. Some poor, wounded, dying creature had perhaps crawled to hide itself, with the instinct of the animal creation at the approach of death, amongst those thick furze bushes close to the east wing of the Grange, and in its dying agony had given utterance to the cry—perhaps one of many—that had so startled the Arden sleepers.

CHAPTER XVII
"NOT PROVEN!"

BY noon next day all the Arden guests are gone, with the exception of Kathleen O'Hara, whose home is far away in the West of Ireland, and the grandchildren and nephews and nieces, who must remain some time longer.

* * * * * *

And all these people leave Arden with the same thought in each breast—though they breathe nothing of it to their host—the conviction, that the girl who shuddered at their story-telling, the girl with the great, dreamy, rapt eyes, which seem to gaze away into vacancy and see what no one else can see—eyes that seem to foretell some great and gathering shadow in the gazer's life—has eloped with Harman, her uncle's steward, a man of infamous character—Harman, who made so rich a harvest before he went—that Mabel Arden has gone forth to meet the word as his wife, or—worse!

* * * * * *

So they read the riddle of this sudden, extraordinary disappearance.

Is it not rational?

Such things are, and such things will be to the end.

"It is very sad, very deplorable, when such an occurrence takes place in a good old family like the Ardens, but" . . . and a shrug of the shoulders completes the sentence.

And thus the girl, Mabel Arden, the idol of her mother and uncle, the beloved of Hugh Denver, the favourite of young and old, low and high, the girl with the sweet, lofty, exalted nature, with the visionary spiritual eyes, flashes out of the life of those around her—vanishes from their sight, swiftly, suddenly, leaving no trace, no faintest hope, seemingly, of a return—disappears in the night, in the darkness, from the safety and security of her uncle's home—disappears awfully, mysteriously; and never again will the eyes that love her best, however weary they may grow with anguished, tortured longing, look into those other eyes—those grey, dreamy ones, with the shadow in their depths of an impending fate, a shadow that has already fallen—on this side of the grave!

And yet, one and all, with the exception of the staunch, faithful-hearted mother, who, at first is kept in ignorance, and who, even when at last given the only solution of the horrible mystery, spurns it with loathing and contempt, keeping her trust in the bright, unsullied purity of her child unspotted to the end—one and all, relatives and friends, after the first shocked, dazed sensation of finding the girl gone from their midst—all agree as to how she went and with whom.

It is a terrible blow, degrading, humiliating; but it must be borne, although Mrs. Derrick declares, with many tears and much self-pity, that she "can never hold up her head again, after such disgrace."

* * * * * *

As to tracing the fugitives, everything is done that can be done; but in vain.

Harman had chosen his time well; he had had many hours start, before even his flight was suspected, and he had got clear away. Where he could have hidden Mabel during those long hours that must have elapsed between her disappearance from the picture gallery and the time of their mutual flight, none could conjecture, save that it must have been far at least from the scene of the robbery. Very possibly at the cottage—and that it was returning from leaving her there he was when he encountered, unexpectedly, all the Squire's guests in the great hall, and this doubtless accounted for his somewhat hesitating, confused manner.

After many weeks, a man answering in some respects to his description, is seen two or three times in different foreign towns at the "gaming tables," but each time disappears suddenly before he can be identified; and to Mabel there is no clue.

* * * * * *

During these first few weeks of the frantic, futile search for the missing girl, Hugh Denver remains at Arden, hoping against hope.

His reason tells him there is but the one revolting solution, of what would otherwise be a terrible mystery; yet he lingers, hesitating to accept it finally.

It seems such desecration of the girl's pure memory. Marriage—if happily it was even marriage—with such a man—a criminal! An actual, common, daring robber, cheat, swindler!

But the trusting, innocent creature did not know, and, with her idealistic, dreamy temperament, invested him, of course, with every virtue, every noble, chivalrous sentiment and aspiration, that would seem in keeping with his handsome poetic face.

So the man who loved her so truly and well, makes excuses for her to himself at times, though always cherishing a savage, furious anger, against that other man who has stolen from him all his joy in this world—the man who has done much more than this, who has deliberately stamped on his darling's beautiful young life, and faith, and purity on her sweet confiding innocence, and crushed them, ruthlessly, to the earth for ever.

Then, at another moment, he will feel a wild rage against the girl—a fierce sense of humiliation, a desperate, stinging shame and sorrow, that she should have deceived him so cruelly, and not merely him, but those, her nearest and dearest, who loved and believed in her thoroughly.

To have sunk so low for that ruffian's sake! If she must have played him false, surely he would not have felt it so bitterly, he thinks, if she had not degraded herself so greatly, in forsaking him for one so debased, so low, so steeped in sin and shameless evil-doing.

But this mood of resentment and anger against poor lost Mabel is always the briefest of any; all personal feelings are swamped and drowned out by a passionate, over-whelming tide of pity, that sweeps all before it; which generally in its turn, leaves a strange, unaccountable impression behind, that, possibly, after all, there is a greater mystery in Mabel's sudden, singularly untraceable disappearance, than is manifest on the surface—that they have taken things too much for granted, and that Harman, with his beauty, and his devilry, does not hold the key to the puzzle, as the world imagines.

Look how positive, how unshakable is poor, weak, suffering Mrs. Arden, in the conviction that her child has done no wrong, that no dishonour or deceit is hers, but that she has been in some unimaginable way deluded; her credulity imposed upon, and decoyed away from her home—never deserting that dear home deliberately, but deceived by some lying tale of woe or sorrow, which her tender heart has swiftly sped to comfort and succour. Mabel—true, loyal, noble-hearted Mabel—made no secret assignations, had no hidden meeting and communications with a lover whom she dared not name openly.

Her child's brow had never flushed with shame, or her pure eyes drooped with the knowledge of her own active treachery and deceit.

No, either she was duped and cheated for some fell, desperate end, that had nothing whatever to do with Harman and the coincidence of his flight and the robbery, or else she was the victim of some awful mystery, and never left Arden on "All Souls' Night."

How strangely persistent and obstinate is the poor, faithful mother, in her belief in her child's loyal uprightness, and that either of these terrible explanations solves the riddle of that sudden, eerie disappearance.

Why does she so determinedly reject what really seems the only reasonable and natural solution of the puzzle?

Is it that the loving, straining mother's eyes, weary and desolate, perpetual watching and sick yearning, see more clearly than his own, that are sometimes clouded with anger and resentment?

And then again, Hugh argues to himself—how could she be right, in either of the surmises she adheres to with such immovable tenacity?

The latter he puts aside as unworthy of attention. How could Mabel disappear at Arden? The idea is outrageous, not deserving of a moment's serious thought.

But the being decoyed away, by some false tale of misery or sorrow, is possible, feasible—and yet, there is no trace of how she went, when—where?

No trace that the most minute questioning of the Grange servants, the most patient investigations at Arden village can elicit, of any stranger having enquired for her or sought an interview, of an stranger having even been seen in the village.

If any one from Bath or Bristol, or elsewhere, had come to Arden with any fell, treacherous motive, they surely would have been seen lurking about the village, or near the Grange, or Dower House, by some one.

The only way of accounting for this, of admitting the possibility that unfortunate Mabel Arden's disappearance was not voluntary, is, that some one, possibly with felonious designs on the house, which were frustrated (as there was no manner of doubt as to Harman's guilt, with regard to the daring extensive robbery) or, still more likely, some one, possibly a "pal" of that same Harman—an accomplice in his evil doing, who had arranged to meet him—had encountered Mabel in that great dusky avenue (Hugh can only think of the avenue and high road), and attracted either by her rare and singular beauty, or by the glitter of her gleaming trinkets as she flitted through the moonlight, then and there improvised some tale of dire distress, some story of grievous wrong and suffering, demanding immediate relief; something, in short, that by some hideous, malignant fate, just appealed to the girl's tender, sympathetic, enthusiastic nature—a nature sweet, exalted, visionary, that dreamt of noble, heroic, self-sacrificing deeds, that was at once ardent and dreamy, confiding, innocent, unsuspicious of evil, and dangerously impulsive.

How easy then to imagine such a creature, duped, deluded, and decoyed away, till she got too far into the net laid for her to get out, however despairing and desperate her struggles.

And when this picture develops before his mental eye, Hugh Denver, strong man as he is, shudders and grows ashen pale.

It returns to him often after the first day he sees it, and he then begins eagerly and furtively, and yet with sickening, shrinking dread, to search the papers for accounts of hidden, mysterious crimes.

But still, no light is thrown on the mystery which surrounds the occurrence of "All Souls' Night," at Arden Grange; still Mabel's going forth from her home remains wrapped in deepest shadow; still the problem of her disappearance remains practically unsolved—or rather, though the evidence is so strong, that all, with one or two exceptions, after the first struggle, unhesitatingly accept it—the verdict with regard to the girl's actual vanishing—how—when—where—still remains "*not proven.*"

CHAPTER XVIII
HUGH DENVER'S VISION

AFTER some six weeks or so of this most wretched life at Arden—perpetual seeking—seeking that is beginning to be felt to be vain—and never finding even the very faintest clue, of sickening, constant fluctuation of hope and despair, Hugh Denver leaves the Grange, about the middle of December, and returns to his lonely stately home . . . He accepts no invitations for Christmas; he is too utterly miserable, too heart-broken, to endure even sympathetic companionship.

In the solitude of Heron Towers (his ancestral estate), he will spend this most joyous season, when happiness seems to brood over the sin-stained suffering earth, and all humanity, save himself—as he morbidly thinks—rejoices and is glad.

How different, how widely, horribly different, from the Christmas he had looked forward to!

He tries, oh so mightily, to harden his heart against her who has blighted his life so savagely, with such cruel, callous indifference, but the hardening will not come; rather, as the time goes on, he becomes more and more tender. Gradually, and unnaturally (as he deems it, and grows fierce with himself at times for his own weakness), does the burning sense of wrong, the bitter resentment, the stinging humiliation, the jealous, angry pain die out—giving place to only a great and supreme pity, an intense and undying love, and a constant, haunting sense of some terrible disaster having overtaken his beloved Mabel.

And so he ponders and broods, and mourns through the short dark days of the closing year.

Christmas comes and goes almost unnoticed, save that the knowledge of its hallowed presence hovering all around seems to add still a sharper sting to the heart-stricken man's sorrow.

Yes! Christmas is past, and the last two or three days of the dying year drag out their slow, dreary length, until the last of all is reached.

It is New Year's Eve, and exactly two months, to the day, since Mabel Arden disappeared.

Two long months, during which time no sign, no faintest token, has reached the despairing, weary-hearted watchers from across that gulf, that awful gulf of silence and unknowingness, which the girl has placed between herself and those who love and long for her, oh!—so yearningly.

"Two months to-night, since she went from us, so cruelly, so suddenly, so strangely," thinks Hugh, as he wanders restlessly through a wild, dreary part of the park at Heron Towers, in the gloaming of this 31st of December.

It has been a dismal, gloomy day, not actually wet, but with a dull, leaden sky, a faint imperceptible mist, a hopeless, brooding dreariness of aspect, infinitely more depressing than honest, heavy rain. As if the day itself, even in its strongest morning hours, had not heart to light itself up, or declare itself really "day," but slunk by, in dim, twilight fashion, grieving for the death-bed it was so soon to see.

Surely, it may argue, it would not be seemly, to smile and look glad, with sunny face and bright, breezy laughter, when the poor old year's breath is already labouring so heavily, and the end is so near.

So it wraps itself in a mantle of decent gloom; and though there seems to be no wind whatever in fact, rather a great calm—yet, far away, high up amongst the tree tops, a strange, faint, yet shrill piping, an eerie, unceasing, wailing sound increases the mournfulness of the day and the hour—adds to the sense of solitude and desolateness that oppresses Hugh with an actual physical weight—and yet which he cannot throw off by returning to the house, where at least he would feel human companionship at hand, and where he could escape from this shadowy, haunting dusk. He feels compelled, by some force as it were outside his own will, to remain aimlessly wandering through those wild and gloomy glades—romantic and picturesque in the summer sunshine, now ineffably dreary fastnesses of Heron Park.

Momentarily the light becomes less—soon it will be quite dark; already he can hardly distinguish objects at a little distance, but even as he so thinks, his restless steps bear him into a more open space; the trees are scattered, there is a greater expanse of sky, here the dying light seems to linger later—opposite to him is a wide natural arch, made by gnarled, mighty, old elms, an arch through which one gazes away into the western heavens.

Suddenly, as he looks, a slight glow diffuses itself across this arched space, like the last faint reflection of a sunset that had been rich in warm and brilliant colouring; but the sky beyond, away towards the distant horizon, is still cold and grey and dead; and yet that glow grows stronger.

It is no light from that bleak and darkling sky, and Hugh gazes at it fascinated—a sort of odd shudder runs through him—and then—as he looks—he seems to lose all consciousness of where he is, the park and the trees, and the wild, tangled glades stretching about him in all directions, fade from his sight, he sees only that breadth of arched space, lit by that strange, unaccountable light . . . And now he is conscious that he is gazing into some dimly revealed interior—yet stay, is it an interior? For as this weird sky-picture grows more distinct, he notices, that though it seems somewhat like a circular enclosed space, yet that a jagged streak of chill moonlight penetrates its gloom in one or two places, but the remaining spaces would be wrapped in profoundest darkness only for that odd glow, that seems to be revealing to him some mystery; and by that eerie light, he sees that the place is damp and decaying, and very old, with strange, fungus-like growths here and there. And now, suddenly, his attention seems all directed to the ground. In one corner, where the gloom would be greatest without that mystic light, he notes a heaped-up mass of what appears like broken fern, bracken, and brushwood—a pile of what had once been fresh and green and living, out in the fields and meadows, but is now stored in this great, gaunt, dreary tomb—for what?

He tries to pierce the dimness and see better, and then, as he does, the whole thing suddenly fades and blurs. He remains for a moment or two perfectly motionless, gazing transfixed on that breadth of dusky sky, on which he has seen painted this strange picture, a photograph of some place on which his earthly eye has never rested; and soon the light grows faintly again, and, by straining through the gloom, he now can discern a shadowy outline of a scarcely defined human figure, gliding through the dim enclosure.

Breathlessly he gazes like one magnetised; while a strange creeping awe seems to fold him in its chill embrace. Clearly, and more clearly outlined grows that mystic form.

It is a woman—a young woman—a slender, graceful girl, with floating hair.

It is—it is—great heavens—it is Mabel!

Yes! Mabel Arden!

That weird light grows stronger: he can see her plainly now, and he looks at the girl as he last saw her, through, as it were, a thin haze.

Quite plainly, though through a sort of thickened mist, he can see her. Her bright hair is loose and flowing; her shimmering, blue-grey dress floats round her as she moves with swift, gliding step; he can even see the cluster of asphodels—his gift—or at least something white glistening on her breast. The figure is now facing Hugh, and apparently gazing at him, with frenzied, wild despair in both look and attitude, as if striving, oh, so terribly, to tell him something. Pleading, imploring—help or forgiveness—which?

Then the light grows less again, and the figure of the girl seems to melt and fade into nothingness.

But once more, before that unearthly lamp goes quite out, it flickers brightly for a fleeting moment, and he sees that phantasmal shape, that simulacrum of Mabel Arden, pointing to a square, dark—unfathomably dark—space at her feet. For an instant she pauses thus, with her head turned towards the aghast, spell-bound Hugh, and shadowy hand out-stretched, and pointing into that dense, impenetrable void—the next moment, she has vanished into its fearful gloom, that hideous, thick darkness has closed over her, the strange, dim, revealing light again fades for the last time, and once more Hugh Denver gazes out on the night sky, dark and lowering, with no throbbing star-light penetrating and lightening its obscurity.

Once again he is conscious of his surroundings, of the tall, swaying trees, now agitated by a moaning, restless wind that has arisen, and of which the shrill, wailing piping of the earlier afternoon was the forerunner; of the tangled thickets and mossy glades of the undulating stretches of wide park land, that he feels rather than sees—as it is now almost totally dark—reaching away beyond that arch of interlacing branches, those bare, winter branches of those gigantic elms.

Through that arch he has seen—*what?*

That weird and mystic picture, on which he has gazed in astonished non-comprehension, with limbs and senses locked, as it were, in a magnetic trance, incapable of movement, of speech, of sound, but with the brain active, unsleeping—that picture—what is the meaning of it?—he asks himself, as he stumbles like a man blindfold, through the dusky, familiar paths that lead towards the house.

He is all thrilled and dazed with the strange experience he has been through. Weak, and faint, and tremulous he feels.

Some extraordinary revelation has been made to him, for some—doubtless—express and important purpose, and he has failed to catch the meaning. This is his first thought.

He has seen Mabel!

Does he not ever see her—with his mental eye—in his thoughts, in his dreams?

But this was no dream; it was a vision. A vision sent to tell him something; perhaps to explain some mystery connected with her disappearance.

He saw her plainly—oh! so plainly—and she looked just as she was on that fatal night; and she turned on him looks of wild, beseeching despair—addressed to him gestures of frantic, frenzied pleading—pleading for what?

Oh, God! he cannot tell.

And then, that awful darkness opened for her, and took her out of his sight.

Was the whole thing a sort of strange allegory, conjured up by his own over-wrought, tortured mind? And was that hideous, black void, which swallowed her in its foul embrace, emblematic of the lot which she had voluntarily chosen—for which she had given up him and her devoted, heart-broken mother, and all her past, with its sweet, and sacred, and tender associations?

Did it represent the dark and shadowed life to which she had sunk. The calm and radiant morning had suddenly plunged into obscure and stormy night—night that did well to be dark and rayless, so as to hide its shame, if she actually was sharing Harman's lot,—as either his mistress, or his wife.

What was the meaning of her imploring gestures? Was she entreating help, as from some physical danger, or beseeching his forgiveness for her cruel treatment and desertion of himself?

Why did he see that painting on the darkling sky? What end could it serve?

He most certainly was not dreaming. He was widely, nervously awake; roaming in restless, purposeless fashion through the park, his thoughts full of Mabel, his whole being concentrated in picturing her, as he saw her going from him down the long, brilliant corridor, with the children crowding round her, on that miserable All Souls' Night, just two months ago exactly. And then—this mystical vision rose up before his eyes.

Was it to mock him? Surely not to comfort, as it shed no ray of light to pierce the oppressive darkness that lay upon that night's occurrence.

No, he must only conclude that it was a wild, fantastic mind picture, that came to harass and perplex.

His brain was saturated with the thought of the girl, bringing back his last memory of her, and he suddenly saw her as she had been—by a strange trick of mind and eye combined—saw her, with certain added circumstances, the creations of his own worried, wearied imagination.

He had simply been the victim, like so many others, of an

optical illusion, a particularly impressive, eerie one, partaking in some respects of the nature of an allegory—but nothing more.

It would be absurd to attach any value to that somewhat singular manifestation.

It was odd, remarkable, even rather weird, above all a proof that his nerves and health were not in the soundest condition; but that is all.

He will think no more of it, and speak of it not at all, as he does not wish to be laughed and scoffed at, as a visionary, superstitious fool.

It is not given to man—say our dogmatists—in these later ages of the world to be accorded prophetic visions, or to be visited by dreams or appearances, that reveal mysteries or hidden sins and sorrows, otherwise unguessed at.

This is essentially a practical age, and dreams and visions are relegated to the limbo of other antiquated monstrosities, belonging to a younger, more innocent, and more credulous world.

And, even if in some rare instances the spirit eyes are momentarily unbound, and the spirit ears unsealed, and penetrate beyond the mists of earth, touching for the briefest moment what is hidden from mortal sight and sense, still, he who has for an instant breathed that purer ether, who has caught one fleeting glimpse of aught beyond the barriers the flash opposes to all things of the spirit, had better be silent as to his experience, unless he wishes to be scoffed at, and derided, and reviled, as either a shameless liar, or else a wild, visionary enthusiast, a poor, imaginative lunatic. And to pose in one or other of these characters is not especially seductive to the mind of the average Briton.

CHAPTER XIX

"AFTER LIFE'S FITFUL FEVER, SHE SLEEPS WELL"

"The air is full of farewells to the dying and mournings for the dead."[87]

MORE than six months have passed away since that November eve that began so blithely and ended in such gloom and sorrow and mystery; and now the fair lands of Arden are smiling under the jubilant May sunshine, the air is jocund with the songs of innumerable birds, and that grand old avenue of chestnuts—that avenue on which Hugh Denver had looked out, noting the fierce swaying of the topmost branches, so pitifully leafless then, is now clothed in the supreme loveliness, in the peerless May glory of its perfection.

What magnificent old trees they are. How splendid is the leafage, how superb the blossoms, those delicate, cream, pink-tipped spirals, or those altogether rose-pink spirals, pointing heavenwards. How beautiful they are. And how noble and peaceful looks the old house itself on this laughing May morning; how hard to think of gloom or despair within its walls. How hard to think that mystery or misery could lurk beneath that honest, gabled roof, those slender, graceful chimneys, behind those beautiful, old, mullioned windows, which seem to smile back at the sunshine, saying, "We, at least, enshrine no secrets."

But lovely as the spring day is without, there is deep sorrow within.

Three hours ago, in the sweetness and freshness of the brilliant

[87] From 'By the Fireside: Resignation' by Henry Wadsworth Longfellow.

May morning, Katharine Arden, Mabel's mother, was laid to her long rest in the Arden churchyard.

Many dead and gone Ardens sleep beneath the chancel of that picturesque old church, as the monumental brasses tell the stranger, but she begged to be laid where the tall, sweet grasses would wave over her head, where the wind and rain and summer sunshine would hold their court.

The Dower House has lost its mistress, and there is gloom and shadow within the walls of the Grange.

A very different gathering from that of six months ago.

The Squire looks ill and aged in his mourning garb; his genial, kindly, old face is pale and worn-looking; he has evidently grieved much for that beloved young niece, who went into the night and the darkness, and has been heard of no more.

The heartbroken mother, whom they so truly mourn for to-day, and yet would not recall if they could—would it not be to never-ending heart-slaying disappointment?—had hoped against hope, until hope itself lay dead, a pallid corpse, and then she had died also.

The belief, the certainty, that her girl would return to her, that all would yet be well, kept the frail woman alive, as no other stimulant could have done.

Her darling child, her precious Mabel, had been decoyed away, deceived, deluded—as to the Harman solution of the mystery, she never would hearken to it for a moment, it was but a hideous, horrible coincidence—but she would return to her mother; nothing could separate them, nothing should separate them—and her child must not find her ill and grieving when she came.

But as the weeks became months and rolled away, and still Mab made no sign, crossed not that awful gulf of silence which yawned between them, broke not that spell of mystery in which she had enveloped herself; when it gradually grew upon the watching, waiting woman that Mabel had disappeared out of their daily life for ever, that she was never to know why her child had gone, or where she had gone, then that stricken woman had turned her face to the wall and died.

Very sad and silent is that small group that sits in the darkened library at Arden Grange.

Mrs. Derrick clad in heavy sables is there, and weeps softly and subduedly;—she loved her gentle, patient aunt very dearly, having lost her own mother when little more than a child—while her husband and Hugh Denver—who is also present—converse at intervals in low tones, sitting somewhat apart from the others.

Hugh is almost more changed than the Squire. He is pale, listless, dejected looking, like a man who has gone through some great trouble which he cannot rally from; yet with all this apparent listlessness and weary hopelessness of aspect, there is a watchful expectant look in his eyes—those intense magnetic eyes—an appearance of listening, or waiting, in his face.

Is it possible that he still cherishes a hope of hearing of Mabel? That he is still watching for a sign, a token, that has been denied the dead mother?

Who can tell?

He never speaks of her except when absolutely forced to do so, but this odd unaccustomed look has only grown in his eyes since the beginning of the year.

At times he tries to banish her from his thoughts. She is unworthy his regard or remembrance, he tells himself—a girl who could act so cruelly, not merely to himself, but to those who had loved her so devotedly and unselfishly all her life.

But then again his heart softens and smites him for his temporary hardness; he thinks how pitifully young she was, and confiding, and innocent; how pathetically unsuspicious of evil. She had been basely deluded, deceived; and when she discovered her horrible mistake, and the true character of the man she had sacrificed everything for, she was doubtless so overwhelmed with despair and humiliation, with a bitter, terrible sense of degradation, as to determine on remaining dead for ever to her friends and kindred.

But besides these four whom we have already met there is a fifth figure in that shadowed room. A tall, slight, worn-looking man, with grey heard and furrowed face, who sits with head bent upon his hand, while slow tears trickle through his thin fingers. It is Richard Ramsay, only brother of her who has been laid in her new-made grave; who has come a long, long way to catch the parting glance, the last faint sigh of the sister he had loved so well in the olden days.

But during the score of years or so that have elapsed since her marriage they have met but seldom—only twice or thrice, when she had been able to go on brief visits to the North of Scotland, as long as her brother still retained his home there, for Richard Ramsay had vowed a vow that he would never enter Philip Arden's house, and he never has, until a week ago. Since her widowhood they have not met, he being altogether abroad, having accepted an appointment in East Africa connected with the Royal Astronomical Society, from which he could not get away till almost it was too late.

But thank heaven he has been in time to see a glad look of recognition in the dying eyes, to hear the familiar words, "Dear old Dick," murmured for the last time by the feeble lips, and he was grateful even for this.

As he stood by the bedside some few hours later on, and gazed down on that worn, patient face, locked in its eternal repose, he muttered between his clenched teeth, "There was a curse upon him and his," as he thought of the child, the bonnie bairn, the winsome lassie—lost, more irretrievably than if she lay there dead beside her mother, and of the mother, still young—as he thought her—still beautiful, worn out with misery and suffering now dead, in the prime of her days.

Although he had met the Squire before and loved him, bitterly contrasting him with his *vaurien* brother, yet never, until this day, has Richard Ramsay been under the roof of Arden Grange.[88]

* * * * * *

And now the Squire breaks the silence that has fallen upon them, saying,

"There's a portrait of our beloved Katharine in the Picture Gallery, Mr. Ramsay, an excellent one, painted just a year or two after her marriage. You have never seen it; would it be too painful to you? You might like perhaps to have a copy of it, or even the original itself. If it would make you happier I would yield it to you; yours is the superior claim."

"Thank you, Squire; I should very much like to see it, if I may. I've no likeness of my darling Katharine in her bonnie youth, and that the dear soul sent me three or four years ago conveys but little to my mind of the brilliant, joyous lass she was when she left me. I shall have it copied, as you kindly suggest, and it will be a very great comfort to my desolate heart, far away in my lonely African home."

Then the Squire rises to his feet and proposes that they adjourn at once to the Picture Gallery. Fred Derrick strolls slowly in their wake,

---

88 *Vaurien*: disreputable, villainous, good-for-nothing.

and Hugh Denver follows the latter listlessly, almost mechanically. He does not know why he goes; he has no particular interest in the poor, dead Katharine Arden's portrait, but those great dreamy grey eyes of her child seem to haunt him, looking at him with a sad, reproachful expression, in their shadowed depths; it seems somehow as if the girl's very spirit hovered around him to-day, and he walks as a man in a dream, conscious only of those sweet sorrowful eyes, of that slender girlish form in the blueish-grey dress—like a cloud, that she wore that fatal night;—she seems to glide on before him in fancy, mocking him, by ever eluding him.

But it is written that these two laggards—Derrick and his cousin Hugh—are not to visit the west wing of the Grange to-day.

The Squire and his guest are already out of sight, having mounted a portion of the grand staircase and turned into the long corridor leading to the picture gallery and the west side of the house. Their voices are still audible, especially the Scotchman's quaint old-world intonation, who has retained the accents of his youth in a great measure in spite of his long residence abroad.

But just as Derrick's foot is on the first step of that beautiful old marble staircase, Dickson, the butler, who, as they learn later, was on his way to the library but withdrew into another apartment on hearing the Squire approach and waited till his master and Mr. Ramsay were out of sight—emerges from one of the doors of the great dining-room—a noble banqueting hall, seldom used, being only suitable for special and state occasions—and approaches Derrick with faltering step and blanched horror-struck face. Scared and terrified as the man looked on the morning he announced the robbery and Harman's flight to the Squire and his assembled guests, it was nothing compared with his aspect now, he is trembling as one palsy-stricken, ashen-faced, and with a look almost of panic in his eyes.

For a moment Fred Derrick is staggered and mute.

What new trouble is coming? The man, though infinitely grieving with the faithfulness of an old attached servant for all the misery that has come to Arden within those last six months, and freshly mourning this morning for her who has been laid away for ever from life and its sorrows, still could never look like that unless some new complication had arisen. Then after a momentary pause he finds his voice:—

"For God's sake, Dickson, what is it? Has anything happened? What have you heard?"

And the man answers with baited breath and whispering tones:—

"Ay, Mr. Derrick, something has happened, something awful bad, I'm fearin'. I don't know the rights of it, and won't say any thing lest I say something too horrible; for God help and protect and save us all, I can't think *how* such a horror could be—up beside a body, as one might say, and we all never to think or suspect anything. But I won't say no more, sir," seeing Derrick make an impatient gesture, which he cannot restrain at the man's want of coherence and slowness in coming to the point—well as he knows the poor old fellow's failing, especially when agitated.

"I'll let you hear it for yourself; you'll be able to understand better than me, just catching a few words through the door as it were. I was coming to the library for you, sir, hoping to be able to get you out unknown to the Squire—the dear, blessed master—it will kill him if he hear it, and if it be true; and keep it from your lady, sir—for the love of heaven, keep it from Miss Constance—Mrs. Derrick, I mean. It will be the death of father and daughter I'm thinkin'. And then—his auditor's patience being well-night exhausted—"they sent me for you, sir—Sergeant Adams, and Dr. Truscott sent me for you to fetch you to the turret; they are both there with that wicked old witch, Meg Morrison, who is a-dying, she came back more nor a fortnight ago; you know, sir, she went off quite suddint one night, about a month after that awful All Souls' Night, takin' the key of the turret chamber with her, and no one knew what became of her; but we all had other things to think of than to be worrying after the likes of her. And then she came back as she went, sneaky and secret-like, the other day—came back to die. She's been mortal bad ever since; and Dr. Truscott, he sent for Sergeant Adams to the village this morning to take her—what do they call it?—her 'dispositions,' I think they said. The doctor first sent for Sir Aubrey Pelham, being a magistrate, but he is away from home, and the only other one near was Squire himself, and he daren't send for him, so he thought the police-officer was the next best; and they have been taking her whole confession down in writing, and they——"

"But what are old Meg's dispositions to us? What have we to do with them?" interrupts Derrick, mystified and horribly alarmed, though he hardly knows why. "If the wretched old creature is dying what can she have to say or confess that can affect us in any way? What can she know of——"

"It's about—I think it's something about Miss Mabel, sir, as well as I could make out; and—and—may the Lord have mercy upon us all, I think it's—I'm fearin'—it's—it's—*murder*!"

Fred Derrick's face grows as white as that of the trembling old man opposite to him, and he makes a sudden backward movement, as though repelling the horrible suggestion, and starts violently to find Hugh Denver at his elbow.

Huh, automatically following Derrick, had seen him accosted by the butler, without noticing anything strange in the old servant's manner, his own thoughts being too much engrossed, too absent and dreamy just then to be very cognisant of small external matters, and seeing Fred engaged he had roamed aimlessly into that great dining-hall from which Dickson had furtively crept the moment before to intercept the Squire's son-in-law, and having strolled listlessly through its stately length, staring blankly at the historic pictures on its wall, emerged by another door, and wondering what was detaining Derrick came round at the latter's back in time to hear the last few sentences. For a minute or so Fred is almost frightened at his aspect; he grows so rigid and stonelike, with a fixed, frenzied glare in the introspective, somewhat mesmeric eyes; then he suddenly shakes himself free of the horror that binds him, and grows rational, collected, practical; his dreamy, visionary state of a while ago gone. He has now to grapple with facts; awful, terrible facts, if old Dickson's words be true, and not with the mere idle fantasies of a sick brain.

"*Murder*," he murmurs in a clear, horrible whisper. "Then Kathleen O'Hara's wild suggestion was true, her attempt to explain the mystery of that night cry was correct."

"Yes," cried Derrick, eagerly catching the thread of the other's thoughts; "in some incomprehensible way our poor, cruelly slandered Mabel discovered that devil at his fiendish work and he silenced her for ever."

"O God!" interpolates Hugh, in louder, clearer tones, "that *this* should be the ending; that thus the mystery should be cleared up—murder!"

"Hush!" cries Fred, "for God's sake, hush. The Squire must not know, at least not yet awhile, until we are sure, quite sure. It may, after all, be only some wild report, a foolish imagination of this old man's here, founded on some half-caught sentence of a dying woman. We'll go at once to the turret-chamber, and hear what

Sergeant Adams and the doctor have to say—and remember, Dickson, for your life, not one word to anyone of what you have heard till I give you leave; breathe not a syllable lest it might come round to the Squire or Mr. Ramsay," and with these words Mr. Derrick, accompanied by Hugh Denver, starts for the ruined turret.

CHAPTER XX
IN THE RUINED TURRET

"Infinite passion, and the pain of finite hearts that yearn."[89]

"THIS is a most serious and terrible thing, sir," speaks Sergeant Adams in grave solemn tones, rising from the seat he has occupied beside the bed in the turret chamber, and advancing to meet Derrick, as he and Hugh enter hastily. "It will be a great shock to the Squire, I fear, coming so immediately, too, on the death of Mrs. Arden. That wicked old creature," pointing backwards towards the bed, "has made a most extraordinary and startling statement and confession this morning, in the presence of Dr. Truscott and myself. I have taken it all down here," flicking the large open note-book in his hand.

"But I fear she's gone before she's completed her terrible story; before she has made the last point clear," breaks in the doctor, who has been bending over the terribly convulsed form of the old woman on the bed, "that is, unless, as I am half inclined to think, the whole thing is the raving of a dying mad-woman.

"The wretched old hag has been not quite right in her mind for some time back I fancy, from what I hear; and this wild tale of a grievous wrong and a remorseless revenge is, very possibly, but a figment of her diseased old brain. The delusion of being guilty of dreadful, deadly crimes is not at all an uncommon form of lunacy, concludes Dr. Truscott, with a resigned sigh, and a glance backwards at the bed, where the working form is growing

[89] From 'Two in the Campagna' by Robert Browning.

less violently convulsed, growing stiller and stiller by degrees.

"But what does it all mean?" asks Derrick, abruptly, who has been too agitated to speak sooner. "Remember we know nothing yet. Dickson seemed terribly upset when he gave me your message, and appeared to think that something connected with my cousin Miss Arden's most singular disappearance six months ago had been discovered. He even hinted at—at——"

"He spoke of *murder*," interposes Hugh, with ghastly face, but with a slow, horribly clear enunciation of the fatal word, that almost makes his hearers start.

"Yes, murder," he reiterates, with a strange, penetrating yet distant, searching yet absorbed look in his eyes, as they wander vaguely round the unfamiliar interior of the turret chamber. "And we are here," he continues in dull, slow tones, as though his mind were far away, "to prove the truth of that awful suggestion."

"Yes," cries Derrick, who is growing calmer each moment, as he reflects that doubtless the whole thing is either the wild imagination of a dying, clouded brain or, at least, some gross exaggeration. "We are come to hear what you have to tell us. Make haste, like good fellows, and don't keep us in the torture of suspense. What has that miserable old crippled creature to do with us? What can she possibly know of Miss Arden? Is she—tell me quickly—is she, or rather was she, in league with Harman?"

"Harman!" ejaculate both men simultaneously, with evident genuine surprise.

"Harman!" repeats the officer. "I had almost forgotten that ruffian and the robbery, in the teeth of this greater horror. No, sir, Harman's no more to do with it—I mean with Miss Arden's disappearance—than I have; leastways, if that old witch's words are true. It was revenge as did it—Mr. Derrick—deep, remorseless revenge, as Dr. Truscott says—revenge for a great wrong done her daughter by Miss Arden's father, Mr. Philip Arden. He was a bad man, he was. Forgive me, sir, for saying it to you. I shouldn't, but it's hard always to remember."

Fred Derrick's face flushes at this allusion to the family black sheep. "But whose daughter are you talking of? Who did the old creature want to avenge, and how did she do it?" He questions rapidly, confusedly; beginning to think that there is a deeper, more complicated meaning in the whole tragedy than anyone had yet dreamed of.

"*Her* daughter—Meg Morrison's daughter, sir," answers the sergeant, pointing to the bed, where the quivering prostrate form of the old woman lies mute, and now almost motionless.

"We were waiting when you and Mr. Denver came in, hoping that she'd recover consciousness enough to finish this," again flicking the note-book in his hand. "She was took two or three times before, this morning, and worked fearful, but got better again, though weaker each time, but the doctor felt almost sure that this would be the last, and he was about right, I think."

"Eh, doctor? any chance of her coming to again?" addressing Dr. Truscott, who has returned to the bedside, and is once more stooping low over the shrunken form that, save for an occasional very slight convulsive thrill, is now almost rigidly still and quiet.

"None," murmurs the doctor, gravely. "It is almost over—she's nearly gone—she'll never speak again. The mental strain of that confession, if confession it be—the declaration of her fearful guilt, has hastened the end, and though she may breathe for another hour or so, life is virtually extinct. She has swiftly escaped from all possible earthly retribution for her great sin."

And for a few moments Derrick and Hugh and Sergeant

Adams remain silent, impressed almost in spite of themselves with a sort of intangible awe of the mystic invisible presence that has glided in amongst them, and is even now waiting to claim its victim.

Then they turn away with a shudder from the contemplation of that flickering expiring life, going out thus, in the thick darkness of unrepented terrible sin; and the police officer says to Fred Derrick—

"I have no right, sir, any longer to withhold from you and Mr. Denver the confession I have taken down this morning. I only waited, hoping that the wretched creature might be able to complete the statement which wants the final link or clause to make all perfectly clear."

The sergeant had taken the statement down roughly in the old woman's own halting, rambling, somewhat dislocated provincial speech; but the following is a tolerably clear and accurate account—minus old Meg's irrelevant discursiveness—of the main points of that strange pathetic story and startling confession made by Margaret Morrison, pensioner on Mrs. Arden's bounty, and chance occupant of the turret chamber, on this lovely May morning, six months after Mabel's disappearance, and by a strange fate on the very day, almost at the hour, when her mother's broken heart was laid away to its last long rest.

Some ten years before that winter day on which Squire Arden's careless wagoner drove over the sleeping form of Meg Morrison just outside the Dower House gates—a most unhappy and singular coincidence, as the old woman's agony and subsequent grievous lameness intensified the bitter deadly feeling of hatred and revenge then burning fiercely in her breast against the Arden family—some ten years before that day Meg's daughter and only child,

Nannie Morrison, was as bright and beautiful a girl as the heart of any mother, whether of high or low degree, could desire; bright, and good, and true, and happy, and lovely as a spring morning.

She worked as a telegraph clerk, but the hours were comparatively light, the work not too heavy, and the wages fairly good. She loved her old mother fondly, and the mother idolised her. They lived together in a little house in a poor district in one of the large Midland towns, and the mother kept a small shop and also knitted continually, which, together with the young clerk's salary, enabled them to live quite comfortably for humble folk.

But besides this quiet prosperity, which was the result of hard work and unflagging industry, pretty Nannie was engaged to a good, steady, most promising young man in the printing trade, who loved her madly. They were to be married in another year, when he might, as he so ardently hoped, have obtained the post of foreman printer to a good local newspaper, and as his aspirations were high, and his abilities excellent, his honest praiseworthy ambition did not even rest here.

But that fair, smooth, prosperous future that seemed stretching in front of Nannie Morrison's feet, where honour and happiness walked hand in hand with suitability, equality as to rank, &c., was never to be realised.

In an evil hour a "gentleman"—looked on Nannie's lovely face—in an evil hour, a "gentleman" came into her life, and the sweet, simple, honest dream fled for ever.

One winter day, just ten years before Meg appeared at Arden, Nannie Morrison vanished from her home, leaving a few lines of passionate, heartbreaking farewell for her mother; an imploring plea for pardon, both from her and him she wronged so deeply—and that was all.

But those two, thus so basely robbed of what was their all, left desolate and despairing, with nought but that cruel bit of cold responseless paper as a last token of her who had been their very life, soon heard whispers about a "gentleman," from Nannie's comrade clerks in the telegraph office.

He had kept himself very quiet, lay as low as possible in fact, but still the girls felt sure that if Nannie was gone, she was gone with him. They knew nothing of him, either name, or address, or anything that could be regarded as helpful or reliable information, only that he was a remarkably fine, handsome-looking man with all the appearances of a real gentleman, "a first-rate fast swell," as they dubbed him; not young, but middle-aged—and they thought his initials might be "P.M.," as one day at the office they had seen Nannie trace these letters many times in the dust and grime of a window that wanted cleaning, as they waited to go back to work after their mid-day meal.

Wild, eager, ceaseless search and inquiries, were made by the man who was to have been Nannie Morrison's husband, who threw up his employment for the purpose, but in vain.

Nearly a month had elapsed since they got that farewell letter, when a little note came with a money enclosure for her mother, and a few loving words, saying, she hoped often to send a similar gift, but that neither her mother nor anyone else must ever seek to find her out, or communicate with her; the great happiness that was now hers was held on this one condition, and if not implicitly obeyed it would cease at once; otherwise her life would be one long dream of joy and delight, and she asked for nothing better in earth or heaven. She had gained perfect love and perfect lasting happiness, and what more could anyone wish for? (poor credulous fool!) and at no very distant day, perhaps, the cause that compelled them to keep apart now would no longer exist, and she would summon her mother to her, never to separate again, and they would rejoice together in her (Nannie's) wonderful happiness. That was all; no address, no name, no faintest clue as to her present whereabouts or condition, save the postmark, "London," which was wide indeed, maddeningly, distractingly wide.

Yet, hopeless as it seemed, almost absurdly hopeless, the unfortunate young man, shamed and heartbroken, determined to make a despairing effort to track the wretched, misguided girl, who had ruined his life as well as her own, to make one mighty effort to save her from the black, bottomless gulf awaiting her, or, if not—

To London he went, and one, two, three months rolled away; more than six months passed, and the mother, wildly grieving in her lonely home, sat watching and waiting, and neglected her little business and got poorer and poorer; and occasionally those brief notes came, always enclosing money that was never used, always loving, but never giving any clue.

At last, when nearly eight months had elapsed, a gaunt, haggard man, dejected, hopeless, miserable-looking, with a settled hungry despair seated in his aged, hollow eyes, walked into the familiar little room at the back of the tiny shop, in that midland town, and she who sat therein looked at him first with non-recognising eyes; then she saw it was he whom she loved as a son, who was to have been her son. Thus he has grown in that desperate quest.

He told her that at last he had found her whom he sought, only the other day. His patience had been at length rewarded, but there was no result from the discovery.

From what he had heard beforehand he knew it would be useless to attempt to influence her—she was infatuated. And then he determined to kill her; that would be the best way to release her from the bonds of sin that were fastened so tightly round her. So he lay in wait, and then one day he saw her—saw her for the first time since—. And the moment his eyes fell on her beautiful face his murderous intention died suddenly. It was not merely her loveliness, which was so great and so enhanced, but the ineffable light of joy and happiness shining in her face, making its beauty radiant, almost supernatural that palsied the hand that would have slain her. No, she was evidently happy—triumphantly, supremely happy; and he would not shorten that bliss by so much as an hour.

Had he seen *him*, that unknown man, whose wickedness had blighted their lives—asked the mother. Yes, he had, he answered, with a shudder. She was with him, looking up into his face, with that rapture in her own. He could have shot him easily as he passed, and he longed oh, so horribly, to do so, but it would have killed her joy, so he let him go on his way. And then—after telling the mother the very few facts he had gathered, the chief one being her daughter's present address, and that, he thought, the man's name was "Marmaduke"—he went to his dreary home, and there, in the solitude and silence of the night, he shot himself through the heart, and there was one promising, hopeful young life less in the world—that was all.

The only use the mother made at first of the knowledge she had gained was to return, in a sealed, blank envelope, all the money she had received from time to time—not one penny missing. But by and by, when no more notes came, with or without enclosures, a terrible craving to see her child's face again arose in her heart. She went to London, and easily found that pretty cottage in one of the suburbs, where she knew her daughter lived; but after long and dreary waiting, with that hunger ever growing stronger, and nothing to appease it, she at last ventured to make cautious inquiries, and heard that a Mrs. Marmaduke had lived there for nearly a year, but that quite suddenly a short time ago she left, and none could tell whither she had gone—it might have been abroad. Mr. Marmaduke, who was constantly at the cottage, though he only lived there occasionally for a few weeks at a time, had gone with her. This was all Mrs. Morrison could glean, but evidently the proof of the girl's whereabouts and identity, as "Mrs. Marmaduke," being known by the return of the money, had put the man on his guard; he desired concealment, and sought to maintain it, doubtless for base, sinister motives.

And from that hour Meg Morrison never saw or heard anything of the child she had borne, the girl she had worshipped, in whose lovely, blameless, honoured life she had hoped to find the crown of her old age, until a few weeks before that winter day when she lay down, spent and starved and frozen, outside the Dower House gates.

CHAPTER XXI
THE STORY OF THE WRONG CONTINUED

"Man's inhumanity to man
Makes countless thousands mourn."[90]

JUST at the beginning of that severe winter she got a little note in the old, dear, familiar handwriting, only weak and faintly scrawled.

It was dated from the infirmary of a workhouse in East London, and in a few imploring words the writer besought her mother to forgive her and come to her at once, if not for her own sake at least for her helpless child's, who did no wrong, and was the innocent, unhappy victim of her sin and folly. She was dying, she said—she could not live many days, and she must see her mother—whom she knew still lived—before the end.

Need we say that the mother, with that horrible void and hunger in her heart unsatisfied all those weary years, responded quickly to that summons? She only waited to realise any money she could by the sale of the few little things she still possessed. She had grown very poor through the years; the small shop had long been closed; she had no heart to attend to it, so custom dwindled and at last ceased, and the shutters were put up, and but that the little house was her own, old Meg would have been obliged to find another home. But there was no rent to pay, and the knitting which she still did mechanically, and which her humble neighbours, pitying the forlorn, old, deserted creature, obtained for her, brought in enough to keep body and soul together—and what more did she want?

---

[90] From 'Man Was Made to Mourn' by Robert Burns.

But now—what would she not have given to have kept the shop together, and to have had some money saved? Now—her child—her grandchild in a workhouse.

She sold her poor little effects, and so hastily that she got scarcely half the value for them; but still by selling everything she had a small sum of money, that might perhaps nurse her child back to life and health, and—thank God—they would be once more together; and so she left the old home in the midland town for ever, and set her face towards that distant workhouse in East London.

Nannie Morrison was indeed dying—dying surely and rapidly of consumption, after almost unimagined suffering and privation, after a ghastly hand-to-hand struggle with direct poverty in that stronghold of misery and squalor—East London; where the unhappy victims of the murderous "sweater" run to earth, trying to hide their shamed and agonised heads in these fastnesses of want and despair and crime.[91]

Hardly quite three years after she fled from the safe, loving shelter of her honest home, to enter on a life—as she thought, poor, deluded, credulous creature—of perfect, lasting happiness, and when her little daughter was barely six months old, Nannie Morrison was basely, cruelly deserted by him who had sworn to her with many sacred oaths, to love and cherish her for life. The girl was naturally pure and good, and never would have been won to dishonour and shame by the mere glitter of wealth and dazzle of surroundings.

No, she believed with the whole strength of her passionate, sympathetic heart the story her betrayer told her—of a marriage formed long ago in his early youth with a woman much older than

[91] Sweater: a harsh, grinding employer.

himself, who had blighted and cursed his life; that only death could free him from her, and that that blessed release could not be very far distant now, but that in the meantime he had never really loved 'till he knew her—Nannie—and would she not brighten and sweeten his shadowed lot through the weary time of waiting for the shackles to fall off? As soon as ever they did she should bind them anew around him with her own hands, and he would wear them proudly and joyfully to the end.

Can we wonder that simple, believing Nannie, loving as she did so intensely, was caught in the cruel, remorseless trap, and easily influenced to cut herself adrift completely from those who loved her and would have rescued her?

Yes, deserted suddenly at the end of three years, left to face and fight the stoney-hearted, scoffing world—alone, with a dishonoured name, a little helpless babe to protect and cherish, and a £50 note between her and starvation. Nothing else in all the world could she call her own but that sullied name that blighted the little life who was born to no name, and that £50; nothing else save an agonised, and shamed, and broken heart.

Time after time she got employment, the old work that alone she could do well; but always after a little, some whisper about the child came out and she was dismissed. And so, lower and lower she sank through the years—and when her mother looked upon her face again, lying on that wretched pallet in the London workhouse, it was on the face of an old woman she gazed with distracted non-recognition.

Yes, actually an old woman, though it still wanted a month or two of ten years since the lovely girl of twenty-one, brilliant and beauteous as daydawn, had passed out of her life and vision; yet now, at an age when other women in these latter days, still call themselves almost "girls," Nannie Morrison was a worn, withered, faded old woman, whose youth and identity were only betrayed by the voice, the dear familiar voice of long ago.

Mrs. Morrison, with the aid of the little money she had scraped together, removed her daughter to a cheap, clean lodging, where at least the dying creature had the bliss of being re-united to her child—who had been, according to rule, cruelly separated from her in the poor-house—the lovely little fragile Ruth, an etherealised Nannie of the distant days, who seemed to have so slight a hold on life as hardly to belong to earth at all. Her mother had lived for her, and had toiled for her from morning till night and from night again till morning, grudging to snatch an hour's sleep—toiled to earn the grinding sweater's fiendish pittance, that would just keep bread in her child's mouth; and now she was dying of the terrible struggle. Small wonder, when cases such as this abound around us in these latter days and flourish so exceedingly, where "might" so cruelly often and in so many varied ways seems to constitute "right"—the right to grind and crush and torture, to blight and betray and destroy—small wonder that the toiling, struggling, driven masses have risen in hot revolt against the relentless cart-wheels of oppression, that sought to roll them down, down in the dust of slavish, unmurmuring submission; are daily striving to shake off for ever the iron heel of wicked injustice, that has cruelly trodden and stamped upon them in the past. And what is the "might," what is the strength, that seeks thus to conquer and subdue, and, above all, to grind—to *grind*?

It is the strength of money and lands and worldly goods.

And what are these things? Do they not belong to all alike? Are they not the inheritance of all who know labour? Not the monopoly of a few drones in the world's busy hive. Are they not the natural heritage of civilised, toiling humanity? In the beginning the Great Creator made no distinctions. He gave the earth and the fulness thereof to man, to have dominion over it, and over all things upon it. This was to man in the aggregate—mankind; not to the swollen capitalist—the human sucker of the people's blood.

* * * * * *

Nannie Morrison had appealed to her mother, whom she dared not turn to before, partly from the unconquerable pride of shame, partly because the poor soul had imagined from the return of the little gifts of money, long ago, in a blank envelope, without word or sign or faintest token of pardon, that her mother was obdurate and unforgiving. But now she had appealed to her for her child's sake.

Her little Ruth would live, she felt sure—the doctor had told her so—if she could have tender rearing, care and nourishment, and be sheltered, above all, from the roughness and storms of life. Her mother could not give her this, she knew; but within the last year, feeling that her end was not far off, she had made tremendous efforts to discover the real name, position, general surroundings, &c., of the man who had so basely and treacherously deceived and betrayed her and destroyed her life.

She had altogether proudly shrunk from any step of the kind before, but desperation on her child's account forced her to what every fibre of her nature recoiled from.

After long and patient efforts she at last gained what she desired to know. She discovered what she had long felt convinced of, that "Marmaduke" was not the name of her betrayer, but "Arden;" that he was the youngest son of an old and most honoured and distinguished family; that there were large estates in the South-west of England, somewhere not far from Bath; that his eldest brother, a good man, was the reigning Squire; that his wife and family lived at Arden, and that all their surroundings were those of wealth and luxury. Also, she heard a report that he whom she sought, Philip Arden (Philip Marmaduke, as she had known him), was dead, but the source through which she gained her information was not certain on this point; and now, what she wanted her mother to promise her was this: that as soon as she was dead—it would not be long to wait, and she could not part with the child for one moment before the end—but when she was gone she wanted her to take the little girl straight away to Arden, even if they had to walk all the way, or to beg their bread on the road, and to tell the whole story of her (Nannie's) terrible wrongs—the base, cruel deception of which she had been the victim—to the brother and to the wife and children who lived there in happiness and affluence; the wife whom the cold, heartless sinner, the conscienceless, remorseless hypocrite had so lyingly and shamefully traduced and slandered to work his own evil end. He was bad, she had heard—irretrievably, irreclaimably bad in all his relations of life—and why should she spare him? Obloquy and censure were his deserts, and to be shunned by all honourable men the natural sequence of his own acts; and this great and added stain upon his sullied life should no longer be hidden.

Her mother should take the child to Arden and when they saw the lovely, little, helpless creature and heard everything, they would feel pity and sorrow, and would provide for her the nameless, innocent, little one, who was really of their own very blood. And the mother swore—while a feeling of deep, undying revenge grew and smouldered in her breast—that she would do this thing, or die in the attempt.

And two or three weeks later poor, unhappy Nannie Morrison

was laid to rest, and the old woman was alone in the world, with her little grandchild, whom she had grown to love with a passionate intensity, almost exceeding her faithful devotion to her daughter.

Alone—an old woman and a frail little child, and, after paying the funeral expenses, with but £2 and some odd silver between them and beggary. For poor Nannie had lingered longer than she herself had expected; quite six weeks had elapsed since her mother came to her, and the mother in her love and unselfishness had not told her how very small was her stock of money, and had insisted on getting all she could to relieve and lessen her child's sufferings. Then the winter had commenced so early and set in so severely, and little Ruth had caught a terrible cold which she could only partly shake off, and had needed doctor's aid and medicine, and many little things that cost money; and now that money was reduced to £2, and they had to go to Bath—all the way from London to Bath. She could not dare to purchase tickets and go by rail, because there was the terrible chance that their journey might be in vain; that poor Nannie might ether have been totally misinformed as to the Arden family, or again, that the world was so cruel and pitiless to the poor, and unfortunate, and unfriended, that that bad man's people might determinedly refuse to hear or believe her story, or to have anything to do with the child. Nannie certainly had furnished her with proofs to produce to verify the truth of her statement, but even so, they might absolutely decline to listen to anything; might perhaps even have herself and the child charged as vagrants and impostors.

"The strong are often as merciless as they are mighty," thought the old woman, while that bitter, deadly, revengeful feeling burned more fiercely and strongly in her breast.

No, she dare not spend that wretched little remnant of her

money on railway fares, that would bring them to their destination in a few hours, when it was all they had to look to, to obtain food and shelter if denied them there and to bring them back again, not to London, but to that midland town where she had lived the greater part of her life, and where at least her poor, humble neighbours would not let her and the child starve, but would get her the knitting again whereby she could buy bread for the little one, and she would work at it night and day.

If the Arden plan failed, this was all she could think of. But still, her thoughts clung around that unknown Arden and its inhabitants with a profundity of vengeful hatred that almost startled herself.

No, they must get to Bath as best they could without the railway, riding in some country cart, whenever they could beg a lift, walking when this failed.

And so they started, old Meg carrying their small bundle of clothes, and for the first couple of days all went fairly well; they got many an odd jaunt with the expenditure of but a penny or two, and by the end of the second night they had left London more than forty miles behind. But the next day was much colder than any that had preceded it; snow fell, and little Ruth was shivering and ill, and could scarcely walk, and the old woman had to try to carry her as well as the bundle; but though she was a light and fragile creature, still she was past seven years old, and poor Meg's progress was very slow, thus doubly burdened. The roads too were deserted; they met no friendly cart to help them on their way a little until it was nearly dark, when they came on a long brake, or wagonette full of returning market-goers who were loud and riotous after their long day in a good market town some miles off. At another time old Mrs. Morrison would have shunned such company; but now, she felt so exhausted it would seem almost heaven to get a rest; it was bitterly cold and getting dark and late, and for a sixpence the driver offered to take her and the child with him to his destination, a village which would bring them some six or eight miles farther on their way. So after a little hesitation, she scrambled onto the crowded car and managed to squeeze herself into a corner, with little Ruth upon her lap, and on they went rumbling in the dusk.

And by-and-by, she was so tired she fell fast asleep like little Ruthie, and no longer heard the quarrelsome voices of the noisy, half-tipsy fellow-passengers; in fact, she did not wake till the driver roused her on reaching the place where he stopped. She then found that the greater number of the travellers had left the car at intervals on the road. She went to a poor little shop in the village to try to get something to eat for the child, but to her horror, on putting her hand in her pocket she found her purse was gone,—stolen from her in that crowded car. Robbed of all she had—penniless she stood in that little shop—save for a sixpence change the man had handed to her out of the shilling she had tendered before stepping into the car, and which she continued to grasp mechanically while she slept. Penniless, and still far from Arden; she was almost stupefied by the blow. The people were sorry for her, but they were very poor and could do nothing save to give herself and the child food and a night's lodgings without taking that last sixpence; and in the early morning when she set forth again, old Meg carried a great hopelessness and despair, as well as the physical heavy burden of the day before; besides a wild, ceaseless self-reproach at not having spent the money and gone by train, and at least reached their destination, leaving the rest to chance. But she had acted for the best; she feared to part with all her money when all was so horribly uncertain; and how could she think that such strange ill-fate should pursue her?

That was a terrible day. The roads were deep in snow. She spent those last few treasured pence in warm food for the child, who was very ill and weak; and when the afternoon was closing in she had made but little way, and found herself in the open country, with apparently small chance of getting shelter. She had no money to pay for a night's lodging, even if she reached a village. What should she do? she thought, distractedly. She had felt sure she was much closer to her destination than she actually was; she had miscalculated; she had hoped to reach Arden the next day, but that was impossible, or the day after that either, she feared. Bath was still a long way off, as she saw by a milestone just before the dusk fell; and what in the name of Heaven could she do, utterly destitute as she now was, with nothing to sell even that would bring them a shilling or two? On and on she crawled and stumbled through the snow and the gloom, weary almost to death. She had begged a lift from a cart that had passed her a couple of hours before, but the man was surly and refused when she had no money, not even a penny, to tempt him with. At last she reached an isolated farmhouse of the poorer sort, and determined to beg, for the first time in her life, for a night's shelter. Food she did not want, as she still carried the remains of what that sixpence purchased: but a bed, any sort of a bed, for the child, who, she feared, was dangerously ill. The cold that the little creature had not been able to shake off a few weeks before seemed to have grasped the weak little frame with an iron clutch; the exposure, being constantly in the open air when the temperature was so low, was hastening the malady with giant strides to a crisis. But when old Margaret Morrison applied at the door of the farmhouse she was told roughly to be off, that they did not shelter tramps; and when she attempted to explain the cause of her pennilessness, and tell about the child's illness, she was quickly stopped by the farmer's wife desiring one of the men to put "the old hag" outside the gate at once, and fasten it securely—she herself waiting at the door to see the cruelty done.

And back on the deserted snow-covered road, in the bitter cold and fast-gathering darkness, with the child moaning faintly in her horribly aching arms, old Meg found herself, with rage, and despair, and utter blank hopelessness, contending with that awful, deadly spirit of revenge, which had now reached stupendous proportions, in her breast—revenge on him who had brought all this abject misery and suffering on her, on her child, and her child's child. Revenge on him, or—*his*. He had murdered her child, and now he—or his acts—were murdering her grandchild.

Each terribly unhappy coincidence of this ill-fated journey towards Arden she laid at his door; and her constantly murmured prayer was that she might not die until she was avenged. The unfortunate old creature was half mad with misery and sorrow as she trudged on into the night with her helpless burden in her arms. At last, just as it was beginning to snow afresh, she saw something like a small shed in the corner of a field near the road; it was, in fact, an old disused cattle shed. She managed to reach it; it would, at least, afford shelter from the falling snow, and protect the child a little from the bitter winter blast. She had a piece of candle in her pocket, and some matches; she lit it, and stuck it in a chink, and looked round; there was a good pile of clean, tolerably dry straw in one corner where the roof was sound, on this the old woman spread the few poor clothes she carried in her bundle, and laid the moaning, half-unconscious child thereon. She then took off the shawl she wore, the only article of any real size or warmth in her possession, and after doubling it three or four times spread it over the little one. She could do no more, she had done her best. She was alone, in the darkness of a snow-covered, unknown country at night, with no habitation near that she knew of, save that savagely churlish farmhouse, more than a mile away. They might be close to a village and help, but she could not tell; she saw no one to ask a question of, and she dared not run the risk of leaving the child and going to seek for aid when the probabilities were so great that she might lose her way and not be able to get back again through that driving snow, having no guide, no knowledge of the place where she was. No, perforce she must remain, inactive, through those terribly long hours of darkness stretching ahead, brooding always on that shapeless, shadowy phantom of "revenge," now her constant companion.

She ate a little of the food she carried, so as not to let her strength entirely go, and then she sat down on the corner of the straw, beside the child, who refused to take any food, beside a few spoonfuls of milk, with her head against the wall of the shed, chilled to the heart's core, having parted with her only warm garment—sat down, with a dogged patient endurance, to wait for the horribly distant daylight, and for what she felt instinctively might come before daylight.

She had given up all hope now—she only lived for revenge.

And through those first few hours of darkness (it was hardly more than six when she reached the shed, and the late December daylight would not come before eight next morning) the little child moaned and murmured constantly as she tossed in restless pain and fever; sharp, shrill moans, sometimes intermingled with incoherent mutterings of delirium; at others, a low, monotonous, infinitely pathetic sound, like the weak fluttering cries of some poor, wounded bird. The little creature's breathing grew horribly distressed, and sometimes the wretched old woman would put her fingers to her ears to shut out the agony of hearing the pitiful expression of the suffering that she was so desperately powerless to relieve. Once, in a wild frenzy of despair, a passion of helplessness, she rushed to the door of the shed, and out on the road a little way in the blinding snow, shrieking aloud on God and man for help; but only the shrill wail of the wind, the dreary soughing of the trees answered her; and even those few yards she had run unconsciously showed her how horribly futile it would be to penetrate into that awful void of darkness around her, with the hope of getting help and getting back; for, as it was, she was long before she could find the shed again. Just as she stepped within its shelter, a shriller, sharper cry of pain than any she had heard, followed by a greater struggle for breath, met her ears. With palsied hands she struck a match—as she had often done during the hours, the candle had lasted but a short time—and gazed long on the convulsed little face with a strange, wild, desperate look in her eyes, an anguished pity mingled with a look of terrible, desperate resolve, while her lips moved silently—was she registering some awful, binding oath?—and then the match went out, and she sank back into her former position, save that she slipped one arm under the gasping child, which raised and relieved it a little. And the time went on and on, and the expressions of pain were stilled by and by, and the moans grew fainter, and gradually ceased, and the sighing breaths slower and less difficult, as it seemed to old Meg, though farther apart. The unhappy, little creature was easier, she thought, not reading these signs aright, and overcome by her great grief and fatigue, exhausted in mind and body and half-numbed with cold, she fell into a profound sleep, from which she did not awake till the sun had long risen, shining on a snow wreathed earth, with chill, ungenial rays.

CHAPTER XXII
THE WOUNDED HARE

"To where beyond those voices there is peace."[92]

IN the first moments of waking old Mrs. Morrison felt strangely stiff and frozen, and quite unconscious of her surroundings; while one arm felt queerly rigid and paralysed as she drew it from beneath some weight under which it was outstretched.

Then, in a moment or two, the torpid, still drowsy faculties roused into life, memory reasserted itself, the weary, haggard eyes clouded with the blessed oblivion of sleep cleared, and she gazed down aghast on the cold, lifeless form of her little grandchild. She had thought it might be so, but never dreamed she would not know when the dread summons came for her little Ruth. That awful, unseen presence had entered that shed and called the child into the great darkness of the unknown, and she had slept unconscious of the mystic change. And now she was gone; the last creature left for her to love was dead, and, thank Heaven, at peace. The waxen little face, anguish-drawn when she last saw it by the light of the flickering match, was calm and placid now, with a dawning smile upon the lovely features.

Yes, at peace—and had left pain and cold and starvation and the misery of the down-trodden and the outcast behind for ever.

And she still lived—lived for revenge—and then she, too, would follow the others into the unseen.

And so, muttering and mumbling like one half-crazed, she made her preparations.

---

[92] From *Expositions of Holy Scripture: St. Luke* by Alexander Maclaren.

Carefully she folded the dead child in the large shawl that lay above her, and then, removing the few poor articles of clothing on which the little creature had died (she would keep those yet awhile), she hollowed down a large deep nest in the pile of clean straw, laid her darling dead Ruth therein, after a last passionate kiss of the ice-cold little brow, and then shook lightly the rest of the straw over her, which covered her completely—a strange discovery to be made by and by. She really was found two or three days later, and was buried at the expense of the vicar of the parish, a good, kind-hearted man, who could not bear to leave the lovely little dead waif to the wretched barrenness of a workhouse funeral. So a pretty mossy spot was chosen in the picturesque old churchyard, by the tender-souled man himself. His children scattered greenhouse flowers upon the little nameless coffin, and planted spring flowers upon the lonely grave, emblems of hope and promise, which they carefully tended, and little Ruth seemed less friendless in her death than in her life.

Then taking a draught of the milk which remained to relieve her parched lips, but forgetting the food, which she could not touch even if she thought of it, old Meg crept out of that miserable shed into the snow-covered country, carrying the little bundle of Ruth's clothes, which seemed somehow to keep the child nearer to her, and by some strange chance or instinct kept to the right road, as she was really beyond taking note of external things. All that day she tramped on unbrokenly, automatically, like a creature moved by springs, still intuitively keeping in the right way; she neither ate nor drank, she had no money, and it did not occur to her to beg. She moved like one in a dream, ever on, on, mechanically, and by the late afternoon of the second day as she had almost reached the gates of Arden, though she was unaware that her journey was so nearly ended, nature at last gave out, and the exhausted, starved, frozen creature, lay down to sleep. We have read how she was aroused from that sleep, that otherwise would have glided into death; and how singular the coincidence that it should have been an Arden horse and cart and labourer that should have inflicted this intense physical suffering and injury upon her.

For weeks she lay unconscious in that turret chamber, and for months was totally helpless; one can imagine how in that vengeful brooding and nature, that had been so abnormally tried, this added affliction of incapacity, wrought indirectly by the family a member of which had wronged her and hers so terribly, and, above all, helplessness—not alone inflicted through them, but which left her dependent on their powers to aid and succour and assuage—was like oil thrown on the angry flames already burning so fiercely in her breast.

The unfortunate, old, heavily afflicted creature grew, in fact, almost mad and hardly accountable for her after-deeds, as through those long months of complete helplessness she sorrowed with a desperate and unending sorrow and nursed her wrath, and ever brooded on the revenge that she had sworn should be hers.

There she lay, plotting and planning impotently, and Mabel Arden came in and out constantly, and cared and tended, and pitied with a supreme pity the miserable sufferer.

Mabel—whom the old woman's deadliest hatred was turned against, especially when she found that *he*—he, who by his base treachery and wickedness, his cold, heartless, savage cruelty in the past, had brought about all this horrible sorrow and sin, had indeed escaped all earthly retribution; Mabel—against whom her wildest rage, and hatred, and fierce desire for vengeance was directed—pure, dreamy, beautiful, angel-hearted Mabel. Mabel—*his* child, loved and idolised, and honoured; surrounded by all that luxury and fostering care, and strong, faithful, protecting affection could provide; and Ruth—*his* child, also—equally lovely and tender, besides being so fragile and frail a creature. And what was her life? And still more, what was her death?

And then again she would compare Mabel with her own child at the same age; equally good, and pure, and beautiful, and what was her fate? She looked at Philip Arden's daughter, and then the face on the pillow in the East End work house rose before her—that face with its terrible index of the suffering that comes from direct want and squalid misery, and unending, life and soul effacing labour.

She looked on Mabel, and remembered the solemn vow she had vowed as she had gazed on the tortured face of her little grandchild wrestling in her death agony, dying of want and exposure, and the terrible hatred in her heart waxed stronger and stronger, and the revenge she so continually dwelt on and sought came nearer and nearer to her hands.

When able to get about, as we have seen, her strange, repellent manner banished all from the dwelling that had virtually become hers so long as she chose to occupy it. In fact, she would permit no servant to cross her threshold. But Mabel went in and out at will, and the old woman rather encouraged her to do so, though she did not show her much welcome.

Then, one day, sometime in the month of August, when she had grown much stronger in spite of the great lameness (stronger than she allowed it to be imagined, leaving it to be supposed that she was weak and incapable of either much action or much effort) she was poking about in the ruin at the back of her dwelling—not from curiosity but from a great restlessness that was upon her—that insatiate thirst for revenge grew daily fiercer and more unconquerable in her now maddened, diseased brain—diseased from the unceasing dwelling on the one subject—the revenge that she had vowed to accomplish and that ever seemed to elude her when she thought out any plan for its consummation, she was "so horribly helpless now," she would mutter with a groan.

Partly she was looking about in the place, now grown familiar, with a purpose. A miserable hare, cruelly wounded by some so-called sportsman, who had wildly aimed at anything he saw living and defenceless, and being nothing of a shot had only succeeded in savagely maiming the creature, without giving it the release of death, had crept painfully into the shadow of the ruined turret, amongst the thick furze growing at one side of the tower, to die lingeringly. Old Meg had found it, and all her sympathies had gone out in a rush to the creature, the helpless victim of cruelty and strength, the defenceless, innocent victim, just because it was harmless and defenceless, of that insatiate, horrible desire to destroy and ruin so strong and rampant in man's evil breast.

She carried the wounded hare into the turret chamber and made a bed for it near the fire, and nursed it back to a feeble life; but as the creature grew stronger the wild, woodland nature declared itself in its painful efforts, at the slightest sound or movement, to crawl into some dark, remote corner, to hide from the light of day. The old woman soon saw that the creature would never rest comfortably in her living room, and would make its escape before it was recovered enough to get back to the woods. So this day she had gone into the interior of the ruin, to seek for a tolerably dry, warm, dusky spot, where she would make a bed for the poor, little, frightened beast. She had searched the long passage leading to the tower—a portion of which passage had been roofed over and formed her home; but it was very damp and cold and exposed, and so she went on into the tower itself and looked about her. There were great niches, or hollows curved in the massive thickness of the walls in its circumference here and there, and as these hollows extended but a few feet in height the ground spaces beneath them had all the advantages of being roofed by the arching walls above; they were also very dusky, and old Meg went about seeking the driest, darkest and warmest. At last she reached one gloomier than the others, as there was no rent in the wall in its near neighbourhood. The tower was lofty, and rather narrowed as it ascended, so in fact it was always dusky in its mouldering interior. She thought it would be best for the hare, and set to work as best she could, poor hobbling creature, to clean it; but though finding it so difficult to get about, being obliged to use two sticks, yet her arms were very strong; she had always been of a very robust and vigorous build, and the strength had returned wonderfully to the upper part of her body. Once she had collected what she wanted near her and got down on her knees, she could work away in a fashion that would have astonished those who thought her so feeble and helpless, and indeed she was really thankful to have something to do to occupy and interest her a little. She had taken care not to be surprised at her work, for she had fastened the outer door; not that anyone would be likely to come but Mabel Arden, but she had taken such an interest in the stricken hare, had such compassion for the creature, and took such a delight in its recovery, trying to pet and make it know her, that she used to run into the turret chamber constantly. So Meg set to work to clean this particular niche of a portion, at least, of the accumulated dirt and mould of centuries. The whole stone floor of the tower was immensely damp, much decayed in parts, with a fungus-like growth flourishing luxuriantly all over it; but in this especial niche, she had noticed, the mildew, and fungus, and mould, and all the numerous offspring of damp and decay, were much less apparent; still, there was a great bed of dirt and earthy deposit that held the damp, and that she set herself to partly scrape away. She was busily thus employed, her thoughts flown back to her little granddaughter, a desperate sorrow and wonder filling her breast, as to what had become of the little creature's body. She had left it that morning, feeling sure that it would not be found, thinking to come back in a few days when she had fulfilled her mission, and hoping that perhaps then they might be buried together; and now it was eight months ago. She had been rendered helpless by a diabolical freak of fortune. Her grandchild, for all she knew, still remained unburied and unavenged—yes, unavenged. Her mission was still unfulfilled. And as she was thus thinking and scraping away at the deposit of damp earth and mould, she suddenly laid bare a little ring, scarce bigger than a lady's finger ring. She tried to pick it up, but could not, it was fast. What was holding it? She tugged and tugged. Then she scraped about it to loosen it, and scraped it, and it began to shine with a metallic lustre. Then she gave another great pull; she might as well have the little thing, whatever it was, and giving still another tug in the same direction, to her great surprise up sprang another ring quite near it, much larger than the first, more bracelet size, but it, too, was fast. Neither of them could she loosen, and in trying to do so she struck the ground near rather heavily with her iron scraper, and to her great astonishment the sound was hollow, and the blow seemed to be struck on metal, not on stone.

She hammered again and again on various spots where she had partially cleared the great accumulation of deposit, and the sound was similar. She now began to grow very excited and interested.

What did it mean, that hollow, metal-like sound?

Again she pulled vigorously at that larger ring, and, at last, pulling it at a certain angle accidentally, a third ring slowly uprose from the soil that had so thoroughly concealed them all; this was larger still than either of the others, but yet the problem was not solved. There were the three rings in a row, standing up on end from the ground—but that was all. What were they there for? What was the meaning of them? If the handle of any hidden treasure, why the necessity of three?

Meg Morrison tugged and pulled them all about in every direction, separately and together, but in vain; no other ring came into sight. She could arrive at no solution of the mystery. She felt sure it was a puzzle of some kind, and if only one had the key to it these rings would open something; of that she felt convinced. Open what? Some concealed, unimagined place. And more and more wildly, tremulously excited she grew.

Nearly two hours passed, and still the old woman knelt there, stiff and sore in every bone, but had discovered nothing further.

At length, unconscious of her act, her thoughts running on what they could be there for, and why that hollow sound in the floor, she accidentally pressed the two outer rings—the smallest and largest, as they stood on end—towards each other in a direct line, and towards the centre one; she had never chanced on this action before, and as she unthinkingly pressed them harder and harder, while she speculated, she felt suddenly a jarring, vibrating movement just beneath where she knelt. Hastily pushing herself back as far as possible, she still leant forwards, pressing the rings together towards each other with all the strength of her aged, trembling hands. Then, there was a strange, grating sound, a harsh creaking and groaning, and a square metal plate some inch-and-a-half in thickness, slid slowly back, rasping horribly as it moved in the disused rusty grooves, and a space of impenetrable darkness yawned beneath the old woman's startled gaze. The opening was about three feet square—*what* lay beneath? Meg Morrison had struggled to her feet as quickly as she could when that mysterious trap-door began to glide open. She crouched back against the farthest wall of the tower from that black void, and from the foul, noxious vapour that rushed forth. For a few moments she remained thus, in a sort of panic. She hardly knew what she feared, and yet she shook in every limb, and a cold sweat of terror burst out upon her brow; then, seizing her sticks, she hobbled off into her own dwelling.

CHAPTER XXIII

BAITING THE TRAP

SHE went straight to a cupboard, where there was a little spirit, some remains of what she had when very ill. She mixed a small quantity with water and drank it. She wanted to feel as strong as possible.

In the bottom of the same cupboard lay a coil of rope, about five yards in length. This she took out, and to one end carefully secured a candle; then, providing herself with matches and making sure that the outer door was quite fast, she made her slow way back into the ruin.

She seemed strangely—incomprehensibly, if there had been anyone present, to be struck by her manner—agitated and excited. Her eyes shone with a wild, baleful light, and she muttered confusedly as she approached that unsuspected opening in the floor of the ruined tower, which she had so accidentally found; discovered by so strange and fatal a chance.

She now lit the candle at the end of the rope, and getting down again painfully on her knees by the side of that black, rayless space, she lowered it cautiously into that mysterious interior. It went out twice immediately, but the third time remained alight, and by the feeble, flaring flame she then saw that she was looking down into a small, circular room or dungeon, about six feet in diameter, and, as well as she could calculate by the length of rope she let out, about ten or twelve feet in depth. The walls seemed of the same massive construction as those around her, and quite perfect, not a chink or crevice apparently to let in a ray of light or a breath of air. In any case, she felt sure that the enclosure was below the surface of the ground. It was evidently one of those fatal, horrible dungeons of the olden times, so often associated with the ancient, feudal castles, where the hapless prisoner was left to die slowly of gradual suffocation and starvation.

Its existence, doubtless, had not been suspected for perhaps centuries; the trick of the rings had been long lost in oblivion, their very presence unknown in more recent times, owing to the thick deposit of soil and damp that had gathered above them.

It was left for her (Meg) to make the strange discovery, she thought, with an odd thrill of terror and exultation combined, as she shrank back again and again from the mouth of that dark pit, whence the foul, fetid, poisonous atmosphere gushed forth; air that had been so long imprisoned that even the candle would not burn it at first. She noticed also that some six or eight steep, jagged, stone steps led ladder-like down into the air-tight vault beneath. Thus the wretched victim doubtless descended to their awful doom, their living grave, in the distant days when the stately castle, of which this turret was but a trifling fragment, was a power in the land, and its lord one of the fierce and mighty barons of the feudal period.

The floor of the dungeon was stone, similar to that of the tower, only less slimy and damp, being so hermetically sealed; a fall from where she stood down on that hard stone might almost kill, she thought. Many times as she grew more calm and collected, old Meg Morrison let down the lighted candle into that unsuspected crypt, lurking beneath the ruined keep; and then she felt that the next thing to be done was to conceal as thoroughly as possible, the strange discovery she had made. She had a desperate purpose, a terrible end in view, and to accomplish that end, to fulfil the deadly vow she had vowed, she must be cautious and circumspect.

None must dream of the existence of this hidden tomb. Ah, yes—tomb was the best word; and so she determined to try to close that horrible gliding door again. She had learnt the trick of the rings, and could easily work them when opportunity offered, when the hour of her revenge had come. Now she sought the manner of closing, and by instinct, more than calculation or ability to argue, she lit on the correct method. As she had pressed and pushed the outer rings towards each other, so now, she pulled them with all her strength apart and from the centre, always keeping the direct line, and had the satisfaction, after a moment or two of intense straining, of again hearing the horrible grating sound, as slowly, slowly the hideous door of that death-trap slid back into its place. And then to hide all outward appearance of an opening, at least those betraying rings, now so apparent.

"Yes, of course, the best way was to keep to her original purpose in selecting this niche; it was just the place for the wounded hare, and the innocent creature's bed could be made above that vault. She would at once get what was necessary. And before evening a large pile of heaped-up fern, and bracken, and brushwood lay above that hideous vault; and the stricken, frightened little animal was transferred to its new quarters which were much better suited to the wild woodland thing than the hearth in the living-room; and during the next month Mabel Arden was constantly in and out of that ruined turret, petting and tending the creature, as her lovely tenderness and sympathy had pitied and tended a little while before the wretched old woman, who was now plotting her murder. Yes, murder—particularly barbaric, awful murder—where the torture of the victim might be slow and terrible, and where, in any case, the agony to the survivors must be the prolonged agony of dread uncertainty, the anguished distraction of mysterious disappearance; never to know what had become of their loved and cherished darling.

And this was what her fearful, fiendish vengeance especially desired to inflict on Mabel's kindred, on those who loved the girl so faithfully and well; to inflict on them suffering similar to what her own had been, through all those weary dreadful years of waiting for news of her child.

And now the means to accomplish this terrible vengeance were put into her hands by a strange chance; put into her hands by the miserable little accident of her finding and succouring that wounded hare.

Who will say that anything is trivial or of small import when such a very trifling incident as this quoted led to such crushing and terrible results?

About the beginning of October the creature had got better, though it never could do much good, and escaped back to the woods, or more probably was allowed to escape, as Meg began to see she could do nothing while the animal was known to be there, and while Mabel was known to go in and out of the ruin so frequently to see it. No, she must bide her time. When the creature was gone and forgotten, and the ruin was left once more to its normal solitude, then would be her time.

How easy to have the girl into the tower in the dusk on some pretence; and acting on this determination she let the month of October go by to its very last day, and then, as she thought, a particularly good opportunity for carrying out her fell purpose presented itself.

Mabel Arden was going to the Grange to spend the evening—that was nothing, it was of frequent occurrence; but what was unusual was, that she was going to stay the night, as she told Meg, and would not be passing again that way. Then the old woman made up her mind.

Not passing again to-night. Then nothing could be suspected.

So she suddenly asked the girl in a half-whisper as if it was something she was very eager about, and did not wish to be generally known—would she like to see something she had away back there in the tower? Something much stranger than the hare.

Mabel immediately grew excited and interested. Aware of the old woman's sympathy with and pity for the hunted, suffering creatures she knew not what this might be.

But Meg Morrison refused to tell her even what she had rescued from the sportsman's toils. She would show it to her, she said, and that would be better than telling; but not now, not in the daylight. Besides, Miss Arden was going to dinner at the Grange, and might be late if she delayed; but if she promised not to mention the circumstances to *anyone*, as she did not want folks from the great house to be fussing and bothering asking to see the creature, and ran in to-night about ten or eleven o'clock—the same time she would be going home another night—why then she, Meg, would stay up on purpose so as to let her see the poor little sick prisoner.

Of course, if she wished to wait till to-morrow, she might, but there was the chance that the creature might escape, and it was a curiosity,—and poor Mabel walked unsuspectingly into the deadly trap laid for her.

She promised faithfully to tell nobody, especially as there were children staying at the Grange,—boys, who would be sure to torment the poor wounded thing whatever it was—and she would be sure to come; it would be nothing strange for her to run off, even if she were missed for the few minutes that she would be absent, which was not likely; she often did so to see her mother, and she could easily slip away unnoticed.

So it was arranged, and the unfortunate girl, who was doomed to expiate so horribly, so unconsciously her father's sins, who had just signed her own death warrant by her ready unsuspecting acquiescence with the old woman's demand, ran off happy, radiant, tremulous, to meet her lover for the first time after their four months' parting.

And the terrible old woman whose nerve did not fail her, whose resolve did not falter at the near approach of the fulfilment of a vengeance more horrible, more utter, more devilish, than any she could have imagined—made her preparations for Mabel Arden's last visit, carefully, methodically—the one excuse to be offered for the atrocity of the crime she thus deliberately planned, being, that too much wrong and sorrow had made her mad.

CHAPTER XXIV
FAITHFUL EVEN IN DEATH

"Yet in these ears till hearing dies,
One set, slow bell will seem to toll
The passing of the sweetest soul
That ever looked with human eyes."[93]

I By and by everything was ready.

She had determined to bring the light only a certain distance into the ruin and then to leave it down, just as they reached the opening to the tower, so as, by-the-way, not to scare the little beast too suddenly with the light up beside it; of course, she felt sure the girl in her haste and eagerness would run in, knowing the niche at once to make for; the gloom was great, she would be just at her back—and——

* * * * * *

About a quarter past ten, as she watched and waited, a soft tapping came at her door. She opened it at once, and Mabel stepped quickly across the threshold, just as she had seen her a few hours before, save that her bright hair streamed on her shoulders, a cluster of white flowers were in the bosom of her frock, which she had not noticed previously, and a soft, small shawl was wrapped around her. As the girl walked towards the fire, with her back to her, Meg managed to slip the bolt on the door unperceived. Then, after a moment or two's pause, she took up the light to lead the way into the ruin.

* * * * * *

[93] Lines from *In Memoriam* by Alfred, Lord Tennyson.

At this point the rambling, incoherent, wildly discursive statement taken down by Sergeant Adams from the lips of the dying woman, and from which the preceding narrative has been briefly sketched, with a view to making the facts of the story and the motives that actuated the central figure as clear and cohesive as possible to the reader, comes to an abrupt conclusion.

The advance-guard of the great All-Conquering King had arrived and cut short that straggling utterance.

The confession remains incomplete—wanting its most vital clause, as the sergeant insists; while Dr. Truscott inclines to the belief that the whole thing is a hallucination—the wild, unfounded rhapsody of a morbid, diseased brain on the approach of death.

For many hours this lovely spring morning Sergeant Adams has been sitting by that bed in the turret chamber, jotting down the strange, halting sentences of the dying woman; and now, when he finishes reading what he has written, which has ended, to him, in so eminently unsatisfactory a manner, he sinks back in his chair, feeling fagged and weary. The doctor yawns heavily; he, too, is tired, having been at the turret since six o'clock and it is now just two.

Fred Derrick, who is usually so energetic, so inclined for immediate action when anything is to be proved or sifted, any mystery to be solved, or discovery made clear, is plunged in distracted horrible reverie.

For the first time in his life he shrinks, with a sick shrinking of the soul, from action. He feels inert, helpless—shocked and horrified beyond expression. What will action reveal, he thinks dully, but the awful proof, that that wild, tangled tale he has been listening to is true—terribly true—true to its final, uncompleted point of a deadly consummated vengeance?

And then he thinks of the poor old Squire, who has been so heavily tried of late; how will he bear more, so much more than all the rest put together? He thinks of his wife and the uncle who hails from distant lands; and then with a rush from his heart to his lips, he murmurs the words half unconsciously as the thought is borne into his brain—"Thank God the unfortunate mother is gone! Thank God poor Aunt Katharine is at rest and cannot hear this horror!"

For not for one moment does Fred Derrick doubt the absolute truth of that pathetic story of a grievous wrong and sin that we have just read, knowing as he does so thoroughly what manner of man was Philip Marmaduke Arden.

And then Hugh Denver, who has been sitting through the reading of the statement in a strange absorbed state, apparently hearing nothing of the earlier part of the story, his eyes fixed and introspective, only appearing to wake, as it were, from some kind of mesmeric sleep when Mabel's name was mentioned, towards the close of the confession, now starts suddenly erect and ghastly, with a strange tense look in his face, and still that distant, magnetic look in his haggard eyes.

"She is there!" he cries, pointing to the lath and plaster wall that divides the dwelling place from the rest of the ruin. "I see her! She is lying on her face—dead—dead. I see her—down in that black pit; her hair streams across her shoulders. We should have found her many months since; she came to me in that vision to tell me where to find her, and I, like a fool, could not read the meaning of the message. She is there—dead—dead! through all these terrible months, and I—I am accursed. I thought her *false*. We slandered her, we branded her with degradation, almost infamy; and she was white and pure as God's angels; she *was* one of God's angels—one of his martyred saints!"

And with these mad, agonised words he strides across the room to the door communicating with the ruin, dashes it open, and finds himself in a long, dismal, somewhat winding passage leading to the turret. He has never been in the place before, yet he appears familiar with his surroundings. Straight on he walks, looking neither to right nor left; straight on as the walls curve, and fall away and curve again.

The others, roused and impressed much by his strange manner and sudden action, follow quickly; shrinking dread and hesitancy forgotten by Derrick, fatigue by the other two.

Into that gloomy ruined turret Hugh turns with intent directness of step that never wavers.

For a moment or two, as he stands within its mouldering interior for the first time, he pauses with a shuddering thrill.

It is the place of his vision.

He saw the exact presentment of the spot in which he now stands in that strange eerie picture limned on the night sky on New Year's Eve.

It is the same in all respects, save that now they are slanting, narrow streaks of glad May sunshine that seek to illuminate its dusky solitude, striving to penetrate the shadowy grim enclosure by one or two fissures in the crumbling walls; yet instead of dispelling the gloom and dreariness that lurk within, those faint vibrating rods of sunshine, seem rather to enhance the aspect of decay, and age, and death, that ever broods within this lonely tower.

In that mysterious vision it was moonlight he saw trying to soften the solemn darkness of night, trying to soften and beautify the harsh, unlovely marks of age and corruption. Yes, moonlight, though there was no moon in that pallid December sky.

But he saw the scene represented exactly as it was on that fearful All Souls' Night, and then the moon had shone unsteadily, wild stormy clouds constantly flitting across her chill face, causing alternate snatches of darkness and white ghostly light.

Yes, in all things the same interior that he saw revealed to him by that odd, mystic glow, even to that great pile of what looked like broken fern and brushwood—and then he suddenly recollects all that he has been listening to. *That* is the fatal spot! Under that innocent growth of the fields lies the terrible solution of that night's awful mysterious disappearance.

Was it not by the pile of bracken he saw that phantasmal figure of the dead girl arrest her gliding steps? Then the light faded and grew again, and she stood beside an unfathomable darkness, which drew her down and absorbed her out of his sight.

With a strangled bitter cry of despairing sorrow and remorse he flings himself upon that piled heap of brushwood. In a moment it is gone—scattered, and there lie the three rings—like coiled, deadly serpents—unconcealed.

He makes a frantic effort to pull and push them, to remember the trick of their use. But the overtaxed heart and brain give out, nature asserts herself, and with a low moan Hugh Denver falls forward across that metal door, that has been the invincible barrier between himself and his love, unconscious; a blessed and timely insensibility, that may preserve the endangered reason.

They lift him up gently, and carry him back to the dwelling-place, and lay him down as far as possible from the bed where the old woman is now stretched in her last sleep.

Dr. Truscott does all that is necessary, but he will not be likely to come to himself for some little time, and so they return to their dread task in the turret.

Derrick's nerve is completely upset, but Sergeant Adams and the doctor are cool and collected, though horribly impressed by the whole terrible tragedy, which even the latter is beginning to feel did indeed take place; Hugh Denver's singular, startling words having almost done more to convince him than did the confession.

They soon manage the rings, the metal plate glides back, as described by old Meg, and a black, yawning space meets their gaze. They retreat from the noisome, foul, mephitic air that rushes out. It is pure, compared to what greeted the terrible old woman who first opened that long-closed door, but still it is noxious. They soon find they can do nothing without light, as the recess where they kneel is dusky, even at mid-day, and no ray of daylight penetrates down into that unseen dungeon.

So, loth from some unconfessed feeling, some thrill of superstitious awe, to descend those steep, jagged steps even with a light, until they get the bearings of the place a little, they follow the old woman's example and swing a candle down a short way into the black chasm. They soon discern the size and nature of the place. They can see the circular shape, the massive, unbroken walls, and then they look down directly beneath them, just at the stairs' foot, and a terrible shudder convulses the three men, while a simultaneous exclamation of horror and conviction bursts from their lips.

Yes, it is even so; they have found what they came to seek. That deadly vengeance was indeed carried out to its bitterest end.

Below the swaying, flickering light, just at the foot of those jagged stone steps, they descry a woman's form lying on her face—a woman's figure, clad in some gauzy, blue-grey stuff, that catches the light even there, and with bright hair streaming on her shoulders.

The lost is at last found.

Mabel Arden, the idol of this house, met a cruel and terrible death, was barbarously murdered almost within its walls—and none had dreamed it.

She had gone straight from listening to that tale of horror, that had blanched her fresh young cheek, to meet a similar fate.

She had doubtless, as Dr. Truscott and another physician declare, who view the poor remains later on—been only stunned by that frightful fall, contrary to the expectation of her who had so cruelly compassed her death, and who had, presumably, noiselessly stolen at her back as the unsuspecting, eager, tender-hearted girl advanced quickly, without hesitation, to where she thought some hurt creature of the woods was crouching, and with one deadly, well-aimed push (perhaps blow, the old woman was strongly made) had sent her into that unseen tomb. Yes, doubtless only stunned, and had lain for hours unconscious.

Then coming to herself in that terrible place, in that poisonous, loathsome air, in that horrible thick darkness, she had possibly struggled up those steps and beat upon that iron door that shut her down—down for ever—and shrieked aloud in her anguished despair. And then, that last terrible cry burst from that rent throat—that cry that rushed through the fissures in the mouldering walls of the lonely tower—pierced the intervening space, and awakened those startled sleepers in the east wing of the Grange—the last cry on earth of those lips that were never again to be kissed, even in death.

And then, probably, merciful faintness, or stupefaction, engendered by the horror and the foul air, stole over her, and she had either crawled down those cruel steps or again fallen, as seemed more likely from the position of the body; and it was to be hoped that the end came soon, and that she did not awake to consciousness again in that ghastly living grave.

* * * * * *

And so the mystery of Mabel's disappearance on All Souls' Night—though it had long since ceased to be a mystery in the minds of her friends who are now racked with wild, passionate remorse at the memory of their foul suspicions—is cleared up, on the very day that her mother, believing in her child's truth and purity to the last, is laid in her lonely grave. Mercifully she was spared that fearful knowledge. For no imaginary fate, however dark and terrible, could be one half as horrible as that which overtook her idolised girl, in the flush of her youth and beauty and the glad dawn of her new-found happiness, in the safe shelter of her uncle's home, and with but that cruel, awful, iron door separating her from life and its joys; shutting her in with death in its most ghastly, revolting shape; shutting her in to meet that grim appalling phantom, in that awful, thick darkness, in that hideous solitude.

Imagination shrinks from picturing the terrible despair of that young heart, as it awoke to consciousness in its living tomb.

When the girl realised that she, Mabel Arden, was destined to meet a fate equally horrible, equally unnatural with that she had fled, with white cheeks and creeping frame, from hearing described that very night, that she was as completely *Walled up alive*, as was ever nun in history or fable—no wonder then that that fearful cry—a cry desperate in its unutterable despair—burst from that agonised throat.

Words are inadequate, even partially to express Hugh Denver's anguish of self-reproach, his passionate, terrible, undying remorse, at having, for a moment, doubted his darling's truth and purity, at having dared to suspect her of treachery and faithlessness.

And his quivering tortured heart is even more bitterly stung and lacerated,—stung at his own failure in a perfect trust, by the pathetic fact, that within what had been the grasp of those fleshless fingers, and just beneath the poor face, was found a small heap of what at first appeared like dust, but on closer examination was proved to be the dried skeleton of flowers. They were that very cluster of fatal asphodels, that the dying girl must have drawn from her breast in her final moments of consciousness, pressing them to her poor chill lips as her last remaining link with love and life.

Huh had given them to her but so short a time ago; they spoke to her of him—she seemed nearer to him even in that awful loneliness thus clasping and touching those frail, lovely, living things, his last gift.

They would die together, she and his flowers, and so—"faithful even in death," Mabel's true and lovely spirit winged its way from darkness into light eternal.

*   *   *   *   *   *

And by and by, by the very force of that strong, pure, faithful love, which she gave not for a time or times but for everlasting, and which through the ages as they roll will grow more lovely and more perfect, (as will all true real love begun here on earth, for the Great Artificer never created that marvellous fountain of inexhaustible, devoted, exalted love, of which the human heart is capable in rare instances, to dry up and become extinct in the grave)—by that mystic, wondrous influence, which is stronger than Heaven or Hell, her released, unfettered spirit impressed itself on the mortal eye of him she loved, and there was revealed to him, by the magnetic power that mind exercises on mind, when love is the tie that binds them, a shadow, a reflex, of the horror that had engulfed her.

* * * * * *

Thus pure, good, innocent Mabel Arden suffered for her father's sin—paid the penalty of his evil acts—"the just for the unjust."

The guilty, in numberless instances, go unpunished to their graves, yet the blameless sufferers by their evil deeds reap not the guerdon of pity, love, sympathy, but a harvest of wrath that should have been the sinner's portion, for we are told in the words of eternal truth that "The sins of the fathers are visited upon the children.".

THE END

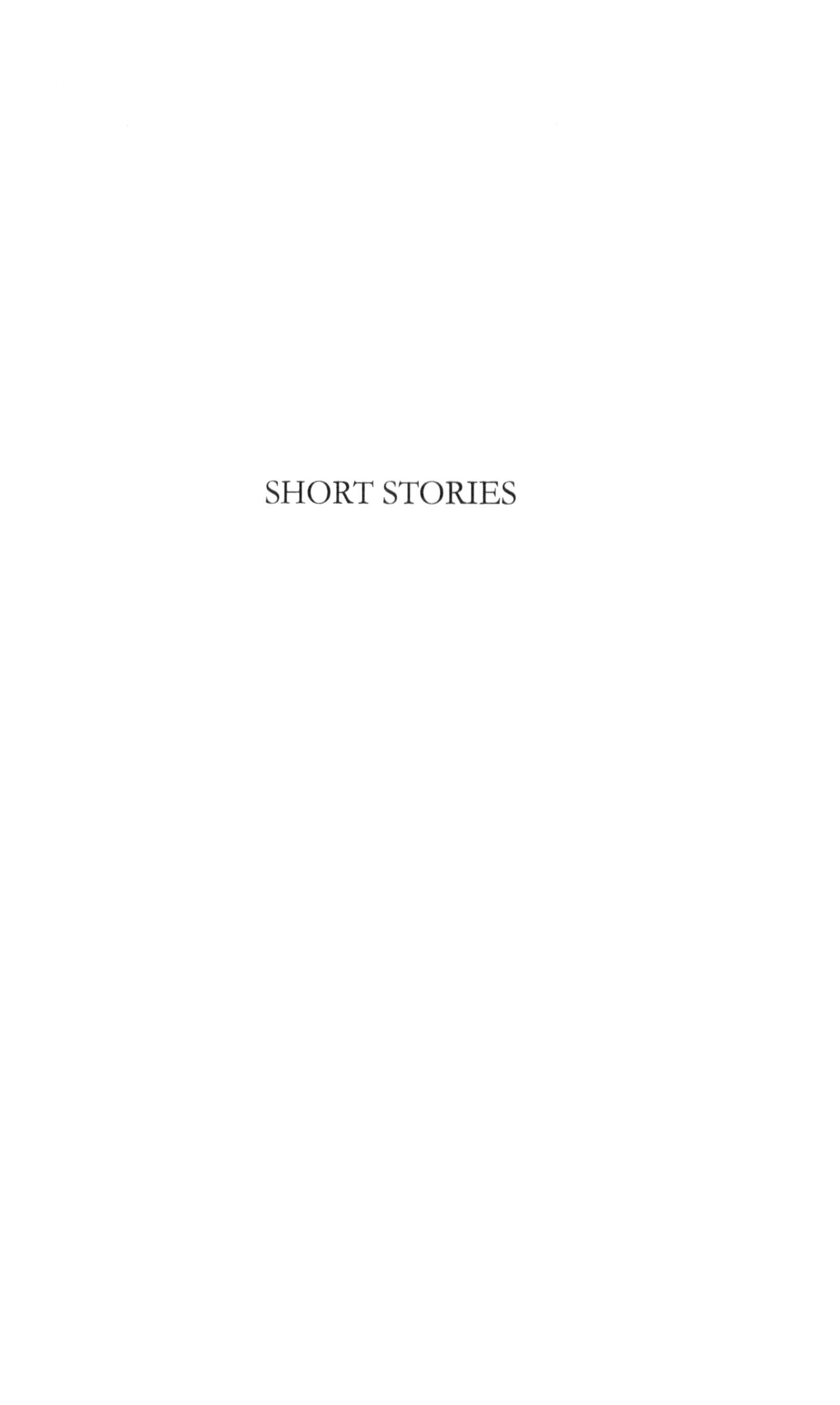

SHORT STORIES

THE COURAGE OF KATHIE

The Sunday Sun (Australia), 28 April 1907.

"WHY, it's Wilmot!" murmured Kathie Ormsby, with a little gasp of astonishment, as she quickly drew in her head and dropped back in her seat in the railway carriage, a rosy flush lighting up the pretty fair face, and making it look radiant.

"I've no right to call him 'Wilmot,' " she added the next moment, in swift self-rebuke, "though I wish I had."

Yes; it was Wilmot Hamilton, the brilliant young barrister, who, a year or so previously, had entered the Russian Diplomatic Service, in which he was already winning distinction.

Kathie's home, during her father's life, had been in London. Dr. Ormsby knew Hamilton fairly well, and valued and appreciated his talents. He always predicted that the young man would go far if he once got a really good start, and he seemed to be fulfilling the doctor's prophecy.

Kathie had not seen Wilmot for more than a year, not since he had gone abroad, and she felt quite faint with a fearful joy. She had always admired him—in fact, though her timid heart would hardly allow her to admit it to herself, she had fallen deeply in love with him.

But she was much too nervous and self-distrustful to try, in any way, to attract or charm the man. She was sweet, and pretty, and lovable, but she was so overpoweringly shy that the very embarrassment of her manner communicated itself to him.

"If I were only like other girls, I think I could have made him like me, but I am such a silly, nervous coward," she would bemoan, and her thoughts rushed back again now to a certain episode as the express train shrieked itself out of the Cardiff station, bound for Bridgend as its next stopping place. It was on one of the last occasions of their meeting, shortly before Dr. Ormsby developed the illness that ran its course in a few days and left her fatherless.

* * * * * *

She had found herself alone in the drawing-room with Wilmot Hamilton for a few moments, who had called to see Dr. Ormsby in the early forenoon.

Kathie had been fitting the flower vases with fresh blooms when he came in, and she continued her occupation, but her shy nervousness was so great when her mother left the room—to see whether her husband had returned from his morning visit to the hospital—that unconsciously she grasped the delicate glass she held so tightly that it shivered in her clasp, and one of her fingers was badly cut.

Wilmot came at once to the rescue, and bound up the wound with his handkerchief with an air of concern, and the girl, feeling almost faint, not from the pain, but from sheer delight at his apparent interest and at his touch, lay back in the easy-chair for a moment or two with closed eyes, and on opening them suddenly she surprised a look in the dark face bent above her—so admiring, so tender (at least, so she thought) that it took her breath away.

The expression in those brilliant dark eyes was actually a caress, she felt somehow almost as if she had been kissed. The glance was so lingering, so penetrating, yet so soft, and the low-murmured "poor little woman" had such a tender cadence-then her mother came back, and the moment of romance vanished.

And when next she met Wilmot she knew that from her sheer nervous embarrassment, her manner was so cold and stiff and distant (though her heart felt just the reverse), that she had disgusted and disenchanted—doubtless offended—him, and perversely killed any little warmer interest that might have been growing.

Since her father's death Kathie and her mother had been living quietly at Gloucester with the girl's grandparents, and now she was on her way to join her grandparents at Llandrindod Wells.

She had no idea that Wilmot Hamilton was in England, and so she was intensely surprised to see him on the platform at Cardiff. He was with three other gentlemen, one a distinguished-looking elderly gentleman of almost gigantic proportions, evidently a foreigner and a person of distinction.

Kathie remembered that she had lately read of the arrival in London on a brief visit to Royalty of one of the Russian Grand Dukes—a man whose name had been prominently and unenviably before the public, connected with the Russian Revolutionary movement of 1905, and especially the horrors of "Red Sunday."

She wondered could this be he—the Russian aristocrat—and if Wilmot Hamilton accompanied him as one of his suite. They had been obsequiously shown to a first-class reserved compartment of the same carriage as that in which Kathie Ormsby travelled. Hers was for "Ladies only" (she had it to herself), next was a "Smokers"—empty, as she imagined—and then the reserved compartment.

The girl peered out cautiously when the train stopped at Bridgend, longing inexpressibly to get another fleeting glimpse of Wilmot, yet shrinking from observation, she was so shy. She saw two porters in the act of putting a foot-warmer into the great man's compartment; she supposed that it had been forgotten at Cardiff, and the day was decidedly chilly.

Then she sat down again, and in another moment was prone on hands and knees on the floor of the compartment—her little luncheon-basket had toppled out of the netting, and its modest contents were scattered broadcast.

As she thus groped and grubbed for the fragments, rather ruefully reflecting that there would not be much left to sustain her until she arrived at her destination, she heard foreign voices just beneath her window, talking excitedly, yet softly.

They spoke in very muffled accents, and in a language that Kathie did not understand, but somehow the tones sounded fierce and threatening; then an English voice speaking German interposed. Kathie knew the latter tongue well, having been educated at Dusseldorf, and the first words gained her horrified attention.

* * * * * *

Then there was more of the rapid, unknown speech (Polish, thought the girl), with an occasional German word. Then another thoroughly British voice broke in, speaking truculently in his native vernacular.

"Look here, Jackson, I don't know what the blazes them deranged furriners are jabbering about; why don't them Nihilists do their own dirty work? That's what I say—but we need have no fear, the bloomin' plot's panned out all right so far. Me an' Bill there just shoved it in. Oh, it's a rare joke, ain't it?"—with the sound of a smothered evil laugh in the voice—"for a foot-warmer to do the trick? Who'd ever suspect a foot-warmer?"

"Whist, ye fool, do ye want to be heard?" from the other English voice.[94]

"What about Bill, as ye call him? Is he square? Is he one of us?"

"He jest knows nuthin', big gaby.[95] He thought it a bit odd I wanted help to put in the blamed thing. Lord, it was mortal heavy, an' I was feered o' my life. If put down wid a crash it might go

94 Whist: be quiet.

95 Gaby: fool.

off sooner nor we wanted, so I jest sez to him, sez I, that I wished to slip in the thing smooth and easylike, out of respec' to the gentlemen, more special the grand old toff, an' he swallered the gammon fine.[96] It wuz a gran' dodge, the extra porter sent on from Cardiff for fear there'd be a rush to see the great Johnnie.[97] It's all in the uniform, you see; no questions asked. And now, the sooner we all sprint the better."

For a few minutes Kathie was transfixed with horror—incapable of thought. But soon her brain was alert and working with extraordinary vigour and clearness.

How to circumvent these murderous wretches. How to avert the impending catastrophe. How to save Wilmot!

Just as the train was beginning to glide into motion again she heard the eager whisper:

"But when's the fuse timed for?"

"This side o' Neath, unless she makes a fast run; at any rate before Swansea."

Kathie raised herself, and stood for a moment or two wildly gazing out with unseeing eyes; she was a transformed creature—brave—intense—determined—strong to do—to dare, every nerve strung to tension point, her pulses hammering with fierce resolve to defy those fiendish assassins—to thwart their plans—to save the man she loved.

Action must be swift and decisive. There was no time to lose; the train was gathering speed. She had turned for a moment at first to the communicator, looking at it irresolutely. Should she alarm the guard and try to stop the train? The next instant she

96 Gammon: nonsense.

97 Johnnie: aristocrat.

rejected the idea. If the train came to a sudden stop the jar might only precipitate the hideous catastrophe.

* * * * * *

The next instant she had slipped off her little, high-heeled shoes, which might have impeded her, and leaning over opened the carriage door, holding tightly to the window-strap, as she did so.

On to the narrow, treacherous, slippery footboard stepped this girl, clinging desperately to the swinging door, trying not to look down. If she did she was undone—the sense of giddiness was so overwhelming. How grimly and steadfastly those weak-looking little white hands clung, each following the other, as she glided on step by step in her stockinged feet.

What a storm had suddenly arisen, thought poor Kathie, as her hat was almost wrenched from her head, in spite of its securing pins, and the wind seemed to whistle ferociously about her ears. The day in reality was as calm as ever; it was the speed of the train that caused the wind.

She thought nothing of this. Her mind was concentrated on the one great end—to save—to save Wilmot! He was in danger—his life in jeopardy, and she must save him, even at the risk of her own.

She clutched wildly at the handle of the next compartment, and cautiously moved along the footboard. Then she paused for breath before resuming her hazardous journey. As she started again the rush of air almost took her off her feet, but she managed to cling on, and in another moment had grasped with one hand the window of the first-class compartment, which was partly open.

There was a hasty, astonished exclamation from within, and just as the other hand joined its fellow a handsome, hatless head was thrust out, and almost came into violent contact with Kathie's wild, disheveled one. It was Wilmot Hamilton himself.

With instant presence of mind he grasped those strained, clinging fingers in his strong reassuring clasp, and in a trice had the girl in safety.

"Why, it's Kathie Ormsby!" he exclaimed in astonished accents. And even in that moment of hideous danger Kathie felt a sting of delirious joy at Wilmot's remembrance and use of her Christian name.

His immediate thought, as also that of the other men, who had all risen to their feet in startled surprise, was—that she had met some terrible fright, or insult, and had thus risked her life to find refuge in another carriage.

* * * * * *

But before a word could be spoken save his first confused exclamations of astonishment, this instant and natural impression was speedily routed from these four men's minds and they one and all—even Wilmot—were inclined to think that it was with a madwoman they had to deal.

Poor, pretty, heroic Kathie! Her wild, distracted aspect, with bright hair floating on the breeze, her hat at a rakish angle on the back of her head—the great grey eyes burning with feverish lustre—the pallid cheeks, compressed lips, shoeless feet, all contributed to give colour to this delusion.

For the girl's first act, after panting for an instant in an effort to speak that failed, was to swoop down on the apparently harmless foot-warmer.

She made a huge vain effort to lift it, the men looking on in consternation.

"Oh, I can't!" she moaned in despair. "Throw it out—at once!—at once!" she then gasped in quick vehemence. "Do you hear?" in imperative yet sobbing notes of appeal, looking straight at Hamilton.

"Dear Miss Ormsby, what is it?" cried Wilmot in quick response.

"Pray compose yourself. You have gone through a terribly trying ordeal, but you are quite safe now. We will let nothing harm you, so——"

"It must go out, at once—at once, I say!" she almost screamed in agony of aghast desperation. "Oh, God! they won't do what I ask, and I can't lift it!" she wailed.

They tried to soothe and temporize as with an unreasoning creature.

"You seem to know the lady," said an elderly man to Hamilton, who seemed to be the Grand Duke's chief friend and travelling companion, speaking in a low voice and in excellent English, as is the way of cultivated Russians. "What is the nature of her insanity, and how is she permitted to travel alone—or has she escaped from her attendant?"

"The girl is no more insane than we are—at least she wasn't," replied Wilmot. "Some fright or shock she has had must have unhinged her mind temporarily." Then, as she again stooped to the thing, trying to drag it along the floor of the carriage, he said softly, "Kathie, dear, won't you tell us all about it? We're all your friends here. What's alarmed you? Leave that beastly old thing alone—don't tire and hurt yourself with it, it's all right."

Then, her breath a trifle calmer, and her mind clearer, she raised herself, and swept a despairing glance round at the four men.

"I've come to save you," she cried in frenzied appeal. "I prayed to be in time, and I am! If you'd only throw it out—now—this minute! Oh, I am not mad!"

Perhaps she saw something in their looks as they gazed at her in a pitying, helpless silence.

"I heard the wicked men's plot, and I thought if I got here before it burst all would be well, and you won't even help me. Oh, for the love of Heaven," suddenly laying her trembling hand on Wilmot's arm, "hurl it out before it is too late! They want to kill him!" pointing a shaking finger at the large and distinguished-looking foreigner, who, she felt instinctively, was the objective of this dastardly outrage.

"It's the Nihilists! I heard it all higher up the line."

"Poor, pretty little soul! Best humour her, and fling the thing out," murmured the great man. "We can explain to the railway people, Hamilton. Do what she asks, toss it out!"

"Oh, thank God! Thank God!" sobbed Kathie, whose hand still clutched Wilmot's arm, while the others spoke, and he looking into her eyes at this close range saw therein sanity and frantic distress.

"There's something in her story, your Highness, I feel convinced," he exclaimed, excitedly.

* * * * * *

Then his strong, sinewy hands seized on that sinister foot-warmer.

"By Jove, the thing's a ton weight. Lend a hand, Rouloff," addressing a young man, the fourth member of the party, and apparently the Grand Duke's secretary, while Kathie implored them to be careful not to shake or jolt it till the moment they were ready to hurl it out.

Having got the door again open, the two young men stood poising the heavy projectile. The line here was running close to a hedge; a green field lay beyond. Then there was a simultaneous, well-balanced swing of the two pairs of muscular arms, and the thing was gone, shot out like a stone from a catapult, right over the hedge.

The train was going at great speed with all the rush and clatter of an express, but the next moment a terrible roar filled their ears, drowning all other sounds; the train seemed to sway, as if the earth were shaken or rent—the other passengers afterwards declared that they had been terror-struck, believing that an earthquake had taken place—half the guard's van was blown away, though fortunately the man himself escaped injury.

And Kathie, her noble work done, fell in a faint into the arms of the man whom she had risked her life to save, as he staggered back in horror when that awful concussion rent the air.

He carried her to the waiting-room at Neath, where she soon revived. They were alone, these two, the Grand Duke and the rest of his suite having gone on to Swansea—their destination.

And when Kathie opened her eyes, and looked up from that shabby horsehair lounge on which she lay, in that bleak, bare waiting-room, into the dark, earnest face bent above her—a face not alone filled with the most vivid concern, the profoundest gratitude, but in which the love-light dwelt so unmistakably—she felt that she had awakened in Paradise! The next instant Wilmot's lips were pressed to hers in a kiss so long, so fervent, that it took her breath away. His arms went round her in a strong, tense clasp.

"Kathie, my darling, my own, you have saved my life, and that life is yours for ever! How did you do it, and why did you do it? Your heroism was grand beyond words. You have saved many lives, and important lives, from a ghastly death—but, oh, if I could only think you did it specially for me? I loved you, dear, more than a year ago, and thought you guessed it; but you repelled me, Kathie, and it seemed, to me, purposely, so——"

"Oh, Wilmot!" she sobbed, hiding her burning face in his breast, "it was only my horrid, awkward shyness. I've loved you, dear, all the time, and I felt to-day that I must either die—or—save you!"

And again she was gathered closely in his arms, and their lips met as if never more to part.

AN AUDACIOUS WAGER

Irish Weekly Independent, 3 February 1912.

The newspaper from which this story was taken suffered damage. A few words in the text are illegible, and they are indicated here as [. . .]

CHAPTER I

"YELLOW hair and brown eyes? Rather a stunning contrast. What was the other girl like, Treherne—tall or short?"

"Can't say positively; make it a rule never to look twice at an ugly woman. Tall, I fancy, but the little one is ripping, perfectly irresistible."

"And she seemed struck, you say?" questioned the older man, with a queer gleam in his eyes.

"Struck? I should think so." And the conceited young captain of the Lancers smiled consciously and twirled his moustache with an offensively blatant air of triumphant conquest.

But Major O'Reardon only laughed while still the odd expression lingered in his eyes. He was very fond of young Treherne. The boy's vanity was so glaringly audacious that it was actually ludicrous, and but provoked a smile; and if he made a somewhat greater fool of himself now than [. . .], perhaps, it would be for his good by-and-by, and might help to cure him of his pet foible.

"Poor little thing," continued the young man. "I feel convinced that she is languishing for an English lover, and knew at a glance that I was not a Paddylander, whom doubtless she finds a set of duffers. No offence to you, old man, you have been so much away from your native land that I look upon you as almost as much of an alien as myself, and they are [. . .] if they don't appreciate a bit of loveliness like that. Well, I'll gratify the little witch and spoon to her heart's content."

Major O'Reardon laughed again, a slightly angry contemptuous laugh this time, while his face bore a somewhat flushed and scornful aspect.

"How will you contrive an introduction? I infer you are not as yet even acquainted with the lady's name?"

"Oh, leave that to me," smiled Treherne with an air of sublime self-confidence. "I'll lay you an even bet that within a week I'll be on a footing of tolerable familiarity with little golden locks, and by the time you return from the North we shall be on terms of loving intimacy."

And then, as they paused outside his brother-in-law's house, before O'Reardon could reply, he continued, "Well, old chap, good-bye; I'll go in and win, and you'll be best man, won't you? If that Irish colleen is a lady, as I feel convinced, ten to one, but I'll throw her the handkerchief. Bet you a pony she won't refuse."

"Done!" cried O'Reardon, with sudden animation, verging almost on excitement. "By the way, Dolly, can't you remember what the other girl was like—why do you call her ugly? dark or fair?"

"Scarlet hair!" tersely responded the lady-killer. "A perfect Gorgon, Medusa's head—anything you like to express what's hideous. Ta-da, dear boy." And Captain Adolphus Treherne vanished within his relative's open hall-door, leaving the Major to wend his way to the railway station en route for Dublin, and Richmond Barracks, where he was then quartered.

A few days later Captain Treherne made acquaintance unconventionally with the young lady whose beauty had so fascinated him, and with regard to whom he had made so outrageous a bet with his friend Major O'Reardon.

And when he discovered that the inamorata was the only daughter of Mr. Ambrose Blennerhassett, of Grove Mount, Kingsdown, then indeed did the vain young fool congratulate himself upon his amazing good luck.

For his sister and her husband, though almost strangers in the place—the latter having been invalided home from South Africa a short time previously—had spoken of this Mr. Blennerhassett as a man of wealth and position.

Good old family—as the name alone declared—plenty of money, and beauty ad infinitum; what more could he, Adolphus Treherne, desire in a wife. He had no qualms on his own account, not one, but only thought it perfectly natural, and in accordance with the eternal fitness of things, that this Irish beauty should at once become captive to his English superiority.

She spoke little certainly—her friend ("The Gorgon," as Treherne had ruthlessly dubbed her) did most of the talking; but she smiled so enchantingly, and encouragingly, smiled with an arch roguish light in the brown eyes, whenever they were turned on him, for which he could not quite account, but which was, nevertheless, delightful and provocative.

The taller and elder girl, who had constituted herself spokeswoman, talked quite frankly and unconstrainedly.

"Before they knew who I was they were inclined to be quite chummy and unreserved," he reflected. "I suppose it is Irish unconventionality; I might have been but a cad and a bounder."

Poor Adolphus! Many a true word spoken in jest. Perhaps the latter offensive term would not have been so inappropriate at this stage of his career, in spite of the good old Cornish family to which he belonged.

* * * * * *

A fortnight went by—the Major being still detained in the wilds of Donegal, during which Treherne saw much of the Grove Mount people—but one thing chafed him abominably; try as he would, using all the finesse he flattered himself he possessed in no small degree, yet, he never could manage to be alone with Norah, something always seemed to happen to prevent it, just at the last moment, in the most provoking, tantalising way. This constant foiling of his pet purpose, he attributed to Miss Delaney's frantic jealousy of his implied preference for her friend.

"An ugly jealous woman is the very devil!" he soliloquised lugubriously.

Late one afternoon he found the Major waiting to see him. He had arrived from the North the night before, and had run down to Kingstown to see some friends. He had but a few minutes to stay, but wished to hear Treherne's latest report and learn how his little affaire-de-coeur was progressing.[98]

"Famously," drawled the other, "there's a dance on at the house to-night. I wish I could take you, old chap, but though I'm on such friendly terms with the young ladies"—with an atrociously unconscious laugh—"yet it would be rather a cool thing to do on so short an acquaintance. But come down to-morrow and I'll introduce you. I'll not afraid you'll cut me out, O'Reardon, your solemn old face would frighten my pretty Norah into fits."

"Norah?"—starting a little, and looking surprised. "Do you call her 'Norah' already?"

"Yes, why not?" Conveying the impression that he spoke to the lady as well as of her in this easily familiar tone. "But, I'll tell you what you can do for me if you're charitably disposed, old fellow—

[98] Affaire-de-coeur: love affair.

take the Gorgon off my hands, do a little platonic love-making and I'll bless you. A few civil words from a fellow, at least from me, send her crazy with delight. It will be no end of fun, don't you know, and will give me the opportunity I want with the little one, and Norah, I can plainly see, wishes the girl at Jericho as ardently as I do."

"Ah! I understand," replied the Major meditatively—"ugly friend jealous, I suppose?" with a queer smile.

"Jealous as the very deuce," laconically drawled Treherne.

"I say, O'Reardon," with greater animation, "even if I had no feeling in the matter it would be an act of actual Christian charity to marry that girl, and take her where her beauty will be appreciated. Would you believe it, I've been visiting there now for three weeks, and with the exception of a few old fossils, I have not met a man at that house. Not one single specimen of the genus homo who could even by the wildest stretch of imagination be construed into a suitor of the young lady's."

"Perhaps we, in Ireland, are not in such frantic haste to get rid of our girls, putting them so glaringly up to auction, as our more progressive friends across the Channel," cynically remarked the Major.

"Oh, that's all rot, you know," scoffed Treherne.

"Then I may take it for granted, I presume, that you have quite made up your mind to make the young lady in question your wife?" slowly enunciated O'Reardon, while his eyes sought the carpet, and a strange smile hovered round his lips, partly concealed by the heavy drooping moustache.

"Well—yes, I think so," yawned the egotist. "Marriage is rather a bore, rotten sort of game, you know; but the Mater, dear soul wishes, as she expresses it, to kiss and bless a grandchild before she dies, and I might as well gratify her when the way is made so smooth for me."

After a few minutes more desultory chat the Major took his departure, and it was not till he had gone that Treherne remembered that he'd forgotten to mention the name of the family he proposed to marry into. "So much the better," he reflected exultantly. "Poor old Lawrence will be all the more impressed. He seemed quite bowled over just now—envious, I make no doubt, of my wonderful luck. What a duffer he must feel himself. He makes no innings with girls, I'd swear, while I've won all along the line, and all off my own bat, without even an introduction. It has been a case of 'Veni-Vidi-Vici,' eh, Adolphus, my boy."[99]

CHAPTER II

WHEN Treherne reached Grove Mount that evening the rooms were full, and for the first time as he looked around, he experienced a slight qualm as to the certainty of his sole pretensions to the hand of the daughter of the house.

"Who were all those men, confound them!" he muttered, none of whom, with a few exceptions, had he seen before.

But his misgivings were soon dispelled. Almost imperceptibly the little crowd of black coats melted away from Miss Blennerhassett's immediate vicinity leaving Treherne in possession of the field.

"Vastly obliging of these 'Paddies' to vacate so quietly; doubtless they guessed how matters stand," he reflected complacently.

"How late you are, Captain Treherne," smiled Norah reprovingly.

"Nearly eleven! With the exception of two other laggards, you have the proud distinction of being last."

[99] Veni-Vidi-Vici: I came, I saw, I conquered.

"Last! Miss Blennerhassett that sounds ominous," drawled Dolly, airing his most silky looks and tone.

"Last horse in the race seldom stands to win, you know, and I would fain hope that I might have a chance of winning, by a length, that race that possibly some of us here are entered for. Be an innovator, Miss Blennerhassett, and introduce the delightful law that is to be established in some good time coming when, as we are told, 'The last shall be first,' etc."

"Don't be irreverent, Captain Treherne. Even if I would I could not do what you ask, and declare you primus (though in what enigmatical race I can't conceive), as you do not belong to either extreme. You forget—I told you that there are still two even greater delinquents than yourself who have not yet put in an appearance."

"Well, at any rate, don't be so unkind as to say that I am too late to claim a waltz or two from Miss Blennerhassett?"

"I am sorry, but I think, indeed I am almost sure, that my card is full. Yes, really," as she consulted her dainty tablets. "With the exception of one square after supper I have not one blank. If you like to put your name down for that you're welcome."

"Oh! that's too cruel. You know how I confided to you how I hate those beastly squares," replied Treherne, hardly believing that she could be in earnest.

But it was strictly true. He glanced at the pretty toy she extended towards him, and saw that each dance had its corresponding complement of initials, save that one hateful square late on in the evening. He also noticed that the same initials occurred four or five times.

Who the deuce could "L.O.R." be who was so favoured? He felt mortified in the extreme. He could have taken his oath that the girl had no lover. He was seized with a bright idea, which his vanity convinced him held the key to the little mystery. It was but a pretty trick, a woman's artifice to try him, to test the strength of his regard, hoping to make him speak, and "L.O.R." was but a myth—the bait used for his ensnaring. Or, again, the "R." was possibly a badly formed "B," and represented a young brother, an undergraduate at Trinity, who had been spending the first portion of "The Long" with friends in Scotland, and may have returned unexpectedly. He—Treherne—had often heard Norah allude to "dear old Len," longing for his home-coming. This initial would just fit, and was, doubtless, the solution of the problem.

"So," he drawled out, "this is quite too disappointing. "I looked forward to a whirl with you. You waltz rippingly, I'd swear. May I ask who is the fortunate individual who signs himself with such compromising initials 'Lor' declaring himself to be in a chronic state of plebeian wonder, doubtless at his own amazing good luck?"

Norah coloured furiously at this somewhat insolent speech, and was about to make a stinging rejoinder when Miss Delaney hurriedly approached, exclaiming:

"Norah! where have you been hiding yourself? I've been looking everywhere for you. They won't be here this evening, I'm certain. Fancy, it's just eleven o'clock, and not come yet. Is it not awfully provoking? Oh! Captain Treherne, how do you do?"—and Kitty Delaney turned to greet that young officer standing sulkily by, with, as he thought, a decidedly melancholy air. She was looking, as he was forced to admit to himself, wonderfully well, better than he could have imagined it possible for "The Gorgon" to look, under any combination of costume, or circumstances.

But then, evening dress does such wonders for a woman whose strong point is in the neck and shoulders line, and Kitty's arms and shoulders were second to none.

"Don't worry yourself about the laggards, Kitty. Believe me when hey come, they'll feel aggrieved if you reproach them for being late. Here's Captain Treherne only just arrived, and seems to consider himself ill-used at anyone's having the bad taste to be before him."

CHAPTER III

PRETTY Norah's dainty plumes were somewhat ruffled, thought Adolphus.

She impatiently declared that she must return to the ball-room, as her partner in the next dance would be seeking her, and Treherne was just about to offer his escort, when a hand placed on Kitty's shoulder made the young lady start, and exclaim joyously as she wheeled around, "Oh, Lawrence, at last! How shamefully late you are. Are you prepared to cry 'Mia Culpa'?"

"Did you give us up, Kitty? It is your province to scold Ringwood and not me"—answered the masculine voice carelessly, but in tones horribly familiar to the listening Dolly—and then unceremoniously swinging Miss Delaney aside, Major O'Reardon (for it was he) advanced eagerly to Norah with outstretched hands.

The girl had started from her seat, while a glorious crimson tide flooded cheek and brow.

"Laurie! I am so glad," she murmured, and the two pretty little white hands were buried in the strong clasp of those brown sinewy ones, which closed over them so lovingly; while the scoundrel and shame-stricken Treherne, who would have felt grateful that moment to an earthquake, a landslip, or any other convenient upheaval of nature that would have promptly removed him from the scene of action, thought he heard a whispered:

"You're not angry, darling?" breathed from behind that great dark moustache, belonging to the man, whom he had mentally dubbed a "duffer" and a "muff," and whose solemn cold face he had averred would "frighten his little Norah into fits."

Pretty Norah did not seem at all scared now, though in such close proximity to that terrifying visage. She looked as Treherne never dreamed she could look—beautiful as she was—the very incarnation of love itself!

"What in God's name does it all mean?" he inwardly groaned, as he tried quietly to remove himself from the immediate presence of those two, so apparently sufficient to themselves, without attracting notice, but he was not to get off so easily. As he made the first step towards effacing himself, Kitty cried. "And where is Phillip, Lawrence?" and the major dropping Norah's hands, glanced back and met the crestfallen Treherne.

"Hallo! Dolly, is it you, well met," he exclaimed cheerfully, adding to the young man's heavy burden of mortification by using that hateful contraction of his name.

"When did you arrive, old fellow? Let me present you to my sister, Miss Delaney. Captain Treherne, Kitty, of the [5?]th Lancers."

"Sister! Miss Delaney, your sister?" stammered the aghast and mystified Dolly, growing frantically red and embarrassed at the discovery of a complication that he could never have foreseen.

"Yes, my sister, or rather step-sister, ain't you, Kitty?" smiled O'Reardon, with imperturbably good humour.

"I wonder you care to claim such a "Gorgon" for a sister, Lawrence," laughed Kitty, with a malicious glance at the disconcerted warrior, whose weight of shame and humiliation grew suddenly almost intolerable, as he realised how he had been sold, and what a terrible mess his outrageous vanity had led him into.

"Well, I think I need not hesitate to claim you as my sister, when such a man as Ringwood longs to claim you as wife," replied O'Reardon, with marked and significant emphasis, wishing fully to enlighten the blundering and discomfited young officer.

"Oh, here he is," she cried blithely, before her brother could say more, and the unhappy Treherne unconsciously following the direction of her gaze, saw—was it possible, standing on the threshold of the room, where he was detained by a lady who seemed loth to let him go, Colonel Ringwood of the Hussars? Phillip Ringwood, of noble birth, distinguished appearance, and handsome fortune—Colonel Ringwood, the gallant soldier, whose military career had been so brilliant, was, actually, the betrothed husband of the [...] Kitty Delaney. The girl whom he had chosen in the [...] of his insolent self-conceit to term a "Gorgon"—whom he had represented as being so desperately jealous of the much coveted attentions which he had deigned to bestow upon her friend, was not alone sister of the man to whom he had ridiculed and belied her—but the future Lady Ringwood of Kingswood—a Countess! into whose charmed circle he could hardly hope to penetrate.

"Was ever fellow plunged in such an ocean of humiliation—and so terrible a fix?" he thought, as he ground his teeth savagely, and looked at the girl with awakened eyes, who, to-night, at least, did not look so very unworthy of the elevated position to which she might attain by and bye.

With a convulsive comprehensive bow, he vanishes from that room, that has proved to him a veritable torture chamber. His one desire is to get away. He feels he cannot breathe freely till he has left the house where such a depth of humiliation has been heaped upon him—heaped deservedly, he cannot but admit, but that conviction makes his shame and mortification all the more bitter.

He worked his way wildly through the crowd, to the destruction of chiffons, thereby calling down anathemas on his head, and rushed out into the night.

He strode along in the shade, avoiding the moonlight, with hat slouched over his face. "Hang it all!" he groaned. "What a cursed drivelling idiot I've made of myself! but who could think, that beast O'Reardon would lay me such a devilish trick—though I deserve it all and more, my infernal boasting has brought it on me. And he prepared the girls, of course, and told them of the absurd insolent bet I'd made; and they—they played into his hands! I can never hold up my head again. It will be all through the service in no time.

"Ringwood is such a pal, as ill-luck should have it, of Colonel Garston of ours. I wish I'd cut my throat before I came here."

He found a letter placed beside his candlestick on the hall-table of his sister's house. He took it up, then dashed it down again savagely.

"From O'Reardon! the treacherous hound. What can he have to say to me? To remind me he won the bed, no doubt, or, rather, that I've lost it," with a hoarse mocking laugh.

"I'll leave this the first thing to-morrow. I could never face the daylight here again. I'll exchange and go abroad, West Africa, and if I get knocked over by fever, or Mauser, so much the better."

After a minute or two, he again picked up O'Reardon's letter, thinking he ought to see what the Major had written.

"Dear Dolly—By the time you read this, you'll be vowing all manner of vengeance against me. But I hope you'll forgive the little trick I've played you, and believe that it's because I like you so well, old fellow, that I've thus tried to cure you of your chief foible.

"It's been a little lesson (a private lesson, as I've carefully refrained from saying anything to Ringwood, who might spread the story to your annoyance) which, I trust, will be taken in the spirit in which it was meant, and save you from falling into the same error, under other circumstances, when the consequences might be seriously unpleasant. And you know you did not mention the lady's name, dear boy; if you had, of course I must have spoken. And I think, considering how matters really stood, that I took everything that was said in very good part. As to the bet, I need hardly add that, knowing what I did when I allowed you to make it, it falls to the ground.

"Hoping, when we meet, that all will be forgotten and forgiven on your side, as it is already on mine, believe me, dear old man, ever yours,

"LAWRENCE O'REARDON."

This kindly candid note did not do much—then, at least—to assuage Treherne's wrath.

"The infernal prig," he muttered furiously. "It's just like him. For my good—curse him—and a 'private lesson,' when both the girls were in the know, and, no doubt, half their circle of acquaintance besides. What woman could resist blabbing about such a rotten joke? And of course it was all 'grin' to them.

* * * * * *

A few hours later saw Dolly Treherne—the crestfallen on board the mail boat bound for Holyhead. He exchanged, went aboard on active service, and when some few years later, he and O'Reardon met again, the latter and his pretty wife hardly recognised in the bronzed and brilliant soldier the vain, silly egotist of the preceding episode—the man who had not alone distinguished himself in the field by conspicuous bravery, but who had also won fame and reputation by his earnest devotion to duty, by his thoroughness, humanity, unselfishness, etc.

"That bitter lesson was the making of me, dear old chap," he murmured, as he gripped his friend's hand with true affection, "and to you I really owe what I am to-day and the success I've won. My absurd selfish vanity that kept me a trifler and a fool was instantly killed. I loathed myself that night and for long afterwards, and to get away from myself and humiliating remembrance I plunged into duty and work, and found in these—forgetfulness. The turning point of my career was when I made that insolent and audacious wager."

GARTH AUSTIN'S STRATEGY

Weekly Freeman (Ireland), 14 June 1913.

The newspaper from which this story was taken suffered damage. Two words in the text are illegible, and they are indicated here as [...]

CHAPTER I

"BUT both girls are equally rapid, daring riders, reckless, if you come to that. They seem completely devoid of fear. There's not a member of the Royden Club in it with them for pace—regular scorchers. Then, they're twins, exactly alike—those who know them best can't distinguish one from the other, I am told; and they get themselves up in duplicate fashion which makes the likeness still more bewildering. And, lastly, they're devoted to each other. Damon and Pythias and all the rest of the classical lot may take a back seat—they'd be out of the running if a prize were awarded for faithfulness, etc. Nell and Bell Freeman would come in an easy double first."

"Ah, I see; twin cherries—and such rot," laughed the speaker's friend, with the sound of a sneer in his voice.

"Twin fiddlesticks," responded the other, gruffly. "The girls are made of sterling stuff, I feel convinced. No idiotic nonsense about them—right down true and loyal to each other. But the reason I dwell on this strong mutual bond, that is said to exist between them, is that I think, if the case goes before the magistrates they will be thoroughly puzzled to convict one of them. They will stand by each other to the death, and nothing will induce either to give the other away."

"Umph! so you imagine that the law will find its work cut out for it to say which of the Sisters Freeman did the deed; and till they can prove which was the guilty one, of course they are both innocent." Again spoke the voice which had in it a suspicion of a sneer, and which belonged to the elder of the speakers.

"Yes," continued the younger man, "[…] not alone that it could not be brought in murder, but not even manslaughter. Just a fine—perhaps a heavy one—for reckless riding, and a caution."

"Ah, but you forget that a public rebuke is almost a keener, more humiliating ordeal—a more dread punishment to a woman (some women) than hanging itself," retorted the other, scoffingly.

The unhappy accident which young Thornton, a journalist on the staff of a morning paper, had been discussing with Dr. Garth Austin, had occurred on the previous afternoon, and resulted in the death of a poor old woman who had been knocked down by one of the Freeman girls' bicycles going at headlong speed. In falling she had struck her head against a stone. She never recovered consciousness, and died in three hours. The pretty little village of Creswell, which lay about half-way between the small town of Royden and the old city of Bodminster, was the scene of the tragedy. There was a somewhat steep incline just outside the tiny hamlet as the road swept on round a sharp curve towards Bodminster; but a few yards below the curve, and where the descent was steepest, a road branched off at right angles to the left; it was really but a narrow country lane, with high, sweet-scented hedges on either side, so that anyone suddenly emerging from its concealing shelter would be, unless gifted with acute hearing and alert, quick observation, directly and dangerously in the way of a vehicle rapidly descending the hill. Ordinary vehicles—unless the pedestrian were very deaf, indeed—would proclaim their presence while still out of sight—not so the ghostly bicycle, and the curve was so sudden and near the turn into the lane that the descending cyclist had scarcely time to ring his bell, unless he remembered to do so, before he shot round the curve, as a warning to anyone who might be about.

The inquest had been opened early on Tuesday, the day following the accident, and before Max Thornton met Garth Austin at the hotel where they dined, the elder man having only arrived in Bodminster that morning. But it had been adjourned till the ensuing Friday, in the hope of ascertaining some further particulars.

At the first inquiry the two or three inhabitants of the village of Creswell who had seen the accident (two respectable married women and a lad), and had gone to the assistance of the injured woman, were questioned as to how deceased came by her death, but their answers were somewhat confusing and unsatisfactory. They spoke of the Sisters Freeman riding through the village, as was their daily custom, and of one dismounting to adjust her shoe-lace, whilst the other continued on her way without pause. They declared most positively that the accident took place as the sister who had lingered behind descended the incline; that the foremost rider could not possibly have had anything to say to it, as her figure was fast diminishing in the distance when the second rider came dashing down the slope, unmindful of brake or bell. But they could not say which of the Sisters Freeman had lagged behind.

"Ah, faix, sir," said one of the women, addressing the Coroner, and by her speech declaring her Hibernian origin, "I hear tell that the young ladies is christened Miss Arabella and Miss Eleanor; but, sure, glory be to God, they might as well have the one name betwixt them for all the differ it makes, as their own mother can't tell which is which. The last one, whether she was Miss Bell of Miss Nell, sorra bit o' me or Margaret Dempsey knows," indicating the other witness, "came racin' down the hill like mad, not ringin' her bell nor nuthin', and skeert me an' Margaret above a bit as she flew past us. An', shure, yer honour, it was all over in a moment: the poor ould crathur was down on the ground niver to rise again, God rest her soul! An' Miss Freeman tarin' down the road for all the world like a steam engine that kills people an' takes no notice. A gintleman was comin' towards Creswell, an' saw somethin' was wrong, threw up his hands an' hollered at her; but 'twas no use at all, at all. An' whether the poor old soul was run down by her wheel or whether she only fell wid the fright not a bit of us knows. Dick there sez that he thinks somethin' knocked agin her sideways-like, but boys 's not to be thrusted."

This was all the information that was gleaned at the first inquiry into the nature of the fatal accident which had overtaken the unfortunate almshouse woman, Mrs. Musgrave, with the exception, at least, of the medical testimony, which proved that deceased was in weak health, and that in falling she had struck her temple against a stone, this being the direct cause of death. But how she came to fall still remained unsolved.

Instinctively all Max Thornton's sympathies were with the Freeman girls. He admired them hugely, though he could not distinguish one from the other—admired their beauty, their character, their devotion to each other, and, above all, their literary talent.

* * * * * *

Proceedings had not commenced on Friday when he arrived at the adjourned inquest. The twins were in their places, close together, and as Max looked at them with a sympathetic, admiring glance he noticed that Dr. Austin had secured a position near the girls where he could study them at his leisure without much chance of being observed by them, and how intently he seemed to regard them even now, before the examination of witnesses had begun.

Max felt somehow resentful of that keen, steady scrutiny, that suggested to his mind treachery and danger to the twins. Austin, he knew, had pursued the study of medicine, but of late years he had grafted literature on his original profession, and to a great extent had given up practice. A work of his "Medicine and Metaphysics," which had appeared a few years previously, had made something of a hit, while a later pamphlet on "Physiognomy, or Character by Countenance," had quite a boom; it revealed the peculiar bent of the writer's mind. Dr. Austin had made brain-study a speciality, and this deciphering of character by head, and facial developments was more or less an outcome of it.

The Freeman sisters were first questioned. Their answers to all preliminary inquiries were promptly and readily given. One declared herself to be "Arabella," the other "Eleanor," though a moment or two later, one girl dropping a small notebook she held, the other quickly stooped to recover it, and in the momentary confusion the twins managed or seemed to change places, so that which was "Nell" and which was "Bell" remained the puzzle it had ever been.

They were four-and-twenty years old, and lived at Royden with their mother and invalid brother. They were journalists.

They passed through the village of Creswell on their way to and from Bodminster on an average four times a day, sometimes only twice. They were generally together, but occasionally alone. They remembered the day in question.

Had they seen the deceased as they descended Creswell Hill?

"No, we saw no one," was the answering response made by each witness, each sister employing the plural pronoun, as was their constant and somewhat confusing habit. It was not that the editorial "we" had become grafted on their conversation, but presumably that the personality of each girl seemed to have a dual existence in her twin sister. The Coroner and his jury, unaware of their habit of speech, felt rather confounded at this daring denial. Two or three times he changed the form of his question, but the reply was always the same in substance.

Then the Coroner changed his tactics. "In riding through Creswell village last Monday afternoon, which of you dismounted to adjust her shoe-lace?" he interrogated.

This question was met by unbroken silence. After waiting in vain for an answer, he repeated it, addressing the girl nearest to him.

"Miss Freeman, I must beg of you to reply to my question—which of you on the day of the accident lingered behind for the purpose mentioned? I insist upon a response."

Then in a low but resolute tone came the reply. "I must decline to answer that question." And the Coroner at last felt hopeful of a solution of the problem—the girl was evidently sheltering her sister; the other twin was the delinquent. But when he addressed exactly the same question to the other girl and received identically the same reply, spoken in a still more determined tone, he felt baffled indeed. However subtly he put the question he failed to elicit any information that could tend to prove which of the twain had been the last to descend Creswell Hill. Evidently, as Max Thornton surmised, neither sister would give the other away—they would stand by each other to the death.

At length the Coroner spoke very gravely and rebukingly, saying that their strange obstinacy would be to their own disadvantage. The case was a serious one. There would be a magisterial inquiry, everything would be thoroughly sifted to prove how deceased came by her death. There was little doubt that the unhappy woman had lost her life through their reckless and wicked infringement of the laws of the County Council. One of them had Mrs. Musgrave's death upon her soul, and which it was would be for the law to determine. "You may give trouble and delay by the unwise policy you have adopted, but that is all. The law is a mighty omnipotent machine against which puny individual effort is useless; and your very action in thus hindering the ends of justice will make justice assume a sterner aspect by and bye."

The Freeman Sisters grew very pale during the Coroner's address, but adhered to their original resolve with unflinching determination.

Max Thornton noticed that Dr. Austin lingered behind as the crowd filed out from the Court, and a few minutes later, on glancing into the almost deserted room, he saw him in close conclave with the Coroner.

Max felt suspicious, and antagonistic, as if mischief were brewing for the twins, whose championship he longed to undertake, yet; in what way could he serve them? Or again, how could Garth Austin possibly injure them? and why should he wish to do so?

CHAPTER II

"I WONDER who is that Dr. Austin, twin love," remarked one of the Sisters Freeman to the other as they drove away from the crowded Courthouse. "He has an interesting clever face, yet, somehow I fear him."

"Why, dear? a perfect stranger."

"I can't tell you, but I instinctively feel, that he'd like to solve the problem of our identity—to force us to confess which is which. Once or twice I caught him watching us with a strange steady gaze—such an intense penetrating look, as if he were trying to read one's very soul—it made me shiver. I began to wonder was he a hypnotist, and was he trying to influence us even in the Court."

"Oh, what a wild imagination! it's easily seen, Sis, that you're the novelist of the future literary partnership, whilst I am only the practical newspaper writer. But, however, if Austin—whoever he is—is against us, young Thornton, of the morning paper, is on our side. I pitied the poor fellow he looked so worried."

"Perhaps," continued the girl who had first alluded to Austin, without noticing her sister's speech, "he wrote that biting cynical article in the paper."

"Is it Thornton?" ejaculated the other, in scoffing disbelief.

"No, no, I am speaking of that Dr. Austin. I think I saw a sardonic gleam in his eyes as he gazed at us so intently, and somehow he looked literary. I am sorry I answered it in that mocking defiant spirit. If he is inclined to be inimical it will set his teeth on edge. I should have liked him to be on our side. I fancy he would be a staunch friend."

"Don't worry abut him, dear," responded the other more optimistic twin. "He's nothing to us." But the other shook her head, she felt much more unaccountably interested in Dr. Austin, a complete stranger—though with the interest was combined a fear—than she did in Max Thornton, of whose friendly feeling there could be no possible doubt.

Next morning, Saturday, as the Freeman Sisters rode at an early hour, and at a very tame and decorous pace into Bodminster, they were surprised to see Max Thornton evidently waiting for them. He was standing at the top of a quiet street through which they always passed. As soon as he saw them, he stepped off the kerbstone into the roadway, raising his hat. Involuntarily they slowed down. In an instant he had placed a note in the hand of the girl next to him, with the hasty words—"Good morning, Miss Freeman, important, please burn"—and the next moment had vanished down a side street, before the twins well knew what had taken place.

It was brief, and ran as follows:—

"Beware of Dr. Austin! He is up to something. I cannot tell what, but I fear he means mischief. He is a scientific physiognomist, and an enthusiast on the subject. A character problem is his delight; the more puzzling the better he's pleased. The extraordinary likeness between you and your sister, will stimulate him to some unexpected effort to distinguish which is which, so, beware an interview, or, an attempt to draw either of you into conversation. Always your friend"

"I told you so!" cried the girl who read, almost in tones of triumph pleased with her own perspicacity.

"I felt sure he was a hypnotist or thought reader or something of that kind. I think if he even gazed long enough at me without speaking, or asking any questions, I should be compelled to confess what I most wish to guard, to keep secret.'

"In my mind he's more of the amateur detective, and I hate and despise the class," cried the other indignantly. "Each thinking he's another 'Sherlock Holmes,' when he's generally only a stupid bungler. But Thornton is a trump to warn us; he's a downright good fellow."

If the Freeman Sisters could have watched Dr. Austin's somewhat singular proceedings on that very Saturday, they might have fairly felt suspicious and distrustful of him.

He seemed to haunt the village of Creswell and Creswell Hill, especially that part of the descent where the green country lane branched off to the quarry.

He would walk slowly down the slope, with his hands clasped behind him, evidently thinking deeply; then, turning into the branch road, and walking a few steps, would face round, and retrace his steps until he again emerged on the high road, where he would pause, as if meditating. It seemed as if he were picturing the accident to himself, and imagining the very spot on which Mrs. Musgrave had stood when she came by her death. He saw how completely any pedestrian in the quarry road was hidden from view—no rider descending the slope could have any warning of an approach.

"It is only a marvel that accidents are not of common occurrence here," he muttered to himself. "It's a perfect death-trap for any unwary pedestrian, not to speak of feeble old women. The only way to account for a tolerably unstrained record in the past is, the want of traffic. I have been here now nearly an hour"—looking at his watch—"and only three traps and two bicycles have passed, well, it is to be hoped that the Parish and County Councils will wake up to their duties, and make alterations in the roadway that will render a similar accident impossible. Those poor girls! I pity them, and I admire their pluck. One interests me more than the other, and that is the reason I am determined to ascertain which is which. I wonder will my plan succeed or am I mistaken in my estimate of the difference in the twins' characters, and will there be no result? If I am successful, I suppose they'll hate me for ever, but it is too rare an opportunity to forego, and I'll take care they shan't suffer through my scientific hobby. If I compel an involuntary confession, and I fancy I will, if Nell is the delinquent (as I believe) I'll pay the piper; and besides, Mr. Leeson approves, a great fact in my favour; he wants to spare the girls getting into further trouble and publicity. And, after all, if I do force an unconscious admission it will be only an anticipatory one, that softer-faced girl would never have the moral courage and hardihood to stick to that quibble of the "we," before the magistrates. She would break down, she has qualms of conscience as it is, I can see. Hers is, I feel assured, a frank, honest, open nature, and it's only a silly sweet cowardice that induced her to adopt that subterfuge. That is what makes me feel almost positive that she was instrumental in causing the accident. If it had been the sister, the bolder, stronger, nature would not have been easily terrified. She would have known it was the merest accident, for which she was hardly at all responsible. The victim may have stumbled without the lightest brush from the descending cyclist, and the rider would have gone back and boldly avowed all she knew, her own forgetfulness of brake and bell being her only crime."

Thus musing and soliloquising, Dr. Austin strolled back up Creswell Hill, and entered the nearest cottage. He had been there earlier in the day, before his strange promenade at the fatal spot, and now returned for a few final words.

"And you're certain they always come home to dinner on Monday, and return to Bodminster in the afternoon?"

"Always, sir. Whatever it may be other days, they're as regular as clockwork on Mondays."

"Ah! and you say you knew the deceased's appearance well?"

"None better, sir. Poor old soul, she was in the almshouse this ten years, though folks say she was a lady once, and that old Paisley shawl that she most wore was a relic of her better days."

"You can easily get the things you say, and you'll take care to be punctual. I'll make it worth your while, as I told you this morning. So don't spare pains or trouble to be as perfect in detail as possible. I'll be in the quarry road a little after two; and mind, no word to anyone, save your neighbour, Mrs. Ryan."

"All right, sir; I'll be in the field waiting for you. But there's no 'tail' in it, sir, if by that you mean a trained skirt. Poor Mrs. Musgrave never wore nuthin' of that sort. It's all in the shawl, sir."

And with this strange and somewhat enigmatical phrase they parted, Dr. Austin turning into the next cottage, where lived Bridget Ryan. He had apparently been also there earlier, as his first words were: "I have arranged all with Mrs. Dempsey. She tells me that Monday is the best day."

"And Margaret'll do it! Glory be to God! She's the brave woman. I couldn't to save me life. It seems, beggin' yer honour's pardon, like mockin' the blessed corpse; but the poor creature 'll sleep no less sound, an', faix, it's a charity to shame them brazen hussies. I think it's them murdherin' bikes that has made the women what they are nowadays."

"I have no wish to shame or punish those ladies you speak of. It was an accident pure and simple—an accident that could scarcely be avoided with such a villainous construction of roadway. I only desire to satisfy myself from a scientific point of view. You will remember to be on the look-out on Monday afternoon, and to engage one of them in conversation, as agreed?"

"Troth, sir, ye may make yer mind aisy. I'll do it as natural as a play actress. Ye may trust an Irishwoman's tongue all the world over."

CHAPTER III

MONDAY was a gloomy miserable day, not actually raining, but with a dank sodden air, and fog shrouding the hills.

At 3 o'clock, when the Freeman twins rode through Creswell, on their return to Bodminster after dinner, it seemed to be growing dusk already. They had nearly cleared the village, when, from one of the last cottages, a woman ran out in front of the rider nearest to her, crying—

"Oh! Miss, a word wid ye."

Such an appeal was not to be disregarded, and both girls pulled up.

"Not you, me lady," said Mrs. Ryan—for it was she—nodding her head to the farther rider.

"I wouldn't be so bold as to trouble ye both. It's yer sister here that I want to speak wid, just a word."

Then as both girls looked incredulous at this bare-faced pretence of distinguishing one from the other, she whispered, while the farthest twin remounted, and proceeded slowly on her way round the curve, with careful adjustment of brake, and repeated ringing of her bell.

"It's the smile o' ye, alannah, that's the kindest.[100] I don't know which o' ye it is, and mebbe it's both, for ye're as like as if ye was yerself an' the lookin'-glass, but sez I the kind smile has the kind heart, an' if I speak to her she'll tell me true. I've heard tell, me lady, that ye've have a brother that's mortal bad in the back; an' I've got a little babby, Miss—he's nigh upon four years old now, praise be to God! He's the youngest of twelve children and nine in the graveyard.

(This sentence was rather obscure and the listener remained in doubt whether Mrs. Ryan was the mother of twelve children or twenty-one!)

"An' I'm sore afeerd, Miss, he's gettin' weak in the back; so I thought I'd ax yer pardon, an', though yer brother's a grand gentleman, would you tell me kindly how the sickness came on him first or was he born so?"

Bridget Ryan knew as well as the twins themselves how poor Ted Freeman lost the use of his limbs, but it served as an excuse for speech, and her ready Irish wit caught at it.

---

100 Alannah: child.

"Oh, my brother was twelve years old when he met with an accident which left him what he is. He had a terrible fall off stilts, and he has never walked since; so you need have no fear that your child can be in any way affected as he is," answered the girl kindly and unsuspiciously, as she prepared to mount again. "You should have a doctor to see your little boy if you think his back is not right."

Little Tim Ryan was about the sturdiest and most incorrigible youngster in the whole village.

"Och! Miss, acushla! but ye're the sweet one.[101] Won't ye forgive me"—laying her hand on the bicycle to delay the rider—"for havin' to speak forninst ye at the court of the poor old soul that's gone. I know it wasn't ye did it, honey. I wouldn't say a word agin ye two grand young ladies; but that old pryin' Crowner, bad cess to him![102] wid his divil's own questions, wud set the dhirty polisman on a dacent woman an' clap a body in jail while a sow'd be licken' her ear."

Miss Freeman grew very pale and scared-looking at Mrs. Ryan's allusion to the inquest, and with a murmured word or two got away from the voluble and hypocritical woman, riding slowly and cautiously, and ringing her bell many times, as she approached the descent.

While the foregoing interview was taking place her sister had disappeared round the curve, proceeding on her way to Bodminster. As she neared the branch road a woman's figure emerged from it, walking feebly and leaning on a stout umbrella. The cyclist swerved slightly at the sudden appearance of the figure, but skirting round it in a wide sweep she continued on her way without pause. When

---

101 Acushla: darling.

102 Crowner: coroner. Bad cess: bad luck.

she had got a little distance it struck her with a thrill of consternation that the elderly woman, walking slowly and painfully, was wrapped in a Paisley shawl. What a singular, almost startling coincidence! That day week, about the same hour, the figure that emerged from the branch road to meet almost instant death on the highway was that of a woman, walking feebly and wearing a Paisley shawl—a very uncommon article of attire in these latter days. She twisted herself in the saddle and looked back. There was no figure to be seen. How strange! How impossible! She dismounted and stood for a moment or two in the road, staring back incredulously. Where had the woman disappeared?

With her slow, halting gait she should take quite a long time to ascend that steep incline. Ah, of course, she had turned back into the Quarry road—perhaps startled by the bicycle, remembering the event of a week ago. Well, thank goodness, the girl reflected as she remounted. She had rung her bell any number of times, and descended slowly with the brake on, and oh!—pausing with an actual gasp of thanksgiving—

"How tremendously glad I am that Nell was delayed. It was most lucky. What a turn she'd have got, poor darling! I am so thankful that I was first!" And then on she sped with a relieved air, not again looking back.

But, as the other girl (who had been retained by Bridget Ryan) cautiously wheeling round the curve, and down the incline, approached the branch road, the same figure which had puzzled the foremost rider, emerged from its green shelter walking with difficulty. It was that of a feeble elderly woman, wrapped in a Paisley shawl, and wearing a large old fashioned black bonnet, and thick veil. After advancing a few steps, it paused, right in the path of the descending cyclist. There was a terrified exclamation—a faint scream—and the next moment, Nell Freeman tumbled off her machine, and lay unconscious on the dusty highway. Then there was another quick smothered exclamation, this time in masculine tones, and a man's figure dashed from the concealing shelter of the Quarry road and strode swiftly to the girl's side. It was Dr. Austin. One keen penetrating glance at the pale unconscious face, told him that he had been perfectly right in his conjecture.

His scheme had succeeded admirably. He had detected, with his expert eye the subtle intangible difference in the faces of the sisters. He had felt almost assured, that the girl, who now lay prone and senseless at his feet, had been the actor in the late tragedy—he determined to prove it, and he had done so! But did he now look like one who was rejoicing and triumphant having scored a success? No, he was filled with swift new-born remorse and [...]. As he gazed at the face looking so sweet and helpless in its unconsciousness, a sudden great pity and tenderness sprang to his breast for the victim of his cruel strategy. Yes, cruel! In his ardent pursuit of his scientific hobby, in his eager desire not to let slip such a rare opportunity of testing his own skill in character-reading, and as a physiognomist, he had ignored or forgotten, the possible result on a fine and susceptible nervous temperament, of the severe and peculiar test he meant to apply.

The girl had, of course, imagined in that one horrified moment of recognition, that she was confronted with the spirit of the woman of whose death she had been the innocent instrument. Yes, Dr. Austin was overwhelmed with remorse as he carried poor Nell up the hill, assisted by Mrs. Dempsey, for it was she who had masqueraded as the feeble pedestrian, but she had hastily divested herself of bonnet and shawl, and flung them out of sight, with an uneasy qualm, as she glanced askance at the still white face of the cyclist. Had she been engaged in laudable work after all? she questioned in her own mind. She never would have consented to take part (the principal part) in the strategy, but that Dr. Austin had told her that the Coroner approved of the plan—and the Coroner to her, just then, represented the whole force of the law. The real facts were, that Mr. Leeson (the Coroner) had caught at Dr. Austin's scheme, unfolded to him immediately after the close of the inquest, when Max Thornton had seen the two men in earnest conclave. He (Mr. Leeson) had a respect for the Freeman family. He had been acquainted with the father, and he wished much if possible to prevent the inquiry into Mrs. Musgrave's death being brought before the magistrates, as they might, very probably, send the case for trial, and he desired to spare the widow the consequent distress, and to save the girls from the injury it would certainly do them. Whereas, if they could be forced to confess now, the matter would end there with the infliction of a fine; and if strategy was necessary to compel that confession, why, then, let it be strategy.

They carried Nell to the first cottage, which happened to be Mrs. Dempsey's, and soon, under Dr. Austin's treatment, she came to herself. When she first opened her eyes she seemed dazed and non-comprehending; but in a moment, with returned recollection, she started violently and gazed wildly round her with a look of horror in her eyes, and this evident terror so impressed Mrs. Dempsey that involuntarily she cried out—"Oh, Miss, won't you forgive me; it was only a joke."

"No, not a joke, Mrs. Dempsey," Dr. Austin quickly interposed. "But I will explain all to Miss Freeman"; and, waving the women from the room (as, of course, Mrs. Ryan had to come in to see the end of the drama in which she had played a part) he and Nell were alone.

In a very few words he told her the whole story, and then begged for forgiveness, heaping reproaches on his own head, and deploring the scientific hobby which had impelled him to a course of action—"which, I know, was unjustifiable, but for the one fact that Mr. Leeson was in favour of it," he continued.

"For your father's sake he was was desirous, if possible, to save any further inquiry. His own good sense told him that you and your sister were blameless, save in the matter of neglecting the injunctions on the notice board at the top of the incline; and——"

"Oh, I am so glad it is all over, and that there is nothing to conceal any more," exclaimed the girl, who had been listening in a half-stupefied, half-bewildered manner to his explanation, and there was a sound of huge relief in the weak, weary tones.

"I had a terrible start, and I shall never forget the horror of that moment before I swooned. I did faint, I suppose?—and for the first time in my life," looking at the doctor interrogatively.

"I thought—I was sure—that the spirit of the poor creature, whose death, I shall always feel, lies at my door, stood before me on the very spot where she last stood in life. Oh, Dr. Austin, you don't know what it is to feel even partly responsible for the death of a fellow-creature!" (This was one of the things best left unsaid to a medical man.)

"I don't know how I have kept up as I have done. I couldn't only for Bell. But, thank God, all deception is over. I feel ever so grateful to you instead of resentful. It seemed a cruel and terrible trick to play one, but I can see that at least Mr. Leeson's motive was a kind one. There need be no further inquiry into poor Mrs. Musgrave's death. Last Monday—only a week ago! Great heaven! it seems almost a year of misery." looking up into the sympathetic face bent over her, with quivering lips and streaming eyes.

"Don't dwell on the sad affair any longer, dear Miss Freeman. It was all the purest accident. If I could have dreamed that you felt as you do nothing would have induced me to subject you to such an ordeal. It was brutal in the extreme, though the barbarous cruelty of it never seemed to strike me till now. So much for allowing oneself to be carried away by any craze."

"No, no," she interrupted. "I am grateful to you, more than I can say, for compelling the confession. It takes away the load of concealment—the necessity for subterfuge."

"It is bad enough to have the sorrow and horror of it all eating away one's life, and not to have the weight of a secret besides."

"Dear Bell will be dreadfully crushed and upset, and she set her heart on braving it out, but I am so glad that all secrecy is at an end."

Then she burst into a fit of hysterical weeping, and Dr. Austin felt more repentant and remorseful than ever. He obtained a vehicle and conveyed her home. He was very sympathetic and tender with her. In spite of his forty years, he had never yet since his adolescent days, had even a passing fancy for a woman. He had been too much occupied with his scientific pursuits to think of the sex; but now his whole heart—a heart that had not been frittered away on a score of objects—went out in a rush to the girl whom he met and learned to love under such very peculiar circumstances.

Her family, and especially Bell, were very antagonistic to him at first for the part he had played. The latter, in fact, hated him with a fierce, jealous hatred.

She felt instinctively that he had come to take her sister from her. The girls had always declared that they would never marry—that their love for each other filled all their heart and life; but Nell, as we see, was weaker than her sister, and she broke her resolution. She had been strangely attracted by Dr. Austin from the first moment she saw him, though with the fascination was mingled a feeling of apprehension which was prophetic.

He exercised a subtle influence over her, an influence which was unfelt by her sister's stronger nature—and strangely it was through her weakness, her failure, her imperfections, so to speak, that she captivated him. As far as beauty and talent went the sisters were equal; and yet, Garth Austin, felt no slightest affinity towards Bell, though he was magnetically drawn to her twin sister, who was, it must be admitted, her inferior in nobility an strength of character, in steadfastness, and courage.

But it was Nell's very womanly weakness—the femininity, so much more accentuated in her temperament than that in her sister Bell, that first attracted Dr. Austin, and, later, won his love.

Max Thornton, though he could not distinguish any difference in the twins' personality also felt most admiration mingled with a warmer feeling, for the girl who betrayed her womanliness in her weakness.

But by-and-by, when he discovered that she was appropriated by the man, with whom he had felt so fiercely indignant—though he grew to see that, after all, Garth Austin had been the girls' best friend, and had saved them from what might have proved serious results of their unwise police—he tried his best to persuade Bell to break her resolution also.

But he was not successful, she was true and staunch to the only great and absorbing love of her life—that for her twin sister.

www.ingramcontent.com/pod-product-compliance
Lightning Source LLC
Chambersburg PA
CBHW020931310726
48980CB00007B/725/J

* 9 7 8 1 9 1 7 1 1 3 0 4 5 *